THE
CRIMSON
THREAD

THE
CRIMSON
THREAD

KATE FORSYTH

**BLACK
STONE**
PUBLISHING

Copyright © 2022 by Kate Forsyth
Published in 2022 by Blackstone Publishing
Cover and book design by Blackstone Publishing
Cover photography © Richard Jenkins
Landscape photograph © GIS/Shutterstock

Printed in the United States of America

ISBN 979-8-200-95024-9
Fiction / Historical / World War II

Version 1

CIP data for this book is available
from the Library of Congress

Blackstone Publishing
31 Mistletoe Rd.
Ashland, OR 97520

www.BlackstonePublishing.com

You would have died in the winding labyrinth
Without the thread I gave you.

> *You said to me, "I swear by these dangers*
> *As long as we live, you will be mine."*

> *We are alive, Theseus, but I am not yours.*
> *Though buried by your deceit, I live.*

Ovid, "Ariadne to Theseus"

For my father Gerry Humphrey
& my grandfather Arthur Humphrey,
who first told me the story of the desperate struggle
to save Crete from the Nazis
&
for my great-uncles
Stan & Jack Humphrey
&
Reg & Gerry Quirk,
who fought on Crete in 1941 & barely managed to escape

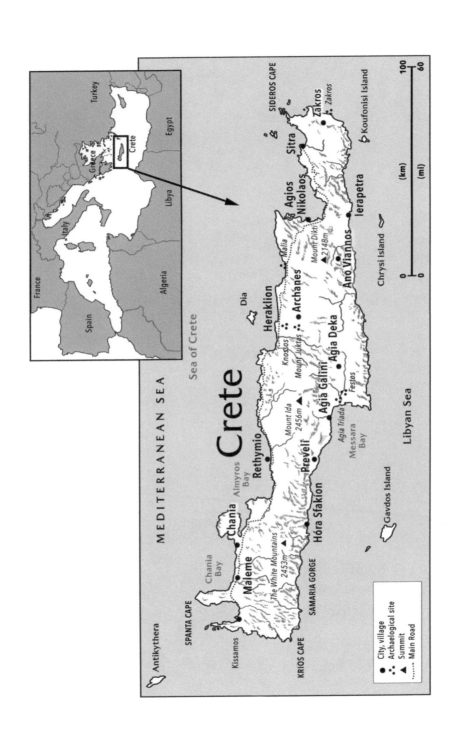

PART I:
THE FIRST STEP
APRIL 1941

O
blessed
pilgrim
the first step
on the spiral path
snaking down to the secret place
the point of pivot the darkness where your
shadow hides

I

25 April 1941

"Red thread bound,
in the spinning wheel round,
kick the wheel and let it spin,
so the tale can begin."

Alenka's grandmother chanted those words to her every night as she told her a story, sewing as she spoke, each stitch as tiny as if set by a fairy.

Yia-Yia knew many stories of gods and heroes, giants and nymphs, and the Three Fates who spun and measured and cut the thread of life. Many of Yia-Yia's tales were strange and terrible. A girl who was turned into a tree. A woman cursed with snakes for hair. Another whose tongue was cut out and who could only tell her story by embroidering it upon a cloth. The story Yia-Yia told most often, though, was that of the minotaur in the labyrinth, for it was the *mythos* of Alenka's home, the ruins of the Palace of Knossos in the island of Crete.

Once, a long time ago, her grandmother would say, a princess lived here. Her name was Ariadne, and she was the mistress of the labyrinth, for she held the key to the puzzle of paths where the minotaur was hidden. Half-man, half-bull, the minotaur was fed every seven years on the blood of seven young men and seven maidens. One day a hero named Theseus came, determined to defeat the monster, and Ariadne showed him the way into the labyrinth and gave him a sword and a spool of blood-red thread so he could find his way out again.

"Is it true, Yia-Yia?" Alenka once asked. "Did a monster really once live here?"

Yia-Yia had smiled, sighed, shrugged. "*Po-po-po*, who knows? Lies and truths, that is how tales are. Perhaps there was no minotaur. Perhaps bulls were sacred to the people who once lived here, and that is why they painted or sculpted them so often. Maybe it was just a sport, like bullfighting, young men and women risking their lives to leap over the bull's horns. Maybe all of it is true, or maybe none of it. Now close your eyes and go to sleep."

Alenka liked to think it was true. One of her greatest treasures was an ancient coin she had found in the ruins, with a labyrinth of seven circuits engraved upon one side and a woman's crowned head on the other. She wore the coin hanging around her neck with a little golden cross and a blue bead, a charm against the evil eye her godparents had given her at her christening.

Every year, in early spring, Alenka's grandmother had woven together red-and-white thread to make her a *martis* bracelet, a talisman against harm. Alenka would wear it about her wrist until the almond tree in the village square began to blossom and the first swallow swooped in the sky. Then she and the other villagers would tie their bracelets to a branch of the tree to encourage a good harvest that year.

But Yia-Yia had died that winter, so Alenka had to weave her own *martis* bracelet. It seemed the magic had failed with her grandmother's death. The coming of spring brought terrible danger. The German army was marching down the flanks of Mount Olympus toward Athens. Soon, Greece would fall to the Nazis, as every other country had done. Only the British fought valiantly on.

It was hard not to lose hope. Why, the King of the Hellenes had already fled. He was here in Crete, at the Ariadne Villa in Knossos, along with Emmanouil Tsouderos, the newly appointed prime minister. His predecessor had shot himself just a week earlier. The official report said he had died of a heart attack, but everyone knew that was a lie.

Alenka worked as a translator and guide for the curator of the archaeological dig at Knossos. He lived in a small cottage in the garden of the villa, which had been built by Sir Arthur Evans, the British archaeologist who had discovered the ruins of the ancient palace. Alenka's mother was the housekeeper at the villa, so Alenka had grown up playing in the ruins, listening to the stories of the archaeologists, and typing up their articles and books. It was her dream, though, to go to Oxford and study history and languages. In her secret heart, she wanted to solve the riddle of the ancient hieroglyphs found on Crete. No one had ever been able to crack the code, though an Australian classicist named Florence Stawell had come close. Alenka had been studying hard for her university entrance exams, but the war had changed everything.

She sighed. Carefully, she set a stitch in the white linen of her *sindoni*, the embroidered sheet that would be pinned to her wedding quilt, as if that act of needlework would keep her family safe against the coming danger. Alenka was sewing a constellation of seven red knots above the dancing figures of a boy and a girl and their mother. Her family.

As she sewed, she silently chanted the charm her grandmother had taught her:

> *By knot of one, the spell's begun.*
> *By knot of two, it cometh true.*
> *By knot of three, make it be.*
> *By knot of four, this power I store.*
> *By knot of five, the spell's alive.*
> *By knot of six, this spell I fix*
> *By knot of seven, angel of heaven.*

She snipped the red thread with her stork-shaped scissors, muttering a familiar prayer, "O holy angel, deliver us from evil!"

Her half brother Axel bounded toward her through the villa's garden, his face alight with excitement. "Have you heard? The Luftwaffe have blown the port at Piraeus to bits! Won't be long now before stormtroopers march into Athens." He began to goosestep around her, one arm held high in the stiff Nazi salute.

"What in God's name is wrong with you?" Alenka cried. "You can't want that! Not even you could be so stupid."

Axel scowled. "I do want that! Why shouldn't I? I'm German."

"You are not! You've never even been to Germany. You're Greek, just like the rest of us . . ."

"My father was German, that makes me German," he shouted at her.

Indeed, he did not look much like a Greek boy. He had ice-blue eyes and curly hair so fair it was almost white. His father had been an archaeologist from Berlin who had come to the Villa Ariadne to help in the reconstruction of the ruins. After he had gone home, Alenka's mother Hesper had discovered she was pregnant. When Axel was born nine months later, as pale as a white rabbit, Alenka's father Markos had been furious.

In Crete, there was no greater insult than calling a man a cuckold.

Markos had beaten Hesper till she could not stand. Alenka had been only seven when Axel had been born, but she remembered that day all too vividly. Her father's raised fist. Her cowering mother. Blood on her mother's mouth, bruises on her skin. The baby screaming. Alenka's mother falling, crawling, curling into a ball. Her father kicking her.

"Get out," he had said. "Get out and never come back."

So Hesper had wrapped the baby in her shawl, taken Alenka's hand, and crept through the night to her mother Galena's house, in the small village of Knossos. Alenka's Yia-Yia had calmed the baby, tended Hesper's bruises, and tucked Alenka up in her own bed by the fire. She had been a tiny, fierce, black-clad woman, as quick to curse as to bless, who wore a black cross on a long black cord about her neck, hand-knotted by the monks, for counting her prayers.

She had told Alenka a thousand-and-one stories and taught her how to cook and clean and scrub and sew. "Alas, you too will need to be married one day," she would say, "and it will be hard for a man to forget your mother's shame. Like mother, like daughter, they will say."

So Alenka had decided never to be shamed by love.

Her half brother, meanwhile, had grown up forged by hatred. He was twelve now and like a boy carved from marble. Perfectly formed but cold through to the core. The only person he did not hate was his absent father. Axel was obsessed with knowing who he was, and pored over old photographs of that summer, looking for resemblances. He tried to force his mother to tell him his father's name, and when she refused, punched her hard. Still, Hesper would not tell.

As he grew older, Axel determined to make himself as German as possible. When he was ten, he realized that he had been born on Adolf Hitler's fortieth birthday and developed a fixation on the führer that was truly frightening. He began to collect cigarette cards that featured photographs of Hitler and would arrange and rearrange them obsessively. Alenka's godfather Manolaki had burned them all one day. Later that day, the shed where Manolaki made his fortified wine mysteriously caught fire. Everyone feared it had been Axel.

Alenka found she was rubbing an ugly puckered scar on her arm. She took a deep breath, and said, "Axel, I know your father is German, but you cannot want Greece to be invaded and defeated . . ."

"I do," Axel said. "The Germans will come, and I will join up and fight for them, and they'll give me a machine gun and I will shoot anyone who calls me a bastard, and they will think me a hero and take me back to Berlin and give me medals, and I will find my father and he will be proud of me."

His voice had quickened as he spoke, his hands balled into fists in a way Alenka knew all too well.

"Axel, that's never going to happen. Didn't you see the photos of what they did to Belgrade? We will be bombed to smoking ruins just like that! People will die. Innocent people, women, and children."

"I don't care! I hate them. They're all mean to me—they deserve what's coming to them!"

Alenka bit her lip. Her little brother did have a hard time of it. She had told him just to ignore it, that the other children only teased him because he reacted so strongly, but Axel just cried, "It's all right for you, they never call you the son of a whore!"

He made things more difficult for himself by punching and kicking the other children or slashing the tires of their bikes. The adults in the village disliked him too, for Axel was always in trouble of one kind or another. Playing truant from school, stealing fruit from gardens, breaking windows with stones. Things had gotten worse since the war had begun, for everyone knew that Axel's father was German. Some of the old women had even spat three times at him in the street, making the sign of the cross over and over again.

She tried to soften her voice. "I know you're unhappy here, Axel, but it won't be forever. If you'd just go to school and work hard, then when you're finished, you'll be able to do whatever you like."

"Which is why you're still here in Knossos, sewing your dowry like a good little Greek girl."

Alenka's face burned. Axel had such a way of prodding sore points. How could she explain how calming she found it, setting one small steadfast stitch after another, watching flowers and birds and dancing figures bloom from the end of her needle? It did not mean she was a good Greek girl. Good Greek girls walked three paces behind the male of the family, stood quietly against the wall and watched while the men feasted, ate only when they had finished, then did the washing up while the men played cards, drank *tsikoudia,* and argued about politics. Good Greek girls wore a headscarf and an apron over a skirt that reached their ankles and married the man their father chose. Good Greek girls cooked and spun and wove and washed clothes and scrubbed floors from dawn till dusk, while their little brothers ran free, indulged from birth simply because they were male.

Alenka had rebelled against all that since she was a child. It infuriated her that Greece was the home of democracy, but she was not allowed to vote. What sense did that make? She was just as intelligent and capable as any man. Her heroines were the poet Sappho, the freedom fighter Laskarina Bouboulina, who had commanded her own fleet during the Greek War of Independence, and the singer Sofia Vembo, whose sultry songs had captured Alenka's imagination that past winter. Sofia Vembo dressed like a Hollywood star, was photographed with bare shoulders and a smoldering cigarette, and was known to have a lover. She had inspired Alenka to pluck her eyebrows and shorten her hems, despite the scandalized looks of some of the older women in the village.

"Axel, you can't really want the Nazis to invade us," she said, trying to recover her poise. "They're so cruel. We'll be enslaved."

"Good!" Axel kicked her sewing basket hard. It flew across the courtyard, spilling her pins, needles, thimbles, and spools of thread over the ground. Alenka jumped up, exclaiming in anger. He seized her embroidery and flung it to the ground, grinding it into the dirt with his grubby bare feet, then evaded her clutching hands and ran off, laughing.

"You are such a little brat!" Alenka shouted after him. She picked up her *sindoni*, shook it free of dust, and put it neatly on her chair. Then she took out a cigarette. Her hands were shaking so much it took her a long moment to light it. She stood, smoking, looking out across the ruins of the old palace.

Axel was right. Alenka was very afraid.

For her little brother, as much as for herself.

II

"You know I've always said the most important possession of a king of Greece is a suitcase," the King of the Hellenes said with a wry twist of his lips.

He stood on the terrace of the Villa Ariadne, smoking a cigarette, while his cousin, Prince Peter, lounged in a deckchair nearby, flipping over the pages of a newspaper.

Teddy Lloyd stood in the doorway, waiting for them to notice him, the morning's dispatches in his hands. He would have dearly loved a coffee and a smoke himself, but he would have to wait until he was off duty. He was not on such friendly terms with the royal family of Greece that they'd ask him to join them at breakfast. Still, he took careful note of everything so that he could give a decent description of it in his next letter home. His mother would be thrilled he was hobnobbing with royalty, he knew.

You've come a long way, Teddy, old boy, he told himself. To think a country kid from Australia would end up guarding a king!

Teddy and his best mate, Jack, had signed up because they wanted to see the world. They had both been studying Classics at the University of Melbourne but had been bored to tears reading about ancient battles in dead languages when there was a real war happening on the far side of the world. So they'd enlisted together.

At first, it had been exactly the adventure they'd hoped for. They'd been drilled with broomsticks, rifles being in short order, and spent a lot of time hiking before dawn and playing cricket, pretending the balls were grenades. An accelerated officer training course followed, at Duntroon Royal Military College, in which the worst danger came from the constant hazing by the regular cadets there. One had tried to lock Jack in a cupboard, thinking he was an easy target because he stuttered like a fool. Jack and Teddy had fought back, much to the cadet's surprise, and later that night, Teddy had shaved off his eyebrows while he slept. No one messed with him and his mate.

After graduation, they were equipped with a stout pair of boots and put on board what had once been a cruise ship, to the blaring sounds of a military band playing "Roll out the Barrel!.' They'd traveled to the Middle East in style, playing endless games of cards and drinking the ship cellar dry.

Again, it was real *Boys' Own* stuff. Marching in the desert, pretending to stab stuffed dummies with their bayonets, while someone rattled a petrol tin with a stick to imitate the staccato sound of machine-gun fire, camping out under the stars.

Everything changed in the new year. They were sent to Bardia, a small fortress on the coast of Libya held by the Italians. Teddy had felt a strange seasick sensation in the pit of his stomach the night before the dawn raid. Half-excitement, half-dismay. Like being caught doing something wrong and trying to think up a way to get out of it. Their weapons were antiquated, and so were their communication methods. There was no radio. If the Aussie infantry wanted to communicate with the Pommie tanks, they had to stick their tin hat onto a bayonet and wave it in the air. He could smell the fear, but everyone pretended they didn't care. Teddy had joked too, but for the first time, he had realized he might die. Or worse, be crippled like his dad.

It was a baptism of fire. A fortress of barbed wire, concrete-lined trenches, and bomb shelters. Dust whirled in tiny tornadoes, encrusting nostrils and ear whorls, turning the seams of their uniforms to sandpaper. Teddy had chalked "look out, Musso, here we come" on the sides of their truck, but he knew—as they all knew—that the Anzac forces had only six thousand untried men attacking an army of forty-five-thousand seasoned Italian soldiers. The whole day was a blur, all *whizz-bang-zap-boom-thwack-ack-ack-arrrrrrrrgh*, like in a comic book.

Afterward, eerie silence and desolation. Sprawled bodies lying in the orange sand, flies clustered on their eyes and mouths and wounds. Thousands and thousands of Italian soldiers stumbling out to surrender, crying, "*Aqua, aqua,*" which Teddy eventually worked out meant "water.' He had to learn another Italian phrase, *Lascie le armi*, which meant "lay down your arms'. He pronounced it "lashay lay army,' but the message seemed to get through. So many Italians were taken prisoner, no one knew what to do with them.

That night, Teddy and Jack found an Italian officer's tent with his uniform all laid out ready for him, a white suit bedecked with gold lace and tassels, a safari helmet waving with peacock feathers, a blue satin sash. The mess tent nearby was piled with tins of baked ham and truffles, jars of cherries, and crates of fine wine and brandy.

Jack found a gramophone and put on some opera, and Teddy forced open some tins of condensed milk with the point of his bayonet. Wearing the Italian officer's gaudy jacket, sash, and hat, they got grandly drunk, singing, "*O mio babbino caro*" at the top of their voices and eating the condensed milk out of the tin with spoons, something Teddy's mother had never allowed him to do. They had a merry old time of it until their commanding officer told them to "Take off those bloody ridiculous clothes and try to look like bloody soldiers."

A string of swift and easy victories followed, and Teddy felt invincible. They cheered when they heard they were being transferred to Greece. "We'll run those Eyties out in no time," he had boasted.

As they marched through the streets of Athens, the soldiers sang:

> *When we meet old Mussolini,*
> *We'll piss right in his eye,*
> *We'd rather shoot him*
> *Than salute him,*
> *That bloody old Mussolini.*

Pretty girls lined the streets, throwing flowers. Teddy caught one and stuck it behind his ear, and the crowd cheered. An old woman dressed all in black pushed a bottle of wine into his hands. "*Niki!*" she said and mimed drinking. Teddy did as instructed, pulling out the cork with his teeth and spitting it into the gutter. The wine was sweet and rich, and he took a few more swigs before passing it to Jack. "I could get to like this place," he said.

"Everything is so old," Jack said in wonderment. "Look, there's the Acropolis!"

"The whole place could do with a lick of paint," Teddy replied.

The crowds cheered. "*Kalimera! Niki! Niki!*"

"Who's this Nicky guy?" Teddy asked Jack.

"It means victory," Jack said, grinning.

They had thought they'd be fighting the Italians, as they had in Libya, but Hitler decided that Mussolini needed a hand. Teddy and Jack and their battalion had to march north, under the Luftwaffe's ceaseless strafing, to fight against the Germans advancing down the Thermopylae pass into Greece.

That night, their commanding officer called the men together. Lieutenant-Colonel Theodore Walker was a tall, lean man, with dark hair parted down the middle as neatly as if drawn with a ruler. He had been a banker before the war, so Teddy called him "the accountant" rather derisively. "I'm sorry, lads, but I'm afraid we've been given our orders," Walker said. "The Germans are on their way, and we have to do our best to stop them. The longer we hold them off, the more of our boys will live another day. So do your bloody best, I know you'll make me proud."

The 2/7th battalion did their best, but the Germans could not be stopped. It was all one hideous blur after that. They had to retreat, using dead mules to fill in bomb craters in the steep narrow roads, hiding in muddy ditches as the Luftwaffe roared overhead, listening to the groans of the wounded, eyes stinging from the smoke of burning army trucks. They were ordered to abandon their supplies and their equipment, smashing up their big guns with sledgehammers so the Germans could not use them. Sand was poured into the engines of the trucks; the horses were shot.

Somehow Teddy and Jack stumbled all the way back to the port at Athens, hoping to find a berth on an Allied ship. The Greeks surrendered on April 20, Hitler's fifty-second birthday, as if wanting to give him a bloody great big present. It didn't matter. The Luftwaffe continued to bomb the city and the harbor, and machine gun the long lines of filthy, exhausted soldiers as they retreated.

Not a single RAF plane in sight. "Rare As Fuck," the men had begun calling them.

A British officer stalked down the road, shouting, "Anyone here speak Greek? The bloody Greek navy has refused to transport the bloody Greek king out of here, so we need to bloody fly him out, and we can't find anyone who speaks the bloody language!"

Teddy knew a sweet chance when he heard it. He jumped up. "I do, sir! *Kalimera!*"

The officer looked him up and down. "Any good?"

"I was studying Classics at Melbourne University before I signed up, sir. And we had a bastard of a teacher at school whose favorite punishment was to make us translate Homer. I was always in trouble, so I got a lot of practice."

The officer did not smile, so Teddy added another quick "sir."

"Very well," the officer said wearily. "Grab your swag and let's go."

So Teddy had caught up his kitbag and gone off with the officer. At the last minute, he had turned and winked at Jack, laughing. It was true that their Classics teacher had often punished him by making him translate Homer. It was also true that Jack had always helped him on the sly.

Luckily, King George of the Hellenes spoke excellent English, so Teddy had not been caught out. And now here he was, guarding the Greek royal family in the comfort of the Villa Ariadne in Knossos, instead of scratching out a slit trench with his tin hat like the rest of his brigade.

He felt a bit bad about Jack, but it was every man for himself. Jack could have spoken up. And they'd not wanted two men. Teddy had to seize his chance.

He glanced at the papers in his hand and realized with a jolt that it was Anzac Day. The rest of his battalion would be down on the beach, getting plastered and playing two-up, paper poppies in their button-holes. Twenty-six years ago, his father had fought at Gallipoli. Teddy felt that he should raise a beer for the old bastard. There was no beer at the villa, but it was well stocked with gin. Surely no one would notice if he slipped a bottle in his pocket when he went off duty. Yep, Teddy had landed on his feet, for sure. Who could have guessed those bloody boring lessons in ancient Greek would end up being of use?

"Funny old place, this villa," Prince Peter said, looking about him with interest. "Like an English country house plopped down in the middle of an old Greek ruin."

"I wish we were in an English country house," King George said moodily. "Or at Brown's Hotel. At least they know how to make a decent martini there."

"Well, you are the king of Greece, Georgie. Your people think you should stand by them in their hour of need."

"Unfortunately, I have a very long memory. They didn't want me in '24, when they deposed me, and stripped me of my Greek nationality. And they were happy for me to be a mere puppet-king dancing to the tune of that damned Metaxas these past five years. Why should I stay and fight and die by their side now?" The king took another deep drag of his cigarette, his hand shaking noticeably.

Teddy didn't understand Greek politics. He didn't think anyone could. Jack had told him to try and remember it in numbers.

Nineteen years since King George had inherited the throne.

Twenty-three changes of government.

Thirteen coups.

One dictatorship.

One Nazi invasion.

Teddy wondered what would happen now. If the Greek royal family was evacuated to Cairo, would he go with them? He didn't want to miss any of the fun, but then again, it could do his army career some good. And his mum would be able to crow about it all over town.

A flash of movement caught his eye. Teddy looked across the garden.

A shapely young woman in a white flowery dress was bending over, gathering up something that had fallen.

His lips formed a soundless whistle. Things just kept getting better and better.

He delivered his dispatches smartly, then went down into the garden where she was folding up her sewing. "Excuse me," he said. "I think we've met before. I'm Teddy Lloyd, on secondment to the king's guard."

The young woman looked at him in surprise. "I don't think we've met before."

She speaks English, he thought exultantly. *And she's a real dish!*

"Oh, sure we have," he said persuasively. "It was just last week. You and I were sitting in a train carriage, along with your mother and my general. Our train went into a dark tunnel, and none of us could see a thing. Everyone heard, though, the sound of smooching, then a loud slap. When the train comes out of the tunnel, the general has a bright red cheek. "What on earth!" the general thinks. "My lieutenant kissed the girl and I get slapped?" Your mother thinks, "Bravo, my girl, you taught that handsome Aussie soldier a lesson!" You wonder why your mother slapped me, when I have come so far and put myself in such danger to fight for your country. He deserves a kiss, you think. Meanwhile, I'm congratulating myself on my cleverness. It's not every day I get to kiss the prettiest girl in Crete and slap a general!"

She laughed. "There are no trains in Crete, you idiot."

"Damn, you've got me there. Must've been a bus."

"Must've been a different girl."

"Can't have been. There is no prettier girl in Crete. Want to come ride a bus with me, find ourselves a long dark tunnel?"

She shook her head, casting him a laughing glance.

Desire hissed all through his body. Teddy stepped closer, smiling down at her. "How about showing me the sights? I get a few hours off later. Go on, make a poor homesick digger happy for a few hours."

She considered him. "I'm not sure I can trust you to keep your hands to yourself."

"Oh, you can't! But why would you want to?"

She could not help laughing but shook her head again.

"I'm not asking you to marry me," he said in exasperation. "I won't be here that long."

"It is good you are not!" she flashed back. "Because I'm never going to get married."

"So what's the harm then, in having a little fun? We might both be dead tomorrow."

That seemed to strike a chord. "True," she answered slowly. "All right then, I'll show you around. But only if you promise to mind your manners."

"Sure, babe," he said easily. "Boy scout honor."

But he crossed his fingers behind his back.

III

26 April 1941

An old Venetian fortress guarded the entrance to the small port of Heraklion, dozens of candy-colored boats bobbing at their moorings. Beyond the fortress, a narrow pier ran far out into the sea. The island of Dia was a dark smudge in the distance. It had once been a dragon, an old fisherman had told Jack, coming to attack Crete, but Zeus had turned it to stone with a thunderbolt.

Jack loved all those old stories. He had read the tales of the Greek heroes, growing up in Cambridge. When he was eight, his nana had come to take him all the way to Australia. He had not had much time to pack, but the first things to be shoved into a suitcase were his favorite books: Andrew Lang's *Tales of Troy and Greece*, *The Secret Garden*, *Treasure Island*, *Peter Pan*, *The Princess and the Goblin*.

It was Jack's keenness for ancient myths which led him to study Classics at university. He had been thrilled when he heard his battalion was being deployed to Greece. *The gods once lived here*, he thought as they sailed toward Athens. *Here Hermes invented the lyre, here Aristotle sat and spoke aloud to his disciples, here Socrates drank hemlock.*

And now here he was, by some extraordinary workings of fate, in Crete, the epicenter of so many myths. The bull-headed minotaur locked within the labyrinth. The hero Theseus who volunteered to come to Crete as one of those to be sacrificed to feed it. The princess Ariadne who fell in love with Theseus, and so gave him a sword so that he might kill the monster, even though it was her own brother. Daedalus, the builder of the labyrinth, who made wings of feathers and wax so he and his son might escape the king's wrath, only to see Icarus fly too close to the sun and fall to his doom. Even the name of Heraklion was mythic, inspired by the hero Hercules, who had come to the island to capture a wild bull and so fulfill the seventh of his twelve labors.

The old town was crowded within high medieval walls. Bougainvillea grew over iron lace balconies where women pegged out their washing on lines strung over the alleyways. A man dragged along a sad-eyed donkey with wooden chairs lashed on top of sacks of cement. Terracotta domes and tall belltowers rose behind an elegant Italianate loggia with rows of symmetrical arches. Jack walked up the road, carefully noting doorways and rooftops that could provide cover and the position of telephone wires and call boxes.

He still could not quite believe that he had been recruited to join Brigadier Brian Chappell's intelligence team here in Heraklion. Or, indeed, that he had survived the nightmare that had been the retreat from the Greek mainland.

The port of Piraeus had been like a hallucination of Hades. German dive-bombers had screamed down like harpies, clawing the fleeing soldiers with machine-gun bullets. Through the smoke, Jack had seen a woman struggling along with a heavy bag, a sobbing little girl on her hip. A boy had stumbled beside her, dragging a suitcase, a teddy bear in his other hand. Jack had run to help them and gotten them to safety.

In return, her husband, the British First Secretary in Athens, had given him a berth on their steamer ship. It had sailed through the night, but at dawn was discovered by the Luftwaffe and blown to bits. Jack had helped tend the wounded, then fixed a broken radio and sent out an SOS. Help had arrived, and they had somehow managed to get to safety in Crete. The British First Secretary had recommended him warmly to the brigadier, so Jack had found himself with a new role, working in the British command headquarters set up in a cave located between the airport to the east and the town of Heraklion to the west.

So far, his duties had been light. The brigadier had introduced him around, told him to get a new uniform, write to his grandmother, and go and check out the defensive potential of the town. Jack had obeyed with alacrity.

The narrow, cobbled street led out into a broad, tree-lined square. In the center was an ornate marble fountain supported by miserable-looking lions with manes set in stylized curls. Jack knew it had been designed by the Venetian doge, Francesco Morosini, in the days when Crete had been ruled by Venice. It was cool under the plane trees, and Jack sat at one of the little tables and ordered a coffee. He was bewildered by a rush of questions and gesticulations from the waiter.

His modern Greek was getting better every day, but most of his practice had been saying things like *yassous*, a general term of greeting and farewell, *kalimera*, which meant good morning, *neh*, which rather confusingly meant yes, and *yamas*, said when raising a glass. But Jack was determined to learn. After a halting conversation, the waiter smiled widely, nodding his understanding, and took his order to the kitchen. Jack took out his battered copy of the *Iliad*. His place was marked with a dried anemone flower that he had plucked on the flanks of Mount Olympus. He laid it carefully on the table, and began to read:

> And the renowned smith of the strong arms
>   made elaborate on it
> a dancing floor, like that which once in the wide
>   spaces of Knossos
> Daedalus built for Ariadne of the lovely
>   tresses . . .

———————

"How apt!" a well-bred English voice said at his elbow. "Reading Homer in Greece." Jack looked up. A tall, handsome young man stood beside him, dressed in impeccably pressed khakis, with thick brown hair swept back from a broad brow and a patrician nose. Jack remembered meeting him earlier that day at the HQ cave. He had one of those posh-sounding double-barrelled names.

"I didn't know I was c-c-coming to Greece when I packed it, but my university tutor gave it to me, pre-presumably so I could keep up my s-s-studies. It seemed a-a- . . ." Jack took a deep breath, carefully enunciating the word that had blocked him. ". . . appropriate to read it here." Jack gestured around him at the old woman in black crossing herself three times before a tiny domed shrine, the bony cats sleeping in the sun.

"I'm surprised you aren't fortifying yourself with some honey-sweet wine," the British officer said. "Coffee isn't very Homeric."

"D-d-didn't Alexander Pope translate the *Iliad* while sitting in a coffee house? I . . . I'm happy to mimic the master."

The officer laughed. "A quick riposte! It seems you speak my language. May I sit, have a smoke?" He pulled out a chair, sat down, crossed his legs—giving a glimpse of plum-colored socks under his khaki trousers—and pulled out a monogrammed silver cigarette case. He offered one to Jack, then lit up, blowing an extravagant plume of smoke. He called to the waiter, asking for a coffee in perfect Greek, then turned back to Jack. "I'm Paddy Leigh-Fermor, by the way. You're Jack Hawke, right? Is it true you saved the First Secretary's wife? And fixed a radio with a rusty nail and a broken pencil?"

"Well, y-y-yes," Jack stammered. "We h-had to send an SOS somehow . . ."

"I wish you could do something about the radio situation here," Leigh-Fermor said. "Some damn fool ordered all the wireless sets to be left on the beach at Athens, and the ones we have are all broken."

The waiter brought their coffees and two tiny glasses of water. "Cheerio!" Leigh-Fermor cried and drank it in a single gulp. Jack followed suit, then choked and spluttered. It was not water, but some kind of pure, heady liquor.

"It's *tsikoudia*," Leigh-Fermor explained, laughing. "A kind of brandy made from the skin of grapes left over after the wine harvest."

"B-b-brandy! But it's not even n-n-noon."

"The Cretans begin drinking *tsikoudia* as soon as they wake. "To kill the microbe," I've been told. It's considered most rude to have guests without offering them a glass. Damn, I love this country! They sure know how to live." He called for a bottle, and the waiter brought one on a tray with barley rusks topped with goat's cheese, diced tomato, and oregano. Leigh-Fermor tossed back another glass of *tsikoudia*, lit another cigarette, and began to talk.

His conversation was a rush of funny anecdotes, clever asides, ruminations on art and poetry, and stories of his wild adventures. He had, he told Jack, walked from the Hook of Holland to Constantinople at the age of eighteen, with nothing but a stick, an old army greatcoat, and a volume of Horace in his pocket.

Jack listened, dazzled, half-drunk, envious. His life seemed so very ordinary in comparison. He tried to say so but could not manage to pronounce his new friend's name. It was the worst kind of tongue twister.

"Please, old man, just call me Paddy. I'm not at all the sort who likes to be saluted. I was expelled from the King's School in Cambridge for holding hands with a greengrocer's daughter, you know. She was, I have to say, of sonnet-begetting beauty . . ."

Paddy seemed able to talk at length, and with great wit and charm, about everything from cricket to Noel Coward. Jack found himself laughing and talking in return, telling Paddy something about his own lonely childhood in Cambridge and how he had lost himself in tales that sounded a clarion call to his soul. Theseus who defeated the minotaur. Alexander the Great who slashed the Gordian knot with his sword. Admiral Lord Nelson, who lost his eye and his arm in battle, but kept fighting to the end. King Henry, making his speech on St. Crispin's Day: *we shall be remember'd; we few, we happy few, we band of brothers . . .*

Jack had no brother. His father was nothing but a cold distant memory, a few curt letters a year. He had no uncle, no grandfather, no cousin. How he had longed for a band of brothers. And so he had followed the dark horn summoning him to war, only to see so many eager young men just like him die on the battlefield.

Paddy nodded in recognition. "Like Childe Roland to the dark tower came, in that poem by Browning. How does the line go? *All the lost adventurers, my peers . . . each of old, lost, lost!*"

They were silent for a moment. Then Paddy sighed, glanced at his watch, drained the last drop of his *tsikoudia,* and stubbed out his cigarette. "I must go. That's the worst thing about being a junior intelligence dogsbody for a bloody brigadier, they expect you to actually do some work! Shall I see you back at HQ?"

"Y-y-yes, I'll c-come now." Jack stood up too, picking up his copy of Homer. He hesitated for a moment, then said shyly, "D-d-do you know where K-K-Knossos is?"

"Indeed, I do. It's only about three-and-a-half miles from here, up in the hills behind Heraklion. You want to go and see the labyrinth where the minotaur once lurked?"

Jack nodded, expecting to be teased, but Paddy said, "It's a smashing place, well worth seeing. Do you know, when I was in Vienna, I met this young baron named Von der Heydte. He was in trouble with the Gestapo for punching a Nazi in the nose, and so had to join the cavalry. Anyway, I had a long drunken conversation with him at a party one night about the minotaur. I had always thought the bull-headed monster was meant to represent the bestial in man; you know, unconscious impulses, repressed desires, that kind of thing. All very Freudian. Von der Heydte had a darker view, though. Perhaps he knew what was coming."

Jack leaned forward, interested. "W-w-what do you mean?"

Paddy stood up, brushing crumbs off his trousers. "He thought the minotaur's real name was 'War.'"

IV

"Crete is the very cradle of civilization," Alenka said. "That's what Sir Arthur Evans believed, anyway."

"He's the guy who owned the villa, isn't he?" Teddy said, gazing about him at the tumbledown ruins of the Palace of Knossos.

"Yes, that's right. One day Sir Arthur was in Athens and went shopping in the flea markets, hoping for antiquities. He was an archaeologist, you know. He found some old stones which had been engraved with mysterious symbols said to have come from Crete. They really intrigued him. He wondered if they were evidence of some kind of ancient hieroglyphic language."

Teddy's eyes were fixed on her face. Encouraged, Alenka went on. "Then his wife died. Sir Arthur was heartbroken. He could not bear to stay in England. So he came to Crete. He heard an antiquarian from Heraklion had found some ancient storage jars in Knossos and wondered if his mysterious engraved stones had also been found here. He came and climbed this hill and saw, among the anemones and wild iris, fallen blocks of stone carved with the same shape as his little stones. The *labrys*, or double-headed ax."

Her voice was full of wonder. She had told this story many times, to many travelers from many lands, but it never failed to enchant her.

Such a curious chain of clues and coincidences which had led to the discovery of the Palace of Knossos.

"Sir Arthur bought the land and wanted to excavate, but he was not allowed. Crete was still ruled by the Turks, you see. He had to wait till we threw off the shackles of the oppressors and won our independence. King George was then the crown prince. He gave Sir Arthur permission to dig. Exactly one week after the first spade was driven into the soil of the site, Sir Arthur found a clay tablet marked with the same mysterious symbols—the double-headed ax, an eye, a snake, branches of leaves, a horned bull . . ."

"What do they mean?" Teddy asked.

Alenka shrugged. "Nobody knows. No one has been able to decipher the language. It's one of the great mysteries of the world. They could be songs, or poems, or spells, or prayers, or they could just be something completely mundane, like a laundry list. I hope one day to solve the puzzle."

Teddy glanced at her admiringly. "You sure know a lot about the old place."

"I should. I grew up here. I met Sir Arthur Evans many times when I was a child. He liked to think he was some kind of a pasha. Did you know he used to send a train of donkeys up Mount Ida to bring back snow to make sherbet?"

"Good God! Did he really?"

Alenka smiled. "No! Of course not. Idiot!"

He grinned. "Well, how am I meant to know? His villa looks like it belonged to an English lord. Have you seen the bath?"

"Imported specially from England," Alenka said solemnly. "With hot water, no less!"

Teddy laughed and jumped down from a wall onto a wide paved area. He then turned and offered his hand to Alenka. She took it, and he swung her down to the ground effortlessly. His eyes were very blue, his grin very engaging, and the sun shone in his blond hair.

It was her job to show strangers around the palace, Alenka reminded herself. She was not meant to laugh with them and tease them and let them hold her hand.

She hurried into her speech. "The last time Sir Arthur came, for the unveiling of his bust, we gave him a laurel wreath and he insisted on wearing it the whole day. He was so funny and very kind. A real lamb. Without him, no one would have discovered that a whole city lay hidden on this hill—a city with a theater and a throne room, the walls all decorated with frescoes of griffins and flowers and dancing girls and a prince carrying a sacred cup and bull-dancers leaping."

Teddy stared around at the tumbledown walls, the broken columns, and yawning pits. "It looks just like any old ruin."

"Oh, but it's not." Alenka leaped lightly onto one of the walls. "Come and see."

Teddy bounded up beside her. He had all the lithe grace of an athlete. *And he knows it*, she told herself.

"Look down at the palace," she instructed, in her best schoolmarm voice. "What does it look like?"

"I'd rather look at you." Teddy made a grab for her hand.

"I am not one of the local attractions! Be sensible and look."

He sighed melodramatically and gazed out over the ruins.

"What do you see?"

"It looks just like an old broken-down maze," he shrugged.

"That's it exactly! When Sir Arthur found the ruins here, he believed he had found the long-lost palace of King Minos. If you remember, he was the ancient king of Crete who ordered a secret labyrinth built to hide the minotaur . . ."

"Is that the thing that was half-bull, half-man?"

"Yes, that's right!" She smiled at him. "Every seven years, seven young men and seven young maidens were chosen to enter the labyrinth as sacrifices to the minotaur."

"He ate them?"

"Yes. He ate them."

"Till some guy came along and killed the monster?"

"Yes. Theseus. It's a very old story, very famous. The thing is, when Sir Arthur saw the palace from above, just like we see it now, it struck him that perhaps there was truth in the old myth. The word *labyrinth* comes from the ancient word *labrys*, you see, which means *double-headed ax*—and that is the emblem of this palace! And everywhere there are frescoes and carvings of bull-leapers—young men and women somersaulting over a bull's back.

"Sir Arthur thought that perhaps the myth of the minotaur was born from some kind of ritual dancing with a bull—and so he named this old ruin the palace of Minos, the king from the myth, and called the civilization which was born here the Minoans."

"That's amazing. Is it true?"

Alenka shrugged. "Who knows? Sir Arthur was a storyteller. He invented a whole history for this place and gave everything names that sounded like poetry. He built something beautiful and profound out of broken fragments. I like to think it is true. Or some of it, anyway."

She smiled at Teddy a little mischievously. She was well aware that he had no real interest in the ruins and had had something else in mind when he had asked her to show him the sights. But he was tall and handsome and came from Australia, a place she had always been curious about because it was so very far away. She had always thought Australia was hot and dry, a place of deserts and red rocks, but Teddy had told her that where he lived in the Macedon Ranges, they had frost and snow in winter and that he and his friend Jack used to build snowmen and have snowball fights.

"So if you grew up here in Crete, how come your English is so good?" Teddy asked.

"Well, my mother has worked at the villa ever since I was a little girl, and of course the curator has always been English, and so that's what everyone at the digs had to speak." Alenka looked back toward the hill where the stone villa had been built among exotic palm trees and Canary Island pines. "When Mr. Pendlebury took over as curator, his wife and children used to come and stay. I played with them and looked after them, and Mrs. Pendlebury gave me English storybooks to read to them.

"As I got older, archaeologists would come from the British School in Athens, and Mr. Pendlebury would sometimes be too busy to look after them. So I would show them around, tell them the stories, translate the Greek signs for them. Mr. Hutchinson is the curator now, and his mother lives here at the taverna with him. She speaks no Greek and is quite old and crippled, so I do a lot for her. There is always translation work to do and letters to type, so I'm kept busy. Or at least I was. They are packing up now, to go back to England."

"Is that little white building at the bottom of the garden the taverna?" Teddy asked. "Does that mean it sells grog? I'm dying for a beer."

Alenka shook her head, laughing. "No, no. It was once a *kafenion*, but now it is where the curator lives."

"So no hope for a beer then?" Teddy grinned at her.

"I can get you some wine. My mother will have some at the villa."

"Only if you will come and drink it with me."

Alenka looked troubled. "My mother would not like me to drink wine with an Australian soldier. She would not think it . . ." she searched for a word, then said with a shrug, "proper." As she spoke she remembered Axel sneering at her for pretending to be a good Greek girl and felt the burn of mortification once more.

"Have a heart," Teddy said. "Here I am, ten thousand miles from home, knowing nobody, fighting for your country. Having a glass of wine with me is the least you can do."

Alenka hesitated. *What harm can it do?* she thought. *I might soon be dead.*

So she agreed and led him the back way to the villa. She could see her mother through the kitchen window, washing dishes, a black scarf bound about her head.

"Your mother is the maid?" Teddy said in disbelief.

"The housekeeper." Alenka frowned at him. "Wait here."

She went through the half-open door. Her mother Hesper looked up. She was dressed, as always, in the color of sorrow. Her face was gaunt, with hollowed cheeks and deep lines engraved on either side of her mouth. Her eyes were as dark as Alenka's, but sunken into their sockets.

"Mama," Alenka said, "the Australian soldier is very far from home and lonely. He wants me to share a glass of wine with him. We will sit out here, in the courtyard, where you can see us. All right?"

The lines about Hesper's mouth deepened. She looked out at Teddy, sprawled comfortably in a chair, hands in his pockets, hat pushed to the back of his head. One work-worn hand crept up and closed tightly about Yia-Yia's hand-knotted black cross, which Hesper had worn about her neck since her mother's death. She spat three times.

"You don't need to worry," Alenka said gently. "He'll not hurt me."

Her mother's look of distress did not ease. Alenka said sternly, "He has come a long way to fight for our country. He is our guest, Mama."

Hesper stood still for a moment, thinking, then she reached out and gently touched the golden cross Alenka wore about her neck, strung with a tiny blue bead and the old coin she had found in the ruins. She looked at Alenka pleadingly, then went to get a tray and some wine.

Alenka twisted the cross about on its chain, biting her lip. Then she tucked it inside her dress and went slowly back into the courtyard.

Teddy smiled at her. "A-okay?"

Alenka nodded but did not speak. She gestured to a small table and chairs set out under the pine trees. It had a view of the garden with glimpses of the valley beyond. It was dusk, and swallows were swooping over the ruins. In a few moments, Hesper came back. She was carrying a tray with a bottle of pale wine, a little carafe of *tsikoudia*, some glasses, and a plate of *mezedes*. She poured the *tsikoudia* into small glasses and hobbled away.

"*Ya-mas!*" Teddy clinked his glass with Alenka's before tossing the *tsikoudia* back.

"*Ya-mas!*" she echoed. Before she sipped, however, she bent and spilled a few drops of the pomace brandy on the ground.

A libation to the gods.

V

Teddy slugged down his wine, watching Alenka. He did not understand why she intrigued him so much. She was not pretty in the way of the girls he was used to. Her hair and eyes were black, her skin brown, her nose strong as a man's. Her hands looked deft and capable, callused from hard work, but she moved with easy grace as if she was a dancer, and her mouth was full-lipped and sensual. When she was talking, her face and hands were so animated and full of life, he could not take his eyes off her. And she spoke English. The first girl he'd met in months who spoke his language and could understand his jokes.

He kept trying to flirt with her, but she only laughed and changed the subject. And when he put out his hand to touch hers, she withdrew it. Perhaps it was because her old crow of a mother was watching.

Teddy began to plot how to get her alone. "Will you come dancing with me? There must be somewhere around here that has some music."

She hesitated.

"Come on," he coaxed. "Where do all the bright young things go?"

"There is somewhere we could go tomorrow night . . ." She gazed at him as if assessing his suitability.

He grinned at her. "Great. Let's go then!"

"You might not like the music. It's *rebetiko*."

He frowned. "What does that mean?"

"It means the music of rebels. It's the blues of Greece."

"Will I get to dance with you in my arms?"

"No," she replied at once. "We Greeks do not dance like that. Why should I let a man lead me? I will dance alone."

"You're a hard nut to crack," he complained. "Maybe I can coax you into a foxtrot on the night."

"Maybe." Her dark eyes glinted with mischief. "Maybe not."

"All right then. I like a challenge. Where is it? I can borrow a motor-cycle and come pick you up."

She shook her head. "No need for that. It is not far. We will walk. It is a secret place, though. You must tell no one."

"A secret place!" The idea intrigued him. "But why? Is it dangerous?"

"Old people do not approve of *rebetiko*. It is for the young only."

The wine was finished. The old crow came out and cleared the table, banging the empty bottle onto the tray, clattering the glasses together. "It seems I must go," Teddy said. "Walk me to the gate?"

Alenka nodded and led him down the driveway to the road. It was almost dark, and the cypresses were black against a thin moon. Teddy waited till the villa was out of sight, then—without a moment of warn-ing—seized Alenka in his arms and kissed her.

Surprise was, after all, the essential principle of any military campaign.

VI

Jack jumped down from the bus outside the Palace of Knossos and strode down the street toward the entrance. Through the pine trees, he could see a glimpse of tumbledown stone walls, half-broken buildings, tall pillars. He felt a deep thrill in the pit of his stomach. At last he would get to see the fabled labyrinth, the place where the fearsome minotaur had been kept captive. The very stones were steeped with story. He sat down on a broken wall and drew out his tattered notebook, scribbling down a few lines of poetry.

A sweet laughing voice caught his attention. "*Po-po-po-po*, Modestine, whatever is the matter?"

Jack looked around.

A young woman in a white dress was pulling on the reins of a small donkey. The beast had all four legs planted squarely on the road. Her ears were laid back, her eyes showed a rim of white. A necklace of bells and blue beads hung about her neck, and she carried a bundle of driftwood and, surprisingly, baskets of flowers.

"Come on, Modestine! We are so close to home. It's not far now. Come on." The young woman coaxed and entreated, yanking on the reins, but the donkey would not budge. Jack dismounted and went to help. He pulled a handful of dry grass and held it out. The donkey eyed it sideways and curled her lip. Jack looked about for something more tempting. He saw some fresh green leaves growing out of the wall and leaned over to pluck them.

A low rattle and hiss. A thick coil of orange scales. A cold, unblinking eye.

Jack sprang backward, caught the young woman by the waist, and swung her away. "S-s-s-s-snake!" he exclaimed.

"Let me go! What's the matter with you?" She picked up a stick and gave the snake a gentle prod. It hissed again, uncoiled itself gracefully, and slipped away through the stones. "It's just a leopard snake. You could not find a gentler creature." Her voice was full of reproach.

"It-it-it had a *V* on its head, doesn't that mean it's a d-d- . . . death viper?"

"Not here. Herakles honored Zeus by destroying all venomous snakes and dangerous beasts on Crete, you know."

He grinned at the way she spoke about ancient gods and heroes as if they were old friends. She laughed too, her whole face lighting up. An electric thrill raced through him. "N-n-no, I d-didn't," he managed to say. "I c-c-c-come from Australia, most of our snakes are deadly."

She gazed at him with new interest. "Oh, yes. So I have heard."

"I-I was bitten when I was a boy." He showed her the deep ugly scar on his arm.

She nodded in understanding. One of her hands rose involuntarily to touch a scar on her own arm. "So you are afraid of snakes now."

"No! I mean . . . I'm not afraid, I'm . . . I'm . . . I'm . . . respectful." Somehow, he got the words out.

She laughed again. "Very wise."

Jack was afraid she was mocking him. Girls often did. He was very aware of how badly his tongue was mangling his speech. He would have liked to have stayed in the cool shadows, talking to this beautiful girl with her great dark eyes and laughing mouth, but he knew he would only embarrass himself. He gave a kind of gauche bow and went on down the road.

"Come, Modestine." She caught the donkey's reins, moving away from him. Every movement was light and graceful. Jack felt his own awkwardness acutely.

Modestine, he thought. *I know that name . . .*

Then he remembered it was the name of Robert Louis Stevenson's donkey, which had carried the young writer's pack on his long hike through the wild mountains of France. Stevenson had wept when he had to leave Modestine to return home to Scotland. It was one of Jack's favorite books. He looked back, but the young woman and the donkey had gone.

Jack walked on slowly, wondering about her. She had looked Greek, with her honey-colored skin and black lustrous plaits wound about her head like a crown. Yet she had spoken English the whole time, even to the donkey. Her accent was quite pure. Only a slight shortening of her vowels and the way she pronounced "Herakles" showed she was a local. And, of course, the way she said "*Po-po-po!*, an exclamation that seemed to express everything from surprise to indignation to sorrow.

What was a Greek girl doing speaking English to a donkey named Modestine?

Thoughts of her preoccupied him till he reached the ruined palace, which lay within a shallow bowl of a valley, surrounded by low bare hills. Whoever built it did not fear an attack, Jack thought. This was a peaceful city, with no sign of defensive walls or bastions. Unlike the old town of Heraklion, crammed inside its thick Venetian walls.

Jack spent the next few hours exploring. A restored fresco of blue dolphins and fish and spiky sea urchins in one room edged with spirals. An earthenware bath in a small antechamber which would not look out of place in a Victorian mansion, and, next door, the world's first flushing toilet, built more than three-and-a-half thousand years ago. A deep stony pit that might have been a well, a great painted gateway, a throne room with frescoes of griffins and lilies, and a white alabaster chair with an unusual sinuous back. An area that looked like an ancient theater with shallow steps leading down to a wide stage. And, in the main courtyard, the famous giant bull horns which framed the distant peak of Mount Juktas, said to be the grave of the god Zeus. Watching the eagles soar about the mountaintop was thought to have inspired Daedalus, the architect of the labyrinth, to build wings made from candle wax and the hollow feathers of birds, so that he and his son Icarus could escape. But the boy had flown too close to the sun. The wax had melted, and he had plummeted to his death in the Cretan Sea.

The maze-like ruins were deserted, though a few workmen's tools lay in corners. The only sound was the twitter of swallows flashing between the Minoan columns. Jack found a shady space under a pine tree, sat and drank from his water bottle, and imagined himself back in time. A long procession of bare-chested men, carrying jugs of wine and platters of grapes, women with long black curls playing on pipes, a musician with a lute, a priestess in heavy ceremonial robes, snakes writhing up her arms. Perhaps, hidden deep in the darkness below, a man with the head and horns of a bull bellowing his fury and despair . . .

Jack pulled out his notebook and scribbled a few more words.

Minotaur . . . longing for the light but so afraid of what is to come . . . sensing the hidden sword . . .

Then he saw the young woman with the crown of plaits coming through the ruins, carrying a box on her hip. Jack could almost imagine she was carrying a *hydria*, ready to draw water from a well. But then she put the box down, opened its lid, and revealed a portable gramophone. She put a record on the turntable, and the familiar strains of Glenn Miller's "In the Mood" rose into the air. The young woman lifted her arms as if embracing an imaginary partner, and then began to practice the foxtrot, dancing backward and chanting, "Slow, slow, quick, quick," just loudly enough for Jack to hear her. He could not help but grin.

Thinking she would not like to know she was being observed, he stood up and walked out into the sunshine.

She stopped, frowning. "What are you doing here? Did you follow me?"

He shook his head. "I . . . I . . . no, I . . ."

Jack could not get the words out. Something about this girl made his tongue more knotted than ever. His blood surged through his veins, his heart raced, his palms sweated, his skin blazed hot, even his ears were burning. He felt as if he was drunk. It must have been the *tsikoudia* at lunch. "M-m-minotaur," he managed to say. "I w-w-wanted to see . . . the-the-the . . ."

"I'm sorry, the palace is private property. You can arrange a tour with the curator, but he is preparing to return to England. I'm afraid I have to ask you to leave." Her voice was cool and remote, her dark eyes stern.

Jack left. He knew Teddy would have said something clever and charming that would have made her laugh, and perhaps let him stay, but Jack was not Teddy.

His best friend was guarding the Greek king at the villa nearby, Jack knew. He asked the way from a small boy with a mop of fair curls who was crouched over a lizard, trying to pull its tail off. The boy looked up at him, grinned, and put out one grubby hand. Jack found a small coin for him. The boy then pointed to a tall gate right behind him and said something in Greek that Jack was sure meant *idiot*.

He was in luck. Teddy was playing cards with a few other men in the courtyard of the small white house that guarded the gate. Drachmas, pound notes, cigarettes, and a can of bully beef were heaped in the center of the table, along with an almost empty bottle of *tsikoudia* and shot glasses.

Teddy leaped to his feet. "Jack! You made it. I was afraid you'd been left behind in Athens." He turned to the other men, saying, "Jack's my best mate from down under. Jack, come and play. I've had the worst losing streak, I need you to win back all my cigarettes for me."

"Nah, I'm out," one of the other men said, in a New Zealand accent. "I have to get back to work. Lloyd, don't forget you owe me for the grog."

Teddy shrugged. "Sorry, mate, I've blown all my cash. I'll have to owe you."

"I've heard that before," the man said sourly, pocketing his winnings.

"Here, I'll c-c-cough it up," Jack said. He found the coins in his pocket and gave them to the soldier, then they headed to the little *kafenion* nearby. The owner brought them the obligatory glasses of *tsikoudia* with their coffees. Teddy slugged his back, then drank Jack's too after he pushed it away. "What I wouldn't give for a cold beer," Teddy said. "Though this does the job."

They caught up on each other's news. When Jack told Teddy about being assigned to the brigadier's intelligence force, he frowned. "Well, you landed on your feet all right. You'll see some action there too, while I'm stuck here babysitting His Royal Highness." He brooded in silence for a moment, lighting another cigarette.

"I saw the ruined p-p-palace. Can you believe how old it is?"

"Oh, yeah, so I got told! I was shown round the place by the dish of a girl who works there. I didn't pay much attention to the ruins, I have to say. She's one hot potato."

Jack's heart sank. "I m-m-might have seen her too. Is she slim and dark, speaks perfect English?"

"Yep, that's her. Her name's Alenka. She sure is something! I'm taking her out dancing tonight, as a kind of goodbye. The king heads to Chania tomorrow, so I'm shipping out. Wish me good hunting, Jack. If I play my cards right, I might get lucky."

Jack looked away. The thought of that beautiful, black-eyed girl being the last in Teddy's long list of conquests was unbearable.

Please, he thought. *Don't let her fall in love with him.*

VII

Alenka looked at herself in her tiny mirror. She wore a homemade dress, spun from her own silkworms and dyed with fruit from her mulberry tree, and a pair of red dancing shoes that had cost her two weeks' worth of pay.

Every time she thought of Teddy, she felt a lurch in the pit of her stomach. She had not known kissing could be like that. He had taken her by storm, breached all her defenses. She had tried to slap him, as her grandmother had taught her, but he had only laughed, caught her raised hand in his, and kissed her again. "Have a heart," he had said. "I've come all this way to fight for you, the least you can do is give me a kiss."

So she had let him kiss her. She did not know why. Perhaps it was because he was so handsome, with his laughing blue eyes. Perhaps it was because of the war. All those people dying, all those lives ruined. She felt such a shadow of doom upon her. At least she had felt alive in his arms, his mouth so hard and demanding, his hands greedy for her. Just thinking of it made her hot and bothered, her blood rushing faster.

Was this what desire felt like? Alenka wondered. Because it felt a lot like fear.

Her bedroom was long and narrow, with stone walls and an arched ceiling. One window looked out onto the village square with its old, bent almond tree. Another gave a view of her garden, planted among tumbled ruins, and beyond, high on the hill, an old stone windmill, its sails turning in the continual rush of wind from the sea. A third window looked down on the Villa Ariadne in its jungle of exotic trees. The sills were so deep she could keep books in them, and so her room was cool even in the height of summer. It had room only for her bed, made up with homespun linen sheets and a warm red blanket, plus an armchair where she could sit and write or sew in the light of a lantern. Her dowry was kept in a battered chest at the foot of her bed.

Alenka heard her mother come through the front door and into the kitchen. She would have been at church. Hesper turned on the radio, as she always did. The announcer was saying, very fast and feverish, "Attention, all Greeks! The capital has fallen into the hands of the conquerors. On the Sacred Rock of the Acropolis, our blue and white flag is no longer flying proud. Instead, it is replaced by the swastika, the banner of violence."

Alenka stumbled out to the kitchen, and into her mother's arms. Gripping each other tightly, they listened together. "The Athens Radio Station must go off the air now. It will no longer be Greek. It will be German and broadcasting lies. Greeks! Do not listen to it. Our war continues and will continue until the final victory. Long live the nation of Greeks!"

A long eerie crackling silence.

PART II:
MINOTAUR
MAY 1941

O
mad
blinded
minotaur
stranger to yourself
lost in your circling labyrinth
longing for light but so afraid of the great
beyond

I

Teddy sat in the shade of a gnarled olive tree, eating cold porridge out of his mess tin and wishing for a slap-up breakfast like his mother used to cook.

He was in the garden of a villa owned by the new Prime Minister of Greece, who had grown up in Crete. King George had been moved here the day before, after several weeks in the ancient town of Chania, the island's capital. Teddy had been ordered to accompany him, and reluctantly he had done what he was told. He had not wanted to leave Knossos. He had unfinished business with Alenka. She'd stood him up! Just because Athens had fallen. He understood she was upset, but she had known he was being shipped out the next day. The least she could have done was kiss him goodbye. But she had pushed him away, crying, "How can you think about dancing or kissing at a time like this? Athens has fallen, the swastika flies above the Acropolis, we are enslaved!"

"I know, I know, I'm so sorry. Bloody Jerries! I wish we'd been able to stop them." He took her in his arms and tried to kiss her, but she leaned away, averting her face. "I guess I just wanted a chance to see you again. We could be dead tomorrow."

That line had worked before, but this time she just frowned.

"Come on, Alenka, let me die a happy man," he had said, pulling her closer.

Alenka had shoved him away with such force, he had been sorry. But the harm had been done, she would not let him kiss her, and now he was stuck out at some tiny village where all the girls stayed well out of the way of the soldiers. At least he had been able to go out to bars and nightclubs in Chania. Out here, there was nothing much to do but drink and gamble.

Most of the other soldiers guarding the king were from New Zealand. They sat nearby, cigarettes hanging out of their mouths, some with bare feet as they darned their socks, others with their shirts off to enjoy the morning sun on their shoulders. The villa was set on a hill overlooking Chania, which lay between the naval port of Suda Bay and the airport at Maleme. Teddy and the other soldiers were watching Messerschmitt fighter planes hammer the town in their usual dawn attack, which was so predictable everyone called it *the daily hate*. Smoke billowed up from the town, staining the cerulean sky.

"Bet you ten drachmas the next one hits the cathedral," Teddy said.

"Done!" a private said at once.

A moment later, Teddy gave a groan of disappointment. "Damn! They missed."

"Pay up, bucko," the private said.

"Sorry, mate, my pockets are to let. I'll write you an IOU."

Teddy pulled out a notebook and pen and scribbled down the value, signing his name with a flourish, then leaning over and tucking it into the private's top pocket.

"I can see I'm never going to get those drachmas," the private said philosophically.

"Mate!" Teddy threw up his hands in mock horror. "Don't you trust me?"

"Not as far as I can throw you."

Teddy grinned and lit another cigarette.

"What's that buzzing noise?" someone said.

Teddy squinted into the sun. Black dots seethed on the horizon. He thought for a moment it was a flock of birds. The drone grew louder and louder, the dots grew larger and larger. He stared, then felt a sudden sick lurch in the pit of his stomach. "Junkers!"

Everyone jumped up and stared. Hundreds of German transport planes, roaring toward them, very low in the sky.

"What's that flying behind?" one of the men asked.

Teddy raised one hand to shield his eyes. "Gliders," he replied in an overawed voice. "They're pulling gliders along."

The heavy transport planes released their cables. The gliders swooped silently to the ground, like vast steel albatrosses. Then paratroopers jumped out of the iron bellies of the Junkers, parachutes snapping open above them. Hundreds and hundreds of them. They looked as if they were dangling from gaily colored umbrellas. Teddy half-expected them to land with a twirl and start singing and tap-dancing along the street. Instead, they landed and rolled expertly, stripping off their harnesses and unbuckling their Luger pistols in smooth practiced movements. More than a dozen landed only four hundred feet from the villa.

"Holy shit!" Teddy cried.

Everyone began to scramble for their weapons. Men pulled on their boots, laces flapping, and ran for the Bren guns. Teddy drew his pistol, shooting up at one glider that seemed as if it must brush the olive tree with its wings. "Goddamit, they're so close!"

"We must get the king away!" Second-Lieutenant Win Ryan shouted from the villa. "Come on!"

The king had been moved to this villa a few miles out of Chania to keep him safe from the bombing. No one had expected German paratroopers would be landing in the fields all around them.

Ryan looked grim. "I knew we should have got His Highness away earlier. Come on, we need to go!"

He was the leader of the New Zealand troops set to guard King George and his party. For days, the generals and the diplomats had argued over what to do with the king. The British generals thought he should stay and give heart to his people. The British diplomats thought he should be whisked to safety. King George did not want to be seen as abandoning his people, but neither did he want to become a German prisoner of war. Things looked bleak for him, Teddy had to admit. His former prime minister dead by his own hand, his capital in flames, his government in chaos, his army conquered, and now the blitzkrieg had struck Crete, the last stretch of free Greek soil.

The king was standing on the terrace in his pajamas and dressing gown, a half-eaten crumpet in one hand. "I had best get changed," he said with admirable composure.

Within minutes he was dressed in full ceremonial uniform, with a stiff high collar, gilded epaulettes, and breeches tucked into long shiny boots, his hair slicked back from his high forehead. Hurriedly, he threw papers from his desk into his briefcase.

Someone shouted in German nearby.

"Your Highness," Ryan said urgently. "Please. We must go. We cannot risk you falling into their hands!"

"I'd much prefer that did not happen," he answered wryly and allowed Ryan to usher him from the room.

The men hurried from the villa and across a small garden to a back gate. Behind them, a burst of machine-gun fire. Teddy cursed under his breath as he ran. He wanted to stay and fight. Some action at last! And here he was running away like a frightened rabbit. Still, his task was to protect the king. Teddy couldn't let anything happen to him on his watch.

"*Ela! Ela!*" A local Cretan called to them to come, then said in English, gesturing wildly, "Away from the sea! To the mountains!"

The king turned and ran as directed, and Teddy followed, swearing as bullets whined about them.

At first there was a fair amount of cover. Stone walls. Olive trees. An old ruined church. A row of vine stumps just beginning to sprout. Gradually the fields gave way to undulating stony ground. A narrow winding goat track led between pine trees and out onto the bare flanks of the mountains, white peaks towering above. The older men were sweating and panting. Even Teddy, who prided himself on always being at peak fitness, was glad to stop in the shade of the pines and gulp water.

Colonel Blunt, the British military attaché to the king, was a man who liked to think ahead. He had organized Cretan guides and mules to be on hand just in case they had to make a quick getaway. They were dressed in the traditional Cretan costume of baggy breeches and tall boots, black fringed scarves bound about their brows, daggers at their waist. The mules were pathetically thin, but the guides soon had them loaded high with weapons and bags. A handful of mules were set aside for the king and his party to ride. Teddy had to suppress a grin at how ridiculous they looked, most of them in formal business suits, sitting on the backs of the tiny beasts, the thin soles of their dress shoes nearly brushing the ground.

German aircraft flew low overhead, circling like carrion birds.

"Please, sir," Ryan said to the king, whose breast was laden with beribboned medals that glinted in the blazing sunshine. "I must insist that you wear something a little less conspicuous. The Germans are hunting you; there is no reason to make their task easier."

The king frowned but nodded his agreement. One of the men helped him out of his jacket, and it was folded and thrust in a bag. Sweat stained his armpits and the back of his shirt.

"We should split up," Ryan said. "We are too noticeable in such a large party. One group of us will head this way over the mountains to the south coast. The other can head west and try to find another way through. I will stay with His Highness."

Teddy looked up at the mountains. They soared so far into the sky the peaks looked like thunderheads. He had never seen anything so stern and remote. A quiver passed through his body. He felt the familiar clench of unease in his bowels. "We have to climb those mountains?"

Ryan glanced at him in surprise. "Yes. It's the only way through to the south coast."

"Can't the boat pick us up along the coast here?"

Even as Teddy spoke, he knew it was a nonsensical question. The island of Crete lay halfway between Europe and Africa and was bisected by immense mountain ranges, some peaks towering well over eight thousand feet. The northern half of the island curved toward the Greek mainland, with a single road running along its edge, strung with ancient walled towns and little villages set in olive groves, vineyards, and gardens. The southern half was blasted with hot, sandy winds from the deserts of Africa, and so was much stonier and wilder as a consequence. The closest port still held by the British was Alexandria in Egypt, so any rescue mission must race through the night and return to safe harbor before the dawn flight of the Luftwaffe. They did not have time to make the long journey round to the northern shore.

"No." Ryan's tone was curt and angry. "Fall in, Lloyd. You're coming with us."

Teddy could not think of a way of getting out of it. Soldiers had to go where they were ordered. He picked up his pack and his heavy gun and pushed his way to the head of the line. He didn't want anyone slipping and falling and taking him down with them.

Ahead, serrated ranks of stony mountains rising into white spindrifts of snow.

Behind, a dizzying void.

II

Teddy kept his eyes on his boots, trying to ignore the sick fear in the pit of his belly. The Cretan guides led the way, rifles held horizontally across their shoulders, their gait sure and light and tireless. The soldiers surrounded the mules, shielding them with their bodies, scouts ranging ahead and behind and around. The path was very narrow and stony and zigzagged in rising switchbacks across the steep slope. The men came to the top of the hill and paused to rest a moment, wiping their foreheads on their sleeves and easing the straps of their Tommy guns. Teddy was parched with thirst and drained his water bottle dry.

Far below, the patchwork of vineyards, olive groves, and maize fields were strewn with the billowing fabric of collapsed parachutes. Teddy could see small khaki-clad figures running toward the fallen crates, tearing them open and dragging out weapons, ammunition, and supplies.

"Look at all that lovely loot we're missing out on," he complained, only half-joking.

"It's not such easy pickings as it looks," the king replied. "The Germans are holding their own."

He passed his field glasses to Teddy, who scanned the landscape below. Allied planes were burning on the airfield at Maleme, but the anti-aircraft guns were spitting fire at the Junkers soaring overhead and quite a few were spiraling down out of control. Paratroopers were leaping out, trying to escape, but their parachutes were caught in the tailspin, and they veered wildly over the sky before crashing to earth. The very thought of it made Teddy feel sick.

He passed back the field glasses. "The Jerries are dropping like flies!"

King George sighed. "I wish I had your optimism." He scanned the view once more. "All the Germans need to do is secure the airfield, and then they can fly in as many troops and weapons and supplies as they need. There'll be nothing we can do about it."

"Nobody's going to let that happen," Teddy scoffed. A frowning glance from Ryan, and he quickly added, "At least, I hope not, sir."

The scout ran back, breathlessly reporting parachutes lying abandoned on the hillside to the west. A quick consultation, and the Cretan guide suggested heading straight up the mountain, a clamber that would make a mountain goat think twice. Teddy glared at the guide but had no choice. Up the cliff they scrambled, over broken scree, dragging themselves up with their hands till their palms were sore and bleeding, ripping their uniforms on thorns. Teddy was laden with his pack, belt of ammunition, and submachine gun. His feet felt as if they were boiling in his boots. There was no shade, no water, no respite. Ryan gave the king his tin hat so that he had some shelter from the scorching sun.

A halt was finally called on a tiny shelf of stone surrounded by plunging cliffs. Teddy pressed his back to the wall, lit a cigarette, and looked at his boots so he didn't need to see the plunging void below.

"I need to check in with HQ, tell them we are," said Blunt. "Who has the wireless set?"

Everyone looked at each other in dismay. No one had thought to grab it.

Blunt was appalled. "How can we let General Freyberg know where we are or what time to pick us up? Good Lord, what a mess." He turned suddenly to the king. "Your Highness! Your papers? The decoded messages I gave you?"

The king patted his breast, then realized he was not wearing his jacket. A frantic search was made through the bags until the jacket was found and the pockets checked. Nothing.

"I had them in my hand," the king said. "I must have put them down . . ."

Blunt gazed at him in horror. "If those papers fall into German hands, they'll know . . ." He stopped abruptly. "I will have to go back."

Blunt quickly chose a few men to go with him. Teddy volunteered at once. He would rather face a pack of ravening wolves than that mountain.

"No," Ryan said. "We need someone with us who can speak Greek. Just in case something happens to our guide."

"But . . ." Hurriedly Teddy tried to find some kind of excuse. "Surely Colonel Blunt will need someone who speaks Greek too?"

"I think I speak it far better than you," Blunt replied curtly. He jerked his head at the men he had chosen, and they turned and began to slither back down the precipitous slope in a rattle of stones.

Teddy watched them go in consternation.

His father had fallen and broken his back when Teddy was a baby. He had spent the rest of his life confined to a wheelchair. Teddy's heart would jerk at the faint hiss of his father's approach. He would quickly hide whatever he was doing and pretend to be studying, but his neck would be prickling, knowing his father was coming. A sickening stench of iodine and infection preceded him. His body slumped huge and soft and heavy, his swollen hands clenched on the steel rims of his wheels, the skin of his face hanging in loose, sour, suspicious folds, bristled with gray from clumsy shaving. Nothing Teddy did ever pleased him. It did not matter how fast Teddy ran or how powerfully he bowled a ball or how many hours he spent swotting.

"You should've seen him before he broke his back," Teddy's mother would say mournfully. "You're so like how he was."

The thought sickened Teddy.

He and Jack often joked in private about their conceptions. They had realized one afternoon, drinking stolen whiskey and smoking stolen cigarettes, that Teddy had been conceived the last time his parents had sex and Jack had been conceived the first time. It was both funny and awful. Both boys had rocked with laughter, muffling their mouths, trying to imagine it, trying not to. Afterward, they had been shamefaced, and yet still shaken with hiccups of hilarity.

Teddy had been conceived in London, his father on leave from the Front, his mother doing volunteer work with the British Red Cross, which seemed to involve knitting a great many socks and serving weak tea to wounded soldiers. Two days after the armistice, when his unseen son was almost exactly three months old, a drunk Clifton Lloyd had climbed a statue in the square of a small Belgian town to jam his digger's hat on top of the curly marbled wig. He had lost his grip, slipped, fell, and cracked his spine. Groaning, he had rolled over, tried to get up, fallen again. Two of his mates had seized him under his armpits, dragged him back to their digs, and tossed him into his camp bed. In the morning, he had been unable to move.

The fear that he too might fall had kept Teddy firmly on flat ground ever since. He didn't like steps or ladders. He never climbed a tree or clambered over a wall. He had hated gym at school, and feigned illness so many times he had been sent home, the worst punishment anyone could devise. Film clips of tightrope walkers crossing the Niagara made him pant like a dog. Sometimes he dreamed he was falling, and woke with a terrible lurch, scarcely able to breathe.

The White Mountains loomed above him like shards of glass. But Teddy could not let anyone know how terrified he felt. He feared the other's men derision almost as much as the fall.

III

Alenka and her mother stood on the terrace at the Villa Ariadne, watching paratroopers drift like thistledown through the sky above Heraklion.

"I can't believe it's happening," Alenka said. "I thought . . . I hoped . . ."

Hesper drew her close, one arm about her shoulders.

The villa was empty now. The curator and his mother had left for Cairo, after carefully wrapping up all the archaeological treasures and hiding them. The king and his retinue had gone, and Teddy with them, not a moment too soon for Alenka's peace of mind. He was not someone who took no for an answer.

The church bells rang out, sounding the alarm. Alenka's godfather, Manolaki, hurried through the garden, an ancient rifle in his hand. He had obviously dug it up out of some hiding place, for it was thick with grime and rust. "Hesper! I need to clean my gun. Where's the gun oil? *Po-po-po-po-po*, I need it now!" His voice wobbled and broke, and he dashed one huge, gnarled hand across his cheek.

"Oh, Uncle Manolaki, no!" To Alenka's dismay, his lined face was wet with tears. She had never seen him weep before.

"Micky is dead," he said. "We had the news this morning."

Alenka felt the news like a blow to her solar plexus. Micky had been his father's pride and joy. He had been studying law in Athens when the war in Greece broke out. He had joined the Crete battalion at once and gone off to fight in Albania, but the general in charge of his battalion had fled back to Crete, leaving his men behind. The general had been murdered in vengeance for his betrayal, but the Cretan soldiers had still been unable to get home. Micky was like a brother to Alenka; it was very hard to hear that he had died.

"Oh no!" she cried. "Oh, Uncle Manolaki, I'm so sorry."

Hesper was weeping, clutching at her cross, her mouth moving as she silently prayed. Alenka put her arms about her mother, feeling her thin frame shake with grief. Manolaki's wife, Kyriaki, was Hesper's dearest friend. They had grown up next door to each other in Knossos and were godmother to each other's daughters.

Manolaki shook his fist at the paratroopers drifting down through the evening sky. "Cuckolds! If only we had our men here to fight you! But we have nothing. No troops, no arms, no ammunition, no aeroplanes, no sons!" He looked down at the old rusty weapon. "Our hearts are all we have left, but they shall not be found wanting."

Alenka put out one hand toward her godfather, her vision blurred with tears. He brushed her aside irritably. "No time for that! Hitler's winged devils are leaping from the sky onto our soil. They think us an island of weak old fools. We shall show them! Get me oil so I can clean the rust from my gun. Go, girl!"

Alenka ran to the garden shed, found a tube of gun oil, and took it back to her uncle. He began at once to scrub at the old rifle, laying it on the table on the terrace, spraying oil onto the paving stones in his desperate haste. Every now and again, a tear slid from an eye, and he dashed it away, muttering prayers. "May the Almighty give me strength today. May he make my aim true!" He put down the gun long enough to cross himself swiftly, three times, then returned to his task.

"Hesper, it is not safe here. The Germans will come. You and Alenka and the boy must not be found here. Go to the ruins, hide there. Take what you need for at least one night."

He tested his rifle, shooting an old clay pot to smithereens. The bang made Alenka jerk violently, and afterward, her ears rang and her legs trembled. Suddenly it all seemed real.

Manolaki slung his rifle over his shoulder. "I must go. May God be with you."

He hurried away, his straw hat on the back of his head, a cartridge belt fastened about his ample waist. Alenka felt sick with anxiety. Her beloved godfather had helped look after her and her family ever since they had fled their home after Axel's birth. He was a gentle, unworldly man, who had spent his life caring for the ruins of the Palace of Knossos. How could he fight the Germans?

Hesper had gone silently to the kitchen. Alenka could hear her opening cupboards, banging drawers shut. Alenka began to think about what they would need. Pillows, blankets, warm clothes, food, wine, a lantern, a box of matches. A rustle in the garden made her jump. She leaned over the stone balustrade. A flash of a familiar striped jersey. "Axel! I know you are there. Come out!"

Her half brother wriggled out of the undergrowth. His fair curls were tousled, his knees and hands very dirty.

"The Germans are coming. We need to hide. Come, we are going to the ruins."

"Shan't! I'm not going to hide like a cowardly girl. I'm going to go and fight." He pulled a carving knife out of his belt and brandished it in his fist. "For the Germans!"

"Axel, don't be silly. You're just a kid. Put the knife down, you'll hurt yourself."

"I am not a kid! I'm a man now. I will go and fight for the Germans, and we shall win and then you'll be sorry."

"Axel! Please . . . I don't have time for this. We need to go."

"I'm going to find the Germans. I'm going to tell them where the king is."

"What?" For a moment, Alenka could not believe what he had said.

"You heard me. They want to find the king, so I shall tell them where he is and then I shall be a hero."

"But Axel . . . you don't know where the king is."

He grinned at her. "Yes, I do. I heard the Australian soldier telling you. I am a good spy! And the Germans will be pleased."

"How are you going to tell them all you've so cleverly spied out?" Alenka mocked. "You can't speak German!"

He stamped his foot. "I can! I've been practicing." Laboriously, he said, in an atrocious accent, *"Der könig ist hier."*

He flourished a hand-drawn map, repeating the words and stabbing his finger at the paper, which was marked with a large red cross in crayon. "See, I have thought of everything."

Axel turned and ran down the driveway. Alenka shouted to him to come back, but he ignored her. So she called to Hesper, "Mama, Axel has run away. He means to find the Germans. I must stop him!"

She needed some kind of weapon. Looking about frantically, she saw her dressmaking scissors in her sewing basket. She picked them up and ran after her brother, the drone of German planes growing louder and louder, almost drowning out the clamor of the church bells.

IV

Axel could hear his sister calling him. He clambered up into an olive tree so she would not find him. Alenka was always bossing him around, telling him what to do. She thought she was so smart. Well, he'd show her. He'd help the German soldiers catch the king, and they would take him to Berlin so he could find his father. He'd be a hero! And then Alenka would be sorry she hadn't been nicer to him.

He watched the planes roaring overhead, paratroopers leaping out and floating down to earth with their parachutes billowing behind them like wings. Axel would like to do that. It must be like flying. You would look down on everyone.

Some of the planes fell, spiraling in flames and smoke, smashing into the ground. Axel tried to steel himself so he would not flinch at the sound. If he wanted to be a German warrior, he had to be tough! He thought of his mother, weeping and praying all the time. Nothing he did ever brought her attention from God down to him. Maybe if he dropped from the sky like an angel, she would see him at last.

Axel peered through the olive branches. A patrol of German soldiers crept through the maize field toward the olive grove. Axel's heart pounded with excitement. His palms were slick with sweat. He wiped them on his shorts, practicing what he was going to say. He had looked up the words in Alenka's German-Greek dictionary. She thought she was the only one who was good at languages!

The paratroopers began to search through the olive grove. Axel liked the eagle on their helmets and their big boots and guns and bandoliers of ammunition. They meant business, all right. He took a deep breath, then dropped out of the tree to the ground, right in front of them. At once they swung up their guns, their eyes hard and suspicious.

"*Guten tag*," he said. "*Willkommen*."

The German soldiers just stared at him in amazement, then looked around as if suspecting a trap.

Axel pulled out the map he had drawn from his pocket and presented it to the leader.

"*Der könig ist hier.*" He tapped the red cross with one dirty forefinger, then looked up at him expectantly. The officer's face was suspicious. Axel scowled and tapped the cross again, saying more loudly, "*Der könig ist hier!*"

"*Der könig?*" the officer repeated.

"*Ja, ja! Der könig.*" Axel smiled and nodded, tapping the cross again.

The German officer suddenly seemed to understand. He took the map and showed it to the other men, jabbering away in German. Axel could not understand a word. He waited impatiently. At last the officer nodded curtly, shoved the map into a pocket, and turned to go.

"Wait!" Axel cried. "What about me?" He spoke in Greek, not knowing how to say the words in German. The officer seemed to understand, though. He rummaged in his backpack and pulled out a slab of chocolate.

Axel grabbed it and began to gobble it down. He did not get chocolate very often.

The paratroopers hurried off down the road toward Heraklion. Axel wiped the back of his hand across his mouth and watched them go. He was filled with fierce triumph. He had found the Nazis and told them where the king was. He had spoken German. He had been rewarded. Chocolate was just the beginning. Other rewards would come. Medals and decorations and parades. He would be taken to Berlin, and the *führer* would salute him. He would find his father and show him all his medals, saying casually, "Oh, yes, well, it was because of me that the king was caught." His father would be so proud. He'd try and embrace him, but Axel would scorn such softness. He would stick out his hand instead, and his father would shake it, and say, "That's my boy. That's my son."

He ran through the olive grove, pretending to shoot with a machine gun. *Ack-ack-ack! Ack-ack-ack!*

Something white fluttered in the corner of his eye. He spun around, his heart banging hard. A German paratrooper hung from a tree, his parachute caught in the branches. His hair was as pale as Axel's and clung to his brow in little damp curls. He was only young, his skin pale and smooth as cream.

Axel went a little closer. He tried to remember how to say "Hello" in German. "*Guten tag*," he said at last.

There was no answer. The paratrooper's blue eyes stared blankly. Blood trickled down his face.

"Are you all right?" Axel asked.

No answer.

The wind rustled, and the olive leaves flickered. The paratrooper swayed back and forth. His body was limp, the toes of his boots drawing little circles in the dust.

Axel's skin crept. He felt suddenly cold, despite the heat of the day. He darted forward and pushed the paratrooper hard. The dangling body swung back, his boots hitting the olive tree with a clunk. Then he swung fast toward Axel, eyes fixed and glazed. Axel screamed and fell backward. He scrambled away. Crouched down and put his hands over his face. He could hear the creaking of the parachute as the dead man swayed to and fro.

After a long while, Axel crept forward. He took the paratrooper's gun from its holster and looked at it. It gleamed. He lifted it high and aimed it at the paratrooper's head.

"Bang, bang," he said.

V

The sun sank through a blood-red sky. All afternoon, Junkers had flown from the north in tight V formations like migrating geese, turning and banking to fly low over the fields outside Heraklion, paratroopers leaping out in perfect order, their chutes opening one after the other as if set to a mechanical timer.

"C-c-cry *Havoc!* and let slip the dogs of war," Jack said grimly.

"Good old Shakespeare," Paddy replied. "He has the perfect phrase for everything."

"I w-w-wonder what he would have made of Nazi paratroopers? They're like . . . like angels of death."

"I've heard the Cretans calling them "winged devils." Indeed, it's a poetic nation."

"How m-m-many more can possibly come? You can barely s-s-see the sky for the parachutes."

"The sun is almost down. The bastards won't be able to fly soon."

"Th-that's something to be g-g-grateful for," Jack replied.

"Though they'll be using the cover of darkness to get their heavy weapons and equipment, and bunker down." Paddy lifted his binoculars and scanned the landscape. "We've got Greeks guarding the wells and springs, so at least they'll have trouble finding water."

"They must be thirsty, poor b-b-buggers."

"I know I am," Paddy replied fervently. "Must be time for a good stiff whiskey."

A young private ran up, red-faced and panting. "Lieutenant Leigh-Fermor! Message for you, sir."

He handed over a crumpled piece of paper. Paddy read it swiftly, frowning. "Damn! We've lost all communications with the east. The field telephone lines have been cut—whether by bombs or paratroopers on the ground, it's hard to tell. And the radio is buggered." He turned to Jack. "I need you to get to the British vice-consul in Heraklion. His name is Captain Pendlebury. He's the man we want. Tell him we need a radio or two. He's got some stashed up in the mountains in case of emergency. Also tell him to let his guerrilla thugs up there know we need them here on the ground."

Jack nodded his understanding. "Where c-c-can I find him?"

"You know where the Morosini Fountain is, where we had lunch?" Paddy drew a little notebook out of his pocket, sat and rested it on his knee. With a stub of a pencil, he drew a quick map, with a doleful lion dripping water from his mouth at its center. "His office is here." Paddy drew a little cross. "If he's not there, try the basement bar at the Knossos Hotel across the road. Or Maxim's. That's a restaurant built into one of the Byzantine arches that surround the fountain. Pendlebury likes to go there. He looks so British no one can believe he speaks Cretan like a native, and so he listens in on all the conversations and knows who is leaking to the Germans."

Paddy made a few other tiny scribbles on the map—a *K* for the hotel, an *M* for the restaurant—then passed the map to Jack, along with the folded message. "Everyone knows Captain Pendlebury. You'll have no trouble finding him. Unless, of course . . ."

Jack turned back.

"Unless you find his glass eye on the desk. That'll mean he's gone off adventuring into the mountains already."

Jack could not help a little double-take of surprise.

Paddy grinned. "Yes, he leaves his eye on his desk as a shorthand message to anyone who knows him. He's quite a character. An archaeologist by trade. Used to be the curator up at the palace at Knossos. I think he's better suited as a soldier, personally. It's very hard to imagine him grubbing around in the dirt and getting excited about an old pot shard. When I met him a few weeks ago, he was wearing Cretan dress, with a dagger in his sash and an eyepatch. He looked just like a pirate! Anyway, good luck, be careful on the road. The Jerries will have snipers set up to pick off anyone that looks like they're on official business. Bloody bastards! Bugger them all."

He turned back to the private, asking him a series of low urgent questions, and Jack hurried off to find a motorcycle. Soon he was racing along the coast road, keeping low to his handlebars, looking out for the glint of light on a gun. The bodies of German paratroopers lay everywhere or hung from trees, wrapped in their parachutes like strange cocoons.

Don't look, Jack told himself. *Don't think about it. Just do the job you are here to do.*

But his whole body shook with the nearness of death.

Gunfire. His wheel swerved. Jack braked to a skidding halt, flung himself into the roadside ditch, and lifted his binoculars. Fighting, to the left, between the airport and the sea. The soldiers called the stretch of land there *the buttercup field*, for it was a meadow of dancing gilded wildflowers. Now it was trodden into mud, all the bright flowers crushed and broken. Allied soldiers rounded up German prisoners, hands held high.

Jack felt a giddy rush of relief. He mounted his motorcycle and sped on down the road. As he came closer to the town, he saw a band of Greek civilians led by a priest with a rifle in his hands, a cartridge bandolier worn over his long black robes. The men were armed with ancient breech-loading muskets, daggers, scythes, axes. A woman—dressed in black, her hair hidden by her headscarf—carried a kitchen knife bound to a broom handle with string. It ran with blood.

They heard his motorcycle and whirled, weapons raised, only to recognize his uniform and step back. Just ahead, a dead German lay in the ditch. The woman ran to strip him of his weapons and his boots. "He has a pistol, Greeks, come and get it!" she cried.

As Jack reached Heraklion, the boom of anti-aircraft guns and the shock of multiple explosions rocked the ground beneath him. His bike veered off the road and crashed into the bank. He scrambled clear and stood for a moment, his heart thumping madly, as overhead three or four enormous Junkers 52s came spinning down out of the sky, flames and smoke spiraling behind them. It was a terrible, awe-inspiring sight. *We've got them,* Jack thought dazedly. And then with fierce pride, *It was the Aussies that got them.*

Jack could not get his bike started again. The kick-starter was jammed. His hands were shaking. He left it in the ditch and ran down the road. His legs felt stiff. They didn't seem to work properly. He made it at last to the New Gate—built sometime in the sixteenth century—where the old aqueduct ran through the thick Venetian wall. It was shut fast. Jack had to shout and knock and show his ID tags before he was allowed in.

Beyond was a long, dark tunnel. It led to a maze of narrow cobble-stoned streets, shadowed by tall stone buildings and overhung by iron balconies. Many houses had been bombed to rubble, which spilled down into the alleyways so that Jack had to scramble over piles of loose stones and scree. Smoke rasped his throat. People ran, makeshift weapons in their hands. Jack stopped one. "L-l-lion fountain?" he panted. The man pointed, then ran on.

It took Jack a good half an hour to find his way there. Nothing looked familiar in the darkness and the smoke. At last he stumbled into the square and saw the famous fountain with its circle of stone lions dribbling water into the pool. He splashed some on his hot face, then got out his crumpled map, trying to orient himself.

Captain Pendlebury wasn't in the British Consul office, and his glass eye was not on the desk. So Jack went to the Knossos Hotel. There, in the basement bar, he found him.

Paddy had been right. Pendlebury was easy to spot. Six foot tall, lean, and athletic looking, with a Cretan dagger at his hip and a rifle over his shoulder, his fair English skin was sunburned, his short hair the color of corn stubble. His uniform was dusty and creased, the jacket discarded, shirtsleeves rolled up, buttons half-undone. A black scarf was knotted nonchalantly about his throat, and he had a glass of *tsikoudia* in one hand. He laughed at something one of his companions said, then tossed the brandy down. As Jack hurried toward him, Pendlebury looked up. One of his blue eyes was slightly miscast.

"S-s-sir, I-I-I have a m-m-message," Jack struggled to say.

Pendlebury raised an eyebrow at the sound of Jack's stutter and slopped some *tsikoudia* into a glass. "Have a drink, man," he said, taking the message which Jack thrust toward him. Jack took a slug and felt the *tsikoudia* burn a path down his gullet. At once fresh vigor radiated throughout his body. Pendlebury grinned at him and topped up his glass. "Have another. Dutch courage."

Jack sipped it a little more circumspectly and looked around him.

The room was dark, lit only by small lanterns hanging from hooks in the ceiling and a few flickering candles in red glass jars. A long wooden bar stretched the length of the room, and giant wine barrels were stacked at one end. The men with Pendlebury were all Greek, dressed in billowing breeches tucked into high leather boots, curved Cretan daggers tucked into mulberry silk sashes, black beaded scarves tied about their heads. One was an old man, oaken-skinned and gaunt, with a neat white goatee. He looked like an Elizabethan pirate, Jack thought, in his long cloak and wine-colored sash.

"This is Captain Grigorakis, better known as Satanas," Pendlebury said. "That's because only Satan knows how many times he has been wounded, or how many bullets are still inside him. I swear he'd rattle if he was shaken."

The old man grinned. Jack noticed he was missing a finger.

"C-c-can you get the radio, sir?" Jack asked. "I'll need to take a m-m-message back to HQ. They're getting w-w-w . . . worried with no news from the west."

Pendlebury shook his head. "Not now, anyway. We've just had word the Jerries are trying to break in through Chania Gate, and so there's no way I can get out now. Nor you, I'm afraid. Things are getting rather hot. We're going now to try and drive them off. You'd best come with me—we need as many men as we can get."

Jack nodded, though he felt a little sick. He was thinking of the battle at Thermopylae. They had fired more than six thousand rounds, a record for a day's fighting. The barrels of their guns had been blackened and smoking with the heat. Many of the gunners bled from the ears, their eardrums burst. And yet the Germans had kept on coming. Like robots. Nothing had stopped them.

Pendlebury put a hand on his shoulder. "Stiffen your spine, lad. It won't be pretty, that's for sure, but we can't allow Heraklion to fall. The cable and wireless offices are here, the harbor, the power station, the telephone exchange . . . and the people. We have to protect the people. They are such good souls, salt of the earth. They know what it is to live! We cannot let them be conquered."

"W-w-why are the Germans doing it? Why do they b-b-bomb and shoot and kill innocent people who want n-nothing more than to live their lives in peace?"

"The lust for power? It's a kind of madness, I think. Certainly for Hitler. I don't know about the soldiers. They seem to love him, Lord knows why. They certainly follow him blindly."

"'Tis the times' plague, when madmen lead the blind," Jack quoted.

"Indeed," Pendlebury answered. "Now, 'Do as I bid thee, or rather do thy pleasure; above the rest, be gone.'"

Jack grinned. "Yes, sir!"

"Good lad!"

The next few hours were a blur. Loading, aiming, shooting. Jack's shoulder ached from the recoil, his eyes stung with smoke. Bright flares shot up into the night sky, lighting up the scene with white intensity, blinding him. The constant barrage of gunshots.

Then the gate was breached. The Jerries were in the town. The Allies were forced to retreat through the rubble. Sharp flare of pain in his thigh. Jack stumbled, fell. He crawled inside a doorway. Put his hand to his leg, brought it away bloody. It wasn't too bad. A ricochet, maybe. He rested a moment, dizzy and sick. Boots pounded past him, and he shrank back into the shadows.

"*Aera!*" a young man shouted, shooting as he ran. "*Aera!*"

It was the Greeks' war cry. It meant *like the wind*. Jack gave a wry grin. Poets even in war. He remembered a story Paddy had told him. When the Germans had marched into Athens, they had forced an old soldier to take down the Greek flag flying over the Acropolis and replace it with the swastika. The old soldier did as he was ordered but then refused to hand the Greek flag over. Instead, he calmly wrapped himself in it and threw himself off the ancient citadel, crying "*Aera!*" His broken body was found hundreds of feet below, still wrapped in the blood-stained flag.

These Greeks, Jack thought, *will fight to the death. They truly are heroes.*

He found the courage to struggle up and run out to join the battle once more.

VI

Alenka stumbled through the darkness, too afraid to call her brother's name. She had searched for him all evening, but it was now after midnight. She was so tired and cold. She could not look anymore. She had to go home.

She saw the flat roof of the taverna behind its high walls. Her breath sobbed out in relief. Quietly, she slipped through the gate and hurried through the garden toward the villa. Alenka had grown up here; she did not need any light to know her way. Her plimsolls were silent on the grass.

Lights flashed through the trees ahead.

Maybe it's Axel come home, she thought. Her steps quickened.

German voices, glass breaking. Alenka froze in the shadow of a pine tree. Powerful torches beamed here and there. Men in uniforms strode about the villa, wrenching aside shutters to look in the low-set windows of the basement, bounding up the stone steps to the double doors, tramping on the shattered glass and wood to get inside.

Alenka closed her eyes and prayed. *O merciful Lord, please let my family be safe, please let my family be safe, please let my family be safe.* She crossed herself three times, then drew her dressmaking scissors out of her pocket. They were sharply pointed, but not much of a weapon against men armed with machine guns. It helped steady her nerves, though, clutching the scissors like a dagger.

"*Der könig ist nicht hier!*" someone shouted. "*Niemand ist hier.*"

Alenka spoke German quite well, for many archaeologists from Berlin and Munich came to Crete, hoping for a great discovery like Heinrich Schliemann's unearthing of the treasures of Troy. So she understood the soldier's shout and knew her family must have taken refuge in the ruins. She had to press her face into the bark of the tree for a moment, she was so dizzy with relief.

A sentry was keeping guard near the steps of the villa. He would see her if she tried to get past him. Alenka carefully unwound her scarf and wrapped it around her throat and face, hooding her eyes. She bent and fumbled about until she found a rock. Then she flung it as hard as she could in the opposite direction. It fell with a satisfying thump, and the sentry at once whipped around, then ran to investigate.

Alenka flitted from tree shadow to tree shadow through the garden, eased open the little portal gate, and then ran toward the old palace.

The ruins truly were like a labyrinth. The Nazis would never find her there.

The underground chambers of the palace were dimly lit with candles and oil lamps so that shadows flickered over the frescoes of blue dolphins and fish and sea urchins. Hesper was looking out for her, white with anxiety. She caught Alenka in her arms in relief but did not speak. Hesper had shackled her tongue a long time ago. She only unlocked it to pray, to chant hymns, to mutter an occasional monosyllable.

"Axel?" Alenka looked about her at the cluster of people camped out on the stone floor. There was no sign of him. Hesper shook her head. "He hasn't come back? Where could he be? I searched as long as I could, Mama. But there are Germans everywhere. They're at the villa. I should go back, try and find him."

She made a motion as if to go out into the night, and Hesper clutched her with thin, frantic hands, shaking her head.

"But, Mama, what about Axel? He's only twelve. He must be so frightened."

Hesper would not let her go. Alenka's godmother hurried up, her round face creased with worry and fear. "Alenka, thank God you are safe. Your mother has been so worried."

"Axel is still out there, Aunt Kyriaki. I need to go and find him."

"It's too dark now, you'll never find him. And the Germans might find you. Please, Alenka, don't upset your mother anymore. Axel is a smart boy. He'll find somewhere to hide. You can go and look for him again tomorrow."

Alenka hesitated, then looked at Hesper's agonized face. She could not understand why her mother did not speak. When Alenka had been a little girl, Hesper had sung to her and told her stories, and taught her how to make *dolmades*. Then, one day, she had just stopped speaking. It was as if she had been struck mute by a curse.

"Mama, perhaps if you came with me and called for Axel? He might come for you?"

Hesper shrank back as if terrified, shaking her head. Alenka tried to persuade her, but her mother's distress was too acute. At last she submitted and wrapped herself in a blanket and lay down next to her mother. She did not sleep much. The palace was a strange and haunted place at night. Every scritch of owl and scuttle of wind jerked her awake, hoping it was her brother, frightened it was Nazis.

She rose in the dawn and put on her plimsolls. Her mother was gone. Alenka crept up the broken steps and into the central court. Smoke smudged the eastern horizon. A black figure sat hunched in the shadow of a pillar. Alenka tiptoed toward her, sat beside her, took her icy hand.

"He hasn't come back?"

Hesper shook her head.

"I'm sorry. I searched for him everywhere. Really, I did."

Her mother squeezed her hand in understanding but did not speak.

"I will go now and find him and bring him back."

Hesper shook her head urgently, gripping her hand.

"I'll be careful, I promise." Gently, Alenka disengaged her hand, tying a black headscarf over her hair. A kind of camouflage. She reassured her weeping mother one more time, then went quietly through the ruins, one hand on the scissors in her pocket, keeping a sharp lookout.

Where could Axel be?

Most of the paratroopers had been dropped down by the sea, near Heraklion. Perhaps her brother had gone to find them down there?

She hesitated. She did not want to go to Heraklion. She wanted to hide away and wait till it was all over, praying for salvation. But her brother was only twelve. He was out there somewhere, frightened and alone and in danger. She could not abandon him.

Trembling with fear, Alenka began to sneak through the olive groves, keeping away from the roads, all her senses on high alert. Every explosion made her jump. The sky was filled with ravens, their croaking calls like a presentiment of disaster. She saw a cluster of them pecking at something that lay in the field, and turned away, sick with horror and fear.

She was more than halfway to Heraklion when the German planes came. Flying low, they bombed the old town mercilessly. Alenka could only crouch down in the grass, her hands over her ears, her face pressed into her knees. The ground shivered beneath her. She prayed with all her might. *O holy angel, who stands by my wretched soul and my passionate life; do not abandon me . . .*

When the planes at last turned and flew away over the sea, Alenka scrambled to her feet and began to run. As she ran, she continued to pray, the words coming in broken gasps. *Save, O Lord, my brother . . . he is only a little boy . . . he does not know what he does . . .*

Most of the gunfire seemed to be coming from the west, and so Alenka headed to the east of the old town. "Axel," she sobbed out loud. "Where are you?"

She thought of his favorite places. The harbor at Heraklion, with its great vaulted Venetian arsenals. The old fortress, with its battlements and spectacular views out to Dia Island. Axel loved anything warlike.

The thought gave her feet wings. She sped toward the old town, so hazed with smoke it was hard to see anything but the occasional church dome above the walls. The road was choked with people. Old women in

black, carrying heavy baskets and bundles tied up with rope. Old men
leaning on gnarled shepherd's crooks, leading heavily burdened mules.
A weeping mother pushing a perambulator crowded with half-a-dozen
children and their suitcases. A little boy trying to drag along a recalci-
trant goat. A priest, gray hair in a bun under his tall black hat, the hem
of his long robe pale with dust, carrying a hatchet. Wounded people
carried on old doors. German prisoners of war, marched along with
their hands behind their heads by grimy-faced Allied soldiers. A limping dog. Two women in black, dragging an old wooden cart in which
an old woman sat swaddled in blankets and scarves, nothing to be seen
of her but one round, soft, withered, bewildered face.

Most were stumbling away from the city. Alenka had to force her
way through them, crying her apologies and asking again and again,
"Have you seen a fair-haired boy? Blue-eyed, striped jersey?"

Quite a few nodded and pointed back toward Heraklion.

Alenka came to the old Venetian wall and ran along its length. She
could hear gunfire. Past the old Lazaretto Gate, where the lepers used
to be taken from the city to the old Lazar hospital by the sea. Past the
Sampionara Bastion. Around the corner. Straight into the arms of a
German soldier.

Alenka struggled to get free. The paratrooper gripped her arm, just
above her elbow. She managed to yank the scissors out of her pocket. He
laughed and took them from her easily, throwing them away. Then he
dragged her down toward the harbor. A company of German soldiers,
in tight formation, marched toward the gate that led into the old town.
A big gun on wheels was being dragged behind them. Pushed ahead, a
human shield of women and children. Alenka was shoved in their midst.

"*März!*" the German soldier ordered, prodding them forward with
the butt of his rifle.

Alenka looked up. The gate was locked shut. Greeks peered over the
wall, rifles pointed. An old woman beside her prayed, clutching her cross.
A very thin woman in a fur coat tottered along in high heels, her mascara
running in black streaks down her face. A young mother, a baby in her
arms. An older woman, a boy whimpering by her side, his hand fastened

firmly in her long dark skirts. A little girl, thumb in mouth, a doll with a broken china face under her arm. The sound of sobbing, praying, pants of fear. The German soldiers drove them all forward, toward the gate.

The Greek defenders lifted their rifles to the sky. They would not shoot. Alenka stumbled in her relief. Then the Germans behind began firing. Men on the wall were hit, bodies tumbling down. The gun on wheels bullied its way through the crowd. It fired. A great bang and crack. When the smoke cleared, Alenka saw the gate was broken, hanging askew. It fired again and again, then the Germans forced them to run, prodding them forward with their rifles, shouting, "*Schneller!*"

Still, the Greeks did not fire. A young man sprang into the breach in the gates, beckoning her desperately, crying in English, "Quick, quick! G-g-get in and then get out of our way, so we can shoot the bloody b-b-bastards!"

Alenka recognized him. It was the young Australian soldier who had tried to save her from a harmless snake. She ran up the cobblestoned road toward him. He reached out, caught her in his arms, and swung her through the broken gate, just as a bullet whizzed past, scorching her skin.

He shoved her behind him, lifted his rifle to his shoulder, squinted along the barrel, and fired. Reloaded, took aim, and fired. Again and again. It was no use. The Germans could not be stopped.

The young man swore and cast down his rifle. "No ammo left." He pulled a pistol from his belt, checked it, flung it away too. "C-c-come on!" He held out his hand. Alenka took it, and together they ran down the street, taking shelter in an arched doorway. "S-s-stay here," he ordered. Alenka obeyed, as he ran out into the street, seized a weapon from the hand of a dead Greek soldier, then fired it toward the advancing Germans. It held them back for only a few minutes, but it was time enough for many of the women and children to stagger out of sight.

Then he flung that weapon down too. "We need to g-g-get out of here!" He put his shoulder to the door and broke it down. As he and Alenka fled down the long, dark passageway, someone cried, "Halt!"

The Australian soldier caught her about the waist and swung her through a doorway, just as a fusillade of shots rang out. Bullets whined about them. A splinter of stone nicked Alenka's ear, and she jerked back in pain.

"H-h-hurt?" he asked her.

Alenka shook her head, wiping away blood.

Together they raced up a short staircase, and through a room where a family cowered under a kitchen table. The young man clambered out the window onto a tiny balcony, then turned to help Alenka scramble through, lowering her down to the ground by her wrists. He then jumped down beside her, looking swiftly both ways. A narrow alleyway led to the main street. They crept to the corner and peered out. Shattered walls, mounds of rubble, twisted metal, bodies lying like broken marionettes. They ran, the sound of pursuit close behind.

A corpse in a gray uniform and jackboots lay sprawled on the cobblestones. The Australian soldier seized his weapons and artillery belt. "Know anywhere s-s-safe?" he asked, swiftly loading the stolen gun.

"My uncle's lyra shop . . . it's not far . . . if it's still there."

"R-r-run, get there if you can. I will ho-ho-hold them off."

Alenka nodded. Just then a German staggered toward them, shooting wildly. The Australian soldier dove in front of her, firing from the hip. Alenka threw herself to the ground and hit the cobblestones hard. Winded, she lay still. The German fell, only a few paces beyond them.

The Australian sucked in a sharp breath. "D-d-damn! I've been hit."

She sat up shakily. Blood stained his khaki shirt and poured down the side of his face. He struggled to his feet, and she rushed to help him. Together they stumbled up the road and into the square. All the shops and *kafenions* were shuttered. Alenka looked under a loose stone for the key to her uncle's shop. Her hands were shaking so much, it was hard to turn it in the lock. As a platoon of German soldiers ran into the square, Alenka shoved the door open. They scrambled inside, and she slammed the shutters shut.

VII

The walls of her uncle's lyra shop were made of rough stone, and hung with stringed instruments of all shapes and sizes. Mandolins, bouzoukis, baglames, zithers, lyras.

Black-and-white photos hung crookedly from nails, a blue shirt and headscarf were flung over the back of a chair, and a shepherd's crook made from wonderfully gnarled wood leaned against the wall. An old table stood in the center of the room, with tools scattered upon it, a lute mold, coils of catgut and wire, tattered rolls of music, curling spirals of wood shavings, a gluepot with a brush still in it. Alenka frowned. It was not like her uncle to leave his shop in such a mess. He had been interrupted at work. She tried the handle of the back door, but it was locked.

The young man sat down on a stool rather abruptly.

"Let me see." Alenka came toward him.

He lifted away his bloody hands. She saw a jagged hole in the smooth olive skin of his abdomen. His tunic was stuck to it in places, and Alenka tried to lift it away, only for him to jerk and curse in pain.

"Wait a minute." She looked around. A wine jug stood on the sideboard. She poured the wine into the old pewter mug nearby, then eased the shutters open. She could see water splashing into the fountain only a few strides away. Yet her legs trembled, her breath was unsteady. She did not dare try and fill her jug. She looked back at the Australian soldier. He was holding his stomach with both hands. Blood was seeping through his fingers. He looked up at her. His eyes were dark and full of shadows. She thought about how he had swung her away from the gunfire, shielding her with his own body.

Alenka took a deep breath and slipped out through the shutters.

The sound of explosions and gunfire. Smoke caught in her throat, stung her eyes. Alenka crept forward. German soldiers were breaking down a door opposite, shouting to each other. Alenka dropped to her knees, crawled to the fountain, filled her jug, then crawled backward, trying not to slop the water. A harsh order made her jump. She looked around. No one had noticed her.

She scuttled back to the safety of the lyra shop. Her heart was pounding as if she had run up Mount Ida.

The dark-eyed soldier was slumped on the stool, hands pressed over his stomach. Alenka cut his shirt away. The bullet had passed through his abdomen, just above his hip, exiting out through his back. She felt a rush of relief. She had been afraid she would have to try and dig the bullet out of him. She made a pad with the cleanest parts of his shirt, then used her scarf as a bandage, winding it carefully about his narrow torso. Then she tended the wound at his temple. The bullet had creased the skin of his scalp and nicked his ear. She washed his face clean, then bandaged it with her uncle's black beaded headscarf.

He was shivering, so she brought him some wine and her uncle's shirt. He drew it on thankfully, buttoning it up.

"Th-thank you." He sipped the wine eagerly, then held the cup out to her.

She was very thirsty. The wine soothed her dry throat and calmed her. She drank deeply, passed him back the cup, and he drank again.

"You saved my life," she said. "Thank you."

"It was n-n-n . . ." He struggled to speak, his face contorting, and at last managed to say, " . . . nothing."

"You might not remember, but we have met before. You know, the snake."

"I-I-I remember. Of course I remember." His dark eyes were steady on her face.

Alenka went red. "I was not very polite to you. You came to see Knossos, and I turned you away. I'm sorry."

"No . . . no . . ." He paused, trying to steady his voice. "You thought you were alone. You were d-d-dancing . . . of course you did not want a stranger watching you. It . . . it's me who is sorry."

"I thought the ruins would be empty and no one would see. It's just so hard to get any privacy where I live. I have a little brother who is always spying on me and telling tales, and, well, my mother does not approve of the foxtrot."

"Nor of amorous Aussie s-s-soldiers, I'm sure."

She blushed even redder. "You mean?"

"M-m-my best mate is Teddy Lloyd. I saw him just after I saw you. He said he was taking you out d-d-dancing. Or at least, I thought it must be you."

"Oh." Alenka had thought the amorous Aussie soldier he meant was himself. "But how did you know Teddy was talking about me?"

"Because you are so b-b-b- . . ." He struggled for a moment, then said in a stammering rush, "beautiful."

Her cheeks burned.

"T-T-Teddy called you a dish. That's the highest possible praise from him, and I . . . I . . . I promise you, he's a c-c-connoisseur."

She busied herself tidying up his torn and bloodied shirt.

He looked contrite. "Sorry, I didn't mean to em- . . . embarrass you."

"*Po-po-po-po-po*," she said. "What's your name?"

"Lieu- . . . Lieutenant B-B-Benedict John Hawke, at your service, ma'am," he replied, trying to smile. "Though my friends call me Jack."

"I like Benedict. It's like a blessing."

He gave a wry twist of the mouth. "It d-d-does not suit me, though. It c-c-comes from the Latin . . . *b-b-bene* meaning good and *dicte* meaning to speak . . . as you can hear, s-s-speaking well is n-n-not something I can d-d-do."

"My mother is the same. She makes me think of that line from Sappho, *My tongue is broken . . .*"

"Yes. That's it exactly." Jack gazed at her in wonder. There was something about the intensity of his gaze that unsettled her. She thought of the rest of Sappho's poem. *And through and through me . . . 'neath the flesh, impalpable fire runs tingling . . .*

"How do you know Teddy?" she asked.

"We c-c-come from the same tiny country town, called Woodend. It . . . it's near Hanging Rock in central Victoria."

"Is it called Hanging Rock because people were executed there?"

He shook his head. "No. It's because there's this rock, s-s-suspended like a lintel over a magical doorway. It's a rather eerie place. Watches stop w-w-working there . . ."

"So how did you become friends?"

"T-T-Teddy's family have a big property there. My nana used to teach his sister piano. I'd go out to the farm with her, 'cause there was no one else to l-l- . . ." He paused, struggling to make the words, his mouth contorting. " . . . look after me. I-I-I-I'd sit on the step and read till she was finished."

He looked very pale. He leaned one elbow on the table and supported his head upon it. "One . . . one day I was sitting there, reading when Teddy came bounding up. He said, "Aren't you b-b-bored?" He didn't wait for me to answer, but yanked me up and said, "Let's go hunt snakes." I was t-terrified of snakes but didn't want him to know. So when he grabbed a big stick, I did too, and we . . . we went and poked our sticks in a hole, and a red-bellied snake came out and b-b-bit me. Snakes are p-p-poisonous in Australia, remember."

She nodded and smiled.

"I-I almost died. Teddy had to help me b-b-back to the farm. My nana cut out the poison which is why I have this s-scar . . ."

He showed Alenka the thick welt on his arm, and she put her hand on her own scar, nearly as wide and jagged.

"Teddy's f-f-father was very angry. He hit Teddy and m-m-made him ride for the doctor. I had to stay at the f-f-farm till I got better. Teddy was swotting for his exams, and I . . . I . . . I helped him. Then I got a scholarship . . . and went to school with him . . . ."

His voice was fading. Concerned, Alenka bent over him.

Suddenly, the shutters banged open. A German paratrooper stood in the doorway, rifle raised. He was very young, but anger and determination were in every line of his face and body.

Alenka gave a little scream and jumped up, hands raised. "*Nein, bitte!*"

He answered angrily. The only word she recognized was "*Englisch.*'

"*Nein, nein!*" She tried to remember the German word for "Greek." "*Griechen,*" she said. He jerked his gun at her, and she repeated the words in desperate haste. "*Nein, bitte, Griechen, Griechen!*"

The soldier moved forward so swiftly she only had time to tumble from her stool and try to fend him off. He seized her collar in one hand and tore it away. Alenka screamed. Jack sprang up, trying to defend her. The German soldier shoved him away. He fell to the floor. Alenka's dress was ripped from the neck almost to the waistband. She covered herself with both hands, scrambling away, sobbing in fear.

"Halt!" The paratrooper caught her and held her still, examining her bare right shoulder. He grunted, then searched her swiftly. Alenka had nothing in her pockets, not even a coin purse. He let her go, then turned his attention to Jack. "*Englisch,*" he said again, his gun lifted to his shoulder.

"*Nein, mein brüder, mein brüder,*" she gabbled, trying to stop him.

He looked from her to him. Jack was black-haired, dark-eyed, olive-skinned. He looked more like her brother than Axel did, she thought wildly, particularly with the Cretan headscarf wound about his brow.

"*Lebst du hier?*" the German asked, gesturing around.

"*Oh, ja, lebst hier.*"

He said something else, and she shook her head, not understanding. He gave a little noise of frustration, then seized one of the biggest instruments hanging on the wall, thrusting it toward her and Jack.

"He . . . he wants us to prove it," Jack said, in halting Greek.

"Prove?"

"That we live here." Jack got up, both hands raised.

Alenka grabbed onto the table for support, faint with fear.

Jack gave her a little reassuring grin. He took the instrument from the German soldier. It was a great lyra. Most lyras were small, about the size of a mandolin, and played with bows hung with hawk-bells. This fat-bellied instrument was much larger, with four strings instead of three. Made from ancient wood taken from Venetian ruins, it was called a *vrondo-lyra*, or thunder-lyra, for its voice was deep and moody.

He chose a bow. Sitting in the chair, Jack rested the pear-shaped lyra between his legs. Alenka felt a stir of hope. He lifted the bow, drew it across the strings, and a strain of delicate music lilted into the air, a phrase of notes repeating itself again and again. It was so fragile, and yet so ardent, so joyous.

A lump rose in her throat. All the hairs on her arms quivered, as if in terror. Yet it was awe and wonder that she felt.

This is what music is for . . .

He played for three or more minutes, the melody climbing higher and higher, in recurring melodic loops, then the music slowed and circled down once more, like a lark coming to rest upon the warm breast of the earth. A few more tremulous notes, then Jack lifted the bow from the strings. Silence fell.

Alenka surreptitiously rubbed the tears from her face.

"Bach," the German soldier said huskily.

Jack nodded.

The German nodded back, cleared his throat. "*Wunderschönen. Danke schön.*" He bowed, looked around the little room. Alenka noticed a spreading blot of blood on Jack's shirt and his unmistakable army-issue boots. A rush of fear unnerved her.

"*Ich habe auch brüder,*" the German soldier said, and left.

I too have brothers.

The relief that followed was so powerful Alenka sank to the floor. She was alive. Strangely, miraculously alive.

She stared at Jack. "But . . . how?"

"It . . . it is like a cello." Jack caressed the silky golden body of the lyra. "My m-m-mother played the cello. I learned—to feel near her, I suppose. She . . . she died giving birth to me, so I never knew her. That's one of her favorite suites. My nana says she p-p-played it every Monday morning, all of it. N-n-not just the prelude."

A long silence, then he sighed, cradling the lyra like it was a baby. "Bach's Cello Suite No. 1 in G major," he said, very low and gruff. "The k-k-key of benediction."

Alenka stared at Jack. "But you are so good . . . you should be on the radio . . . playing at Carnegie Hall."

"No." Carefully, he laid down the lyra. "I started too late. It is far too late for me."

The blot of blood was now a flood. He pressed one hand to his side, then swayed and fell heavily to the ground.

He lay motionless in a crimson slick of blood.

Alenka did not know what to do. She knelt beside Jack, her hands pressed over the bloodstained bandage wrapped so inexpertly about his abdomen. He moaned in pain. Relief weakened her limbs. She got up and rushed to the doorway at the back of the shop, banging on it with both fists. "Uncle Dimitris," she cried, but nobody answered. So she slipped to the front door and peered out through the shutters. She could hear gunfire, but it was some distance away. Down near the port, she thought. Trembling, she ventured a little farther out.

Suddenly, gladness rushed through her. A tall figure with cropped fair hair stood leaning on his sword-stick nearby, conferring with a group of men, a map spread out between them. A boy stood by his side, his arms filled with old-fashioned black telephones with crank handles, obviously salvaged from the bombed-out shops nearby.

"Mr. Pendlebury!" she cried.

He turned at once. "*Kyria* Alenka? What are you doing here? It's not safe."

"I'm looking for my brother. He ran away, and I thought he may have come here, to my uncle's house."

"This is no place for a child, nor for you, *kyria*."

"I know, but . . ."

"The general was looking for a safe place to set up a field hospital and I suggested the villa. The doctors and nurses are preparing to head up there now. You'll be able to get a lift home with them. The trucks are all marked with the red cross, so you should be safe."

"There's an injured soldier in there. He saved my life . . ."

"He had best go with you. Boys, wrench off one of those shutters, use it as a stretcher." Pendlebury issued a few quick orders, then turned back to Alenka. His eyes narrowed as he saw her torn dress. "My dear girl, are you hurt? What happened to you?"

Alenka looked down at herself, not understanding the sharp note in his voice until she saw the ripped bodice. "A German soldier tore it . . . I don't know why . . . he didn't hurt me."

"Looking for bruises, I guess. From the recoil of a rifle. I heard they were killing anyone who tried to resist, regardless of age or sex." Pendlebury's voice was grim.

"Do they expect us to sit by and do nothing?" Alenka cried. "They are invading our home! Shooting our people!"

"I think they do not know the character of the people of Crete. They will be sorry, I promise you that, *kyria*."

"Yes," she answered, her voice full of conviction.

He smiled and turned back to his map.

Alenka caught his elbow. "Excuse me, sir, can you tell me . . . are we winning? Can we drive them off?"

He hesitated, then said, "For now, *kyria*, we have driven them off. It's hard to know for sure, with our telegraph wires all down and no radios working. They've lost at least half-a-dozen Junkers and thousands of men. Hopefully, they will decide the cost is too high and withdraw. It depends on whether we can hold the airfields. As long as they cannot land, we shall win."

She smiled in her relief and thanked him.

Two men came out of the lyra shop, carrying Jack on a makeshift stretcher. He was still unconscious.

Pendlebury bent over him. "Oh, it's the young Australian soldier. What was his name?"

"Jack Hawke," Alenka told him.

He nodded. "That's right. He fought bravely today. Look at him, he's scarcely more than a boy! Well, he'll be all right. The doctors shall fix him up."

To go and fight again, Alenka thought but did not say.

Wearily, she followed the men through the piles of rubble and smashed masonry. Jack lay motionless on the old shutter, his face smeared with grime and blood, his eyes shut. One of the stretcher-carriers stumbled on the uneven ground. Jack was jerked awake. He looked around in sudden panic and cried out.

Alenka hurried forward, taking his hand and bending over him so he could see her face. "*Po-po-po*, it's all right. I'm here."

PART III:
THE HIDDEN SWORD
LATE MAY–JUNE 1941

O
swift
twirling
chain dancers
leaping to your deaths
the last to come the hidden sword
the subtle thread unspooling back into the
blackness

I

22–23 May 1941

Teddy had never been so high above the world. It made him feel as if the ground was reeling under his feet.

The White Mountains rose and fell as far as he could see, a few thin pines clinging with misshapen roots to rocks. Above, the high ridge was encrusted with snow. It was bitterly cold, and the wind sliced through his sweat-damp clothes like a scythe.

The last few days had been the most difficult of his entire life. The terrible mountains. The yawning abyss. The sick terror.

Teddy and the king's party had spent the first night of their flight in the tiny village of Therisso. It nestled between high snowy peaks, at the head of a deep winding gorge, with a dozen or so weather-beaten stone houses huddled together as if seeking protection from the biting wind. The only sound was the tinkle of goats' bells. An old woman crouched on a step, spinning wool with a drop spindle. She creaked upright at the sight of them and began to harangue them in a shrill voice.

"What is she saying?" Ryan asked, his hand near his gun.

Rude words and insults were the only Greek Teddy had studied closely. "She's calling us soft," he said uncomfortably. "Unmanly."

"But . . . why?" one of the other men asked.

The old woman gestured toward the coast. Teddy caught the Greek word for "fight" and "German.'

"She thinks we should be down fighting the Nazis, not fleeing like yellow curs with our tails between our balls," Prince Peter said bitterly. He dismounted from his mule and answered the old woman with a flood of Greek. The king also dismounted, though he did not speak. His jaw was set, his face downturned.

Other old women came out of their houses at the sound of the raised voices. They began to shout and gesticulate too. Again and again, they pointed away from the village. "*Po-po-po-po-po!* Go back and fight!" they cried. Hunched, swathed from head to foot in black, they looked like witches from a pantomime.

"*Gorgonas,*" the king muttered.

"*Malakas!*" they answered him.

"What does that mean?" Ryan demanded, looking about uneasily as the gathering crowd pressed closer around them.

"A man who masturbates too much," Prince Peter answered. He gestured toward the king and shouted something. Teddy recognized one word, for it had been said so often in his hearing in recent weeks. *Vasiliás.* It meant king.

One old woman spat. Another thrust out both gnarled hands, palms forward, fingers outstretched, smacking the back of one hand with another. Yet another shouted a word Teddy would never have thought an elderly woman would know, let alone speak. Ryan motioned to his men to close ranks around the king.

"They do not care much for royalty here," Prince Peter explained. "When my father was high commissioner in Crete, the people of Therisso rose against him and forced him out."

"It is a village of revolutionaries," the king said. "And I suspect our guides sympathize with them, bringing us this way."

An old man in a goatskin cloak hobbled out, making shushing motions with his hands. The others argued with him, but he spoke with stern authority and they fell back, scowling.

"Please forgive," the old man said in broken English. "All our young men lost, fighting. Much angry. Please to come?" He gestured toward his home, breaking into a flood of Greek as he spoke to the king.

A single room, with an earthen floor and a sleeping bench built near the fire. Onions, garlic, and paprika pods hung from low, smoke-blackened beams. Candlelight gleamed on gilded icons hanging in one corner, on the silver fittings of an ancient rifle leaning against the wall, and on the furrowed face of the old man. He offered the king the only chair and brought them bread and olives and wine. There was only enough for each man to have a few mouthfuls and a swig. There was nowhere to lie but on the floor. Exhausted from the hard day's climb, most of the men soon slept. All but Teddy, who had felt such darkness within him he could not rest.

"How goes the battle?" the old man asked the king anxiously. "Have we eaten them?"

"Yes, we have eaten them," the king lied.

The words made Teddy shiver. It was like something out of Homer. There was one line in the *Iliad* he always remembered: *Would to God my wrath and fury might bid me carve thy flesh and eat it raw* . . .

The morning dawned cold and red. King George borrowed a heavy sheepskin coat from the village headman. For the first time, he looked Greek. He did not move with the lithe grace of their guide, however. His mule's hooves slipped on the snow, and it often halted, legs splayed, refusing to go on. Teddy knew how it felt.

Colonel Blunt caught up with them around noon. His face was grave. The villa had been occupied by German soldiers, he said, too many to try to engage. The wireless and the king's papers were in enemy hands.

The news cast a pall over them all, much like the haze of black smoke that hung over the sky to the north. The good news was Blunt had managed to ring headquarters with a civilian telephone and confirmed a ship was being sent to evacuate them the following night. It meant they had only thirty hours in which to climb the White Mountains and descend the other side. Shouldering their weapons, wrapping scarves about their mouths against the needle-sharp flurries of snow, the men grimly marched on.

Teddy was so cold, his feet and hands felt like clumsy blocks of ice.

Pain shot up his legs with every step. *Frostbite*, he thought. *Amputation. Crippled.*

It was hard to hide his terror.

At dusk the guide had led them to a tiny round hut built of stones against the cliffs. It belonged to a shepherd and his wife. They exclaimed with dismay at the exhausted men stumbling through the snow and hurried to help them.

The shepherd caught one of his ewes, and his wife swiftly milked it. She brought them a bucket of warm foaming milk and a single wooden mug, which they passed from hand to hand, king and commoner alike. Teddy had never heard of a ewe being milked before, even though his father ran sheep on his property in the Macedon Ranges. He was so thirsty, he drank down his mugful as if it were beer and then wished for more.

The shepherd killed the ewe and swiftly skinned it and hacked it up. The men gathered fallen branches to make a fire and filled the empty milk bucket with snow to melt. Mutton broth was soon simmering away in the men's mess tins, shoved around the fire's edges. Teddy and the men crowded around the flames. When Teddy gingerly took off his boots, he found his socks stiff with blood. His heels and toes were a mass of broken blisters, but he was so cold he could feel nothing. He began to massage his toes to get the feeling back, but Ryan stopped him.

"Better to soak them in warm water," the New Zealander said. "Else you might lose a few toes."

So Teddy and the other men filled their tin hats with snow and set them around the fire to melt, then bathed their hands and feet in the warmed snowmelt. Feeling returned in a roar of pain.

The hut was very small, but the king, his cousin, and the dignitaries crowded in as best they could with the old shepherd and his wife. Blunt, of course, had thought to bring his sleeping bag and groundsheet, but he gave these to the king and wrapped himself in his greatcoat. Everyone else had to sleep out in the bitter-cold darkness. They huddled around the fire or hunched into rock crevices. Some of the men were dressed only in shorts, and they were given the spots by the fire. Teddy was—unfairly, he thought—given picket duty.

Blunt took him aside. "The king must not fall into German hands, whatever the cost. Do you understand me, Lloyd?"

"Do you mean . . ." Teddy began incredulously.

Blunt gave him a hard stare. "You have your orders, Lloyd."

It was a long night. Teddy could only keep from freezing by stamping his feet constantly, his hands shoved deep in his pockets, his chin buried in his collar. The mountain peaks frowned down on him, black against the starry sky. The moon was little more than a sliver.

Close to midnight, a great orange glow lit up the horizon far to the north, pierced by flares like bright shooting stars. Teddy stood and watched. He hoped it was the German navy that was being clobbered so hard and not the British.

————————

Dawn stained the snow-dusted peaks of the mountains, and Teddy's breath blew white from his mouth. There was nothing to eat or drink except snowmelt.

Only his anger warmed him. Guarding the king was meant to be soft duties, not this exhausting slog through a wild and remote landscape. He did not believe the guides when they assured them they were not lost. The people of Crete had no love for the king, Alenka had told him. They were rebels and republicans by nature. The local guides had probably led them the most difficult way on purpose. Perhaps they intended to leave them here to die.

"It is time to go on, Your Highness," Ryan said. "We have a long way to go today if we are to make the evacuation point tonight."

The king nodded. He was so stiff, Ryan had to haul him to his feet.

They labored on and on, climbing ever higher. Teddy wondered if he could duck down behind a boulder and hide, then make his way back. He did not want to be labeled a coward and a deserter, though. His mother would be so ashamed.

At last the path reached the highest point of the ridge. From there, the ground fell away in a series of sheer cliffs, down, down, down to the stony floor of a gorge, many hundreds of feet below.

"How far to the coast?" Blunt asked.

One of the guides shrugged and raised both hands, all ten fingers splayed. "At least ten hours," Blunt translated. "Maybe more."

It was then that Teddy decided he had had enough. The Cretans were quite mad, he thought, to think they could get down those cliffs in one piece. What if he slipped and fell, breaking his back like his father?

"There's no way we can take the mules down there," Ryan said. "And we'd best lighten the load. Better leave the heavier guns."

"I'll take them back," Teddy volunteered. "They'll be needing them at the fight."

Ryan looked surprised but nodded. "Very well. Seymour, you'd best go with him."

A group of ten men—the ones with the worst blisters—were chosen to go back to Chania. The king bid them all farewell formally, shaking their hands and thanking them for their service. "I hope you're not jumping out of the frying pan into the fire," he said to Teddy.

Secretly, Teddy scoffed. He had seen the paratroopers being shot down out of the sky, and the Junkers coming down in flames, and the long lines of German prisoners of war being marched along the road. A piece of cake, he told himself.

But he nodded, smiled, told the king what an honor it had been serving him, then gladly turned away from that dizzying fall and headed back toward the white peak. They spent the night at Therisso and made it to Chania as the sun was going down over the bay in a fierce orange blaze. Everywhere, smashed planes, smoking wrecks of ships, blackened trucks, and long lines of bodies waiting to be buried. The air smelled of death.

Teddy felt sick. He stopped a soldier, stacking corpses in a ditch. "What's happened? Have we won?"

"Won?" the soldier answered bitterly. "No. We've lost the airport at Maleme, and the Germans are pouring in. It's a bloody shambles."

II

23 May 1941

Alenka crouched by the fire, unable to stop her shivering. She had got home the previous evening to find her mother on her knees, praying before the flimsy gilt icons in the eastern corner of their kitchen. "Axel?" she had asked at once.

Hesper had shaken her head.

"Have you gone out looking for him? Where did you go?" Alenka had demanded, thinking that if she knew where her mother had searched, she could go elsewhere.

But Hesper had only shaken her head again.

Alenka could not believe it. She had searched for her brother all day, even going into the bombed and smoking ruins of Heraklion, where the battle was still raging. Axel was only twelve. Hesper should have been half-demented with worry for her little boy. Yet here she was, silently praying instead of searching for him.

"I don't understand!" Alenka cried. "Why don't you *do* something? Why don't you *speak?*"

Her mother had raised her harrowed face, her mouth contorting as she struggled to articulate. She croaked a sound. Alenka had seized her shoulders, shaken her. "Why? Why?"

Hesper had answered, so low that Alenka had to bend to hear

her. "He forced me."

"What?" Alenka responded uncomprehendingly. "Who? What do you mean?"

Her mother just looked up at her with huge, dark, haunted eyes.

Then Axel had come home. His curls ruffled, chocolate smeared on his face, a paratrooper's rucksack on his back. He'd tossed it casually onto the table. Out spilled cans of liverwurst, a German pistol, a flick knife, a slim packet of cigarettes, hand grenades.

Rage had flashed through Alenka. "Where have you been? I've been half out of my mind with worry for you!"

Axel just grinned. "I can look after myself."

Alenka caught him by the shoulder. "How can you be such an idiot? You're just a kid. You could've been killed."

Axel had gone crazy. He had punched and kicked her, shouting at her, "They would not kill me, I am German too! My father was German, I look nothing like you, I look like my father. I will go to Germany and I will look for him and I will find him. He will be pleased to see me, he will be proud, he will *love* me!"

Sudden realization hit Alenka like a blow to the stomach. She looked from her half brother, his hair as white as fairy floss, his eyes as blue as the sky in spring, to her mother, hunched over as if she was ill, her hands pressed to her mouth. *His father*, she thought dazedly.

She had pulled herself together, scolded Axel, confiscated his loot, held him off as he tried to kick her again, subdued him with threats of sending him to bed without any supper, but all the while her mind had churned and churned, trying to understand.

Hesper's silence. Her lack of loving warmth for her son. Her terror at the German invasion. The worried glances and anxious solicitude of Kyriaki, her oldest friend.

Alenka hardly slept that night. She felt as if the black earth of Crete, trampled by German jackboots, was her body, that her throat was as choked with horror as her mother's. She rose in the morning to find that Axel had broken open the cupboard in which she had locked the German haversack and stolen it all again. She did not know what to do, how to help him. *My father will be pleased to see me, he will be proud, he will love me,* her brother had cried. His words were like stones. *I have failed him,* she thought.

Alenka inched closer to the fire. It was almost summer, but she felt as if it was winter. Shaky in all her limbs. The words kept replaying, like a scratched record. *He forced me.* Hot tears spilled down her face, and she scrubbed them away.

I have to do something, Alenka thought. *I have to help somehow.*

She went to the battered chest at the end of her bed and opened it. Within lay her dowry, the quilts and pillowcases and tablecloths that she had been making since she was a child. Without a dowry, no Greek girl could marry. She lifted the folded linen out. On top lay her *sindoni,* the sheet she had been embroidering when word had come the Germans were invading her homeland. She ran her finger over the seven crimson knots of protection she had sewn over the heads of her family. She could not bear to cut them. She laid it back, picked up the pile of other linen, and carried it out the door, down the cobbled laneway and through the narrow portal gate into the garden of the Villa Ariadne.

Large tents had been set up on the tennis court, and wounded men were being carried inside on stretchers, their uniforms torn and bloodied. Doctors in white gowns and masks bent over them, working swiftly. Their hands were stained scarlet to the elbow. A giant white cross had been made in the garden with sheets, the edges secured with rocks so that the Luftwaffe knew not to bomb them. Overladen jeeps and trucks crept up the driveway, past a long line of stumbling, filthy, exhausted men, many with arms in slings or makeshift bandages about their heads, using their rifles as crutches.

Alenka came into the sitting room of the curator's cottage, crammed with rows of injured soldiers lying on low cots. A young nurse was tending them, a white apron tied over her uniform. Her dark hair was pinned up in smooth ornate rolls under a white nurse's cap, and her lips were scarlet to match her cape.

"So many of them," Alenka said. "I have brought you some linen to cut up, if that would be a help?"

"Thank heavens!" the nurse exclaimed in a broad Australian accent. "We are desperately short on supplies."

Alenka saw Jack lying in one of the beds. He had lifted himself up on one elbow at the sound of her voice and was gazing at her eagerly. Gladness rushed through her, and she hurried toward him. "You're all right! Oh, I was so worried. How are you feeling?"

"Better," he croaked. "Thank you for saving me." He caught hold of Alenka's hand.

"I didn't do a thing," she said, flushing. "It was you who saved me."

"We might have lost him if he didn't get here so fast," the nurse said. "He's lost a lot of blood, and he's not out of the woods yet. Lie back down now, lieutenant, you need to rest. Come into the other room, *kyria*."

Alenka gently retrieved her hand, and Jack lay down again. She smiled at him over her shoulder as she followed the nurse into the next room.

"But these are too fine to cut up for bandages!" the nurse said, beginning to go through the stack of linen. "Did you do all this beautiful embroidery?"

Alenka nodded. To her shame, her vision blurred with tears. "It's my dowry. Here in Crete, a girl starts making her dowry as soon as she can sew."

"But there must be years' worth of work in this pile," the nurse said. "Are you sure you wish to sacrifice it?"

Alenka began to cut one of the tablecloths into strips. "What's the point of a dowry if we are to be ground to dust under the Nazi jackboot?"

Her voice was so full of despair, the nurse laid a hand on her arm in sympathy. "Don't lose heart. They've not won yet."

Alenka thought of the ancient town of Heraklion, bombed almost to rubble. Her uncle, weeping as he scrubbed clean his ancient gun. Greek women and children forced to march ahead of German cannon.

"So you and that handsome young soldier you brought in . . . are you two going steady? He's not taken his eyes off you since you came in."

"Gosh, no." Alenka colored hotly. "I've only just met him. He saved my life." She thought of the exquisite music Jack had played, his own blood pulsing out with every note; the way the young German soldier had said *I have brothers too.* Tears welled up again, and she had to scrub her face with her handkerchief.

"It's very hard, I know," the nurse said. "Come, sit down, I'll make you a cup of tea."

Alenka sat down gratefully. She felt weak and shivery as if her fear and grief were some kind of life-threatening illness. She took up her scissors and began to slice through delicate embroidered flowers and birds.

"So much pain, so much waste," the nurse said, filling a kettle with water and putting it on a tiny portable gas ring. "These men! Shooting each other to pieces, and then we have to patch them up so they can go out and shoot each other again."

She lit the gas with a little whoosh. "Your English is very good. You work here at the villa?"

Alenka nodded. "Yes. At least I did. I do not know what will happen now."

"Me either. I suppose it will all depend on who wins the battle."

Alenka crossed herself fervently. "Let it be us, God willing!"

The nurse put out one hand and gripped hers. "God willing, my dear."

Another rush of tears overwhelmed Alenka. She wiped her eyes and blew her nose. The kettle whistled, and the nurse made the tea. Alenka drank a few mouthfuls thankfully and managed to compose herself. "I'm sorry," she whispered. "It's just . . . I've never seen . . ." She gestured with one hand at the rows of wounded men, the bucket of bloody swabs, the doctor with the saw in his hand.

"Don't be sorry. I used to weep every night when I first began nursing. But my matron would never let me go on the floor with a red nose and swollen eyes. 'The least you can do for those poor boys is give them a cheerful smile and a steady hand,' she'd say."

Smiling, the slender young woman slipped her hand into her pocket and drew out a small powder compact and a tube of lipstick, passing them to Alenka. "Now I'm always prepared! The nurse's motto."

"I thought that was the motto of the Girl Guides." Alenka began to powder her nose.

The nurse laughed in surprise. "It is, but I didn't expect you to know it."

"English school stories. The Pendlebury children came here most summers, and I always read their books." Alenka applied the lipstick as best she could with such a shaky hand, then passed the make-up back to the nurse. "Thank you . . . I'm sorry, I don't know your name."

"I'm Faith Naughton-Green, but please, just call me Faith. Sisters-in-arms, you know." She stuck out one hand, and Alenka shook it, laughing a little.

"I'm Alenka Klothakis. Please, will you let me help you? I feel so powerless, not knowing what to do."

Faith nodded. "Of course. We need all the help we can get. You'll need a strong stomach, though. And skin as thick as a rhinoceros."

Alenka soon understood why. She had never seen such pain and suffering before. On every side, men held out pleading hands, some weeping. She carried buckets of water in and stinking bedpans out, rolled bandages till her hands ached, scrubbed blood off floors, boiled surgical instruments in one pot and soup in another, and held the hand of one poor young man till he died.

It was hell.

She was amazed to realize the nurses and doctors were tending injured Germans, as well as British and Anzac soldiers. They were brought in by their comrades, who then hurried away to join the battle once more. The doctors put the German wounded in a tent on the tennis court, out of sight of the main hospital in the villa.

"How can they?" she asked angrily. "The Germans are the enemy!"

Faith sighed. "I know, Alenka, but they are wounded too. It is our job to care for anyone who is hurt, regardless of religion or nationality."

"Well, I can't," Alenka cried. "I won't!"

"Perhaps you could come and help with the poor locals being brought in? None of us can speak Greek, and we need someone to translate for us."

So Alenka had gone to help tend all the children and old people with bloodied clothes, bruised faces, broken limbs, lacerated flesh. One told her that John Pendlebury had been put up against a wall and shot by the Germans. He had been wounded and unarmed. She could not bear it. He had always been so kind to her. She thought of his lovely wife, Hilda, left a widow, and their two little children, left fatherless, and it all became too much to her. She sank down, buried her face in her arms, and sobbed.

Faith brought her a handkerchief and a cup of tea, and sat down beside her, comforting her. "It's all right, you have your cry. You'll feel better for it. No, don't get up. Sit and drink your tea. You've been on your feet for hours."

Alenka noticed dazedly that it was dark outside.

Faith kicked off her shoes and rubbed her aching feet. "What a day!"

"Thank you," Alenka said, scrubbing at her face with the handkerchief. "Not just for the tea. For being here." Her voice cracked a little, but she was determined not to cry again. Faith was so calm and cheerful all the time.

"I signed up just as soon as I could," Faith said. "Had romantic notions of what a nurse was, I suppose. Still, I wanted to help, and they won't let a woman fight."

"But to come all this way . . . it is a brave and noble thing to do."

Faith laughed at her. "You've been reading too many of those *Girls' Own* stories!"

Alenka smiled weakly. "I do not know how else to say what I mean. It is brave and noble."

"Not at all," Faith said briskly. "Would you like me to sit at home knitting socks instead? It wouldn't feel right. I just wish there was more I could do."

"How did you end up in Crete, of all places?"

"Well, we go where the army tells us to go." She smiled wearily and lit a cigarette. "We were in Athens, you know. Ended up getting out just ahead of the Germans and brought here. And now the bastards are here too."

"Will nothing stop them?" Alenka's voice was full of despair.

There was a long pause. Then Faith unpinned her white nurse's cap, throwing it on the table. "Do you like how I've styled my hair?"

Alenka was bewildered. "Well, yes, but . . ."

"It's called a victory roll. It's named for the way pilots spin their planes when they've shot down an enemy, leaving a spiral of smoke in the air. It's a sign of triumph. One more German shot out of the sky, one more Nazi dead. We women can't fly planes or shoot guns, but we can fight just as hard in our own way. We have to just roll up our sleeves and our hair and get to work. Do you see?"

Alenka nodded.

"I know it's only a hairstyle," Faith said, "but every morning, when I look at myself in the mirror, I think, *Each new day we are still fighting is a victory, each day that we are alive is a victory.*"

III

Jack drifted in and out of nightmares. A cold hand, gripping his, dragging him along. A sharp voice, saying, "You wicked child! Such bad blood in you! Your mother's blood!"

A door opening. Darkness yawning. The key turning in the lock. Banging on the door till his fists hurt. Trying not to cry. Feeling out with his hands, afraid of what might bite him. A sudden sound. Soft and low, humming near his ear. He turned, reached out again. His fingers touched something smooth. He traced its shape. Hard, and yet satiny, like polished wood. A deep curve, a fluted edge, a rounded flank. Then something taut and strong, tense as an arrow string. It leaped under his fingers, and a note of music sang out. The string quivered. Under his hand the smooth wooden body vibrated as if stirring to life.

Wood smashing, splintering, strings jangling, snapping . . .

A window starred with frost. Puddles iced over. Wind keening. So cold. Ears aching. Face pressed into black cloth, smelling of mothballs. The world rising, falling, swelling, surging, heaving. Yellow fields, a burning sky. A laughing face, daring him to poke a snake. Hissing, uncoiling, forked tongue flickering. Striking. Hot poison in the blood. Teeth chattering like castanets.

"*Po-po-po*, he has a fever," a soft voice said. A cool hand on his brow.

Jack opened his eyes. He saw Alenka leaning over him, her dark eyes intent on his face.

He smiled at her and reached up to touch her cheek.

Her eyes widened.

Another young woman said briskly, "His wound is infected. Some dirt must have got in. We must try to get it clean, keep him cool. I'll call the doctor."

A man in a white coat and mask came, leaned over him, smelt his wound. Probed him with something sharp. Jack cried out, flinched away. Hands held him down. The doctor shook his head. Darkness nibbling at his edges.

"Jack?" Alenka's voice called him back. "I'm going to find something I hope will help you. I need you to hold on for me. Jack, can you hear me?"

He nodded, though his neck was stiff as a rod, his head heavy as a cannonball. Pain flared through him. He closed his eyes.

The nurse said doubtfully, "There's not much we can do for him now."

"He saved me!" Alenka's voice was fierce. "I cannot let him die. Faith, will you watch him for me? I'll be back as fast as I can." Then she bent over him again. He wanted to see her face one more time. He opened his eyes.

She smiled at him. "Jack. Just wait for me. Please."

"Till I die."

She frowned. "You're not going to die. Don't say that. I'll be back as soon as I can."

The night was an ocean of pain. Her promise a long bright thrumming string to which he clung. Each wave a dark memory he had thought long forgotten. But he concentrated on breathing, allowing the rhythm of the waves to lift and lull him like music. He imagined playing the Chaconne, one of the most difficult passages of music ever composed. Bach had originally written it for the violin, but Jack's mother had been determined to master it on the cello. She had played it every Sunday morning.

He imagined his bow sweeping over the strings, each low note vibrating out, the chords repeating, repeating, repeating, like running steps, like a living heart. Sixty-four times the four-bar phrase recurred, lifting, sinking, changing, transfiguring each time. When Jack reached the crucial turning point, the shift to D major, he imagined each note as a step upward toward the light.

When dawn came, so did Alenka, breathing fast, her hair tumbling down her back. She carried a bunch of silvery-gray greenery in her hands.

"Faith, is he still with us? Quickly, boil me some water!"

"What have you got there?" Faith asked, moving swiftly to obey.

"Dittany. It's a wild herb that grows only on Crete. Aristotle said that when goats have been wounded by an arrow, they seek dittany out and eat it and are healed." As she spoke, Alenka was rapidly pounding some of the leaves with a pestle. "We use it for everything. To ease childbirth, to help new skin grow over a wound, to make love potions."

"Love potions!"

Alenka smiled wearily. "Dittany is said to spark the flames of passion. One name for it is *eronda*, from Eros, the god of desire. It has heart-shaped leaves, you see. It's very dangerous to gather as it only grows on the highest crags, and so young men climb up and pluck it for their beloveds, to prove their passion. They are called love-seekers."

"How romantic."

"And this dittany is the most potent of all because it grows on Mount Juktas, where Zeus sleeps. It will heal him." Alenka made a poultice from the bruised leaves and laid them over Jack's wounds in his temple, his thigh, his abdomen. He clutched at her hand, saying her name. Faith brought a kettle of boiling water. Alenka put the remaining leaves in a cup and poured the water over them. A fresh, vitalizing fragrance rose into the air. Alenka let it steep a while, then added some honey. She lifted Jack up and held the cup to his lips. He drank it down. It was warm and strong and sweet. As she laid him back on his pillows, he lifted one hand and slid it through her loose dark tresses, cupping the nape of her neck. "Alenka," he whispered, then drew her down to kiss her.

For a moment, their lips clung. Then she pulled away, pressing one hand to her mouth. He shut his eyes, his hand relaxing. As Jack slipped away into sleep, he could still taste her—honey and flowers and a tang of something bitter.

When Jack woke, he remembered only snatches of dreams. He thought kissing Alenka was just one more fevered figment, but when she saw him, she flushed hotly and fled.

Alenka did not come near him for the next few days, and Jack lay in his narrow hospital bed and fretted. The Australian nurse checked his pulse and shook her head at him. "You need to rest," she said. "You almost died. It's a miracle you didn't."

"Alenka," he whispered through dry lips. "D-d-did I . . ."

"Don't you worry about anything you might have said and done while fevered," she replied. "Nurses know not to put any store in what patients say when they're off their heads."

But Alenka was not a trained nurse. And she was his best mate's girl. Jack was tormented with guilt and regret. The nurse took his temperature and clucked her tongue. "Rest up and drink your soup, and when your strength has returned, you can go and talk to her."

The next day the nurse brought him a crutch. "Don't exhaust yourself," she warned him. "And be careful of that wound in your side—I don't want you opening it again."

As soon as she was gone, Jack seized the crutch and limped around, looking for Alenka. The villa was so crowded, patients lay on mattresses in the garden. A Greek man sat on the steps, wrapped in a bloodstained greatcoat, staring at nothing. Two doctors bent over a German soldier who lay screaming on a stretcher, amputating his leg below the knee. One of the doctors injected him with a syringe, and the screaming died away into sobbing. Another man wandered about, trailing a bloodied sheet from his naked body, talking nonsense in a thick Scottish accent, his eyes dazed.

Jack saw a young girl carrying soup in an earthenware mug to an old woman who lay in a tent, one eye swollen and bruised, her skinny arm in a sling.

"*Syngnómi?*" he asked carefully, a useful Greek word that meant both *sorry* and *excuse me*. "*K-k-kyria* Klothakis?"

The girl stared at him with huge, solemn eyes, then turned and pointed toward the villa. He thanked her and limped on. Already he was growing tired.

The villa had been mortared. There were huge craters in its walls, and the windows had been blown out so glass lay on the ground. A fair-haired boy was sweeping it up. Jack asked his question again, and the boy pointed toward a door that stood open on the other side of a small courtyard.

Inside, a black-clad woman was standing at the stove, stirring a steaming pot of lemon-scented chicken broth. She was very thin, with shadowed eyes and hollowed cheeks, and a strong straight nose like that of an ancient Grecian statue.

"*Kyria* Klothakis?" he asked diffidently.

She turned and gazed at him. "*Neh.*"

Jack was confused for a moment, then realized she had said "Yes."

"Alenka?" he stammered.

She hesitated for a long moment, then said something in slow, halting Greek.

Jack thought she had said, "in the garden," but he could not be sure. The ancient Greek he had learned at school and university was very different from the modern Greek spoken in Crete. She must have seen the puzzlement on his face, for she hobbled forward, laid a claw-like hand on his arm, and pointed away from the villa, repeating the phrase in strongly accented English. "She is in the garden. That way."

He stammered a thank you, then followed the winding path through the pines. It led past a tennis court, crowded with white hospital tents, to a narrow gate in the wall. He stepped out onto a steep cobbled lane that ran down toward the Palace of Knossos to the left and climbed up toward the stony hills to the right. Ahead was a hamlet of small stone houses, built higgledy-piggledy around a village square with a well in the center. The windows were shuttered against the heat of the day. An old woman sat in the shade of an old almond tree, spinning wool. He asked her the same question, and she answered with the same Greek phrase Alenka's mother had used.

In the garden.

The old woman pointed up the narrow laneway toward the hills. He walked past a few small stone houses. Beyond were low ruined walls, then bare rocky hills. An old windmill stood on the crest, white canvas sails turning slowly. A stream cascaded down a channel of ancient stones and disappeared into a round tunnel under the road. The donkey Modestine was tethered to an iron hook in a dilapidated stone wall overhung with ivy.

Jack patted the donkey. Her gray hair was soft and plush as fur under his fingers. A thick black stripe ran down her spine, crossed by another at her shoulders. Jack remembered the story he had been told at Sunday School when he was a little boy, living with his father and grandmother in Cambridge. The faithful donkey that had carried Jesus into Jerusalem had wished it could shoulder the burden of his crucifix. It had stood vigil throughout Christ's long suffering, the setting sun casting the shadow of the cross upon its back. The cruciform marking was a remembrance of that donkey's faithfulness.

There was, no doubt, some rational explanation for the donkey's marking, Jack thought. Still, the sight of it gave him a strange superstitious shudder.

Stories cast long shadows. Like sins.

Modestine had been drinking from a bucket but had knocked it over with one hoof. The water had split across the dry stones. She nosed it with a dripping muzzle, then raised her head and looked toward the wall, ears pricked forward. Jack followed her gaze with his own. A small wooden door was hidden beneath the curling tendrils of the ivy. Jack pushed it open, bent his head, and stepped through.

Within was a garden built among gray ruins. Alenka knelt at the edge of a rock-hewn cistern, drawing up a bucket of water. Jack limped forward to take it from her. His hand brushed hers. She flushed scarlet and snatched her hand away, scrambling to her feet.

He had to apologize to her, before she fled from him again.

"I . . . I . . . I'm sorry. I . . . I was . . . was . . . n-n-n-not . . ." As always, the more deeply he felt, the more mangled his words became.

Her eyes flew up to his, startled.

"I did not m-m-mean to . . . I mean, I sh-should not . . . not . . . have . . ." He stammered to a halt, then blurted, "Please forgive m-m-me."

She hesitated, searching his face with her great, dark eyes. Then she smiled. "*Po-po-po-po-po!* Forgiveness granted."

His heart gave a great bound. His head swam. He dropped the bucket, splashing water everywhere, and gripped the gnarled trunk of an olive tree, its leaves flickering like tiny silver flames. *I've walked too far*, he wanted to say. *It's hot. I'm weak from the loss of blood and the fever.*

But that was not the whole truth.

I think I'm falling in love with you.

Jack could not say such a thing to Alenka. He had met her only a few times, exchanged only a few words. And every syllable from his mouth had been but poor, stilted, crippled things. Why would she look at him, when she had met Teddy, with his eyes as blue as forget-me-nots and his easy grin?

"You look like you're about to faint—you must sit down!" Alenka led him to a rickety table and chair, set on a stone terrace shaded by a grapevine. Jack sank down gratefully, and she brought him a cup of water. It was surprisingly cold, given the heat of the sun now high overhead. He drank deeply, looking about him with interest.

At the far end of the garden stood an ancient mulberry, its branches propped up by immense wooden crutches. Skeins of softly colored silk hung from its boughs, in loops of pale yellow, green, indigo, pink, and crimson. Silvery olive trees stood along the southern wall, underplanted with rosemary, thyme, sage, oregano, and parsley. Beehives stood beneath a lemon tree, and tiers of straw baskets looked as if they might be the homes of silkworms. Roses grew everywhere, pink and golden and red, and wildflowers danced in every cranny: poppies, anemones, tiny native peonies. All was contained within the high stone walls, hidden away from the outside world.

"It's a s-s-secret garden," Jack said in wonderment.

Alenka clasped her hands together. "That's my favorite book! Mrs. Pendlebury gave it to me to read one summer. I began working on this garden after I read it."

"It's my . . . my . . . my favorite book too. I always felt a bit like Colin. My m-m-mother died when I was born, just like him, and I was sick a lot, and, well, nobody really wanted m-m-me."

She leaned forward, her face warm with sympathy and understanding. "I felt just like Mary. Not that my parents were dead, or anything like that, just . . . I was so lonely, I suppose. I really wanted to have Dickon as *my* friend, piping birds and animals to his hand like Pan . . ."

"Foxes and squirrels and robins," Jack said, remembering.

"Yes, all the wild creatures. And he helped them save the garden."

"I always wished his m-m-mother was mine."

"Me too!" Then Alenka's smile faded away. "I shouldn't say that."

Jack thought of the silent, black-shrouded figure with the sunken, tragic eyes. She was nothing like Dickon's warm-hearted, laughing mother, the giver of good food and good advice. He could understand Alenka's guilty longing. It was so like his own. He was grateful to his nana, but she had been embittered with grief and struggle and poverty.

"I'd have liked to have planted all the flowers in the book here in my garden," Alenka said, "but this is Greece, not Yorkshire. And I cannot afford to buy many seeds. I can only grow what I can collect from my rambles in the hills and gorges, or what people give to me. And, of course, plants that feed us must come first."

"I've always wanted a s-s-secret garden of my own," Jack confessed. "Any yard would have been g-g-good. My nana lives in a few rooms above a shop. I always envied Teddy, who g-g-grew up on this big farm with a huge old garden . . ."

The mention of Teddy reminded Jack that he had kissed his best mate's girl, the worst kind of betrayal. He felt the scorch of shame and humiliation once more. He looked away. *Don't tell Teddy what I did*, he wanted to say, even as another part of him said rebelliously, *It's not fair, all the girls fall for Teddy, why did he have to pick the one girl I like?*

Suddenly, the door crashed open, and a young woman rushed into the garden. Her hands were held out stiffly before her, her arms caked to the elbows with dirt. She was crying. "Alenka! I . . . I found Papa . . . he's dead! Oh, Alenka!"

She flung herself into Alenka's arms, sobbing.

"Oh, no, Phyllia!" Alenka hugged her close.

"He was just lying out there on the hillside. I could not bring him home, he's too heavy. I tried to bury him, but the ground was too hard. I had to cover him with stones . . . but it was so hard, I did not know what to do. I did my best, but he's still up there. I broke all my nails trying to cover him—oh, Alenka, the ground was too hard . . ."

"Oh, Phyllia, not Uncle Manolaki."

"What are we to do?" Phyllia wept. "Papa dead, Micky dead, Minos gone to fight, only me and the children left to help Mama."

The two young women wept in each other's arms. The intensity of their grief shocked and disturbed Jack. In his world, sorrow was silence, an absence, a hanging sword. He did not know what to do or what to say.

"I knew something was wrong when he didn't come home. He would have sent word, he wouldn't have wanted us to worry. I went out, searching for him . . ."

"Into the war zone? Oh, Phyllia, you could have been killed! Or worse!"

"What would that matter? I had to find my papa!"

"Does your mama know yet?"

"Oh yes. Evangeline is with her now—oh, oh, I cannot believe he is dead."

"I hate them," Alenka said with a passion. "I hate them. He was such a good man. I will make them pay."

Silent and forgotten, Jack followed the two young women as they hastened away from the green hidden garden and back into the stone-strewn world of sorrow and death.

IV

Alenka brought her godmother a bowl of soup, but Kyriaki just shook her head, her face furrowed with grief. She was dressed in unrelenting black, her hair hidden by a scarf, her fist clenched upon her dead husband's gold cross, which Phyllia had brought down from the site of his fallen body. Her three daughters sat close around her, and her youngest son, Alekos, knelt with his face in her lap, trying hard to master his grief.

"*Po-po-po-po-po*, what will we do now?" Kyriaki whispered. "How are we to live?"

Alekos lifted his tear-stained face. "I will work, Mama, I will do Papa's job."

His mother's face contorted. "You are a good boy," she managed to say.

Alenka knew—they all knew—that the dig at the ruined palace was finished now, the curator and his mother gone back to England. There was no work left for any of them. It was impossible to imagine any future, with the Germans storming their island, their homes, their livelihoods. Nobody spoke, though Kyriaki's lips moved as she prayed.

Heavy with grief, Alenka went slowly out the door and into her own home, which was just next door. Whitewashed and black-beamed, the kitchen was dominated by a huge domed fireplace. An iron pot sat on a trivet above glowing ashes, with a few battered pewter jugs and a massive stone barley grinder on the mantelpiece. A jug of thorns was set in the deep sill of the window, spun around with cobwebs to catch insects. In the center of the room, a pillar made from a gnarled juniper tree was hung with bunches of dried herbs, strings of sun-dried tomatoes, ropes of onions and garlic. A few flimsy gilt icons hung in the eastern corner, and one wall was taken up with her mother's sleeping shelf, neatly made up with red handwoven blankets and an embroidered counterpane and pillows. Otherwise, the only furniture was a small table with three chairs, her mother's loom by the fire, and a rickety ladder up to the loft room where her brother slept.

"Axel?" she called. "Where's Mama?"

Her brother looked over the loft railing. "Gone out. I'm hungry. When's supper?"

"Where did she go?"

He shrugged.

Alenka fed the chickens and the pig, chopped tomatoes and oregano, rinsed out the white beans which had been soaking overnight, made a fire on the hearth. Still no sign of her mother. Alenka felt dread creeping through her. Where could Hesper be?

The sun had set, the light was fading. Alenka wrapped a black scarf about her head and shoulders, then crept out into the street. She did not know what she would do if she saw any Germans. They must be close. Her godfather's body had been found on a hillside above the palace, and wounded paratroopers had been left at the field hospital, only a short walk away. She was so afraid, she felt sick.

Alenka went to the church. It was the third point in the small triangle that made up her mother's life. Home, work, worship.

The arched door was locked, and the window of the priest's little house was dark. Alenka hesitated. She saw a low line of flickering lights in the cemetery and pushed open the iron gate and went within.

Along the back wall, one long trench had been dug. Makeshift crosses stood in a row, German helmets set on top, marked with an eagle carrying a swastika in its claws. A small candle had been set into the freshly turned earth at the foot of each cross. Hesper bent and lit the last one, then fell to her knees, praying. Tears trickled down her bent face.

Rage flared through Alenka. She ran forward, seizing her mother's thin shoulder. "What are you doing? How can you light candles for them? They are our enemy! They killed Uncle Manolaki!"

Hesper turned to face her. For a long moment, she was silent. At last, she said, with difficulty, "They are still . . . somebody's son."

V

The sun was setting, and the shadow of cypress trees stretched across the road. Teddy put his foot down, the clapped-out old jeep veering from side to side. He kept his shoulders hunched, his gaze sweeping the stony hillside nervously. Not that he'd see any sniper lying out there, squinting down his sights at Teddy. He wouldn't know till the bullet hit him.

All the other runners had died or gone missing. The telephone wires were cut, the radios kaput. The poor bloody buggers at the airport at Maleme had even tried semaphoring for help, Teddy had heard. It was time for the Allied forces to cut their losses and get out.

Teddy had arrived in Chania to find the town in utter chaos. The Germans had been bombing the small town ruthlessly. The bodies of civilians lay lifeless in the rubble, the sickening stench of death quavering in the hot air. The Allied soldiers sat, heads bent, hands hanging, defeat and exhaustion in every slumped line of their bodies.

Miraculously the crescent on the tall muezzin's tower and the cross on the cathedral's belltower were untouched, rising high above the smoking ruins. Old women in black knelt, praying and weeping, crossing their breasts feverishly.

Teddy's first thought had been for Jack. It was impossible to get news, though. All communications with the east were cut. So when their commanding officer asked for volunteers to try to get a message through to Heraklion, Teddy had put his hand up. The lieutenant-colonel had been surprised. Most runners were lowly privates, not lieutenants.

"I can't fight, sir," Teddy had said. "My feet are a mess. I can still ride a motorbike, though, sir."

So he'd been given a map and a sealed envelope, and strict instructions to keep his head down. Hearing gunfire, he had taken a potholed back road but after a few hours his motorcycle had broken down. So he had hitched a ride with an old farmer in his mule-drawn cart, but the slow pace had infuriated him. So he'd borrowed a bicycle from outside a village *kafenion*, and made good speed till some Jerry had jumped out of a ditch and shot at him. He'd veered, wobbled, and crashed into the ditch, and taken off like a hare over the fields, blistered feet forgotten. He swore one of the bullets the Hun fired after him had parted his hair on the wrong side.

He'd found another back road that seemed to be heading in the right direction. It was easy to steer a straight course in Crete, with the sea on one side and the mountains like an icy wall on the other. Teddy kept limping as long as he could. When it was too dark to see, he had rolled himself in his greatcoat and slept under a tree and woken stiff and sore in the morning, his feet so swollen it was hard to force his boots back on. He had limped on down the dusty road to another village set among olive groves. A woman gave him some bread dipped in olive oil and a hard-boiled egg. He sat eating, his throbbing feet in the cool water of the street fountain, while she arranged a lift for him with a man taking chickens in wicker baskets to market.

After that, he went by foot, making his way east toward Heraklion. The main road was blocked by the Germans, and a pitched battle was taking place near an old stone building that had been turned into a kind of fortress by the enemy. He watched for a while through his binoculars, then decided to give it a wide berth, creeping through endless olive groves and over the stony flanks of hills. He was glad when he managed to hitch a ride on a truck full of exhausted hollow-eyed soldiers heading back to the old Venetian town.

Brigadier Brian Chappell, the commanding officer at Heraklion, was taken aback, and then indignant, to hear they were pulling out. "We've done our job here—what the bloody hell has gone wrong down east?" he barked.

"They lost the airport at Maleme, sir," Teddy said. "The Jerries are flying in a dozen planes an hour."

"Bloody fools!"

Teddy had asked after Jack and heard from some British toff that he had been wounded in battle and taken to the field hospital at the Villa Ariadne. His first feeling of relief was pierced at once by a jab of acute jealousy.

Jack had better not be trying to make any moves on Alenka, he thought. Teddy had seen her first.

A moment later he grinned and eased his shoulders. Poor old Jack, always so tongue-tied around girls. He wouldn't have a chance with a hot potato like Alenka. Still, the idea troubled him. Jack was good-looking enough, even if he was so dark. And he liked the same kind of old rubbish as Alenka, all those musty, dusty myths and ruins. Teddy volunteered at once to take the news of the impending evacuation to the doctors and patients of the field hospital.

The British toff gave Teddy a jeep, and he was heading up the road to Knossos with orders for the field hospital to be dismantled, and for anyone who could to return to Heraklion. Battleships were being sent to take as many men as they could away but could only sail at night so the window of opportunity was very narrow.

As darkness fell, Teddy had to drive more carefully. There was no moon, and all the houses were shuttered and quiet. A German sniper could be lurking behind every wall or bush. He passed the church, where hundreds of tiny candles flickered in the dusk, and parked on the road outside the villa gate. Walking up the driveway, he could not believe how different everything was, after just a few weeks. What had been a beautiful garden was now a muddy field filled with trucks, tents, and wounded men. Teddy put his head in a few tents, but the smell of blood and rot and disinfectant made him feel sick. He moved on quickly.

The villa's windows were all shuttered, but he could hear English voices issuing swift orders. Teddy went around to the little courtyard outside the kitchen, where he had drunk wine with Alenka the first night he had met her. He was keen to see her again, though he also dreaded having to say goodbye to her. Girls did weep so when you said goodbye.

Mingled in with his eagerness and trepidation was the wish that he'd had more time with her. She was a sweet armful, and he was sure he had sensed her resistance weakening. The very thought aroused him painfully. Then he saw them in the shadow of the pine trees. Alenka was in Jack's arms, his head was bent over hers.

Rage exploded through Teddy's body. He took a few swift steps forward, seized Jack, and hurled him away. Taken by surprise, Jack staggered and fell, crying aloud in pain.

"What the hell are you doing? Alenka's my girl!"

"I . . . I . . ." Jack began to stammer some kind of explanation, but Teddy didn't listen. He seized Alenka and kissed her passionately.

"Teddy, s-s-stop it!" Jack pulled at his arm. "You've g-g-got it all wrong! I was just comforting her. Her godfather has died . . ."

Slowly the words penetrated the red mist clouding his brain. Teddy released her.

"I am not yours!" Alenka cried, one hand pressed against her mouth. "I'm not a possession! You have no right."

"I'm sorry," Teddy said lamely. "I've had such a rotten time getting to you. The Jerries were hunting the king. We had to hustle him away over the White Mountains. I could have escaped to Cairo with him, but I came back. I had to see you."

He tried to kiss her again, but she pushed him away and turned her back to him.

Jack sat down on the wall, one hand to his side.

Teddy felt bad. "Sorry, mate. I thought . . ."

Jack gave a jerky shrug. "You were w-w-wrong." He didn't look at Teddy.

"Come on, mate, don't be mad. I said I was sorry."

Jack did not reply. Teddy began to realize he might have made a mess of things. Alenka was scrubbing at her eyes with a handkerchief, and his best mate had as angry an expression on his face as Teddy had ever seen. He didn't know what he'd do if Jack was truly pissed off with him. They'd done everything together since they were eight years old.

"Hey, I really am sorry. I shouldn't have jumped to conclusions." Teddy's voice was full of contrition. "You know what I'm like when I lose my temper. And it's been a bloody awful few days."

"That's an understatement."

"If you knew what I went through to get here and warn you, you'd forgive me. I just about rattled my bones right out of my skin."

Jack smiled reluctantly, as Teddy had hoped he would.

"I heard you copped a bullet."

Jack shrugged. "N-n-non-vital hit."

"I didn't hurt you, did I? Damn my filthy temper, when will I learn to think before I act?" Teddy got out a crumpled packet of cigarettes and lit one up for Alenka who shook her head. She still would not look at him. He put it in his mouth and lit up another for Jack who took it silently. "Don't be sore at me, babe," he begged Alenka. "I can't help feeling jealous. You know I'm mad about you. I'm sorry I grabbed you. I didn't mean to act like a caveman. It's this bloody war, it makes us all crazy."

He offered the pack of cigarettes to Alenka, saying disarmingly, "Smoke a peace pipe with me?"

She half-smiled and shrugged and accepted a cigarette, letting him light it for her. As she took a deep drag and blew out a plume of smoke, Teddy felt another fierce surge of desire, but he looked away, telling himself to stay cool. "Sorry about your grandfather," he said. "Hard lines."

"He was my godfather," Alenka said.

"I'm sorry," Teddy said again awkwardly. He was not good at comforting people. He glanced at Jack, who was gingerly feeling his side. Guilt stabbed him. "I'm a damned fool, Jack. I should've known you'd not do the dirty on me. Mate, I came back to get you. We've got to get out of here. The Jerries are pouring in, and we've orders to evacuate."

"You're going?" Alenka cried in dismay. "But what about the Germans?"

"If we stay, we'll end up in a Nazi prisoner of war camp," Teddy said. "If we get away, we'll be free to fight another day."

"But does that mean we've lost?"

Teddy did not answer. He hated losing, and he hated admitting it.

Alenka was white and shaking. "Oh, God, what will become of us?"

"I'll come back. I promise. As soon as I can, I'll come back. Will you wait for me?" Girls liked to be given promises, he thought.

Alenka did not answer. She was frowning. He saw her glance at Jack, who was watching and listening quietly, his thin face troubled.

Teddy jerked his head at him. "Could you give us a minute, mate?"

For a long moment, Jack did not respond. Then he got to his feet, his body crooked with pain. "I'm s-s-so sorry, Alenka. I wish . . . I wish things had been different. That we had w-won for you. That I . . . I . . . I . . ."

"Jack, for God's sake!" Teddy cried, his patience breaking.

Jack half-lifted one hand, then turned and limped away. Teddy looked at Alenka. "I've made a mess of things, I know. It's the war. Each day might be our last. I meant what I said. I don't know what's going to happen. I'm a soldier—we have no control over our own lives. But if I can, I'll come back for you one day. Will you wait for me?"

Her face had softened. She shook her head, made a bewildered gesture with her hand. "I don't . . . I don't know. How can I promise such a thing? I hardly know you. Anything might happen. You might never come back. Am I meant to wait all my life for you? How can you ask such a thing?"

"If I can, I will come back," he swore.

Alenka gazed at him doubtfully. He smiled at her and stepped forward, taking her in his arms. She did not melt into his embrace, as he had expected. Instead, she pushed him away with all her strength. "Stop it! You've got no right. Just because I kissed you once does not mean you get to kiss me anytime you want. I'm not yours, I'm not anybody's. I'm grateful to you for coming and fighting for my country, but that does not mean you own me."

He stared at her, his jaw hardening.

She lifted her chin, squared her shoulders. "I'm sure you've left a heartbroken girl behind in your own country. You'll go home to her and make a life together. I have to make my own life here. Maybe we will see each other again one day, who knows? The Fates will decide."

It was a dismissal. Teddy laughed and shrugged, but he was angry. Girls didn't usually brush him off like that. He answered lightly, "Sure. Whatever will be will be. Good luck." Then he walked away. He sure as hell hoped Jack had not heard what she said. But Jack was waiting some distance away, his back to them, smoking his cigarette with jerky motions.

"Come on, Jack, let's go!"

As they drove away, Jack said, "I can't believe we're leaving them to their f-f-fate. I feel like such a . . . c-c-cad."

"Can't be helped," Teddy said. His blood seethed with frustrated desire and anger. "We have to save our own lives so we're free to fight another day."

VI

As far as Jack could see, stony peaks stretched to the sky. The road was steep and rutted with deep craters and potholes. It looked like a long black winding millipede as an endless stream of exhausted men stumbled along under the blazing sun. Many had heads and limbs wrapped in bloodstained bandages, arms in slings, rifles used as crutches.

Jack and Teddy had ditched the jeep when it ran out of petrol, then joined the retreat over the White Mountains. There was no one to report to, no one to issue orders. Just panic and chaos. The Germans had seized the airport at Maleme and were flying in reinforcements. The Luftwaffe hunted the retreating men mercilessly, bombing and machine-gunning the road.

Each time, someone would call out a warning, "Aircraft, take cover!"

"Get down! Here comes Jerry!" The cry would be taken up by a hundred throats, and the retreating men would dive into the ditch or creep behind a bush, only to crawl out and resume shuffling forward again once the planes had soared past.

"I thought we had them," said a soldier with a bandage covering most of his face and one eye. "I thought we had them for sure."

They rested for a while in the shade of a rock, unable to take another step. The bandaged soldier told them that he had been part of the final defense at Galatas. They had few weapons and even less ammunition, and two old lumbering Matilda tanks. All the wireless sets had been buggered, and their commanding officer had had to use the old-fashioned Cretan telephone service to issue his orders. They had improvised their own grenades by filling empty jam tins with broken bits of concrete and gelignite. Orders had come to retake the town, so they had charged the Germans from behind the cover of the two old tanks. Both tanks foundered, and there was fierce hand-to-hand fighting with bayonets and rifle butts. Casualties had been heavy.

"We did our best," the soldier said, slump-shouldered with weariness. "But there were too many of the buggers."

"I know, mate," Teddy said, and gave him one of their last cigarettes.

An abandoned truck blocked the way. It was riddled with bullet holes and could not be started. Jack and Teddy and the other men had to push it over the edge of the cliff to get past. It hurtled down and exploded in the depths of a narrow gorge, sending up a great plume of black smoke.

"Bloody fool!" an officer shouted. "Do you want to bring the Jerries down on us?"

"I think the Jerries know where we are, sir," Teddy replied, deadpan.

Some of the men marched as a unit, in tight columns. Most just straggled along. The road was strewn with discarded blankets, kitbags, tin hats, boxes of cartridges, hand grenades, gas masks, guns.

Jack and Teddy walked in a daze. Each step cost them. The narrow road rose before them, vertiginous cliffs pressing them close to the edge, gut-wrenching falls beyond. Jack had never seen such mountains. They seemed otherworldly, so gaunt and gray and ancient. The road seemed to promise them a summit at every sharp turn, only to reveal another great flank that needed to be traversed, another soaring peak. His steps wavered, his head spun. Beside him, Teddy pressed himself to the cliff face, clinging to cracks and crevasses with the fingers of both hands, his face turned from the dizzying fall of space.

"Thanks for c-c-coming to get me," Jack said.

"No worries, mate," Teddy answered.

Every hour, they stopped to rest for ten minutes, as they had been taught. At dusk, they salvaged a tin of bully beef and a can of sardines which they opened with the point of an abandoned bayonet and ate with their fingers. The setting of the sun brought a blessed cessation of the German strafing. The silence rang in Jack's ears, a kind of tinnitus, he supposed. He could feel a trickle of blood running down his hip from his wound. He pressed his hand against it.

"You right, mate?" Teddy asked.

"Sure," he managed to say.

"I'm sorry I shoved you," Teddy said. "I thought . . . well. You know."

"Yeah." Jack could not look at him.

It was growing cold. Jack found a discarded blanket and draped it over his shoulders. It stank of sweat and fear and smoke and cordite, but its warmth was strangely comforting.

Around two hours after midnight, they came down into a bowl-shaped valley. The village had been bombed by the Luftwaffe. Flames still danced among the blackened timbers. Unable to walk another step, Jack and Teddy lay down near the embers of a burned-out house. Jack stared up at the canopy of stars, set like a dark twinkling jewel in the encircling ring of snowy peaks. His whole body ached, but it was nothing compared to the pain in his soul. He had not felt so low and bleak since he was a little boy. Life held no meaning, no purpose, no hope. They were defeated, Alenka was lost to him, everything was broken.

Jack woke, stiff with cold, before dawn. His throat was parched, and hunger gnawed his sunken stomach. Teddy found a well, and they lowered their tin hats down on strings to fetch water so icy it made the bones of Jack's skull ache.

Teddy examined his feet. They were a mess of broken blisters and raw seeping skin. "Damn. I don't think I can put my boots on again."

Jack's feet were sore too, but it was the wound in his side which bothered him the most. It had broken open, and his shirt was stiff and brown with blood. Each movement seared him with pain.

A low drone on the horizon. "Oh, no," he said.

A formation of Stukas appeared over the snowy peaks. Soon the scream of their dive and the thump and boom of their bombs echoed throughout the valley. Then came the sound of submachine guns, scarily close.

"Jerries on our arse," Teddy said. "We need to get out of here."

He wrapped his feet in his torn shirt and hung his boots by their shoelaces around his neck. Barefoot, bare-chested, wincing with every step, he picked up his rifle and limped forward. Together they hobbled, supporting each other as best they could, along the winding stony path.

On and on, step after painful step, the sound of battle clamoring ever closer. Other men hurried along the track, crowds of them, casting fearful glances behind them. They came at last to a bluff that jutted out over a steep fall. Far below, the azure waters of the Mediterranean gleamed. Jack felt such a weakening rush of relief, he almost sank to the ground. He tightened his grip on his rifle and began to carefully descend the steep goat track. After a moment, he realized Teddy had not followed. He looked back.

His friend stood, frozen, white-faced, at the edge of the precipice.

"T-T-Teddy?"

"I can't."

"Come on, m-m-mate."

Teddy shook his head.

Jack tried to retrace his steps, to climb back up to where Teddy stood, but the stream of men pushing past him was strong and swift as water swirling down a plughole.

"*Halt!*" someone cried.

Teddy swung around, reaching for his rifle. A shot. An explosion of blood. He fell.

"T-T-Teddy!" Jack shouted his name again. He struggled to get to him, but it was impossible—the retreat had turned into a stampede. A bullet scorched past his cheek. Jack flung himself down the steep slope, catching at rocks to keep himself from falling.

A snapped order in German, then the sound of heavy boots thudding as the Jerries raced in pursuit. Jack ran, fell, scrambled up, ran again. At last he reached the floor of the canyon. A narrow river foamed over boulders and fallen logs. Cliffs soared on either side. Bullets whined past, chipping off splinters of stone that were as sharp as any ricochet. Jack copped one in his arm, and another hit his helmet, bouncing on his back. He kept on running.

Some way down the gorge, there was an ancient temple surrounded by tall cypresses. The Allied soldiers took refuge there, fighting till they had no ammunition left. The Germans hung back, wary to approach, and Jack and some other men slipped away down a side path and crossed the river, running when they could, keeping low. Past a narrow wooden bridge that led to a deserted village, the doors and shutters all closed.

The cliffs towered so tall here, the ravine was deep in shadow. It was as if some god had long ago struck the landscape with a terrible sword, cleaving it in two. The pound of jackboots echoed eerily. Jack ran at full pelt, knocking himself against the cliff. The canyon narrowed, the walls so close he could almost touch both sides with his hands. The river foamed through, fierce with snowmelt. Jack struggled through and scrambled out the far side, drenched to the skin, shivering with cold and blood loss. His boots were sodden and weighed a ton. His head spun.

Jack stumbled and fell to his knees.

VI

"Come on, mate, get up! Run! Run!"

A soldier in a tattered Australian uniform beckoned from behind a boulder at the end of the ravine. Somehow Jack found the strength to race forward. A strong, brown hand caught him and pulled him to safety, then the soldier raised his rifle and shot with deadly precision. After a few hot minutes, bullets flying everywhere, the Jerries drew back.

"Come on, let's get out of here." The Australian soldier hauled Jack up, then gave him the rifle to use as a crutch. Jack limped along. His legs were trembling uncontrollably.

"You're just about done in," the soldier said sympathetically. "Come on, let's get you some help."

The path led down toward the village of Hóra Sfakíon, huddled on the edge of the sea with great stony mountains looming behind. A tiny stone wharf created a small tranquil harbor where fishing caïques were moored. Wounded and exhausted men sat or lay in groups wherever there was shade from the blazing sun. The British command had set up headquarters in a cave, its roof so low they could only crouch—maps and papers spread on the ground.

The soldier who had helped Jack was a lance corporal named Reg Saunders. Jack had seen him before. He was the only Aboriginal soldier in the whole Australian imperial force. He had a reputation for being quick with his fists, after beating up an insubordinate soldier who had called him "a black bastard." He was just as quick with a gesture of kindness, Jack discovered, as Reg brought him some cool water in his tin hat, then tore up his tunic to bind his wounds.

"W-w-where you from?" Jack asked, leaning against a rock.

"I'm a Gunditjmara man," Reg said. "Grew up on the reserve near Framlingham in western Victoria. What about you?"

"Woodend, near Hanging Rock."

"Wurundjeri country."

Jack nodded, though he had never heard the word before.

Reg felt in his pocket and found the stub of a cigarette. He lit it, took a few drags, then passed it to Jack who took it gratefully. The action reminded him acutely of Teddy. Tears overwhelmed him. He lifted his arm across his face, stifling his sobs in his sleeve.

"Lost a mate?" Reg asked.

Jack nodded jerkily.

"That's hard. I've lost a few too. Bloody Jerries."

As Jack struggled for composure, Reg told him that he'd signed up with his local Aussie Rules team. Most of them were dead now. "My people are warriors, you know. Before you white fellows came, and after too. My dad and my uncle fought in the Great War, and my uncle copped it in France. I wanted to do my bit too. Had to walk for bloody miles to sign up."

He had fought in Libya and Greece, just like Jack, and then had retreated to Crete where his battalion had been stationed at Chania, now nothing but a smoking ruin. Then he and some other Australians had been sent to reinforce the 28th Māori Battalion at a road nicknamed Forty-Second street.

"We were the rear guard," Reg said. "Trying to keep the Jerries off our heels. I was patrolling with my unit when suddenly a Jerry pops up his head only thirty yards away. I didn't even think about it, I just lifted my rifle and fired. He dropped, dead as a stone. It was the first time I'd actually *known* I'd shot someone dead, if you get what I mean. I ran up to him and turned him over. He was about the same age as me. I kind of wanted to say to him, "Come on, old fellow, get up, let's get on with the bloody game." But we weren't playing footy, we were at war. Because of me, that kid was now dead."

"Th-th-that's rough," Jack managed to say. He passed the cigarette back to Reg, who took the last deep drag before flicking the butt away.

"Yeah. But you know what? That kid was the scout for a whole squad of Germans, hunting down our poor old blokes who were running like all the demons of hell were after them. And when we saw those Nazi bastards, fresh and neat as new pins, shooting our men in the back as coldly as you please—well, we all got mad as hell.

"We went charging down that street, firing our Brens from the hip and hollering at the top of our voices, and the Māoris did that *haka* war dance of theirs, pounding their chests and pretending to cut their throats with their fingers, and, blimey, if those Jerries didn't turn tail and run for their lives."

Reg laughed and settled himself more comfortably against his kitbag. "Theo Walker, our CO, said it was the first time the Germans had ever retreated from a battle. Jesus, that felt good."

Jack nodded. He had felt the same conflicting rush of emotions himself. Pity, rage, joy at some stranger's death. Now all he felt was an immense weariness and a torn gaping hole where Teddy had once been.

All day the men hiding in the gorges and caves around Hóra Sfakíon were hammered by the scream of the divebombing Stukas and the incessant strafing of machine guns. Jack drifted in and out of feverish nightmares. Somewhere, someone was screaming in pain. When the sun set, the German planes veered away and flew back over the mountains. Reg went to forage for food and came back with a few bashed-in cans of bully beef and a jar of jam.

"It's not looking good," he said. "The Royal Navy's on its way, but they only have a few ships left undamaged. The evacuation fleet from Heraklion was bombed by the Luftwaffe. Quite a few lost, poor buggers."

Jack closed his eyes. It hurt to breathe.

A few hours to midnight, four British destroyers came offshore and dropped anchor. Barges were rowed in to the beach, and thousands of men shoved and jostled, trying to get on board. It had been decided that men who had borne the brunt of the fighting would be evacuated first. Only the walking wounded could be taken. It was too hard to get men on stretchers off the beach, so they would be left, as would any man who had become detached from his brigade.

Men desperately searched for their comrades or improvised new composite units. Some wrapped their heads and limbs in bandages, hoping to be counted among the walking wounded, while others helped their injured mates to their feet and half-carried them to the water. A band of desperate stragglers tried to storm one barge and had to be fought off.

Jack and Reg found the tattered remnants of their battalion, nick-named "Mud over Blood" for its brown-and-red striped insignia. Their commanding officer, Lieutenant-Colonel Theo Walker, told them to look smart and line up neatly. "We should be taken off soon," he said, "since we've been on the frontline and then fighting the rear guard. Make me proud and step smartly, show the other men how it's done."

A cordon was formed around the beach, keeping the stragglers at bay with weapons drawn and bayonets fixed. In desperate haste, the barges were loaded and rowed back out to sea. The landing crafts were overloaded, soldiers crammed in. Some men splashed into the water and swam alongside them, holding onto the sides. The sailors hauled the exhausted soldiers on board, then one by one the destroyers pulled up anchor and slipped away into the darkness. They had to race more than three-hundred-and-forty nautical miles to reach the safety of Alexandria before dawn, when the Luftwaffe could fly once more.

The long queues of men on the narrow, pebbly beach did not seem to get any shorter. Jack watched the destroyers leave with rising panic. Anyone left behind would become a prisoner of war. Then a small cruiser chugged in out of the darkness, hastily dropping rubber dinghies down into the black heaving waters. Men waded into the water and scrambled aboard, desperate to escape. Reg helped Jack limp forward.

"Last boat!" one of the sailors shouted, as the crammed dinghy was pushed out into the waves. "No more!"

"But my men!" cried Theo Walker, standing up in the dinghy and looking back at the shore. "They were promised passage!"

"Sorry, mate," the sailor said. "We can't fit in another bean."

Walker dove overboard and swam toward the beach. Jack suddenly realized their CO meant to stay with them and be taken prisoner with them. He felt a great surge of pride and gratitude. The 2/7th Battalion rushed forward to greet Walker as he struggled up the pebbly sands, his uniform and boots drenched, his usually immaculate hair hanging in dripping strands across his eyes. "I'm sorry, boys. No one deserved a berth on that boat more than you!"

Jack did not think he had ever heard such an awful sound as the rattle of the cruiser's anchor chain being pulled up. They all watched the boat disappear into the night.

"What will happen now, sir?" Reg said.

"The Jerries will be here in the morning. We'll have to surrender. Find anything you can that's white and be ready to wave it."

The men muttered mutinously.

"Never mind, lads," Walker said. "We fought honorably and were defeated honorably—there's no disgrace in it."

But Jack felt a deep corroding shame. He could not bear the thought of sitting out the rest of the war in some filthy prisoner of war camp.

"But, sir," Reg protested. "Do we have to? Can't we just take to the hills?"

Walker looked troubled. "It'd be hard," he said slowly. "This is poor country, not easy to forage here. And the local people may not dare help you—the Germans are known for their brutal reprisals. You don't speak Greek. How will you survive?"

"Can't be any harder than going bush back home," Reg said.

Walker smiled wearily. "I will not order any of you to surrender against your will. You fought like lions, and I'm prouder of you than I can say. If you think you can get away, and not be caught, go for it. Perhaps you will find a way to get free. I hope so."

A junior officer came up to Walker, saluting him. "I'm sorry, sir. I have here the official surrender. I was told to find the highest-ranking officer left on the island and tell them to give it to the Germans. I'm afraid that's you."

Walker took the crumpled piece of paper reluctantly. "So this is how it ends."

"I'm buggered if I'm going to let myself be taken prisoner by the Germans," Reg said to Jack.

"M-m-me either."

"We'd better split up," Reg said. "We have less chance of being taken then." He flashed a wide grin. "Good luck, mate!" Silently he melted into the darkness.

Jack limped away from the shore, heading east.

His only thought was: *Alenka, Alenka, Alenka . . .*

PART IV:
THE WOUNDED LAND
JUNE–DECEMBER 1941

O
bright
goddess dancing down
the serpentine path
toward the deepest secret place
only the spilling of blood can heal the wounded
land

I

It was a moonless night. The houses around the square were all dark and shuttered. The only sound was raucous singing in German from the Villa Ariadne.

Alenka carefully wriggled through her bedroom window, then crouched in the darkness, all her senses strained for any betraying sound or movement. When she was sure it was safe, she ran across the square to the shadows under the almond tree where Phyllia waited for her. They did not speak, but their hands met and clung a moment. Their plimsolls silent on the cobblestones, they crept through the village.

The gate to the old palace was locked, but Alenka and Phyllia knew a secret way in. They went carefully through the dark ruins, not daring to use their torches, then down the steps into the throne room.

The low-roofed hall was lit with candles, set on old stone benches that lined the walls. The walls were painted dark red with battered frescoes of griffins crouching among lilies. The ancient alabaster throne stood in the center of one wall, a round basin at its foot. A lamp had been set upon it, shining its light across to the deep sunken pit on the other side of the room, thought to have been used long ago for some kind of ritual. Young people stood in groups, smoking and drinking *tsikoudia* from jam jars. The air was blue with smoke.

There were only a few young men, some little more than boys. They were not old enough to have joined the army, so they had not been trapped on the mainland when the Greek army had surrendered to the Germans in April. Most had fought during the street battles in Heraklion, though, and were now trying to find some way to survive under occupation, with so much of the land lying in ruins. All were thin and hungry and defiant.

Four young men perched on the bench, playing musical instruments. Cosmo, the eldest brother, played a *bouzouki* with a plectrum made from the feather of a Cretan griffon vulture. The quill was black on its upper side and white on its lower side, and the musician chose which edge to use according to the song that was being played. The black side of the quill was stronger and fiercer and used for songs about war and sorrow and loss. The white side had a sweeter, softer sound and was used for love songs and lullabies. Tonight, Cosmo was playing with the black edge of the plectrum.

His brother, Angelino, played a smaller lute called a *baglames*. The fingernails on his left hand were grown long to strum its strings. Next in age came Yannis, only fifteen years old. He played a Cretan lyra, the hawk-bells on his bow chiming sweetly. Athos, the youngest brother, beat out the rhythm on a chalice drum set between his knees, while their sister, Phanessa, sang a tragic tale of unrequited love in a deep, husky voice.

A boy danced, spinning and swaying, a cigarette in his mouth. He staggered, then dropped almost to the ground, slapping one hand against the floor, before rising and twirling unsteadily once more. Every now and again he gulped from a glass of *tsikoudia*.

Before the war, Alenka and her friends had come together once a week, in secret, to listen to *rebetiko*, the music of rebels and misfits. This was, however, the first time they had dared to meet since the surrender of Crete. It was Midsummer's Eve, one of the most important religious festivals of the year, for it celebrated the birth of Saint John the Baptist. The day was usually spent in feasting and singing and dancing. At sunset bonfires would be lit and the dried wreaths of flowers plucked on May Day flung onto the flames to drive the witches away. Young men leaped over the flames three times to prove their virility. Everyone drank *rakomela*—brandy made with honey and spices—for John the Baptist was the patron saint of beekeepers.

But not this year. Public gatherings were banned in Nazi-occupied Crete.

For the Cretans, at least. The Germans were celebrating *Johannistag* with raucous good spirits, a great deal of beer, and food they had stolen from the larders and cellars of the conquered Greeks.

Alenka had been helping Faith tend the wounded when the soldiers had come. A German command had caught her by surprise. She looked up from her bucket of bloody swabs to find herself at gunpoint. A squad of gray-clad officers had entered the tent. They barked angry orders, gesturing with their guns. Alenka had put down her bucket and raised her hands, her heart thumping so fast she felt suffocated. The senior officer had been polite, but inflexible. Within minutes, the makeshift hospital was being dismantled, and all the Anzac doctors and nurses taken prisoner, along with their patients.

It had been awful to see Faith marched away. She and Alenka had become good friends as they had worked side by side to help the wounded. The Australian nurse had kissed her goodbye and told her to be brave. "Write to me care of the Red Cross," she said. "When this is all over, you must come and visit me in Australia!" Alenka had smiled through her tears and promised, even though such a thing seemed an impossible dream.

The Nazis wasted no time in grinding their jackboots into the faces of the Cretan people. In the month since the surrender, more than two thousand Cretans had been executed. General Alexander Andrae had been appointed the commander of Crete, with Major-General Julius Ringel the divisional commander for the Heraklion area. A stout Austrian with an imperial beard and a brisk, no-nonsense manner, Ringel had made the Villa Ariadne his headquarters. The walls around the old stone house were fortified with barbed wire and sentry boxes, searchlights probing the night. When Ringel first arrived at the villa, all those who lived and worked nearby had feared for their lives. But the general had heard how the field hospital had tended wounded German soldiers and buried those who had died in the graveyard, so he had ordered that the village be spared the brutal reprisals so many others had suffered.

"I have heard reports that candles were lit on the graves of the *Fallschirmjäger*," he had said. "Who was responsible for that?"

Hesper had been pointed out to him. "She does not speak, though," the priest said.

"Then she will be the perfect servant," the general had replied with a hearty grin, though his eyes remained cold and watchful.

So Hesper was employed once more at the Villa Ariadne, though she now mopped up after German officers rather than British archaeologists. Alenka was given work too, as a translator, a job she hated, as she heard so many stories of atrocities. Her German was quite basic, but most of the officers spoke English or French, and she was studying hard to brush up on her *Deutsch*. Axel managed to earn a few coins too, running errands after school or acting as a guide. Even with all three of them working, life was very hard. All mules and donkeys had been requisitioned, so Alenka had lost her beloved Modestine and had to carry water and wood herself. Fishing boats had been commandeered too, and stores of wine, olive oil, flour, lentils, and dried beans. If it was not for the little garden hidden away behind stone walls, Alenka and her family would have been close to starving.

That afternoon Alenka had come home from the Wehrmacht headquarters in the nearby village of Archanes to find an eagle feather tucked into her bedroom window. Her stomach gave a weird lurch. It was the secret signal of their underground *rebetiko* club. A meeting had been called for that night. Alenka knew she would go, despite the danger. She needed to see her friends, needed to drink and dance and pretend her homeland was free.

The *rebetiko* club met late at night in the old palace. It was the perfect place, being far enough away from the village that no one would hear their music and laughter, but close enough that everyone could walk. Alenka had waited till her mother and brother were asleep, then dressed herself in her mulberry-red dancing dress and climbed out her bedroom window.

She now accepted a glass of *tsikoudia* from one hand and a cigarette from another and took a deep gulp of one and a deep drag of the other. A glad rush of giddiness.

"Heard about the students in Athens?" asked a handsome young man named George Doundoulakis. He was six months older than Alenka, and spoke English even better than she did, having been born in Detroit. He and his brother Helias had moved back to Crete when they were little boys, so their parents could care for their blind grandmother. Despite living in Crete for sixteen years, everyone called him American George. He and Helias were considered real cool cats and had set up the *rebetiko* club.

She perched on the bench beside him. "No, what happened?"

"They climbed the Acropolis and tore down the swastika, right under the noses of the Nazis."

"*Po-po-po-po-po!*" Phyllia cried.

Alenka was thrilled. "So brave! Were they caught?"

"Not yet."

"Of course, the cuckolds simply put up another swastika in its place," Helias said.

"But still! It's a symbol," Alenka said. "Of defiance and rebellion."

"We should do the same. Steal the flag they hung from the cross of the cathedral in Heraklion!"

"Such sacrilege! I'm surprised the blessed saint did not strike them down with lightning," Phyllia said.

"Perhaps the saint did not want to damage the dome?" said a girl called Zephyra. She sat on her boyfriend's lap, dark smudges of mascara under her eyes from weeping.

"It was a miracle the cathedral was not destroyed in the bombing," her boyfriend Giannis said. He was a short, broad-shouldered young man with striking hazel eyes.

"I heard a story about that," Alenka said. "Apparently, a Luftwaffe officer went to the cathedral the week after the surrender. He was full of questions about our Saint Minas. When the churchwarden asked why he was so interested, the German said he had been ordered to drop bombs on the cathedral, but every time he flew over, his hands shook so much he could not pull the lever and release the bomb."

Everyone crossed themselves three times, murmuring blessings.

"Indeed, our saint is great!" Zephyra cried.

"It truly is a miracle," Phyllia said.

"We could climb the dome at night and pull down the swastika?" George suggested.

"It's too dangerous," a young man named Kimon argued. "They would kill us all."

"And our families too."

"Or just shoot the first dozen Greeks they saw."

"They took all the boys and men from Hóra Sfakíon and shot them in the balls," Kimon said. "Then doused them with petrol and set them alight. They burned them alive!"

"The monsters," Phyllia whispered.

"They razed the village of Kandanos to the ground," Alenka said somberly. "All the men shot, all the boys over fifteen, the women left homeless and destitute."

"They shall pay for their crimes, the cuckolds!"

"How?" Phyllia cried. "They have won, and we have lost."

"We have to do something!" Alenka said.

"Might as well get down on all fours now," Giannis said. "The cuckolds have us by the balls."

Everyone was silent.

Alenka could not bear it. She drank another glass of *tsikoudia* in a single fiery gulp, then called to Phanessa, "Sing us 'Children of Greece.' I want to dance!"

Phanessa nodded and gestured to her brothers. The familiar tune by Sofia Vembo rang out. It had become an anthem for them all. "Children of Greece, children who fight so hard in the mountains, children to sweet Mother of God, we pray for you to come back again . . ."

Alenka raised her chin high and lifted her arms up like wings. She began to dance, slowly, alone in the middle of the floor. Spinning, bending, touching one hand to the floor, kicking out one leg to slap her heel, stamping her feet, leaping high, spinning again. People began to clap and call out to her. Amber worry beads tapped against glasses gave her the percussive beat.

The *zeibekiko*—known in Crete as the 'Icarus Dance'—was traditionally only danced by men. But this was *rebetico*, where all were free to do as they pleased. The only rule was that *zeibekiko* be danced with intensity, with passion, with pain. It was about leaping high and falling to the floor, only to struggle up again. It was a prayer for strength, a public display of courage. Icarus had dared to soar toward the sun, he had risked his life for that moment of boldness and triumph, he had blazed high.

No one must ever interrupt someone who danced the *zeibekiko*, nor join them. To interrupt the *zeibekiko* was to provoke bloodshed.

The music quickened, and so did her step. Alenka spun, her red skirt flaring, alone in a crowd of shadowy watching faces. Suddenly, a man stumbled into the room. He was gaunt, his dark eyes glittering with fever, his bloodstained khaki uniform hanging in rags.

"A-A-Alenka!" He took a few steps toward her, then stumbled and fell.

"A spy!" George drew his dagger.

"Stop!" Alenka flung herself down on her knees beside him. "Jack? Holy Virgin preserve us, he's burning up." She could not believe he was here. She had thought him and Teddy safely evacuated to Egypt. And he was so thin, so ragged. She laid her hand on his brow, smoothing back his sweat-damp, tangled hair. "Quick, someone! I need water, *tsikoudia*."

"You know him? Who is he?" George hurried to her side.

"He's an Australian soldier. He was here, fighting the Germans. He saved my life! He must've been left behind." Alenka had such a lump in her throat, she found it hard to speak.

Exclamations of fear and amazement rang out. It had been almost a month since the Allied forces had been evacuated from Crete.

"He must've walked here all the way from Hóra Sfakíon!" George cried, passing her a bottle of *tsikoudia*. She dribbled a little into Jack's mouth and he swallowed weakly, mumbling a protest.

"But why?"

"What are we to do with him?"

"We should hand him in to the Germans," Zephyra said, looking about nervously. "There's terrible reprisals for anyone who shelters an Allied soldier."

"We can't hand him in," Alenka protested. "He came here to fight the Nazis. He's sick, wounded. We have to help him."

All her friends looked at each other, worried and afraid.

"Yes, it will be risky!" Alenka gazed about imploringly. "But better to risk all and die than live as a slave. We must fight for our freedom! We must resist with all our strength. And that means we must hide him from the Nazis, whatever the danger."

II

Jack opened his eyes.

He did not know where he was.

Stone floor beneath him. Beamed ceiling above. Walls as red as blood.

Was he in some kind of prison?

He tried to sit up, but his head swam. Sharp pain in his side. He touched it. Bandages wound tight. He managed to push himself up with his other hand. A cup of water sat on the floor. He drank it down greedily. Then he wondered, *Should I have saved some? What if no one brings me any more?*

The last few weeks were a fevered blur. Hiding during the day, stumbling through the night, snatching berries from brambles, stealing eggs from under roosting chickens, devouring them raw. His stumbling steps had beat out a song. *Alenka, Alenka, Alenka.*

And now he was here. Where was here?

A door creaked open. Footsteps.

Jack tried to get up. He was too weak. He looked for a weapon. Nothing but the plate. He broke it against the floor and seized the sharpest shard.

Alenka came through an old wooden door. "You're awake!"

Jack could only gaze at her. She was dressed in black. Her face was pale, her eyes shadowed, yet she was still the most beautiful girl he had ever seen.

She saw the broken plate, the shard in his hand, cutting his palm so that he bled.

"*Po-po-po-po-po*, you are safe," she told him, softly, as if to a child. "No need to fear. You're in the old palace."

He looked around and recognized the alabaster throne with its strange, sinuous back, the ancient paintings of griffins and lilies.

He stared at her, not speaking. She smiled tentatively. "You've been very ill. I've done my best to tend you, but . . ." She made an expressive gesture with one hand.

"I-I-I found you."

"Yes. You must've walked half of Crete, given the state of your boots."

He looked down at his bare feet. "My . . . my boots. Where are they?"

"Ruined."

"M-m-my clothes?" He looked down at his body. He was naked except for a pair of billowing Cretan breeches.

"Torn to pieces and infested with lice. I burned them."

Jack realized she must have stripped him naked, washed him, and clothed him. He burned with embarrassment and shame. He tried to ask her how he came to be here, but his strength was failing, his tongue knotted.

She understood him, nonetheless. "I was here, in the throne room, with my friends, and you came stumbling in from the darkness."

"You were d-d-dancing?"

"Yes."

"I remember."

Jack had thought it a dream.

She knelt and busied herself unpacking her basket. A battered tin bottle of water, some fresh bread wrapped in a cloth, olives in an oily twist of paper. Jack seized the water and gulped it down. It was cool and sweet.

"W-w-what happened? Did the Germans win?"

She shot him a look of surprise. "Yes. How could you not know?"

"It . . . it was all such a n-n-n-nightmare. We had to . . . to retreat?

Over the m-m-mountains? That was real? Then . . ." He began to shake. "Then it's real? T-T-Teddy was shot?"

"Teddy was shot?"

"Yes." Jack's chest was tight like iron bands squeezed his ribs. "I s-s-saw it . . ."

He heard her sharply indrawn breath.

"He was shot? Killed?"

Jack nodded.

"Oh, no! It's all my fault. He came back for me. He could have gone with the king, but he came back for me and now he's dead." Her voice broke.

Jack reached out and drew her close. She turned her face into his shoulder, her tears dampening his bare skin. Gently, he stroked her hair.

Teddy was his best friend, his only friend. For years, Jack had been the shadow to his light, the tide to his gravitational pull. He did not know how to be without him.

Yet crouched here, barefoot on a pile of dirty old straw, hollowed out with hunger and pain, his best friend's girl cradled in his arms, Jack felt something he had never felt before.

Love deep enough to shake his very soul.

His nana had grieved when Jack told her he and Teddy had signed up.

"War is not an adventure, my boy," she had said. "It hurts you somewhere deep down, and the wound never heals." And she had sighed deeply, in the way she did whenever she thought of her daughter Celia, Jack's mother.

But Jack had not listened. What twenty-two-year-old listens to his nana?

Yet she had been right. War had wounded him in ways he could not see. He did not know the panacea. Nightmares startled him awake, drenched with sweat. No amount of dozing eased his bone-deep weariness. Even dressing himself was exhausting.

Alenka came only briefly. Breathlessly she would unpack her basket, apologizing for how little food she had been able to find, gather up his dirty crockery. "I'm sorry," she said. "It is Axel. He is suspicious. He watches me."

Jack spent many hours alone. As his strength slowly returned, he explored the palace, limping along with the aid of a gnarled old shepherd's crook. He found steps leading down into deep underground crypts, built around heavy stone pillars inscribed with the symbol of the double ax. Sometimes there was a dark-stained drain below it. Elsewhere he found rooms lined with gigantic earthenware jars, like something out of Ali Baba, with stone-lined pits set into the floor like traps. In one chamber, the walls were stained black with the shadows of smoke, blowing to the north. In another, a broken fresco showed a boy—as dark and slim as Jack himself—somersaulting over the back of a stampeding bull. His body was bent almost into a circle. It seemed impossibly dangerous.

The future was dark and terrifying. Jack could not hide in the old palace forever. Alenka brought him a pamphlet the Luftwaffe had dumped out of a plane above the maize fields and olive groves, written in broken English:

Soldiers of the ROYAL BRITISH ARMY, NAVY, AIR FORCE!
There are MANY OF YOU STILL HIDING in the
mountains, valleys, and villages.
You have to PRESENT yourself AT ONCE TO THE GERMAN
TROOPS.
Every OPPOSITION will be completely USELESS.
Every ATTEMPT TO FLEE will be in vain.
The COMING WINTER will force you to leave the mountains.
Only soldiers, who present themselves AT ONCE
will be sure of a HONORABE AND SOLDIERLIKE CAPTIVITY
OF WAR. On the contrary who is met in civil-clothes will be
treated as a spy.

THE COMMANDER OF KRETA

Spies were shot. Jack's only hope of evading capture was to fool the Germans into thinking he was Greek. Yet the smallest mistake would mean disaster for Alenka and her friends. *Festung Kreta*, the Nazis called the island now. Fortress Crete. No one could get in, no one could get out.

On the evenings when her brother was busy about his own concerns, Alenka could stay a little longer. She had brought Jack a Greek-English dictionary and an old phrasebook and insisted they speak only in the Cretan dialect. He studied the books diligently during the day, and it was not long before he began to sound less like a foreigner. One night, when Alenka rose to leave, she asked, "Is there anything else I can bring you?"

"B-b-books?"

She smiled and nodded. The next day, she brought her copy of *The Secret Garden*. Jack read it for the first time since he was a child and found himself in tears at the end. *I shall get well! I shall get well! And I shall live for ever and ever!*

"I . . . I'd like to go into your garden," he said to Alenka.

"As soon as you are strong enough, you shall," she answered, though her eyes were shadowed with fear. *What if the Germans find you?* they seemed to say.

"Can you bring me another book?"

She hesitated. "I am worried a soldier will stop me and search my basket. They search everywhere for Allied soldiers. If they see me carrying food and water and English books, they will guess one is nearby."

Jack's heart fell. He did not think he could bear to keep on hiding if he had nothing to read.

"Don't worry, I will think of a way," she said.

The next time Alenka came, she untucked her shirt and drew out a book she had hidden inside the waistband of her skirt, next to her skin. It was a book of English translations of her favorite poet, Sappho. The leather cover was warm and smelled faintly of roses. After she had gone, Jack lifted the book to his nose. When he touched the soft pages, it could have been her skin. When he read, it could have been her voice who made the promise: *And if she loves not, shall soon love . . .*

One morning, before dawn, Alenka helped him limp to the secret garden. She left him there, closing the door in the high wall behind her. Jack swam in the cistern and sat under the mulberry tree, listening to the bees singing in the thyme flowers. He read a Sherlock Holmes story, scribbled poetry in his journal, watched the shadows lengthen, felt at peace.

That evening, Alenka brought her embroidery to the garden and sat on the grass, sewing. Jack lay on his stomach nearby, pretending to write in his journal but covertly watching her. She sewed a row of tiny crosses in red silk.

Like kisses, he thought.

He liked the mathematical precision of her stitches. Someone had once said that geometry was the archetype of beauty in the world. Jack loved that. As a child, he had seen geometry in everything. The bilateral symmetry of a butterfly's wings, the parabolic curve of a cricket ball, the hexagonal shape of honeycomb within the hive, the fractals of pine cones. Mathematics was a kind of perfection that made sense in a world that was otherwise chaos.

One of the reasons he loved music so much was because it was like math. Mathematics was, after all, a study of patterns. Music was simply a pattern of sound. He liked poetry for the same reason. Poetry was as precise as geometry, each syllable as necessary and right in its place as a seed in the spiral of a sunflower.

Jack had written poetry since he was a boy, given Robert Louis Stevenson's *A Child's Garden of Verses* to read by his nana. He could still quote bits of it: *And sometimes for an hour or so, I watched my leaden soldiers go . . .*

And now he was a leaden soldier too. He was like the steadfast tin soldier in Hans Christian Andersen's story, in love with the paper ballerina who pirouetted on one toe and did not know he existed.

Alenka looked up and met his gaze. "What is it? What's wrong?"

"N-n-nothing." Jack looked away in confusion. "I was just w-w-wondering about your embroidery. What . . . what are you sewing?"

She flushed. "It's my *sindoni*. Part of my dowry."

"You . . . you're getting m-m-married?"

"*Po-po-po-po-po*, no! Not ever, probably. Who wants to be bossed around by some good-for-nothing man? Not me."

"Then . . . w-w-why sew a dowry?"

She shrugged. "I like sewing. I find it very calming and . . ." She hesitated, then said in a rush, "I like the way I can create beauty with nothing but a needle and thread."

"M-m-may I see?"

She unfastened her oval wooden hoop and unfolded the white linen sheet, explaining that it would be pinned to a quilt to protect it, only removed for washing or special feast days. One edge of the *sindoni* was embroidered with a design of dancing men and women and musicians, amid a frieze of trees and birds, flowers and beasts, double-tailed mermaids and writhing snakes, all bordered by stylized Greek spirals. The exuberant design had been created with tiny stitches of great precision, with silk spun by hand from the silkworms in her garden and dyed with roots, leaves, petals.

"W-w-why, you're a true artist," Jack said.

Alenka smiled radiantly. His heart gave a great thump in his chest.

Shyly, he asked her about the design, and she began to explain the symbols. Snakes for renewal. Flowers for passion and the fleeting beauty of life. Trees of life for strength and vitality, birds for freedom, the spirals for the labyrinth and the soul's journey. Jack listened quietly.

"See here? That is me and my mother and brother. I embroidered seven knot stitches over our heads for protection, when it became clear Greece was going to fall."

"Why are the knots red? Is that for Ariadne?"

Alenka looked at him in pleased surprise. "You know the story? And that the spool of thread she gave him was red? In Greece, the color red is very important. It's the color of life and blood and passion and magic. Where you say 'touch wood,' we say 'grab red,' *piase kokkino*. And our fairy tales begin *kokkini klosti*, which means *red thread*. She chanted the formula for him: "Red thread bound, on the spinning wheel round, kick it to spin, let the tale begin."

"I didn't know that," Jack said. "Though I did know that *clew*, the original word for Ariadne's ball of thread, is the source of our English word *clue*, meaning a piece of evidence used to solve a mystery."

Alenka opened her eyes wide in exaggerated amazement. "And I didn't know that!"

They smiled, ridiculously pleased they each had something to teach the other.

"I have always loved the story of Ariadne," she said. "See here, on my *sindoni*, how I gave myself a crown of stars? That is because the god Dionysus gave her a crown of stars for their wedding day, and she flung it up into the sky so that anyone who was lost could see it and navigate their way home through the darkness. I always thought that was so beautiful."

He frowned in puzzlement. "I d-d-didn't know Ariadne married Dionysus. I thought she fell in love with Theseus, who a-abandoned her."

Alenka said hotly, "People only know part of the myth. They think Theseus is the hero of the myth, but it was really Ariadne. She was the one who knew the minotaur had to be slayed so no more young people would be sacrificed, she was the one who chose Theseus to do the deed, and she was the one who was clever enough to think of the tying one end of the thread to the entrance so he could find his way out of the labyrinth. Yia-Yia said Ariadne was a priestess who danced with snakes and spoke prophecy in a trance. In the oldest myths, she was the earthly face of the bright goddess, and her labyrinth was a sacred dancing ground. And my name means *bright*, and I love to dance, so I gave myself a crown of stars too. It's silly, I know, but I like the idea of every stitch having a secret meaning."

"It's not silly. It's b-b-beautiful." Jack took out his journal and stub of pencil. *O bright girl, dancing . . .* he wrote.

He was sick with longing for her.

"Would you . . . would you t-teach me how to do it?" he asked hesitantly.

She looked up at him in surprise.

"The hours when I do not see you are very long," he said carefully, not looking at her. "I-I-I need something to do. I like the s-s-symmetry of it and the idea of making something beautiful with my hands."

She nodded. "All right. I will bring you an embroidery hoop and some material next time I come."

The creak of the wooden gate brought them to their feet, eyes wide in terror.

There was nowhere to run or hide. Jack thrust Alenka behind him. A garden fork was plunged in the soil nearby, and he snatched it up.

A man in a tattered Greek army uniform stepped through into the garden. He was about thirty years old, short and strong, his black hair tousled, his jaw bristled.

"Micky!" Alenka flew across the lawn and into his arms. They kissed each other's cheeks three times, embracing and talking volubly in Greek, too fast for Jack to understand.

A sharp pang of jealousy pierced him. He repressed it savagely. What right did he have to be jealous? Alenka had never looked at him with even the slightest trace of warmth. She thought of him as an ally, perhaps as a friend. No more.

Alenka looked around. "Jack, this is my godbrother, Micky. We thought he was dead!"

"I'm hard to kill," Micky said with a grim smile.

The young Greek man came forward, one hand stretched out in greeting. His face was somber, but his brown eyes were full of fire. "Phyllia told me you were here," he said in English. "I believe we owe you thanks. You came to fight for us, and now you're trapped. We're grateful and will do what we can to help you escape."

"But how, Micky? The Germans are everywhere."

"*Po-po-po-po-po!* I got home, didn't I? Fortress Crete is not so secure as they think."

"Micky, you know . . ." Alenka's voice trailed away.

"About Papa? Yes. I will see him buried properly. It's been more than forty days since he died. We shall have a service for him, so his soul can be at peace in heaven."

"The Germans are here, at the villa," Alenka said. "You must be careful, Micky. There have been terrible reprisals."

"The cuckolds will pay." Micky spoke with utter certainty.

III

Alenka and her friends crouched over a makeshift radio which Jack had built from rusty razor blades, a coil of wire, and lead pencils. The old throne room was lit by only a few flickering candles jammed into old bottles so that the painted griffins seemed to rustle their wings in the uncertain light.

"I've m-m-managed to get it to work, though it's temperamental," Jack said. "I'm hoping, with a little f-f-finessing, that I can get the BBC."

He made a few delicate adjustments, then lifted the improvised earphones. The others scooted closer, laughing a little as their knees bumped. A faint crackling sound, then the faraway sound of music.

"It works!" Phyllia cried in delight.

"Pipe down, you idiot," Micky told his sister. "We don't want the Krauts to hear us."

"This is London calling," a British voice announced, sending a stir of excitement through them. The radio played some triumphant organ music, then the news was announced.

Everyone listened hungrily. They had been without a radio for so long. Their only news came from the German radios that blasted from every *kafenion* and taverna, shouting about the latest Nazi victories.

A new voice came on the air, calm, measured, and very British. He announced himself as Colonel Britton, and then spoke about the significance of the letter V, the first letter of the word victory. "The V sign is the symbol of the unconquerable will of the occupied territories and a portent of the fate awaiting Nazi tyranny. So long as people continue to refuse all collaboration with the invader, it is sure his cause will perish, and Europe will be liberated."

A thrill ran through Alenka. Liberation. It was what she wanted with all her heart.

The people of Crete had three great passions: love of country, love of freedom, love of life. The Nazis had brought subjugation, enslavement, death. Alenka was determined to fight them, but she did not know how. She did not want to die unnecessarily or put her family in danger. But to do nothing, to bow her head and submit, was intolerable. Here, at last, was a way to resist that would not bring brutal reprisals down upon those she loved.

"Britain and its Empire stand alone now in this war," the radio announcer said. "They intend to fight on, but they need your help. Become part of the V army. Join the battle. Draw the letter V wherever and whenever you can. Tap out the sound of the letter as you work. Whistle the opening bars of Beethoven's Fifth Symphony as you walk. Pound it with your feet, clap it with your hands. Let the Nazis know fate comes knocking on their door."

The sound of a drumstick beating out a rhythm on a drumskin. Da-da-da-DAH! The rousing opening chords of the famous Beethoven symphony began to play.

A babble of conversation broke out.

Micky declared he would buy a bucket of whitewash the very next day. "We'll daub V signs all over the town!"

"You'd best be careful," Phyllia said. "Don't leave a trail of white footprints back to our door."

"I'm not a complete idiot!"

"That's a matter of opinion," she answered, laughing.

Micky laughed too but sobered quickly. "I will be careful. I'm no use to anyone if I'm dead."

"What did he mean, tap out the letter?" Alenka asked. "How can you tap a letter?"

"In M-M-Morse code." Jack tapped his fingers four times on her knee. "Dot-Dot-Dot-DASH spells V."

Alenka remembered reading about Morse code in one of her English school stories. Someone had flashed SOS with a torch. She didn't know anyone who knew how to do it, though. She asked Jack, and he grinned and nodded.

"I t-t-taught it to myself when I was just a kid. It's a kind of secret code, a way of m-m-messaging without . . ." He struggled for a moment, his jaw contorting. " . . . words."

She smiled at him, understanding at once why he might like that.

He smiled back. "This is *A* for Alenka." He tapped twice on her knee, one short, one long. Alenka realized both Micky and Phyllia were watching them. She drew away, smoothing her skirt down her knees.

Jack also drew away, color rising in his face.

Alenka searched for something to say. "So why Beethoven?"

"It's v-v- . . . very clever," Jack said. "*V* is the Roman numeral for five, and the fifth symphony begins with four notes that are the same p-p-pattern as the Morse c-c-code for *V*."

He sang them out. *Da-da-da-DUM.*

The others mimicked him or tried tapping the code out with their finger.

"The f-f-fifth symphony is sometimes called the "Symphony of F . . . Fate,"" Jack said. "B-Beethoven said the four opening notes were like the hand of fate knocking on the door."

"Then we shall go in the middle of the night and bang out that rhythm on the door of every Nazi in town," Alenka declared. "We shall let them know that our victory and their defeat is their destiny."

She thought of the Three Fates. The spinner, the measurer, and the cutter of thread, the oldest sister who chose the time and the manner of each human's death. Her name meant "the inevitable one.'

We must be like the cutter of thread, Alenka thought. *Inescapable.*

The old man sat, a black beaded scarf bound about his brow, a lyra perched on his knee, his gnarled fingers moving surely over the three taut strings. In a deep, sonorous voice, he sang:

> *Crete, O my love, my beautiful, Crete to whom we're*
> *beholden,*
> *Ela, ela, Crete to whom we're beholden,*
> *All our rocks are diamonds, all your earth is golden,*
> *Ela, ela, ela, all your earth is golden.*

Jack sat on the sun-warmed wall, listening intently. The old man's bow was strung with tiny bells that chimed sweetly. All around him, men in breeches and boots were drinking wine and eating olives, spitting the stones out on the ground. Phyllia and Alenka moved quietly about, offering more wine and bread with salt and oil. Jack had spent the day working with Micky in the vineyard. He was pleasantly tired, his muscles sore. Alenka smiled at him as she refilled his mug of wine. *This is happiness*, Jack thought to himself. *A day spent with my hands in earth, eating and drinking what I have sown and grown, good food, good friends, music, poetry . . .*

There was only one thing in the world that could have made him happier. To have been able to hold out his hand to her, and have her take it, bending her mouth to his, her black hair falling about him like night. His yearning for Alenka was so acute, it was like a sickness in him. Yet he had nothing to offer her. He was a fugitive, hiding out like a coward, always at risk of being captured and shot. He risked her life, just being here, but he was so lonely he could not even keep away for her sake. He was a burden on her.

> *Is there a man who will not fight, who lets himself be*
> *beaten?*
> *Ela, ela, who lets himself be beaten?*

He has no right to dwell in Crete, he is no more a
Cretan!
Ela, ela, ela, he is no more a Cretan!

After each line, the men all sang the chorus. Micky grinned at Jack and urged him to join in. Rather hesitantly, Jack lifted his voice. He had sung in the church choir as a boy, but his English grandmother had not approved of him "showing off," as she called it, and had forbidden it. Jack thought it was because she had hated his mother so much, and the music in him was his mother's only legacy. His Australian nana had done her best to encourage him to sing, but then Teddy had laughed at him and told him that singing was soft, so Jack had kept silent.

The men of Crete did not think singing was soft, though. Music and dance were woven into every part of their lives, vibrant proof of their strength and virility. Every house had a lyra or mandolin propped against the wall, and every man strummed it and sang a few verses as the women prepared and brought their food. Sitting silently was a sign that he was a stranger, that he did not belong here. Jack had to look Cretan and act Cretan if he was not to be caught by the Germans. Tentatively he began to sing. The men all nodded and smiled in approval. Jack had a strange sensation in his throat as if invisible throttling fingers had been unlocked. He breathed deeply and laughed as he sang.

At last the old man lifted his bow. Everyone shouted acclaim and clicked their amber beads against their glasses. More wine was poured, and the old man drank deeply, then came to where Jack sat under the olive tree.

"You sing well, my child," he said. "You like the *mantinada*?"

Jack did not know the word. The old man chanted, with a wide grin that showed only a few stumps of teeth, "A Cretan does not say in plain words what he feels, but with *mantinades* he weeps or with laughter he peals!"

He held out the lyra to Jack. "Here, you try it."

The other men gathered around, laughing. They knew, of course, that he was not Cretan. They expected him to shake his head and stutter an excuse, and then they would mock him and call him a *malakas*.

"It's easy enough," Micky said encouragingly. "Two lines that rhyme."

Jack took the lyra and drew the bow across it gently. He knew the tune, for he could play by ear any music he had heard, and he knew the words for he had heard it sung many times since he had begun working in the vineyard. After taking a few moments to accustom himself to only three strings, he began to sing the final lines of the song the old man had sung:

> *Dig where you will in the soil of Crete, even with a*
> *needle rake it,*
> *Ela, Ela, with a needle rake it,*
> *Blood of a hero stains the point, bones of a hero break it,*
> *Ela, ela, ela, bones of a hero break it.*
> *Crete, your brave sons are far away or fallen, why can't*
> *you keep them?*
> *Ela, ela, why can't you keep them?*
> *Far, far away and fallen, we are left to weep them,*
> *Ela, ela, ela, we are left to weep them.*

There was a long moment of surprise, then the men gathered around Jack, roaring their approval. He was clapped so hard on the back, he almost fell off the wall.

"*Po-po-po-po-po!* This boy, he has a Cretan soul!" the old man said, seizing both of Jack's hands in his own. "And he can play the lyra! How is this so?"

"Benediktos can play anything," Alenka said.

Jack looked at her. She was smiling at him, her eyes full of pride.

She and her friends all called him *Benediktos*, since *Jack* was far too British and therefore dangerous. Jack had always hated *Benedict*, the name his father had chosen. He associated it with coldness, dampness, unkindness. He loved the way Alenka said it, though. Benediktos, the good speaker. He wished it was true, that he could speak without shaming himself, that he could woo her with his words.

Flushing hotly, Jack passed the lyra back to the old man. He tried to say something but mangled the words so badly he could scarcely get a syllable out.

The old man began to play and sing again, but Jack got up and shrugged on his haversack. It was time he went back.

"Stay!" Micky cried. "Eat with us. You've worked hard, you deserve a feast."

Jack knew there was little to eat. He also knew that the Germans were more likely to raid in the evening when the work of the day was done. So he shook his head.

"You'd be very welcome," Alenka said.

He tried to say, 'It's not safe,' but once again made a fool of himself.

She said, very gently, "Benediktos, you didn't stutter once while you were singing, did you know that?"

He stared at her, his throat thick.

She smiled. "You should sing more often."

"I . . . I sh-sh-should g-g-go."

"See you tomorrow!" She turned back to the circle of lantern light, everyone eating and drinking and laughing. Jack limped into the darkness alone.

The old man was singing: "How am I to part from you and leave? How am I to live without you when we part?"

The next afternoon Jack sat in the sun, reading an Agatha Christie story that Alenka had brought him. A boy's voice rang over the ruins. "This way, sir! The treasure trove is this way."

Jack scrambled up and dove behind a broken wall. His heart was pounding. Luckily, he had not let the book fall.

"Good lad," a deep voice responded. The speaker spoke Greek with a thick German accent. Jack risked a peek through a crack in the stones. He saw a portly man with an imperial beard and a cocked gray cap. A swastika was pinned to the breast pocket of his uniform, and an iron cross between his gold-embroidered collars. A barefoot boy in shorts was leading him by the hand. He was angelically fair. Jack remembered seeing him outside the Villa Ariadne. He wondered if he could be Alenka's brother.

Jack watched until they had disappeared down a flight of steps, then thrust the book inside his sash and limped, as fast as he could, through the maze of broken walls till he had reached the safety of the secret garden. Alenka and Phyllia were working together in the vegetable patch, harvesting tomatoes and eggplants for the evening meal.

"Benediktos!" Alenka scrambled to her feet. "What's wrong?"

He told them about the German officer and the fair-haired boy, and the two young women exchanged meaningful glances.

"Axel," Alenka said unhappily. "I should've guessed he'd tell the major-general about the storerooms at the palace."

"He called it a t-t-treasure trove."

"Well, it is! But not gold and jewels."

"Mainly pot shards," Phyllia said. "Some lovely gold-and-ivory statuettes, though."

"I remember the curator was very worried about leaving the dig," Alenka said. "He told his mother that the Nazis stole a lot of art and artifacts from the museums in Athens. He said he would hide what he could. Axel must have told him about it."

"The palace won't be safe anymore. The Nazis will swarm all over it if they think there's anything of value to steal." Phyllia's voice was bitter.

"We need to find you a new hiding place, Jack," Alenka said. "There's a little abandoned church not far from here. There are caves in the cliffs there, where the monks used to go and pray, where you could hide if anyone came. I will come back after supper and take you there."

She and Phyllia hurried away, waving their hands to him in farewell. He weeded the garden, swam in the cistern, read his book. The sun set, and she did not return. Jack dared not return to the palace. He was hungry, having eaten only a handful of tomatoes. He heard boots marching past and crouched low, scarcely daring to breathe.

The hump-backed moon rose. Tiny bats flitted across its shadowed face. Far away, an owl hooted. Jack shivered. *But at my back in a cold blast I hear . . . the rattle of the bones . . .*

Sometime after midnight, the door creaked open. A dark shadow slipped through. In a heartbeat, Jack had one hand over her mouth, the other holding a rusty pruning knife to her carotid artery. He felt the familiar curve of her body, smelt her familiar scent of roses, and let her go.

Alenka was trembling, her breast rising and falling rapidly, her hands at her throat. He wondered if he had cut her.

"We . . . we need a secret signal," Jack said roughly. "S-s-so I know it's you."

She muttered something, a prayer.

"C-can you whistle?"

"What?" she whispered.

He whistled the first four notes of Beethoven's Fifth, *da-da-da-DUM*.

After a few moments, she managed a shaky approximation. He whistled it again.

Together, in the moonlight, they whistled back and forth to each other like lyrebirds.

"M-m-music is a universal language. No one will s-s-suspect you if they hear you whistle just a few notes."

She nodded.

"I . . . I'm sorry if I hurt you."

She shook her head. "I could not come before. Axel was watching. He suspects me."

Jack frowned. "But surely your b-b-brother . . ."

"I don't know. I hope not. I cannot risk it. He is . . ." She paused a long moment, then said, "he's half-German, you see."

Jack did not see, but now was not the time to ask her.

"I will take you to the little church now. It's about half an hour away, but the road gets steep. I will help you."

She slipped one arm about his waist and let him brace one arm across her shoulders. Together they limped slowly through the darkness, the moon lighting up the pale road through the cypresses, nightingales singing.

It was sweet pain to have her warm body so close to his. They did not speak.

IV

19 August–9 December 1941

"I've heard rumors of a British submarine coming at night to the south coast," Micky said, pouring *tsikoudia*. "They want to rescue stranded soldiers. The holy monastery at Preveli is helping them."

Alenka and Phyllia automatically made the sign of the cross.

"If we can get you to Preveli in time, Benediktos, perhaps you too can be saved."

"It is a long walk," Alenka said. "And he does not know the way."

"I would take him." Micky looked troubled. "But I have got a job in a law firm in Heraklion at last, and I cannot get away. Perhaps Alekos can guide him."

"Alekos fell out of an olive tree today," Phyllia said. "He's hurt his foot."

"I will take Benediktos. I know the way," Alenka said.

Micky shook his head. "That would not be fitting."

"Benediktos is a good man. He will not lay a finger on me."

Micky's brows drew together. He flipped his worry beads over and over in his hand. "What about your brother? Will he not wonder where you are?"

"It's school holidays. Axel's gone with the German archaeologists to help with a dig near Chania."

"Your mother?"

"She knows about Jack. You need not worry she will tell anyone." Alenka smiled faintly.

Micky's frown did not lift. "The people in the mountains follow the old ways. They will not like to see a young woman traveling alone with a man."

"I will tell them we are brother and sister. And I will wear a long skirt and a headscarf, and Jack will wear breeches and boots. Do not worry, Micky, we will be careful."

Micky scowled at Jack. "If you touch her, I shall kill you."

Jack stammered a promise, and Micky grunted. There was no other option, though. Jack's presence endangered them all.

In the cool of the following dawn, Alenka came back to the little church. "I have identification papers for you," she said without preamble. "I went to my father for help."

Jack drew his brows together. She had never mentioned her father before. He had assumed her mother was a widow.

"He is a gendarme in Heraklion," Alenka said. "He gave me a blank ID card but stamped and signed it. I have given you a name. See?"

She had written *Benediktos Hatzidakis.*

"*Hatzidakis* means *pilgrim,*" she told him. "I thought it a good name since we walk to the holy monastery. And easy for you to remember, yes?"

"Y-y-yes, thank you. P-p-please thank your f-f-father for me."

She turned away from him. "I do not speak to my father."

Jack followed Alenka along a narrow mule track into the hills. A seemingly endless chain of mountains rose beyond, bare and blasted as a desert of stone. The air was scented with wild thyme, and the only sound was the distant tinkle of goat bells. Far above, an eagle soared.

Alenka leaped nimbly from rock to rock, steadying herself with a walking stick of gnarled olivewood. As the sun was setting, they came to a mountain village. Everyone they passed asked the same question: "What news?"

Alenka told them what they had heard on the makeshift radio. The Germans had bombed Moscow. Saigon had fallen to the Japanese. Estonia had fallen. The shadow of darkness was eating the world. In return for this unwelcome news, the villagers gave them food and wine and warmth and shelter.

Jack did not sleep for a long time that night. Alenka lay near him, wrapped in her shawl. Jack could have reached out his hand and touched her. He could have pressed his body against her, he could have driven into her, he could have released the unbearable tension of wanting her and never having her, in one glad, shuddering spasm.

Benediktos is a good man, she had said. *He will not lay a finger on me.*

So Jack lay still and rigid, unable even to relieve himself with his hand in case she heard him. His dreams were full of her, and the waking into the absence of her an agony.

They walked on through ever-steeper mountains. After a long way, they came to a fork in the road. The wooden signpost was so worn, no words could be read. Alenka hesitated for a while and then followed the road that led higher into the mountains. They came to a tiny roadside shrine, and Alenka crossed herself three times, murmuring a little prayer. A few small houses clustered about a well. Three men sat playing cards and smoking at a table under a mulberry tree, its trunk limewashed against insects. They stared at Alenka and Jack with dark suspicious eyes. Alenka asked for directions from an old woman who was drawing water up from the well.

"*Po-po-po-po-po?* Preveli?" the old woman repeated. She pointed back the way they had come with one thin claw of a hand, then hoisted up the two heavy buckets on a pole braced across her hunched shoulders. Jack sprang forward at once, offering to carry the buckets of water for her. She stared at him in amazement. Alenka caught at his arm and drew him away. They hurried away from the village, everyone turning to stare after them.

"Here in Crete, the women do the work," Alenka said. "If you offer to carry her buckets for her, everyone will know you are not Cretan."

"I'm sorry," Jack said. "I . . . I d-d-didn't know."

She gave him a strained smile. "How could you? It was good of you to offer. Just not the Cretan way."

Alenka turned often to look behind her, but no one seemed to be following them. She did not let them rest, though, till the last light was almost gone. They found shelter in an old stone shed, both so weary they barely had the strength to chew on the last of their rusks.

The next few nights were spent sleeping on rough beds made of wild sage spread with blankets, under a canopy of stars, shivering in the bitter wind that blew off the snowy peaks. The mule track wound along sharp-edged ridges, down precipitous slopes of shale and pebbles, and through steep gorges.

They saw the sea and—many hot, footsore miles later—the white walls and domes of the monastery. A black-clad monk came along, leading a small donkey laden with firewood. He was only young, but his beard was already long, his hair tied up in a bun beneath his stove-pipe hat.

The monk looked stern when Alenka spoke to him, but his features softened when she told him about Jack. He said in a deep, sonorous voice, "Welcome to Preveli. Many soldiers come here. We shall hide you till the submarine next comes."

"W-w-when will that be?" Jack asked eagerly.

The monk tilted his hand one way, then the other. "*Avrio, methavrio.*"

Jack sighed. He had heard those words many, many times since he had been in Crete.

Tomorrow or the day after tomorrow.

They followed the monk wearily along the road. The thick white walls and narrow austere towers of the monastery were set against the backdrop of immense, grim mountains. It looked ancient.

"Tenth century," Alenka told him. "Pilgrims come from far away to stay here. It has a most beautiful crucifix, plated with gold and studded with jewels. It is said to heal the sick and help the suffering. The monks have always carried it into battle . . ."

"Into b-b-battle?" Jack said. "The m-m-monks fight?"

"But of course," she replied in surprise. "When they fought against the Turks, more than a century ago, the cross was lost. Some sailors tried to steal it, but their ship stopped dead in the water. The sailors could not sail away until after they gave the cross back to the monastery. It was a miracle." She saw his skeptical expression. "It's true!"

"Being becalmed at sea happens."

"Not in Crete. In winter, the *tramontara* blows from the north and finds every crack in the wall and we all shiver in our beds. Then we have the *levante*, which blows from the east. It brings rain, storms, high seas, shipwrecks. The *zephyr* blows from the west, cold and bright and sharp as a dagger. In summer, the *sorokos* blows south from Africa, hot as fire, laden with dust. Everything bad happens when the *sorokos* blows. Fist-fights and murders and suicides. They say it blew when Knossos fell." She paused, frowning. "My brother was born in the *sorokos*."

Jack looked at her, troubled. He had always longed for a brother. Yet Alenka spoke as if her brother's birth was a terrible thing.

After a moment, she went on. "The wind is never calm here. It was the miraculous cross which kept the ship still and unmoving on the sea, not the lack of wind."

Her certainty silenced him.

The monk led them through an arched gateway into a paved court-yard. Chickens scratched in the dust, and a goat was tethered under a palm tree. An old church with a domed terracotta roof was guarded on all sides by high walls with only a few narrow, slitted windows. It looked more like a fortress than a monastery.

"Crete has been invaded many times," Alenka said, shrugging. "They come, we fight, in the end they go."

Jack followed her and the silent monk through an archway, the walls several feet thick, down a low, cool, stone-paved corridor and into a vast kitchen. It was filled with unshaven men in ragged khaki. A few whistled at the sight of Alenka, who flushed and drew her scarf more tightly about her face.

"I . . . I guess this is goodbye," Jack said with difficulty. He did not know how to say what was in his heart. He held out his hand to her. "I . . . I . . . I wish . . ."

"Jack?"

He spun around at the sound of a familiar voice.

It was Teddy.

Teddy stared at Jack incredulously. He almost didn't recognize his best mate.

Jack was dressed like a Cretan, in breeches and wine-red sash, a black beaded scarf bound about his head. His dark hair was long and tousled, his jaw shadowed. It made him look wild and dangerous.

Teddy's first emotion was one of overwhelming relief. He had thought Jack must be dead. He rushed forward to thump him on the back. Then he saw Alenka standing close beside Jack, gazing up into his face. Teddy fell back a step, suspicion and jealousy uncoiling in his belly.

Jack looked around at the sound of his name. "T-T-Teddy! Holy cow!" He strode forward, a huge grin lighting up his face. "But . . . how the hell? I saw you being sh-sh-shot!"

"Thank the Lord Christ and all his saints, it's a miracle." Alenka crossed herself, even as she ran to greet him.

"How d-d-d-did you get here?"

"What happened to you?"

"We thought you were d-d-dead and in the grave!"

"Is that why you didn't come back for me?" Teddy asked Jack, unable to help a little hurt creeping into his voice.

Jack stared at him in amazement. "I-I-I saw them shoot you, point-blank! B-b-blood sprayed everywhere. I d-didn't think there was a chance in hell of you surviving. And everyone was running . . . it was like a stampede of mad bulls. I t-t-tried to get back to you, but it was im-im-impossible."

That made Teddy feel a bit better. "I'm hard to kill!"

"T-t-tough as an old boot," Jack said with a grin. "I still can't b-believe you're alive. Or that you are here!"

"Me either," Teddy said with feeling. "Trust me, it was touch and go for a while. I got taken to a prisoner of war camp. It was a frigging filthy place. I got out of there just as soon as I could walk again."

"But how in heaven's name did you get out?" Alenka asked.

"An old woman came to the fence with some eggs for us. She said, "Go to Therisso," and gestured up at the mountains. I knew where Therisso was, I'd been there with the king. So that night I wriggled under the barbed wire like a goddamned goanna. Tore my uniform to shreds, but I got out. The sentry walked past just a few seconds later when I was hiding in the bushes. He flicked his frigging cigarette butt onto my head. So I got a burn to match my bullet hole! I waited till he was gone, then set out. Then I just kept walking till I got to Therisso."

"God must have had his hand over you," Alenka said.

"You always were a lucky d-d-devil," Jack said. "Remember the time you po-poked a snake and it bit me?"

Teddy laughed. He did not tell them how hard he had found it crossing the White Mountains again. He made the journey sound like a wild adventure, with him in the starring role. He described how he had been fed and sheltered at every village, the young women giggling and flirting with him, and the young men glaring at him with faces like thunder. Teddy had arrived at the monastery a few days earlier and had been hidden by the monks in their cellars in the hope a submarine would come soon and take the stranded soldiers away to safety.

"The monks have been hiding diggers here since the battle," he said. "One of them went out every night and blinked an SOS into the darkness, just in case a British sub might be cruising by. Incredibly, one did and saw the message and some Tommies came ashore and made contact. They managed to get seventy-eight men off the first night, and then a hundred and thirty a few nights ago. Apparently, it's a world record." Teddy laughed. "Now we're all waiting for it to return. Every day we ask, "When will the submarine come back?" And every day the monks tell us . . ."

"*Avrio, m-m-methavrio,*" Jack said, making the tilting gesture with his hand.

Teddy grinned. "So we wait. There are so many Aussies and Kiwis here, we're calling it the Anzac Club. A few of them escaped the camp like me, but most of them are blokes who just got left behind on the beach."

"That's what happened to me," Jack said. "Alenka's b-b-been hiding me for weeks."

"You went back to Knossos?" Teddy looked from one to the other, frowning.

"I d-d-didn't know what else to do. I've been holed out in the ruins m-most of the time, and then in an old, abandoned church in the mountains. Alenka brings me supplies when she can, which is not very often. It's just too d-d-dangerous."

"So you must be hungry?" Teddy said, pretending he did not care. "The grub is good here, and the wine not half bad either." He ushered them to a corner of the long table, then called to the young monk to bring them some food. He nodded, looking hot and harassed, and brought bread, lamb roasted in lemon and garlic, wild greens cooked in olive oil, and a pitcher of red wine.

Jack and Alenka both murmured something in Greek and made a swift sign of the cross. Teddy stared incredulously. Jack went red. "Alenka's been teaching me how to act like a Cretan. So I don't betray myself by doing something stupid."

"Which is hard for him," Teddy said with a grin to Alenka.

"He's a quick learner," she replied with a flashing smile at Jack.

Teddy felt another sharp twinge of jealousy. He didn't like Jack liking Alenka, and he didn't like Alenka liking Jack. He knew it was unreasonable, but that was how he felt.

"Better get some shut-eye," he said abruptly. "In case the sub comes tonight."

He and Jack found a patch of floor to lie down and try to sleep, surrounded by other ragged young men. Alenka was led away by the monk, turning to give them a wan smile.

Teddy could not get her and Jack out of his mind. She's mine, he thought. I saw her first. And one day she would say it. One day she would surrender herself utterly to him, crying out loud, "I'm yours! I'm yours!"

Teddy couldn't rest, thinking of all the things he would do to her.

After a long while, he got up and stepped barefoot around the sleeping bodies on the floor. Gray light was seeping in through narrow window slits. He needed fresh air, he told himself. A splash of freezing water. Some kind of vigorous exercise.

He wondered where Alenka was.

Teddy stopped to listen at a door. Heavy snoring. Not in there. He heard a distant rumble. He opened a shutter and looked out.

Snaking up the narrow road came a convoy of tanks and trucks loaded with helmeted soldiers. For a moment, Teddy was frozen in surprise.

Then he ran back toward the kitchen, bellowing, "Germans! Germans are coming! Wake up!" He grabbed his boots and kitbag, shook Jack awake. "Bloody Jerries on our doorstep! Quick, move!"

Tousle-haired, heavy-eyed, the men snatched up their belongings. The young monk rushed in, his long hair loose down his back. "Come, follow me. Hurry!"

Jack caught him by the sleeve. "Alenka? The girl I came with?"

The monk pointed. Jack turned and ran, pushing against the stream of men. Teddy ran after him. They raced through a maze of dark rooms, calling Alenka's name. At last they found her. She sat up, sleepy and bewildered, her black hair hanging in wild disarray around her face. Then she heard the marching of boots, the sound of a terse order in German. Fear galvanized her. She leaped up, wearing nothing but a thin cotton slip. She threw on her dress, snatched her haversack and shoes from the floor, and fled barefoot down the corridor, the two young men close behind.

An elderly monk was being hustled down the corridor, his grizzled beard reaching almost to his waist. A small door, flung open, led out to the bare stony hills, furrowed with shadows. Teddy ran up the slope, shouting at Jack to hurry.

Smoke began to billow from the ancient church.

Traveling at night, hiding by day, begging for help from frightened villagers, they made their way back to Knossos. No one ever refused to shelter them. Teddy could not understand it. Any Cretan who hid a fugitive soldier was executed. Yet no one hesitated. Their courage and generosity astonished him.

The monks were all arrested, they heard, the monastery ransacked. Even the miraculous cross had been stolen. Then the Germans had blown the ancient buildings sky-high. There would be no more submarines coming to Preveli.

At last, footsore and exhausted, they made it back to the tiny church where Jack had camped before. Alenka stayed only long enough to see them safely inside before she hurried back to Knossos, afraid her long absence would arouse her brother's suspicions.

Teddy and Jack lived like hermits, hiding from sight, foraging for food—thin, ragged, half-starved. Once or twice a week, Alenka brought them supplies in exchange for news from Jack's radio. The food was always welcome. The news was not. The German army had surrounded Kiev and besieged Leningrad. It would not be long, it was feared, before Russia, too, would fall to the Nazis.

One day in mid-September, Alenka came swift and light-footed, her face glowing. "The cross has been returned!"

Teddy did not understand her. "The cross?"

"The golden crucifix of the holy monastery at Preveli," she answered as if it were obvious. "They tried to send it to Germany. The plane would not fly. They put it into another plane. It would not fly either. It was the eve of the feast of the Exaltation of the Holy Cross. The Germans were afraid. They returned the crucifix!"

When Jack and Teddy did not respond, she laughed.

"Do you not understand? It's a miracle! God has shown he is on our side. Soon, soon, we will be victorious!"

But the leaves turned orange and dropped, the nights grew frosty, and snow fell on the mountains. It seemed impossible that the Germans could ever be defeated or that Teddy and Jack would ever be able to escape.

V

It was the blackest winter Alenka had ever known. Every morning she woke to find her windows starred with frost. It was hard to find the strength to get out of her bed. She had to break the ice on her jug of water with the handle of her hairbrush. She could not stop trembling. Perhaps it was the news that chilled her to her core. The Japanese had bombed Hawaii, and now the whole world was at war.

There was little to eat. The Germans had stolen everything. Long queues for foodstuffs made shopping an exhausting ordeal. Bread was made from acorns, and they ate meat only with their eyes. Every night, Alenka went out into the bitter wind to search for snails, shining her torch about in the hope of glimpsing a silvery trail of slime. She would come home just in time for curfew, shivering and blue-lipped, with the snails trying to climb out of her bucket. Alenka boiled them again and again in heavily salted water, before poaching them in a little white wine, bottled tomatoes, and a handful of thyme leaves.

One evening she took a clay pot of the stewed snails up to the old church to share with Jack and Teddy, having nothing else to offer them.

Teddy screwed up his face at the sight. "What in God's name?"

"Snails," Alenka said, ladling the stew into three bowls.

"Snails? Do you think we're bloody Frogs?"

"It's the only meat we have. The Huns have taken everything else, don't you understand? You don't need to eat it if you don't want."

"I w-w-will," Jack said. "Thank you."

Teddy unwillingly took his bowl. "I wish I had a gun. I could catch us something better than this to eat!"

"No one's allowed a gun except the Germans," Alenka said wearily.

"L-l-look at the perfect logarithmic spiral," Jack said dreamily, holding an empty snail shell up against the candlelight. "I wonder if it's a *spira mirabilis*?"

"Oh God," Teddy said. "Not bloody geometry again."

Alenka held up one of her empty shells too, examining its spiraling shape. "What does that mean?"

"*Spira mirabilis*? It m-m-means the marvelous spiral. S-s-see how the size of the spiral increases with each circle? It's a p-p-perfect natural demonstration of the golden ratio."

Teddy groaned theatrically.

"Tell me more," she invited, casting Teddy a reproving glance.

Jack told her about the Fibonacci spiral, growing outward in a precise mathematical relation to every ninety degrees of rotation. "It . . . it's the sh-sh-shape of whirlpools and hurricanes, and of our own galaxy."

"What does that mean? Fibonacci?"

She stumbled a little on the unfamiliar word. Jack smiled at her. "It's n-named after the man who d-d-discovered it. It simply m-means each new number is the sum of the two numbers that came b-b-before. So if the first number is n-n-nought, the second number will be one, and the third number will be t-t-two. Then three, then five, then eight." As Jack spoke, he drew the numbers in his journal that she could see how each new number took the mathematical sequence leaping forward.

"So thirteen is the next number, and then twenty-one?" She frowned over his figures.

"You've g-g-got it! It's easy once you get the idea. The same m-m-mathematical principle can be seen in shells and the arrangement of leaves and branches and petals and s-s-seeds. Some p-p-people call it nature's secret code."

Teddy had had enough. "You can be such a drip, Jack. Didn't we get enough of that boring stuff in school?"

"I don't think it's boring," Alenka protested, but Jack put away his notebook and pencil. She got to her feet. "I'd better get home. I can't be away too long." She picked up her basket and went to the door at the far end of the church.

"Let me walk you home." Teddy jumped up, following her.

She shook her head. "It's not safe."

"Oh, come on, Alenka, no one will see. We could have some time alone together. You know, have some private conversation." He winked at her suggestively.

Alenka shook her head. "It would not be . . ." She searched for the right word, then said hesitantly, "seemly?"

"Oh, for God's sake. Really? It's the twentieth century."

"Teddy, if I am seen walking alone with a strange man, at night, it would cause talk, can't you see that? Talk will see you killed."

"We could go somewhere no one will see us. Come on, Alenka. I'll walk you to the aqueduct, it's got a nice dark tunnel."

"No. I can't. I'll come again tomorrow night. See you then." Alenka pushed him away and hurried into the darkness.

———————————

Teddy watched her go, his jaw set. He could never get her alone anymore. Bloody Jack was always there, watching. No wonder Alenka did not let him kiss her. He would have to sneak out one night, catch her somewhere unawares. Thinking about it made him so hard with desire, he almost groaned aloud in pain. He went back to their camp beds, pouring himself a slug of *tsikoudia* and slamming it down.

Jack looked up. "W-what's wrong?"

"Well, actually, now you mention it, you could be a bit more tactful, mate. Always hanging about me and Alenka, it's getting on my nerves, and on hers too."

"D-d-did she s-s-say so?"

"Yeah. She did. You're being a bloody third wheel, mate."

Jack looked away. "S-s-sorry. It's j-j-just . . . I . . . I . . ."

"S-s-s-s-sorry," Teddy mocked. "So you bloody well should be."

Jack bent his head over the chess piece he had been whittling with his penknife. It depicted a young woman with a crown of plaits. The white queen.

For the first time, Teddy realized it looked like Alenka.

Anger boiled up inside him. Bloody Jack. He had no right to muscle in on his girl. Teddy had seen the way Jack gazed at Alenka when he thought no one was watching. He never said anything, but Teddy knew he was remembering the time Alenka had said to him, *I am not yours!* The memory still annoyed him. Teddy had never wanted more than a bit of fun. The moment Alenka had told him off in front of Jack, though, his interest in her had hardened into something more than just desire. He wanted her to melt into his arms, to succumb everything to him, to say, *I am yours . . .*

Teddy lay down with his back to Jack. He had to do something, he decided. Tomorrow night, he'd walk down to the arch of the aqueduct and waylay Alenka there. It'd be dark, no one would see.

No one would know.

Axel had a wobbly tooth. He pushed at it with his tongue, so that it rocked in its cradle. He tasted blood.

The sound of pickaxes and shovels rang in the wintry air. Greek prisoners of war were hard at work, excavating a pile of old stones, guarded by German soldiers who stood around, smoking and laughing. Axel wished he could have a rifle like theirs.

The Germans had been digging up the ruins for weeks now, and Axel was getting bored watching them. He had expected to find coins and jewels and golden swords, not a pile of old rubbish. The general was disappointed. He wanted something like the figurine of a goddess that Sir Arthur Evans had found, with snakes crawling up her arms.

Axel wiggled his loose tooth with his tongue. It suddenly came free, and he flicked it away into the ruins, muttering the little rhyme Alenka had taught him: "I give you bone, you give me gold."

Then he remembered you were meant to toss it onto the roof of your house to make your wish. Axel went in search of it. He saw a gleam of pale ivory under some stones and went to investigate. It was bigger than he expected. Maybe a bone instead of a tooth. He dug with the end of a stick, then sat back on his heels, holding something small and broken and dirty in his hands.

It was an ivory statuette of a man with a bull's head.

Axel rubbed the grime away and saw the horns were made of gold. The figurine carried a sword in one hand that was also gold. In his other hand was the carved shape of a bobbin of thread, reddened with ocher. As Axel examined the bull's head, he saw it was made in two parts, one overlaying the other. With one dirty fingernail, he carefully lifted it up. Underneath the bull mask lay a man's face.

Axel had always liked the story of the bull-headed man, fed every year with seven young men and seven maidens. He could imagine how terrified they would be, locked in the labyrinth, the minotaur crouching in the shadows, licking his chops. He played with the little statue for a while, making it prance and roar like a bull, lifting and dropping the mask so the figure changed from a minotaur into just a man, and back again. Then he slipped it into his pocket and ran up to the villa, his breath huffing white before his face.

It was very cold. The mountains wore white nightcaps, and in the morning the grass would all be hard and silvered like tiny knife blades. It might even snow here in the village. Not that any of the other children would build a snowman with him or let him join their snowball fight.

Axel came to the villa gate and begged the sentry to let him in.

"I've got something to show the major-general," he bragged.

"What?" the sentry asked.

Axel wanted the minotaur to be a surprise, so he opened his mouth, showing the gaping hole where his tooth had been. The sentry laughed and let him in. The guards took him to the general's bedroom, where

Ringel was giving instructions as his manservant packed his bags. Axel saluted him, crying "Heil Hitler!"

Ringel smiled. "You cheeky rascal. How did you get in here?"

"Where are you going?" Axel demanded.

"Home for Christmas."

"To Berlin?"

"Yes, to Berlin."

"Oh, take me, take me!"

Ringel laughed. "Berlin is no place for a boy, particularly one who can't even speak German."

"I can speak German!" Axel shouted his favorite phrases. "*Seig Heil! Achtung! Blitzkrieg!*"

The major-general laughed again and ruffled his hair as if he was a little kid. "And very good German that is too. But no, my boy, I'm sorry, I can't take you with me. Berlin is being bombed by the RAF, you know. It's too dangerous."

Axel stared at the major-general in disbelief. "But you promised you'd take me!"

The major-general's face hardened and his gaze turned cold. "I made no such promise."

"You said you'd reward me."

"And so I have."

"A stupid old cigarette card is not a reward! I want to go to Berlin and meet the führer!"

The major-general seized Axel's shoulder. "I let you and your family live. That's reward enough, you stupid little mongrel. Now get out of here before I have you whipped."

Ringel let go so abruptly that Axel fell to the ground. He stared up at the major-general, his breath coming short. Then he scrambled up and fled. He ran all the way home, tears of rage flooding down his face. He tore into the house like a tornado, slamming the door so hard the bowls on their shelves rattled.

Alenka was kneeling on the hearth, stirring something in a pot. She jerked upright. "Axel, what's wrong?"

"Nothing! Just shut up!"

He hurtled up the ladder to his loft room and flung himself on the bed. Something jabbed him sharply in his thigh. He pulled the minotaur out of his pocket. He was about to hurl it to the floor when Alenka climbed up the ladder. "What is it, little monkey? Has something happened?"

Quickly, he hid the minotaur under his pillow.

She frowned. "What have you got there?"

"Nothing. None of your business. Go away."

She came toward him. "What's wrong?"

Wanting to deflect her attention, he cried, "Papa Ringel is going back to Berlin! And he won't take me! He called me a mongrel. It's all your fault."

As Axel spoke the words, they blinded him with their truth. It was her fault, and his mother's. If only they had told him who his father was, he could have gone in search of him long ago instead of being stuck here in Crete, living as an enemy of his father's people.

Alenka sat beside him on his bed, stroking his shoulder in comfort. Axel bit her.

His sister wrenched her arm away with a startled cry of pain. "You little beast! Why did you bite me?"

"Because I hate you! I hate all of you."

"But why? What have I done?" Alenka cried angrily.

Axel thought about the way their mother lifted a gentle hand to tuck a lock of fallen hair behind Alenka's ear, how she looked up and smiled when Alenka came home from work, how Alenka knew who her father was, knew where she belonged.

But he did not know how to say what he felt. So he bit her again, hard enough to draw blood. It tasted salty-sweet.

Alenka lay curled on her bed, examining the angry red circle of teeth marks on her arm. She could not believe her brother had bitten her. She had tried so hard to be loving and kind. Yet again and again she failed.

Alenka wanted to crawl under her blankets and never come out again. What was the point? Another day of digging through frost for weeds to make soup, another day of grinding acorns to make bread, another day of shrinking away every time she heard the stamp of German boots.

Tears slid down her face. She wiped them away, but still, they persisted. Her brother had bitten her so hard. Would it leave a scar? Like the welt on her other arm. Axel had given her that when he was only nine. She had been sitting at the kitchen table, chopping onions with the big kitchen knife, trying to make her brother do his homework. She had put the knife down so that she could lean over and correct his maths. He had picked up the knife and sliced open her arm.

"Why? Why?" she had asked him then too, weeping and struggling to stop the blood. He had shrugged. "I wanted to see what was inside."

Flesh, muscle, sinew, nerves, veins, capillaries, arteries, intestines, lungs, heart.

Alenka had been afraid of her brother ever since, no matter how much she pretended not to be.

She lay still, listening to the thudding of her heart, watching the blood seep through the tiny crescents her brother's teeth had made in her skin. It was dark outside. She could hear the bare branches of the almond tree creaking in the wind. If she did not get up now, it would be too late to go to the little church and be back before curfew. Jack and Teddy relied on her for everything. They would be looking for her, hoping she would come, fearing something had happened to her. Alenka could not lie in her warm bed feeling sorry for herself when the lives of two young men depended on her. If she failed them, she was letting the Germans win; she was letting terror and death win.

Slowly, Alenka got up, put on her shabby coat, wrapped an old black scarf about her head, and pulled on a pair of battered boots soled with the rubber from old tires. At least they were soundless on the stone floor. She crept into the kitchen, lifted the pot of lentil soup, wrapped it in a cloth to keep it warm, tucked it under her arm, and crept out into the bitter-cold blackness.

Axel was roused by the furtive sound of the front door opening. He peered out his shutters. Alenka was creeping down the laneway. At once he got up, put on his coat and shoes, and slipped out after her.

He knew the general was angry people kept painting huge white Vs on the walls of the villa. Perhaps it was Alenka. If he followed her, he might catch her in the act. Then he could tell Papa Ringel. He would be so pleased; he would have to take Axel to Germany.

But Alenka was walking away from the villa, heading south into the hills. It was hard to see her, so Axel had to creep close to be sure not to lose her. After about half an hour, the old Venetian aqueduct loomed ahead. The road led into the archway, swallowed by darkness.

Alenka trudged into the shadows, her head bent. Suddenly she gave a cry of surprise. It was cut short as if a hand had been clapped over her mouth. Axel hurried closer.

"Teddy, no," Alenka was saying. "Please, stop it. I don't want . . ."

Again her voice was muffled. Then a loud yelp.

"Hell, Alenka, there's no need for that," the man's voice said.

Axel stiffened all over. The man was speaking in English.

"Yes, there is," she answered in the same language. "Here's your food. But you'd better get good at catching snails because it's the last I'm bringing you."

A low murmur. Axel sidled right up to the archway, trying to make out the words. "Okay, okay, I'm sorry," the man said. "I just wanted some time alone with you. Is that such a crime? It was just a kiss."

"Now is not the time for kissing. There's a war on, remember?"

"All the more reason for it, we might be dead tomorrow."

"We will be if you don't stay hidden. Now I'm going home, and you should too." Alenka came quietly out of the shadows, and Axel had to duck down so she wouldn't see him. She hurried past, her scarf drawn close about the pale oval of her face. Axel waited. He wanted to see who she was meeting.

The scrape of a match being struck. Axel turned back. In time to see the flare of light illuminate the face of the man as he lit his cigarette. Fair hair, blue eyes.

Axel recognized him. It was the Australian soldier who had guarded the king.

He grinned.

VI

15 December 1941

When the birds at last began to shriek, Teddy pulled on his coat and boots and went out into the misty morning. He was hungry. What he wouldn't give for his rifle! He could have gone hunting and caught a rabbit or some pigeons or something. But he had nothing but the small knife Alenka had given him. Teddy kicked angrily at a stone, and it skittered sideways and fell over the edge of the ravine. He could hear it tumbling down, and his stomach lurched.

After that he kept well away from the edge.

The track wound along the cliff face then turned toward the Venetian aqueduct which soared over the chasm like a narrow bridge, its parapet not much wider than his hand. It then sliced across the countryside like a medieval wall, its massive stone ramparts pierced with arches. The road to Knossos ran through one of the arches. He had waylaid Alenka there last night, only for her to slap him hard across the face. At the memory, his rage seethed up again.

As Teddy approached the archway, a man stepped out of its shadow. He was fair and blue-eyed, like Teddy, and wore a khaki uniform. "Please help me," he said in a clipped upper-class English accent. "I am a British officer. I need to escape the island and return to my regiment. Can you please be showing me the way to the rendezvous point for the British submarines?"

Teddy hurried forward, his mouth opening in words of welcome. Suddenly and most unexpectedly, someone sprang down from the arch of the aqueduct, knocking the officer sprawling. He went down hard, hit his head on the stony road, and lay still. Teddy hauled the attacker up, ready to punch the life out of him. Then he dropped his fists in amazement.

It was Alenka.

"What did you do that for?" Teddy demanded.

"It was a trick. He's not British. He's German!" She was panting and disheveled, one hand pressed to her ribs.

"But he spoke such good English."

"Look at his boots! No British soldier would have such good boots after so many months in the mountains." She bent over, trying to catch her breath. "Quick, check him. Is he . . . is he dead?"

Teddy bent over the unconscious soldier. "No, he's just knocked out."

She heaved a sigh of relief and caught Teddy's arm. "I think I've cracked a rib. Ow, it hurts."

Teddy looked up at the immense rampart of stone above them. "I can't believe you jumped down from there. It's so high!"

"I had to stop him. Another second, and you'd have spoken to him in English. Can you tie him up somehow?"

Teddy knelt down, efficiently binding the German soldier's hands behind his back with his belt. "How did you know?"

"My brother . . . I saw him coming out of the German compound this morning, looking very pleased with himself. He was eating chocolate."

Teddy frowned. "You think your brother informed on us?"

"He must've followed me here last night. I saw the German soldier come out after him, dressed in a British uniform. Axel said something about the aqueduct. So I took his bicycle and rode here as fast as I could. I saw the soldier go through the archway and guessed he was lying in wait for you. So I rode the other way and dumped the bike on the other side of the gorge. I walked across the top of the aqueduct."

"Hang on." Teddy stared at her then looked at the slender stone rampart which arched across the ravine. "You crossed over on top of that? Are you crazy?"

"I didn't know what else to do. I had to warn you and Jack . . . but I barely got here in time. I saw you coming, and I knew it was a trap. So I . . . slid down the wall, to that little outcrop above the arch, then jumped down on him."

"You could have been killed!"

"I had to stop him," she answered simply.

He gazed down at her. "You saved my life."

"I couldn't bear the thought of you being captured again. You came so far to fight for my country. You could have gotten away in time but you came back to warn me. How could I let you be seized? They would have shot you as a spy, I know it." Her voice quivered.

Teddy kissed her. For once, she did not resist, but clung to him, trembling. His arms tightened about her, and she gave a little cry. He kissed her cheek, her throat, her bare shoulder inside the collar of her dress.

"Stop! Please, stop." She shoved at him. "Don't. Please. I'm sorry, I'm just . . . a little shaken up. It was so close."

He wouldn't let her go. His blood sledgehammered through his body. He kissed her again, and when she opened her mouth to cry out, kissed her more deeply.

She jerked her head back. "No, please, Teddy, stop. You're hurting me." One hand was pressed against her ribs. "Please. There's no time. We have to think what to do." She looked down at the German soldier, who groaned and moved.

Teddy kicked him hard, and he subsided. "We'll have to dispose of him. Shall I . . ." His hand moved to the dagger at his waist.

Alenka caught his hand. "No! If he disappears, they will come looking for him, and then there will be reprisals."

"But what can we do?"

"I know! I'll get Micky to help us. We'll take him back to the garrison and hand him in as a British spy. You know there's a reward? We'll claim it! What can they do? We were just doing our duty capturing him!"

He laughed and tried to kiss her again. But she evaded him, pushing him away, saying, "Go and get your things. Tell Jack. I will meet you at the secret garden in a couple of hours. Leave no evidence behind!"

Every breath hurt her. But Alenka could not stop. It would soon be dark, and she must get Jack and Teddy to safety. She did not think the new divisional commander at Knossos would believe Micky's story about capturing a British spy. As soon as the German soldier recovered consciousness, he would tell them he had seen a blond, blue-eyed man at the aqueduct. And the Germans would come looking for them.

She and Teddy and Jack had hiked narrow goat tracks for the past two hours and were now heading down a steep slope toward the sea. She could see Heraklion in the distance, on the far side of the airport, and the island of Dia floating in the sunset haze.

"Civilization!" Teddy said. "At last!"

"You must not go into town," Alenka said. "It is too dangerous. Your Greek is not good enough, and there are many German soldiers there."

"I-I-I know where we are," Jack said. "Our HQ was in a cave near here. Is that where we are going?"

"To another cave," she answered. "It's well hidden. The British School excavated it a few years ago, but not many people know about it."

She limped on, leaning on a gnarled stick. Every breath stabbed her. Her eyes scanned the hillside. It had been a long time since she had been to the cave. She hoped she knew how to find it. "Look for an old fig tree. It hides the entrance."

"There's one!" Jack pointed to the east.

She sighed in relief and clambered down the bracken-covered slope. A narrow chasm was hidden behind the fig tree.

"We're meant to climb down there?" Teddy said dubiously. "It doesn't look big enough to hide a mouse."

"Looks can be deceiving," Alenka said.

One by one, they clambered down into a long narrow cave. Water trickled past their feet. Jack lit his lantern, and at once there was an agitated rustle and stirring somewhere in the darkness. Alenka exclaimed and clutched at his arm, as tiny black shapes flittered about in the shadows.

"Bats," Jack said.

"Great," Teddy groaned. "Just what we need."

The ceiling was so low he had to duck his head. Suddenly, he jerked back in alarm. "Someone's there!"

Jack swung the lantern up. "It's just stalagmites," he said in relief.

Dramatic white spikes of stone hung from the low ceiling or rose from the ground in strangely human forms. One was tall and slender, like a woman dancing. Crouched nearby was a smaller stone, like a child reaching for its mother. A simple stone altar had been built before it.

"They think it's an ancient temple," Alenka said. "Many offerings were found nearby. Some of them from Neolithic times. Women used to come here to pray. It's a sacred place."

"It's bloody cold." Teddy rubbed his hands together and blew on them.

"I know. I'm sorry. I can't think where else to take you. The Germans will search all around the aqueduct." She put down her haversack. "I have some food, but not much. It is a long way from Knossos, so I will not be able to come often. You will need to forage and hunt for yourselves."

"Without a gun?" Teddy said.

"It is too dangerous; the sound of gunfire will attract attention. You will need to make a snare. I will ask my friend George to get you some wire and show you how."

"Who?" he demanded. "What friend?"

"George Doundoulakis. He works as a translator too, at the German HQ in Archanes. We are very old friends." Alenka did not like the jealous way Teddy had spoken. He thought he owned her just because she had let him kiss her. How could she explain that she had been so worn out, so shaken, that she had surrendered, just for a moment?

It meant nothing, she told herself. It was just a kiss.

Though if the *gorgonas* of the village knew she had kissed him like that, they would be scandalized. They would try to make her marry him.

Alenka did not wish to be married and she was certain Teddy didn't.

He had quite different intentions. She had to be careful not to give in to him again, else she'd find herself bringing an illegitimate child into the world to be taunted and ostracized like her little brother.

"Could we not have hidden somewhere closer?" Teddy asked. "It won't be much fun being stuck in a cave, miles away from anywhere. I'll never see you."

"No. It's too dangerous."

"I'll be a good boy and study my Greek."

"I hope you do."

He frowned at the chilliness of her tone. "You could teach me."

"I can't come here all the time, someone will see. You'll have to be much more careful here, it's near the road."

He tried to slip his arm around her waist. "But when will I see you again?"

She stepped away from him. "I don't know. Not for a while."

Teddy scowled. "Great. Thanks a lot."

She did not speak, and his frown deepened. "I suppose if we're stuck in this bloody damp hole, I'd better get us some firewood, or we'll freeze to death."

He swung himself out of the cave, looking surly.

Alenka bit her lip and glanced at Jack. His face was troubled.

She did not want him to know she had kissed Teddy. She began to speak quickly before he could ask her what was wrong. "This place is called the fairy cave. The two figures there, they are meant to be a *naiad* and her child. You know the word? It means a water nymph."

Jack nodded but did not speak. Alenka came a little closer. "My grandmother told me a story about them. It's about a young man who wanted to be the best lyra player in the land. He knew that if he went to the crossroads at midnight and played his lyra, the fairies would come to dance. They're dangerous, though. They can bewitch you into playing till you are driven mad or die. So you must draw a circle around you with a black-handled knife, and then they cannot hurt you, and, if you play well enough, they'll give you your heart's wish."

Something in Jack's face changed. The air between them was charged and electric. Alenka felt as if she could not get enough air. She put one hand to her cracked ribs. "So the young man sat within the enchanted circle and played so well the fairies blessed him. But one of the dancing fairies was so very beautiful, the young man fell in love with her. He wanted her for his own. He went to see an old wise woman, and she said that he must go and play for the fairies again and play so well that they danced all night. As soon as the cock crowed, she said, he must seize the fairy by her long hair and not let go, no matter what. So the young man did as she suggested, and at dawn, he grabbed the fairy by the hair. She transformed herself into all different shapes—a snake, a bird, a flame—but he did not let go. At last, exhausted, she returned to her own shape. He made her his wife, but she did not speak again. She was mute."

Alenka thought of her own mother. A lump rose in her throat. "After a year the fairy had a child, but still, she would not speak. So the lyra player went to the old wise woman again. She told him to light a fire and pretend to throw the child in it. So he did this, but the mother screamed and snatched up the child and fled to safety here in this cave. The lyra player came searching for them, but the fairy turned herself and the child into stone so he could not drag them back. So she stands here for eternity, weeping for the life she had lost."

To her consternation, Alenka found she was weeping too.

"W-w-what's wrong? Why does the s-s-story make you cry?" His dark eyes were intent on her face. "Is it . . . Teddy? Or . . . or s-s-something to do with your m-m-mother?"

The words came tumbling out of her. "You know how she hardly ever speaks? I asked her why. She did not answer, and I was angry. I spoke harshly to her. And she said . . . she said . . ."

Jack waited.

"She said, 'He forced me.'"

Jack's eyes widened. "Does she m-m-mean your brother's father? The German archaeologist?"

She swallowed, grateful he understood so quickly and did not need her to explain more. "I think so."

"You think that's why she n-n-never speaks?"

"She used to sing to me and tell me stories when I was a little girl. But something made her stop. I never understood before, but . . ." Her voice broke.

Jack drew her close. "I'm sorry, Alenka. It's . . . it's very wrong." Gently, he wiped the tears from her cheeks with his thumb. "D-d-don't cry, Alenka. Please. I can't b-b-bear it."

"Not crying," she answered in a stifled voice. She turned away from him, unable to catch her breath. He went to the back of the cave, leaned down to the little spring that gushed there, and brought her water in his cupped hands. She bent and drank, holding his hands steady with her own. The water was so cold, it numbed her lips and throat. She splashed a little on her face and said, in a constricted voice, "Thank you. I'm sorry."

"You . . . you have n-nothing to be sorry for." He stood silent for a moment, then asked in a low voice, "W-w-what did the women who came here p-p-pray for?"

She shrugged. "For love, I suppose, or children. To keep their loved ones safe from harm."

"Can m-m-men make offerings here too?"

She glanced at him in surprise. "I suppose so."

Jack slipped his hand into his pocket and drew out a carved chess figure. It had her face. He bent and laid it at the foot of the stalagmite.

She gazed at him, and he gazed back. Neither spoke.

Alenka heard Teddy stamping down the steps into the cave, his arms full of firewood, and stepped away. "I need to go. I need to get back."

She fled past him into the twilight.

VII

Christmas Eve. The village was dark and silent. No candles in the windows, no church bells ringing in jubilation. No children singing carols and tinkling metal triangles in return for roasted chestnuts and honey cakes. No delicious smells, no prospect of a feast the next day to break the long winter fast. No laughter and music as the family piglet was slow roasted on a bed of lemon leaves, its bones made into broth, its bristles turned into brushes, its skin tanned to make shoes for the winter, its bladder inflated into a ball for the boys to kick.

The garrison had stolen all the village pigs, an unspoken punishment for the German soldier in British uniform who had been delivered, bound and glowering, back to the barracks at the Villa Ariadne. The new divisional commander, Josef Foltmann, had been forced to reward Micky for the capture of his own man, and he had not been pleased at all. Raids and retributions had made all their lives miserable these past ten days. Micky had wanted to give Axel a good thrashing, but Alenka had convinced him to leave her brother alone. "We must give them no reason to suspect us," she had argued. "Let them think Axel made a mistake."

Now the smell of cooking meat tortured all those who lived in the shadow of the villa's barbed-wire-fortified walls. Alenka did not think it was possible to hate anyone as much as she hated the Germans.

Axel had gone to the villa, hoping for some scraps, so Alenka was free to sneak out. Micky was having a gathering of friends in the vineyard. They had little to eat, but there was always song and wine and olives.

She hurried through the silent village, careful to keep to the shadows. The road wound up the hill, and down again, through long lines of bare clipped trellises. Braziers burned in long rows between the vines like golden fairy lights. A crowd of young people huddled about a bonfire, wrapped in heavy coats and goatskin cloaks. Overhead, a thousand stars glittered.

Micky and Phyllia and her friends welcomed her eagerly, kissing her three times on the cheeks and crying, *"Kalá Christoúgenna!"* The ramshackle table was spread with platters of bread, bowls of olive oil and salt, and a few small parcels of rice and herbs wrapped up in vine leaves. Alenka added her contribution—spiced rolls made with crushed acorns—and went to the bonfire, where George was stirring the *rakomelo*, pomace brandy heated with cinnamon, cloves, and honey.

"Here, let me warm you up." He grinned at her, serving her a mug of the honeyed brandy. "I've been gathering together all the weapons that were dropped during the retreat. We've stockpiled them in a cave, ready for the day we can rise and fight the cuckolds."

"How many?" she asked eagerly.

"A lot. But many have no ammunition or are broken. We need to practice shooting with them, but it is hard when there is so little ammunition."

Alenka became aware of a frisson of excitement among the other young women. She turned and saw Teddy coming toward her. The firelight glinted in his golden hair, and he stood a full head taller than any other man there.

"If it's not the prettiest girl on Crete! Merry Christmas!" He kissed her on the mouth right there in front of everyone, taking her by surprise.

Alenka blushed hotly and extricated herself. She was aware of Micky glaring at Teddy. As her godbrother, he thought it was his job to defend her honor. George was scowling too. If she was not careful, there would be violence. The young men were spoiling for a fight.

So she responded coolly and turned back to George. "Is there enough ammunition for us girls to be taught how to shoot too?"

Teddy was not daunted. "What's this about ammunition? I can teach you to shoot, Alenka. There's nothing I don't know about guns."

"*Po-po-po-po-po*," George said disdainfully. "A Cretan is taught to shoot in his cradle. You British know nothing compared to us."

"I'm not British," Teddy pointed out. "I'm an Aussie. And we're born with a gun in our hands."

"British, Australian, what's the difference?"

"About ten thousand miles, you cretin."

The subtle difference between the English pronunciation of *Cretan* and *cretin* was a sore point with the young men of Crete. George at once bristled, ready for any excuse to let a punch fly.

Alenka quickly towed Teddy away. "Where's Jack? I have some presents for you."

"For me?"

"For both of you."

A few young men had gathered under the gnarled olive tree, beginning to strum their instruments and sing. Jack was, of course, listening, a look of such yearning on his face it tugged at Alenka's heartstrings.

She led them to the table where she had left her packages. "It's Christmas Eve, and you are both so far from home, you must be missing your families. I thought I'd give you a little something to cheer you up. For you, Teddy!"

"What is it?" He took the paper she passed him, and his face lit up. "ID papers!"

"You must practice your Greek, though."

Teddy spun her around, kissing her. "You little beauty! Thank you." Putting her back on her feet, he asked, "What's my new name? Theodore Kynigos? What does that mean?"

"Hu- . . . hunter," Jack translated.

"I thought it'd be easy for you to remember," Alenka said.

He tucked the ID papers away, then took up the bottle. "What's this?"

"It's walnut juice. You can use it to dye your hair and skin. But be careful, it stains like anything. You'll need to wear gloves, or you'll get black fingers."

"Heraklion, here I come!"

"Please be careful. I could not bear it if you were caught. Either of you," she added quickly. "Jack, I have something very different for you." She bent and picked up the lyra case she had hidden under the table. Jack's dark eyes lit up. "Merry Christmas and happy birthday, Benediktos!" She passed him the lyra case.

"How did you know it's his birthday?" Teddy demanded.

"I saw it when I burned his army ID papers. It is hard to forget such a date. Being born on Christmas Eve is to be blessed indeed."

Jack undid the clasp and opened the case to show the golden curves of a lyra, a bow nestled beside it. Color rose in his thin face. He stammered a fervent thank you.

"Someone who plays as well as you do needs something to play on," Alenka said. "It has four strings so you can play it like a cello, but it's still small enough that you can carry it about easily."

"Damn it all to hell, now I'll have to put up with him practicing scales all day. Oh, well, I guess I can always go out now I've got me some ID papers! Let's celebrate!" Teddy tossed the cup of brandy down his throat and turned back to the crowd.

Music was lilting into the freezing air. The young men had taken off their coats and formed a long line, arms flung over each other's shoulders. Faster and faster, they danced, kicking and stamping their feet. George was on the end of the line. Braced by the man beside him, he began to leap and cavort and kick high into the air. The women clustered by the fire, clapping their hands.

"*Po-po-po-po*, Aussie!" George called. "Can you dance as well as shoot?"

"In Australia," Teddy said derisively, "we dance with women, not with other men."

He caught Alenka by the waist and began to spin her about. She had seen dancing like this in Hollywood movies but never done it. In

Greece, men and women did not dance so close, hands all over each other's bodies. She broke free of his hold, shaking her head and pushing him away.

Teddy shrugged and smiled invitingly at the cluster of admiring young women. Zephyra, laughing, ran out and caught his hand. He grinned and began to teach her how to jitterbug. Soon she was daring enough to let him swing her up and over his shoulder. A circle cleared around them, clapping and cheering. Other young men and women began to try it out, laughing and shouting encouragement to each other. "Don't you know how to swing?" Teddy shouted at George, who looked thunderous.

Alenka walked away from the bonfire, huddling her arms about her against the cold. She did not know why she felt so stung. *What do I care if he dances with another girl?*

She did care, though. It was vanity, she realized. Alenka liked being called the prettiest girl on Crete and having all the other girls be envious of her. She was ashamed of herself, being so petty-minded when her country was enslaved and her people were starving.

Alenka heard the faint, eerie notes of a lyra carried to her by the wind. She followed the sound and found Jack sitting alone on a low wall under the stars, playing the lyra. She stood motionless, in utter enchantment, till at last he lifted the bow from the strings.

"That was beautiful. But it's so dark. How can you play when you cannot see?"

She saw the white flash of a smile. "My m-m-mother used to play the cello from memory every morning with her eyes closed. If she was ever t-t-tempted to open her eyes, she'd blindfold herself with a scarf. It's awfully hard to begin with, but once you learn how, it's wonderful. It's like you are the m-m-music."

"What were you playing?"

"Bach's Chaconne. It w-w-was my mother's favorite."

Alenka frowned. "Bach is German."

Jack gave a little shrug. "My grandfather was too. He was put in an internment camp during the Great War, even though he'd lived in

Australia since he was a little boy. You cannot help where you are born, only how you choose to live."

Alenka's frown did not lift. Her hatred of the Nazis ran so deep, she could not bear anything that was German. She could only whistle the opening motif of Beethoven's Fifth by telling herself it was Morse code, not the music of a German composer.

"If it was n-n-not for Bach, I would never have been born."

She came to sit beside him. "Why? What do you mean?"

"When my m-m-mum was just a little girl, she heard a cellist playing Bach's Chaconne on the radio. She t-t-told my nana she wanted to learn to play it. So Nana saved all her p-p-pennies and bought her a cello."

Celia had played her cello every second she could, Jack told her. Bach was her great love, and her hero was the Spanish cellist Pablo Casals, who had discovered Bach's six lost cello suites in a rundown music shop in Barcelona when he was only thirteen. Casals had played one of the six suites every day, repeating the last on the seventh day. Celia had done the same, though she played her beloved Chaconne on Sundays. She was determined to be the best cellist in the world. She played even when it caused her pain. When her fingers cramped so she could not hold the bow, she would close her eyes and practice in her head, counting the notes, wielding an imaginary instrument.

"When the Great W-w-war broke out, she gave it all up. She joined up as a nurse."

"But why?"

"Her f-f-father was sent to the internment camp. He . . . he was a gentle man who would never have hurt a soul. He wasn't allowed to take his violin. M-m-my mother was heartbroken. She wouldn't play if he couldn't."

Celia had been sent to the Western Front. There was no music there. Just the thunder of heavy artillery, the blare of sirens, the shrill whinny of terrified horses, the screams of the wounded. She was working with a team led by an English doctor named Ralph Hawke. Forced into retreat by a massive German offensive, Celia and Ralph took refuge in an old château. Celia found a cello lying amid the rubble.

"I think I must have been conceived that day," Jack said, "for she wrote to my nana: *I played the Chaconne, and now I am to be married.* I was born eight-and-a-half months later."

"But why? Why did she play that song in particular?"

"It m-m-must have been a Sunday. She always p-p-played the Chaconne on Sundays. It's . . . it's v-v-very long and intense, fiendishly difficult to play, quite transfiguring to hear. She called it a . . . a cathedral of music. Bach wrote it after his wife d-d-died, it's full of grief and anguish but in the end, there is a kind of deliverance, hope, and maybe even joy . . . a kind of hallelujah."

"Is that why you play it for her at Christmas?"

He did not speak for a long while, then, stuttering badly, said in a low voice, "My . . . my m-m-mother d-d-died giving birth to me. I was b-b-born blue, but my fa- . . . fa . . . father resuscitated me. He c-c-could not save her, though. So my birthday is her d-d-d-death day. I . . . I play it in m-m-memory of her."

Alenka did not know what to say. She leaned forward and entwined her fingers in his.

He gripped hers tightly. Their white breath mingled in the small space between their mouths. "He . . . he never forgave me. For her death, I mean. And I was . . . sick all the time. I almost died quite a few times."

"Like when you were bitten by the snake."

A faint smile touched his mouth. "Y-y-yes."

"And then again here in Crete. You were so close to death then."

He nodded, squeezing her hands in silent thanks.

"God must have some purpose for you," she said with absolute conviction. "That is why he has saved you from death so many times."

He stared at her.

"It must be fate. There is something you are meant to do. Maybe it is being here, fighting to free us?"

"Fate?" he asked, his voice so low she had to lean in to hear it. "You think . . . fate b-b-brought me here . . . to you . . ."

"What are you two doing?" Teddy demanded, his voice thick with suspicion. Alenka started as violently as if she had been scalded. She had been so deeply engrossed in her conversation with Jack that she had not heard Teddy approaching.

"N-n-nothing," Jack said, at the same time as she blurted, "Just talking."

Both let go of the other's hand.

Teddy was standing over them. He reached down and caught Alenka's arm, pulling her to her feet. "Well, it's Christmas Eve, you shouldn't be skulking out here in the cold. Come and dance!"

"You go dance with Zephyra again, you two seemed to be having a ball! I will dance with Jack." She held out her hand to him.

Jack made a small movement toward her. Then he checked himself, looking at Teddy. He shook his head. He picked up the lyra and began to play again.

Alenka's cheeks flamed as hot as if he had slapped her.

PART V:
MASKED HERO
APRIL 1942–FEBRUARY 1943

O
fierce
hunter
masked hero
the clock is wound tight
time to look into the mirror
of that sharp blade and see your own black eye
gazing back

I

15 April 1942

The coming of spring to Crete was a miracle made manifest, Jack thought. The stony fields and bare crags burst into life. The almond tree in the Knossos village square was festooned with snow-colored blossoms, and wildflowers sprang out of every nook and cranny. Wild thyme, sage, camomile, delicate pink Cretan rock roses, golden-hearted daisies and black-hearted scarlet anemones, said to have been sown from the blood of Adonis. In the vineyard, he wove the fast-growing tendrils into the trellis, creating symmetry from disarray.

Jack had seen very little of Alenka during those dark winter months. He was afraid he had offended her by not dancing with her on Christmas Eve. Silently, he tried to explain to her. *Teddy is my best friend. We've been mates since we were kids. He stuck up for me when no one else would. You wanted to make him jealous, I get it. But it'd only have made him angry. He'd have seen it as a betrayal. And he would have been right. Besides, I cannot dance like him. I'd only have made a fool of myself.*

But he said none of these things out loud, not to Alenka and not to Teddy.

She had come to the cave of the naiad on the last day of February with some food and thin bracelets of red-and-white yarn that she had woven for them. She said they were protection against demons and Nazis. Teddy had not wanted to bother wearing his, and she'd told him that he must—all Cretans did, it would look suspicious if his wrist was bare. "You can take them off at the sight of the first blossom or the first swallow," she told them, "and then tie them to the branch of a fruit tree or a vine to make sure the harvest is good."

Her charm seemed to have worked, for somehow, they had survived the winter despite the bone-penetrating cold and dampness of the cave, their never-ceasing hunger, and the troops of Germans scouring the countryside. Jack and Teddy watched from their hidden cave as the soldiers marched along the coast road, or raced past on their motorcycles, goggles over their eyes, rifles at the ready. It made them sick to see the Luftwaffe taking off from the airport every morning, carrying troops and supplies to the German army in North Africa.

Every morning Jack would go down to the ocean and plunge into its exhilarating freshness, the water so clear he could see the shadows of eagles flittering over the pale ridges of sand far below. He would swim till his arms ached, then walk to the vineyard and work all day alongside the men. As the sun began to set, he would eat and drink and sing with them. He was sure that the singing was helping him speak more fluidly. Perhaps it was because each note was drawn out, flowing effortlessly into the next. Perhaps it was the way rhythm and rhyme worked together so he always knew what words his mouth must shape next. Perhaps it was simply because singing was all joy for him, while speaking had been for so long a struggle and source of shame.

Jack walked home in the twilight, his lyra on his back, gathering firewood and wild greens as he went, hoping Teddy had managed to catch a hare with a wire snare, or perhaps some fish. Sometimes they would walk down to Heraklion and eat at a taverna. Both had been studying their Greek hard, and it was a good chance to practice passing as Cretan, in the cheaper establishments where the Germans seldom went. Jack took his lyra and would sing a few *mantinades* in return for their supper. Teddy would play backgammon or cards, and make the old men laugh with his jokes. He was in a much better mood since Christmas. Jack did not know whether it was because of the freedom of movement brought by his new ID card and walnut-dyed hair, or because Jack had refused to dance with Alenka. Either way, Jack was grateful for it. It made their life as cavemen much more bearable.

They had been on Crete for close to a year and felt they had been forgotten.

Every morning as Jack walked to the vineyard, he stopped and knelt by a roadside shrine that looked like a tiny church for fairies, being only a few handbreadths high, mounted by a cross and crammed with gilt icons. He and Alenka left messages for each other there, for no one would suspect a young woman laying down an offering of flowers or a young man stopping to pray for a moment.

One morning, as Jack knelt beside it, pretending to pray, he saw an eagle feather lying next to a twig of the evergreen holm oak. It meant a secret meeting of the resistance was to be held at midnight in the old church built on the peak of Mount Juktas, where the sky god Zeus was meant to be entombed. Seen from the west, the mountain had the profile of a man lying on his back. It had once had a peak sanctuary built on its highest point, where Minoan priests and priestesses held ancient rituals rumored to have involved human sacrifice. A tiny, whitewashed chapel was built there now, right on the edge of the cliff. It had commanding views over the countryside and down to the sea. No force could approach the church without being seen, and so it was a perfect place for a meeting of the resistance.

Jack felt a thrill of excitement and told himself it was the chance to hear news of the war that caused his pulse to accelerate, and not the prospect of seeing Alenka. He turned back to pass the message on to Teddy, then hurried to work in the vineyard. All day he felt the hum of suppressed excitement and anticipation.

It was a long walk to the church, and it was past midnight when they arrived. Outside the air was crisp and cold and deliciously scented with wild thyme, oregano, sage, mint, and dittany. Inside, it smelled of stale incense, cigarette smoke, and sweat. The nave was crammed with *andartes*. Most were Cretans, dressed in heavy goatskin cloaks, rifles slung over their shoulders. Some of the younger men wore flannel suits and flamboyant ties. Quite a few were stranded soldiers, still in their tattered khaki and slouch hats. A tall man with dark hair brushed back from a high brow stood quietly against the wall, beneath the gilded figures of grave-faced saints, listening to the rapid Greek of the crowd. He was dressed in breeches and a cloak but had a good pair of boots and a revolver tucked into his sash. He was guarded by George Doundoulakis and his brother Helias, their dark eyes scanning the crowd for any sign of trouble.

Alenka and Phyllia were talking quietly at the back of the room.

"*Yassous*, Alenka!" Teddy cried, making his way to her side. "How's the prettiest girl in Crete?"

"*Yassous*," she answered quietly.

"What is it? What's going on?"

"There's a British officer here. He's come from Egypt and wants to talk about helping us fight the Germans."

"What about us? Is he going to help us get away?"

"I think so. We were told to pass the message on to any stranded soldiers."

"About bloody time!"

Jack did not speak. He gazed at Alenka, thinking how thin she was. She acknowledged him with a nod but did not smile at him. He wished he could make her laugh like he had the first time they had met.

"Jack!" A dark young man in a tattered khaki uniform came toward him, grinning broadly. "Do you remember me? Reg Saunders."

"Reg! G-g-good to see you. I wondered what had h-happened to you. I was afraid the Jerries got you."

"They almost did a couple of times. Jack, this is my mate, Arthur Lambert." He beckoned forward another young soldier, dressed in the dilapidated remnants of a New Zealand uniform.

Jack introduced Reg and Arthur to Teddy and Alenka, explaining that Reg had helped him escape the Germans after Teddy had been shot, and that they had been left behind together on the beach at Hóra Sfakíon, when the last British boat had sailed without them.

"We seem to have a knack for missing boats," Reg said. "So many times, we've almost got off the island, but somehow we always get left behind."

"It was my fault last time," Arthur said. "We walked practically the whole length of the island on a rumor some Poms were landing at a beach to the east. It was a bloody long way, especially by shanks's pony. We were almost there when my frigging boots fell to bits. I tried to go on, but the stones cut my feet up pretty bad. So I told Reg to go on without me. Reg just bent down and said, "Get on my back." As if he could carry me for miles and miles on those damned goat tracks!"

"I would have given it a bloody good go!" Reg said with a grin.

"Couldn't be done," Arthur said. "So I told Reg not to be an idiot and go ahead and leave me behind. So he turned to our guide and told him that we'd liked it so much here in Crete, we'd decided to stay."

Everyone laughed.

"Well, I wasn't going to walk out on you," Reg said. "There'll be other subs."

"I bloody well hope so!" Teddy said. "It's not much fun living in a goddamn freezing cave with water dripping down my neck."

"We are lucky, having such good friends to help us," Reg said with a gallant little bow toward Alenka. "We'd have been captured long ago if not for the bravery of the Cretans."

"We are grateful to you for coming so far to fight for us," Alenka said. "We hope you get home soon."

"We have to beat the Jerries first," Reg said.

"And we can't do that cowering in a bloody cave," Teddy said. "We should join forces and attack the garrison."

"What with?" Arthur said. "Our bare hands?"

"Besides," Reg said, "they'd just shoot the Greeks in reprisal. I've seen them do it to a family who was caught hiding a soldier, and I've never felt so bad in my life."

"I just want to do something," Teddy said, moving restlessly. "It's the waiting around that pisses me off."

"Well, that's why we're here, isn't it?" Reg said. "That guy over there is full of grand plans, I hear." He gestured toward the tall officer, now listening to a group of older men who seemed to be arguing hotly over something.

"Who are they?" Teddy wanted to know. Alenka quickly filled them in. The bear of a man with an impressive upcurving mustache was named Manoli Bandouvas, a sheep farmer who headed a resistance group to the southeast. The man with the thick black beard was Georgios Petrakis; he owned an olive oil mill and soap business and had been recruited by John Pendlebury before the Nazis had invaded. He led the resistance group centered around Mount Ida. The man shouting the loudest was Andreas Papadakis; he was a lieutenant-colonel in the Greek army and so thought he should be the one in charge. The thin, stooped older man with the pointed white beard was Antonios Gregorakis.

"They call him Captain Satanas," Alenka whispered. "They say he rattles with bullets if you shake him, and that he shot off his own finger to stop himself from gambling, only to later realize the finger he rolled the dice with was also his trigger finger."

"That's w-what Teddy should do," Jack said.

Teddy grinned at him. "You're always happy to help me smoke the cigarettes I win!"

Just then, George clapped his hands and called for quiet. "I want to introduce you all to our visitor. He's got something he wants to say to you."

The officer stepped forward. "I am Captain Tom Dunbabin, and I am very pleased to be here in your beautiful island of Crete once more," he said in perfect Greek. "Some of you will know me from the dig at Knossos. I worked there for quite a few years with the British School. In fact, I got engaged to my wife on the terrace of the Villa Ariadne. It's too bad it's in the hands of the Jerries now. Let's see what we can do to shove them off."

A resounding cheer from the crowd. Tom smiled. "I am here to do whatever I can to help you in your brave resistance to the German occupiers. I have been authorized by the British government to offer practical assistance . . ."

"What we need is guns!" Bandouvas shouted. "Not talk!"

Tom turned to him courteously. "I will certainly do what I can to convince the British command that you are in need of weapons. My first task, though, is to extricate those Allied soldiers still remaining on the island." He looked back at the khaki-clad soldiers in the crowd and spoke to them in English. "I am afraid you must think you've been forgotten. The British are hard pressed by Rommel and his army in North Africa. Nonetheless, I am hoping that when they hear my report, they will take action on your behalf."

"Tell them we're starving, sir!"

"We have no bloody boots!"

"Or blankets."

"Tell them to airdrop some frigging louse powder, the lice are eating me alive."

Tom grinned at the chorus of complaints. "I'll be sure to tell them I met some Jolly Good Chaps putting on a Spiffing Show in Bloody Awful Conditions."

His mocking of a British officer's upper-class accent raised a shout of laughter from the Anzac soldiers. They called out a few more jeering comments, while the Greek *kapitanioi* wanted to know when they would be given machine guns and hand grenades and dynamite.

Tom was courteous but made no firm promises. He was in Crete, he said, to gather information. The Germans were using the Cretan airfields and ports to support Rommel's Afrika Korps in their advance into Egypt and to attack British ships in the Mediterranean. The more the British HQ knew about Nazi operations in Crete, the more likely they were to send weapons and supplies to the Cretan resistance. His calm reasonableness was in stark contrast to the fiery demeanor of the *kapitanioi* who each wanted to be named the leader of the *andartes*. More bottles of *tsikoudia* were passed around, then Tom came up to Jack and Teddy.

"G'day, diggers," he said. "You're a long way from home."

"You're an Aussie too!" Teddy cried.

"Yep, from Tassie," Tom answered cheerfully. "You?"

"Jack and I are from the Macedon Ranges, an hour or two outside Melbourne. When do you think we can get away from here? It's been almost a year!"

"I know. I'm sorry. Trust me, we are doing our best. It's hard to get a boat or a submarine to the island, except under the cover of darkness. The waters are so clear around Crete, any vessel is easily spotted by the Luftwaffe. And it's been pretty hot in Africa—Rommel's men are pressing us hard."

"We want to go and fight," Teddy said restlessly.

"I know. And we need you! Do not fear, plans are afoot to send another boat soon."

"Tomorrow or the next day, I suppose," Teddy said cynically.

Tom grinned. "Most unlikely, I'm afraid, no matter what the Cretans say. In the meantime, tell me everything you know about German movements in the area. We want to strike a blow against the airports if we can."

"We're hiding out in a cave not far from the airport at Heraklion," Teddy said. "We watch their planes take off and land every day."

"Tell me more!"

They told him all they knew. Tom said with great satisfaction, "This is all bloody good. It won't be long before you see some action, I hope!"

II

"Very homelike," Tom said, looking around at the naiad's cave with approval, noting the beds made with armfuls of wild sage and animal skins, the rabbit cooking on a sharpened stick over the driftwood fire, the clean washing strung on a line between the stalagmites. "You've adapted well to living like cavemen."

"We've been here bloody long enough," Teddy said. "Have you come to tell us we've missed another bloody boat?"

"I've come to ask for your help. It might lead to something."

It had been more than two months since Jack and Teddy had met Tom Dunbabin, but they were no closer to getting off Crete. The Germans knew British officers had infiltrated the island and had built outposts all along the south coast, manned by sentries who watched for illicit landings and searched out any sign of resistance. In late April, they heard Arthur Lambeth had been betrayed and captured. Everyone was very afraid of what he would reveal if tortured. Teddy talked wildly of staging a rescue, but there was nothing they could do. A month later, Reg and another thirty stragglers managed to escape on an old fishing trawler that had been requisitioned by the British navy. Soon after, the *kapetans* shot six men they suspected to be informers. In retaliation, a dozen Cretans were executed in Heraklion in early June.

"W-w-what can we do to help?" Jack asked eagerly.

"The people of Malta are close to starvation," Tom said. "They've been under siege for almost two years. It's the only RAF and navy base we have left in the Mediterranean. If we lose it, we'll lose the war. The top brass plan to send a convoy of ships with provisions from Alexandria to the island, but the Luftwaffe is bombing any boat it sees. It's our job to sabotage as many German planes as we can here on Crete so that the convoy can get through."

As Tom spoke, he pointed with his dagger at a map of the Mediterranean. "The plan is to smuggle four teams into Crete, each aiming to sabotage one of the four major airfields, including Heraklion here in the east. I will meet and assist the commando teams landing on the south coast, but I need someone in Heraklion, someone who speaks both Greek and English. Will you help?"

"Of c-c-course!" Jack cried.

"They will arrive by submarine on the night of the tenth of June. I was thinking this cave would be a good base for them—it really is impossible to find unless you know of it."

Both Jack and Teddy nodded eagerly.

"I also need someone to watch the airport for us and pass on any intelligence that may help the commandos." Briefly, Tom told them what was needed. "Afterward, they'll have to get across the mountains to the south coast to be evacuated back to Egypt. There are only three roads and they will all be closely guarded, so they should go via goat tracks. I believe you've both done the journey before?"

"Far too often," Teddy said. "But not from here. I crossed the White Mountains, behind Chania."

"And I-I-I went to Preveli."

"They are much further west," Tom said, frowning over the map. "Our rendezvous is the beach below Krotos."

"A . . . Alenka might know the way. She's a translator, her English is very g-g-good."

"Does she speak French?"

"French?"

"Yes, most of the commando team are Frenchmen."

"I-I-I think so," Jack said. "She worked as a translator at the dig and speaks quite a few languages."

"Then she will be very useful to us," Tom said.

The cave of the naiad was lit only by the dull gleam of a low fire. There were no candles or lamp oil to spare. Jack sat quietly, strumming his lyra. His nerves felt as tightly wound as its strings. He heard a light step and looked up. Alenka clambered down the narrow crack into the cave. She smiled when she saw them, but it was clearly an effort. Jack could not help feeling they were abandoning her by leaving the island. *This is not our home*, he reminded himself. But he did not believe his own words.

She had brought some food, and wine in a goatskin bag. They ate hurriedly, exchanging news in a low murmur. She knew about the commando raid, but not that Teddy and Jack were leaving Crete with them afterward. "We're a danger to you here," Teddy said. "The Germans will be on the hunt after the sabotage attack and are quite likely to find this little cave. Besides, things are happening out there in the world, and we want to be part of it. We can't beat Hitler here . . ."

"Can anyone beat him anywhere?" she asked in a low voice.

"We have to hope so. Come on, chin up. Your life will be much easier once we're gone. No more worrying about how you're going to feed us!"

She gave a little shrug. "I only wish I could have done more."

The last few weeks had been busy. Jack and Teddy had taken turns watching Heraklion airport. They kept a log of the landings and take-offs of all aircraft, noted the numbers of sentries, the positions of the machine-gun nests and the spotlights, mapped out the telephone systems and the roads, and made a timeline of shift changes and inspections. They also drew up a grid reference of every German garrison and guard post on the coast around Heraklion and looked out for isolated beaches where the commanders could land by submarine. Each evening

they wrote up their reports and left them in the little shrine for Alenka
or one of the other runners to collect for Tom Dunbabin.

It was wonderful to have some purpose and shape to their day.

Jack did not know how he felt about leaving Crete. More than a
year, hiding, fearing every unexpected footstep, pretending to be Greek,
yet knowing a single misstep would reveal his sham, the nasty jolt of
adrenaline every time he saw a German soldier zooming past on a motorcycle, rifle slung over his shoulders. Yet he loved the wild eagle-haunted
mountains with their towering peaks, the tiny churches painted with
gilded Byzantine saints, the villages with their stone-cobbled streets and
cats sleeping on every sill, men drinking at the *kafenion* and laughing,
women in headscarves spinning wool on handheld spindles like they
must have done for thousands of years.

And Alenka, Alenka, always Alenka.

She sat now, legs tucked beneath her, her hair hidden beneath
an old rag of a headscarf, her black dress like a sack upon her thin
body, the tiny golden cross with its blue bead and antique coin glim-
mering about her throat. Her face had been sharpened by the long
months of hunger. Her eyes were deeply shadowed as if bruised, and
her thick dark brows were drawn together, in an expression of trouble and sadness that smote his heart. He remembered the laughing
young woman he had first met. It seemed so long ago, a lifetime ago.
He would do anything to turn back time for her, he thought. Return
her to a world before the Nazis.

How could they be so blind, he thought, to the harm they have
done? How could they be so cruel?

She looked up, met his gaze. Her eyes were so fathomlessly black,
he could not read her thoughts. There was a sternness in the set line of
her mouth, though, a kind of challenge in the tension of her jaw. Go
then, she seemed to be saying. Go back to your own land, to your own
people. We do not need you. We do not want you.

Then he saw her eyes were full of tears.

If he had been alone with her, he might have spoken. He might have
stretched out his hand and touched hers.

But Teddy was there, telling them all the things he planned to do once he was free of Crete. It seemed Teddy was always there.

Jack looked away with a kind of bitter shame.

Dawn came with no sign of any submarine. They scouted up and down the coast. At last, they found the commandos far to the east, hunched over a map, compass in hand.

Six men, disguised as Cretans, but carrying Beretta machine guns with heavy packs on their backs. Four of them were from the French Free Army. Commander Georges Bergé, a strong square man with a strong square face, was accompanied by three of his countrymen, Jack Sibard, Jacques Mouhot, and Pierre Léostic, the youngest at only seventeen. Captain George Jellicoe, the British liaison officer, was only a year older than Jack, and spoke French fluently but had no Greek. Lieutenant Kostis Petrakis, on secondment from the Royal Hellenic Army, spoke English fluently but had no French. So Alenka did her best to translate between them all. She did so with her eyes kept lowered, her body tense, and turned away. Jack realized for the first time that it was hard for her, a woman alone with so many men.

The raiding team had been dropped by the submarine but found their rubber dinghies swept far to the east by the swift currents, Jellicoe told them. They had sunk their craft and were now trying to find their way back to Heraklion.

"It is too dangerous by day," Alenka said. "There are many, many Germans. We'll have to lie low today and travel by night."

They finally reached the cave of the naiad the following night and looked down over the airfield with binoculars. Some kind of night maneuver was going on, and the airfield was lit up with bright lights. Reluctantly, they decided they had to wait another day. Alenka busied herself with her sewing, while Teddy and the Frenchmen played cards and Jack played chess with Jellicoe.

The next night, the five commandos crept down to the airfield under the cover of darkness. Lieutenant Petrakis stayed behind at the cave, not being trained for the task.

"I'd like to go and blow up a few German planes," he said gloomily.

"Me too," Teddy said. "I wonder how you get to be a commando."

"The SAS have a training school in Palestine," Petrakis said. "But it's bloody tough."

"I'm tough," Teddy said indignantly.

"Are you crazy too?"

"What do you mean?"

"Everyone in the SAS is crazy." Petrakis laughed, stubbed out his cigarette, and got to his feet. "Let us go and watch the show! They will be in by now."

He got up and wriggled out of the cave, the binoculars in his hand. Jack and Alenka followed, and the three of them lay down and took turns to watch the airfield below.

"There they are!" Jack cried. "I c-c-can see them creeping across the field."

Two dark figures crouched under a plane. One man lifted another high, planting something under the fuselage, then he dropped lightly down, and they ran to the next plane. Meanwhile, another dark figure was running across to the fuel depot.

"Let me see!" Alenka implored. Jack passed her the binoculars. The brush of her cold fingers was an electric shock.

Planes began to explode, catapulting debris across the runway and lighting up the sky with flames. Teddy shouted with excitement.

Pandemonium erupted on the airfield. German soldiers raced out, dressed only in singlets and light shorts, trying desperately to put the fires out. An officer was calling orders and pointing, and men were grabbing arms. Searchlights swung into action, probing the darkness. At last Jack saw four black figures, wriggling through the bracken toward them.

"Mission accomplished," Jellicoe said with a grin, his white teeth flashing against his blackened face. "Let's go!"

Alenka was on her feet in seconds. She had already planned the best escape route and led the way along a mule track that followed the winding route of a river high into the mountains. Before dawn, they found a secluded wood in which to hide. The horizon to the south was smudged with smoke. It gave Alenka a thrill deep in the pit of her stomach to see it. She hoped the attack had done the Germans some real damage.

Jellicoe was writing up a report, to be radioed to Cairo. "At least twenty planes destroyed, plus various vehicles, fuel dumps, and a bomb depot. Jolly good work, fellows!"

Teddy grinned sardonically at the expression.

Commander Bergé said something in French, shaking the hands of the other men. "He said they'll all be awarded the Croix de Guerre for their night's work," Alenka translated.

"If we get out alive," Petrakis said, in Greek.

Alenka had packed a little food, and they ate eagerly, the commandos only having dry rations. When the sun had sunk down behind the towering mountain peaks, they shouldered their packs and set out once more. The path was a steep scramble, and the men were soon short of breath.

"This is ridiculous," Commander Bergé said. "My boots are being cut to pieces. Is there not a road?"

"*Oui*, but it is very far from here," Alenka replied in her very best French. "The Germans will be searching for you. They will stop any traveler and question them. We must go the back way."

"Where is the nearest town?" he asked. "We need to hear the news, make sure all is well with our colleagues."

She showed him Archanes on the map.

"Take us there," he ordered.

"But the German HQ is there. There will be soldiers everywhere. It is too dangerous."

"They will not be expecting us to be on the road," he retorted. "Always do the unexpected. Besides, they will think us Cretans—why else are we wearing these stupid crap-catchers?"

Alenka did not like to tell the commander that he and his companions looked nothing like Cretans, even wearing the traditional billowing breeches. They were too quiet and watchful, for one thing. They did not laugh enough, or cross themselves three times and spit, or call on the Virgin Mary every few sentences, or cry, "*Po-po-po-po-po!*" They did not have the light, springing step of men used to walking long distances every day. And their boots were too good.

But it was never any use arguing with a man.

Alenka shrugged and led them cross-country to Archanes. The town square was lined with *kafenions* and tavernas, tables and chairs set out under the trees. Bergé led the way to one, telling Alenka to order wine.

She shook her head. "I cannot, women do not sit and drink with men in tavernas. I will wait outside."

"I will wait with you," Jack said.

She made an impatient gesture. "That would be suspicious too. Men drink in the tavernas, women wait for them to be finished. That is how it is done in Crete."

She was glad she did not have to go into the glare of the lamps. There were quite a few German soldiers drinking and eating at the tables nearby. They seemed belligerent. Ever since the invasion, Alenka had tried to keep herself hidden in the shadows, dressing in black, keeping her headscarf wound close about her face, never catching the eye of any German. She was so afraid of what they might do to her. She was nearly as afraid of what the *andartes* would do if she was thought to be fraternizing with the Germans. They shot traitors and shaved the heads of Greek women who slept with Germans, willing or not.

Alenka drew her *sindoni* out of her shoulder bag. She fastened her embroidery hoop over the section of fabric she wished to sew next, being careful not to crush any of the stitches already in place. She sketched the shape of leaping flames with her tailor's chalk, then threaded her needle with orange silk. As she methodically drew her needle in and out of the white linen, she felt herself grow calm and strong again. *We have struck a blow*, she told herself. *We have lit a flame.*

A few other women were waiting outside the taverna. One was weeping, another was praying, another sat hunched, tearing at the quick of her nails with her teeth. When a young man came out, she flew at him and cast herself into his arms, sobbing. "They shot them! Oh, Antonis, so many killed!"

Dread crept over Alenka. Who had been shot?

Then Jack came out of the taverna. "B-b-bad news," he whispered to her. "There's been reprisals in Heraklion."

"They shot townsfolk? How many?"

"F-fifty."

Her stomach lurched. For a moment she could not take it in. Fifty people murdered in retaliation for a few planes and jeeps. Her thoughts flew to her father, her aunt and uncle, her cousins, her childhood friends. Had any among them been shot? She half-turned as if to flee back down the road to Heraklion, to search through the bodies, to look for familiar faces.

It was then she saw her brother. He was coming down the road toward the taverna, chatting away to one of the German archaeologists. He had a soft gray German garrison cap drawn down over his fair curls. It was embroidered with an eagle carrying a swastika. She shrank back.

"W-w-what is it?" Jack whispered. "What's wrong?"

"Axel. If he sees me here . . . Lord have mercy."

Jack stepped in front of her, drew her into his arms, shielding her from view. She pressed her face against his chest, hearing the thunder of his heart. Her legs were weak, the ground seemed to sway beneath her. His arms were strong about her, holding her steady.

"They have gone into another café. I will g-g-go and get the others. We have the news we came for. The raid on Maleme airport was successful, b-b-but the other two failed, we don't know w-w-why."

"Was it worth it?" she asked bitterly. "Fifty innocent people shot!"

He was quiet for a moment. "One of the J-J-Jerries had a note . . . w-w-written by a man who was to be shot . . . he scribbled it to his wife on the inside of a cigarette packet. The Jerry read it out. It said . . . it said . . ." For a moment Jack could not go on. She waited, held safe within the circle of his arms. "It said, 'To my darling wife, your only care will be to keep the children on the path I set them on. You must all be proud . . . proud that I am d-d-dying for my country. I kiss you all.'"

She could not speak for tears. Gently, he wiped them away. "It's w-w-worth it. To fight, to resist, to risk your life for freedom, for those you love, it's w-w-worth it, Alenka."

Alenka nodded and looked up at him. For a moment she thought he might kiss her. Her heart stopped.

He moved away. "W-w-wait here. I'll get the others."

Alenka turned and leaned against the wall, wiping away the tears she could not stop.

He is going away.

She thought of her silent black-clad mother. She thought of her brother, jauntily wearing a cap studded with the swastika when fifty of his fellow countrymen had been mercilessly shot, their bodies flung out like garbage. She thought of her friends, her godbrother and godsister, risking their lives every day to resist. She thought of the mothers and children, the wives and sweethearts, of the men who had died.

I cannot go with him. I must not go with him. Crete is my homeland. I must stay and fight for her. Even if I die for her.

III

23–24 June 1942

Teddy kept thinking he heard someone behind them. Once or twice, he jerked his head around, but it was too dark to see anything. At least that meant the plunging abyss beside him was not visible either. He kept his eyes on Jack, one hand on the cliff, the other clenched on his stick, his foot testing each step forward.

Just one more night, he told himself, *and I'll get the hell out of here.*

Dawn came. The path plunged toward the sea, twisting and turning like a white snake through the bare, blasted landscape. At times it was almost perpendicular, dropping in steep falls of rock that must run with cascades when the rains came.

Teddy's legs were trembling so much, he had to sit down. His palms sweated, his ears roared, he could not catch his breath. He shut his eyes, gripping the ground. It seemed to tilt under him.

He heard the others drop their packs and sit down. Everyone was so tired they could scarcely lift their water canteens to their mouths. Only Alenka and Petrakis seemed unaffected. *I guess they've spent their lives leaping from rock to rock like mountain goats,* Teddy thought sourly. He hated anyone showing him up.

Far below was a tiny village, no more than a handful of cottages and a church. "That's Krotos," Petrakis said. "We are to meet our contact there, to guide us down to the cove below. It is at least an hour more."

Bergé wiped the dust and sweat from his beet-red face. He was a good fifteen years older than everyone else, and it had been a long and exhausting hike through the mountains. He said something in French, and Jellicoe nodded.

"We are to go down to the village and check all is well for our evacuation tonight," he told the others. "The commander and his men will stay hidden here and keep a lookout. If all is well, I will flash a message this evening, and they will come down and join us."

"I'll stay here with the commander," Teddy said. "Just in case anything goes wrong, they should have someone with them who speaks Greek."

"Surely Miss Alenka . . ."

"It would not be fitting," Teddy said. "You know the French."

He did not want to admit he was afraid of the steepness of the slope. *If I sit for a while, I'll be better*, he told himself.

Jellicoe raised his brows in surprise but did not argue. He too must have noticed young Pierre Léostic's glances of admiration at Alenka.

Teddy could not watch Jack and the others as they struggled down the slope. The sound of the rattling stones and their sliding boots turned his stomach to water. He scrabbled away from the Frenchmen and took refuge behind a rock some distance away. His stomach cramped, and he retched. Thin bile scalded his throat, burst from his mouth. His eyes stung with tears of humiliation.

A faint rattle of pebbles. He glanced around suspiciously. A teenage boy was peeping over the rock, grinning at him. In a flash, Teddy leaped up. The boy disappeared, but Teddy raced after him. In a few strides, he caught him by the collar of his shirt. Like any Greek boy, he wore shorts tied up with string, and grubby plimsolls resoled with rubber from an old car tire. His hair, though, was as fair as Teddy's, his eyes as blue.

"What the fuck do you think you're doing?" Teddy said.

"You scared of the mountains, Englishman? You scared of falling?" the boy taunted. "You should be. Many Englishmen die here already. Maybe you the next."

Teddy shook him like a rat. "Have you been spying on us? Who are you?" Sudden realization hit him. This must be Alenka's brother. "You little snake!" he growled. "You're the one who dobbed us in to the Jerries."

He gave Axel a swift blow across the ear that sent him sprawling. The boy cast him a look of hatred and scrambled up, ready to sprint. Teddy caught him again and swiftly went through his pockets, checking for a weapon. He drew something out of the boy's pocket. It was an ivory figurine of a man with a bull's head. The horns and sword were made of solid gold.

"Well, well, what do we have here?" Teddy had heard enough of the treasures of Knossos to guess the little minotaur was both very old and very valuable. He smiled in satisfaction and slid it into his own pocket.

The boy began to swear and curse at him in a flood of Greek. Teddy frowned. Something about the boy's expression unsettled him. He remembered himself when he was a kid. Always stealing money and cigarettes from his old man, making catapults so he could sling stones at cats and dogs, carving his initials into trees and walls with his penknife, burning ants with a magnifying glass, setting fires to see the flames devour the dry grass. Anything that made him feel powerful, the world bent to his will.

This kid would not let his prize go willingly.

Even as he thought this, the boy charged at him, head down. Teddy was knocked to the ground, all the breath driven from his body. He gasped. He felt the boy's hand in his pocket. The boy dragged the minotaur out, then kicked Teddy hard in the balls. He took to his heels, racing away over the rocks. When he was a safe distance away, he turned and made a rude gesture with one hand. Within moments he had disappeared from sight.

"Little bugger!" Teddy got up shakily. "You are so going to pay!"

He trudged back to the others, simmering with rage, thinking, *If I ever catch that kid again, I'll give him the thrashing of his life.*

The Frenchmen were dozing in the shade of an olive tree, Pierre Léostic on guard. He glanced at Teddy curiously. Teddy did not want to tell him he had been bested by a mere kid. Besides, it would be too hard to explain when they did not share a language. He'd tell Jellicoe later, he decided. About seeing the brat, not about being knocked over by him and kicked in the balls.

The afternoon passed slowly. Cicadas buzzed. The heat was relentless. Slowly, the sun sank down over the mountains to the west. Then they saw the brief flash of light from the village so far below. Bergé gave the order to pack up. Teddy had to face the descent. At least Alenka is not here to see me make a fool of myself, he thought.

Refreshed by their nap, the four Frenchmen set off at a quick trot. Teddy followed much more slowly, picking his way down with the help of a stick. He tried to keep his gaze on his feet, refusing to look at the dizzying fall. Soon they were far ahead of him. Pierre turned a few times, looking for him, but irritably Teddy waved him on. He didn't want anyone watching him.

Come on, old man, you'll be fine, just take it slowly . . .

Suddenly, a cry of alarm, then a burst of gunfire. Teddy flung himself behind an outcropping of rocks.

On the slope below him, the Frenchmen had been ambushed by a squad of German soldiers. They were surrounded and outgunned. Pierre lay sprawled, unmoving. The other commandos were dropping their revolvers, putting their hands up. A small figure in a striped jersey and gray field cap was with them, looking about him, pointing back up into the mountains. Teddy ducked his head down.

One of the Germans barked a question.

"*Non*," Bergé replied, shaking his head.

The Germans searched the hillside but did not climb up to where Teddy crouched, his heart threatening to hammer its way out of his chest. He was too high above them. After a while, they gave up the search. The officer ordered his men to cover Pierre's body with rocks, which they did perfunctorily, then the other three Frenchmen were marched away. He waited, head low, till all was quiet again. Then he scrambled down the hill as fast as he could, stumbling and slipping, heedless of the risk of falling, till he had reached the village below.

The others were keeping watch from behind a low wall, their faces grim and set. "We heard gunfire. What happened?" Jellicoe demanded.

"Germans," Teddy panted. "Ambushed us."

"Where are the others?"

"Pierre was killed. The others captured." He turned to Alenka. "Your brother ratted on us, the little traitor! I'll kill him if I find him."

Tears fell down her cheeks, but she did not speak. There was no time. They had to get out of there. Jellicoe led the way in a low crouching run. The way was steep and rough, and they often fell and skidded down in an avalanche of stones. By the time they reached the shore, all were dusty, bruised, and exhausted.

The beach was only a sliver of pebbles and sand. Caves pockmarked the cliff. It was growing dark. A voice hissed a question, and Petrakis gasped the passphrase.

A small rubber dinghy was bobbing toward them. Teddy could see the black shape of a ship out to sea.

"Alenka," Jack said urgently, "you must c-c-come with us. Your b-brother knows you helped the mission! It will n-not be safe for you."

"I must stay. My mother needs me. My country needs me."

"They might k-k-kill you!" Jack exclaimed.

She shook her head. "I can't."

"Quick!" Jellicoe cried. "Jump aboard."

There was no time for a romantic farewell. Which was just as well, really. Teddy hated goodbyes. He said awkwardly, "I'm sorry, I've got to go. Good luck!"

"Goodbye. Godspeed. I will not forget what you did for my country," she answered, her hands clenched together at her breast. Teddy bent toward her, but she turned her face away so he could only kiss her cheek.

Then Teddy was clambering aboard the rubber boat, wet to the knees. Behind him, Jack had seized Alenka's hand, saying something in a low voice. She looked up at him, then suddenly flung her arms about him. They clung together.

"Jack, come on!" Teddy cried.

In a moment, Jack was beside him, holding his lyra high to keep it dry.

"What did you say to her?" Teddy demanded.

Jack only shook his head, looking back to the dark shore.

The British sailors pushed the rubber dinghy out into the rough surf.

"By God, we really are getting away!" Teddy could hardly believe it.

Halfway to the caïque, they passed another rubber dinghy being rowed to shore.

"Ahoy!" a drawling upper-class voice called. Peering through the twilight, Teddy could just see a tall young man with hair brushed back from his brow and a patrician nose.

"Ahoy!" Jellicoe called back.

"Is that you, Jellicoe? Good hunting?"

"Mission accomplished," Jellicoe said. "Though we were betrayed by a local. Léostic was lost, the others captured."

"Oh, bloody bad luck."

"Shame about Léostic, he was just a kid, really. The Jerries shot fifty civilians in revenge."

"Bastards! Bugger them all."

To Teddy's surprise, Jack leaned forward eagerly. "P-P-Paddy? Is that y-y-you?"

The young man laughed. "My God, is that you, Jack? I thought you must be dead. Well met, old chap."

"N-n-not dead. Not yet anyway. We've b-b-been hiding out in a cave, waiting for rescue."

"Troglodyte! What a lark. How rummy that you are leaving just as I am arriving. Give my regards to the fleshpots of Cairo!"

The rubber dinghies had slid apart, and Paddy's last words were called over the heaving waves that separated them.

Then Teddy was swarming up a rope onto the fishing caïque, rough hands hauling him up onto the deck.

He looked back at Crete, just a black mass on the horizon now.

The fleshpots of Cairo, he thought exultantly.

IV

Egypt lay before them. There were no trees as far as Jack could see. Only sand billowing in the wind.

"Tobruk has fallen!" someone yelled up at the boat. "Rommel is on his way."

The port was a fever of activity. He and Teddy were hustled ashore and into a covered army truck. A portly pink-cheeked man in the uniform of a British officer warned them not to look out through the cracks in the canvas.

"Why?" Teddy wanted to know.

The officer did not answer.

"W-w-where are we?" Jack asked.

"Mersa Mutrah. But not for long. The Jerries are racing toward us, damn them."

More soldiers piled in the back. They stared at Jack and Teddy with undisguised interest. Jack had become used to his Cretan clothes, but now he felt as self-conscious as if he was the only one to bother to dress up at a costume party.

All anyone could talk about was Tobruk, less than two hundred miles to the west.

"Hitler must be crowing," someone said disconsolately.

"Those poor bloody Aussies must be feeling sick. They held the place for bloody months, and now Rommel took it in a day!"

"Hang on," Teddy said. "What was that about the Aussies?"

They looked at him in surprise. "You speak English?"

"As bloody well as you do!"

Jack could not help laughing. Teddy looked as villainous as any Cretan *andartes*, with his billowing breeches and wine-red sash, a beaded scarf bound about his walnut-black hair.

"Tell us everything," Teddy commanded. "What's all this about the Aussies in Tobruk?"

"Where you been?" a soldier jeered. "Hiding under a rock?"

"Something like that."

"Well, the Aussies held Tobruk for months last year . . ." One of the soldiers began.

His mates talked over the top of him. "Two-hundred-and-forty-one days, living like rats in tunnels under the city."

"Pounded by the Jerries on all sides."

"They finally got evacuated last December, and the brass put some poor greenhorns in their place."

"Now Rommel's just waltzed on in and taken the place."

"Thirty thousand poor buggers taken prisoner. Worst loss of the war."

"Except for Singapore."

"Libya's lost now and looks like it won't be long before Egypt is too."

Jack and Teddy looked at each other in horror.

"But where are the Aussies now?" Teddy said.

"That's enough. Not another word," the British officer said.

"Do you think we're German spies?" Teddy said indignantly.

"Egypt is full of spies. Do as you are told, else I'll have you court-martialed."

"I thought I'd missed the army," Teddy whispered in Jack's ear.

The truck drove for hours along a road as straight as a ruler, through bare desert sands. Jack and Teddy ignored the rule about peering through the crack in the canvas. The hot wind blasted their faces. At last, Jack saw what looked like an oasis ahead. Palm trees and mina-rets floating in a golden haze. "Is th-th-that a mirage?"

"That is Alexandria," the officer said. "The delta of the Nile. Please do not look out anymore."

He kept a stern eye on them to make sure they did not peer through the cracks in the canvas, so they saw little of the city. They were taken to a military camp, given a small cell-like room each, and told to strip off all their clothes so they could be burned.

"Wash and shave and change," the officer ordered.

Jack hardly recognized himself when he looked in the mirror for the first time in more than a year. He looked like a medieval hermit, with tangled hair and beard, dark burning eyes, hollow cheeks. Yet, after the dirt and hair had been scraped away, his face was still that of a stranger. He was given a British uniform to wear. It hung loosely on him.

A private brought him fried bacon and eggs, a pot of tea, and a Red Cross parcel. He devoured it all, wiping his plate with fresh white bread, then looked through the cardboard box. Chocolate, biscuits, cigarettes. In Crete, tobacco had been so rare that he and Teddy had rationed it with great care, sharing the stub back and forth between them till it burned their fingers. It was an unimaginable luxury to smoke a whole cigarette, lying on a bed with a pillow and a soft fresh-smelling blanket, reading an Agatha Christie novel he had never read before.

Mersa Mutrah fell to the Germans only hours after they left. Rommel and his Panzer tanks were now only a hundred-and-fifty miles away. Jack was not allowed out of his room, but he was given more books to read. The orderly who brought him his meal trays told him there were rumors Mussolini had flown from Rome, with a white charger to ride in the triumphal procession into Cairo. Jack slept uneasily, sure he heard a distant rumble.

In the morning, the British officer put his head in the door and said, "Pack your things, quick smart, we're off to Cairo." Jack simply picked up his lyra and tattered journal, and said, "Ready to go, sir."

As the truck rattled out of the military base and turned to the south, Jack saw a thunderhead of orange dust on the western horizon. "Rommel," Teddy said quietly. "Jeez, he's close."

The road was choked with overloaded donkeys, honking cars, crowded buses with stretchers strapped on the roof, a horse-drawn cart laden with veiled women, sheiks in long white robes and headdresses in chauffeured open limousines, creaking ox wagons piled high with furniture, army trucks full of exhausted-looking soldiers, and long strings of camels led by barefoot children. All were heading in the same direction. Away from Alexandria.

At last, more than four hours later, they reached the capital city. Huddles of flat-roofed houses below pale domes and soaring minarets. Elegant department stores with signs saying "By Appointment to Queen Mary" on one side and, on the other, narrow alleys crowded with street vendors in long robes and skullcaps shouting and holding up bird cages, baby prams, saucepans, trays of cigarette tins, hookah pipes, and brass lamps that looked as if a rub might conjure a genie. Streetcars rattled past, people hanging out the doors, and in every gutter lay a beggar in rags with suppurating sores. Great crowds surged and fought outside the banks, and a long line of people waited outside the British embassy for escape visas. At one café, the staff were hanging up welcome signs in German.

The air was full of smoke and ashes. Scraps of scorched paper. Jack reached out a hand, like a child trying to catch a snowflake.

"They're burning all the sensitive files and secret codebooks," the officer said.

The truck took them to a British military compound just outside the city. It had a view of the Great Pyramid, a shadowy indigo shape against the rapidly darkening sky. Jack gazed at it till the very last moment the door shut behind him. So ancient, so immense, so perfectly symmetrical.

The next morning, the British officer came and began to ask questions. He spoke only in Greek and told Jack to answer him in the same language. He wanted to know where Jack had been born, where he had lived and studied before the war, about the rules of cricket, about whether or not Mickey Rooney and Judy Garland were in love. He ordered Jack to draw him a map of the harbor at Heraklion and wanted the recipe for snail and thyme stew. He demanded the names of all the *kapitans* and Jack's thoughts on their political affiliations. He asked about his lyra, and requested he play a *mantinade*.

Many of the questions were designed to trip Jack up in a lie, and they continued—with regular breaks for food and sleep—for the next two days. Jack answered politely, truthfully, and sparingly.

Afterward, the officer shook his hand. "Welcome to Cairo, Lieutenant."

"Thank you."

As the officer gathered up his papers and went to the door, Jack asked a question of his own. "Was all that really necessary?"

"Yes, unfortunately."

"Is Egypt really full of spies?"

"Is a camel full of fleas?"

Only sixty-six miles from the Suez Canal, Rommel's advance was halted at a tiny railway stop called El Alamein. Despite heavy losses, the Allied forces held firm. Rommel's supply lines were stretched to breaking point. Eventually, he had to retreat.

For the next few months, everyone existed in a kind of limbo as the two armies licked their wounds in the blazing heat of the Egyptian summer. Then, in the final week of October, the Allied forces launched a last desperate offensive. Jack and Teddy were glued to the radio in the mess hall, following the ebb and flow of the battle. The famous "Rats of Tobruk" were in the midst of the firestorm and, by all accounts, fighting with immense verve and dash. Teddy was restless and discontented, wishing that he could be with them, winning glory.

By early November, the German and Italian forces were in full retreat. A combined British and US task force made a three-pronged attack on French North Africa a week later, the first time American soldiers had grappled with the enemy in the war. Two weeks later, Tobruk was recaptured by the Allies.

It was the first big triumph against the Axis in the war. Both Teddy and Jack got joyously drunk. Their salary had been piling up in their bank accounts for more than a year, so they could afford to buy ice cream at Café Groppi, go to the cinema, watch the polo at the Gezira Club with white-clad servants offering trays of gin and bitters, have a slap-up dinner at the Auberge des Pyramides, then move on to cocktails at the KitKat Club. The stark austerity of Crete seemed like an alien world.

Both had been given extended leave. It seemed no one knew what to do with them. They had been asked if they wanted to be sent home to Australia for their furlough, but Teddy had said, very quickly, "No."

Jack knew how much Teddy hated his home. His mother with her shrill laugh, her constant smile, his father with his huge burly shoulders and weak useless legs, slithering about in his wheelchair, fists always ready to strike out. The smell of rot and iodine.

He would have liked to have seen his nana, who must have been sick with worry over his long absence. He wondered what they had told her. *Deepest regrets your grandson has been reported missing in action.* He wondered if she had wept. He had never seen her weep. She was too fierce, too proud. He had written to her as soon as he had arrived in Cairo, and she had replied by the return post, *I always said you were a cat with nine lives. Take care, as you must not have many left . . .*

He remembered how she had come to Cambridge and rescued him. She had sent him a book for his eighth birthday, and he had written a thank-you letter. Usually, his other grandmother, the English grandmother, read through all his letters, correcting his spelling mistakes and saying to his father, in her cold, high-bred voice, "I do not suppose it matters—she can probably hardly read herself. But one must do one's best for the boy. Surely, eventually, some learning will get through that thick skull of his?" That Christmas, though, Granny had taken to her bed with a chill. His father was, as always, busy. So Jack had written:

Dear Nana
    Thank you for the book, I like it very much. I like to read about Norah and her aventures I wish I had a pony called Bobs

and a brother like Jim who would not let anyone be crool to me. I
would like to live somewhere like Billabong.
    It is very cold here and I do not like it in the cubard.
                                        Yours sincerely
                                        Your granson
                                        Benedict

Nana must have booked the next ship to England because she arrived unannounced with the spring. Some harsh words were said, then she helped Jack pack his trunk and they left a few days later. A ship across the ocean to New York, a train across the United States to San Francisco, another ship to Melbourne via Los Angeles, Honolulu, Pago Pago, Suva, Auckland, and Sydney.

In all those long weeks, Jack was not caned once, nor locked in a cupboard. His nana did not speak much, but she read him a story every night and sang him to sleep, drawing circles on his forehead. She did not interrupt him when he tried to talk but listened patiently as he struggled to force the words out. She let him read as much as he wanted.

Jack would have liked to see Nana, but he knew if he left the Middle East now, he might never be able to make it back to Crete. He wanted to with all his heart. He could still feel Alenka's arms about him, her slim body pressed against him from breast to thigh, her breath shuddering through her.

"What did you say to her?" Teddy would ask sometimes, suspiciously, when he had been drinking too much.

"Nothing," Jack would lie.

Cairo was bursting with nightclubs, cabarets, brothels, and gambling dens, and Teddy was determined to sample the goods at each and every one. Many a night, he came in drunk and broke, begging Jack to lend him some money so he could go back again. At first Jack agreed, but after a while, he shook his head and said no.

Teddy laughed at him. "Come on, mate, stop being such a bore. Lend me a tenner."

"Not till you pay me back what you already owe me," Jack replied.

"You can piss off," Teddy said, and went out, slamming the door behind him.

Jack did not see him again for days. Alone, he explored the crooked old streets, listened to the muezzin's call for prayer, climbed the pyramids, and sat at the foot of the Great Sphinx and wrote love poems to Alenka that he could never send.

One day in late November, the stocky British officer who had debriefed Jack on his arrival in Cairo found him reading in the officers' club library.

"Ah, you're a Sherlock Holmes fan," he said.

"Isn't everyone?" Jack replied.

"In my line of work, yes. But it's not your usual soldier's fare, I promise you."

"S-so what is your line of work?" Jack asked.

The officer dropped his cap on the coffee table. "May I join you?"

Jack put down his book. "Of c-c-course."

The officer ordered them some drinks, then said, "I don't think we've been formally introduced. I'm Jack Smith-Hughes. I fought on Crete and was stranded just like you. I eventually got evacuated, but then they shipped me back there last year so I could work on putting an intelligence network together."

"That explains why your Greek is so g-g-good."

"Unfortunately, there is nothing I can do to look Greek. No matter how well I disguised myself, everyone always knew I was British."

Jack grinned. Smith-Hughes just needed a bowler hat and an umbrella to be the perfect English gentleman.

"You, however, managed to go incognito for fourteen months, living right in the shadow of the German divisional commander's residence. You lived and worked among the Cretans and made friends there. You can pass as one of them."

"N-n-not to someone born in Crete," Jack said honestly. "I'm too quiet and too polite. And I can't d-d-dance the *pentozali*."

Smith-Hughes laughed. "Maybe I should add dancing lessons to our curriculum."

"W-what is this all about, sir?"

"I think you may be useful to me. I have just one question for you. Would you be willing to go back to Crete?"

Jack nodded emphatically.

Smith-Hughes smiled and held out his hand. "Then welcome to the Firm."

Jack packed his bag that night, excitement thrumming in his veins. Then he went out to look for Teddy. He searched all the usual officer haunts. Shepherd's Hotel, the Mohamed Ali Club, Madam Bardia's, where a Charlie Chaplin lookalike was doing an anti-Nazi skit up on the stage, and Mary's House, the famous brothel. Teddy was nowhere to be found. So Jack walked down the dark and crumbling alley known as Sister Street in the red-light district of the old town. Many drunken men in uniform. No Teddy.

A boy accosted him from the shadows. "Hey, mister! You want sex with my sister? She's very clean, all pink inside like Queen Victoria."

The girl could not have been older than twelve and had a bruised face. Jack shook his head, wishing he could do something to help her. Even after all these months in Cairo, he was still shocked by the beggars and prostitutes.

At last he found Teddy in a seedy gambling den, drinking whiskey and losing steadily. Jack paid his tab, and steered a stumbling, swaying, protesting Teddy out into the street. He stank of alcohol and hashish smoke.

"I . . . I'm heading out tomorrow." Jack realized it was dawn. "Today, I mean. Couldn't go without saying goodbye."

Teddy looked at him blearily. "What? Where?"

"I c-c-can't say."

"Whaddya mean?"

"I m-m-mean I can't say."

"Why not?"

Jack shrugged.

"Whatcha going for?"

"I d-don't really know," Jack admitted. "Extra training."

Teddy's eyes narrowed. "For what? Commando training?"

Jack considered this. "Maybe."

"How did you swing that?"

"The officer who d-d-debriefed us dropped by. They need someone who can speak Greek."

"I can speak Greek!"

Jack made the tiniest of shrugs. Teddy laughed. "Okay, so my Greek's not so hot. It's still better than those poor old Frogs they sent to Crete. If they can go and blow up German airports, why can't I?"

"I th-think this is more a long-term proposition."

"So how come they asked you and not me?" Teddy sounded genuinely hurt.

"M-m-maybe they c-c-couldn't find you. Maybe they thought . . ."

"What?"

"M-m-maybe they thought you were a little . . . unsteady."

"Hang on! There's nothing wrong with blowing off a little steam."

"N-n-not at all. When it's only a little."

Teddy's ears reddened. "I'll go see 'em. Convince 'em to take me. Where is this guy?"

"I don't know." When Teddy looked incredulous, Jack laughed. "I m-m-mean it! He came and found me. All I know is I have to catch a train to Palestine in a few hours."

"Palestine!" Teddy seemed to come to some kind of decision. "I need coffee. Lots of it. And a bucket of water." At Jack's look of query, he laughed. "To shove my head in."

"W-what are you going to do?"

"Go ferret them out, convince them to send me too."

"But . . . how will you know how to find them?"

Teddy laughed. "I'll ask one of the cabbies. They know everything that's meant to be secret in Cairo."

V

"Oh, sure, ok, *aywah*," the cab driver said. "You want the Secret House? *Ma alesh.*"

He drove at high speed through the crowded streets, his hand on the horn, then came to a screeching halt in front of a tall, gray block of flats in the diplomatic quarter of Garden City. Teddy clambered out of the cab and wiped his sweaty palms on his uniform jacket. His head thumped and his throat was dry. All he could think of was finding some way to make sure he was not sent back to his father's farm. He could not bear the thought of it.

In the cab, Teddy had thought about how he was going to convince the British officer to send him to whatever commando school Jack was being sent to. It couldn't just be because Jack's Greek was so much better than Teddy's. Some of the agents sent to Crete had not spoken a single word of the local language and had been indignant that the Cretans did not reply when asked questions in English. And Patrick Leigh-Fermor was just as tall and fair and blue-eyed as Teddy, so it couldn't be because he didn't look very Greek. Maybe it was the drinking, he told himself. But what else was he meant to do in Cairo?

The receptionist directed him to a small office, where Smith-Hughes was working away diligently, his coat off. He looked up as Teddy came in, and said in a neutral voice, "Lieutenant Lloyd. How can I help you?"

Persuasive arguments jostled in Teddy's head, but he knew at once that this young man would not be easy to charm. So he said rapidly, "Please, sir, don't let them send me home. I came here to fight Hitler, and he's not beat yet. I want to be part of it. And Jack and me, we're best mates. We've been mates since we were kids. We've done everything together. I know you think I'm a bit wild, but I promise I'll steady down if I'm just given a chance. It was tough on Crete, we felt we'd been forgotten. And then there was nowhere here for us, we weren't deemed fit for desert fighting. But I want a go, sir! I want to have a proper crack at the Jerries. Please let me go wherever it is Jack is going. I promise I'll make you proud."

There was a long silence. Smith-Hughes tapped a pen against his cheek thoughtfully. Then he sighed. "Very well. God knows we need all the men we can get."

He scribbled on a piece of paper and thrust it toward Teddy.

"Why don't you head out to D-School, let them test your mettle? If they think you're made of the right kind of stuff, they'll let me know."

"D-School?" Teddy blurted. "What does "D" stand for?"

"Some people say demolition, some people say danger," he answered with a wry smile. "I like to call it the School of Dirty Tricks."

After a long, wearying journey, the train finally drew into the station at Haifa, in the British Mandate of Palestine. It was a grand old building, with a Union Jack fluttering from its flagpole. A young private in khaki shorts and long socks greeted them, reading out their names from a telegram, then showed them out to an army jeep, parked askew half on the pavement and half on the road. The drive through the crowded streets of Haifa was slow, but they soon left the city behind them and began to climb a steep hill.

"This is Mount Carmel," the private said. "Not far now."

At last the jeep turned through a pair of huge old gates set in high walls. Within was an imposing building with a dome topped with a cross, set on the very crest of the hill with commanding views of the wide bay.

"It's used to be some pasha's summer palace, and then it was a monastery," the private explained. "Now it's our training school."

Young men in shorts and singlets were doing star jumps and push-ups in the courtyard. A sudden explosion nearby made Teddy jump, and the private grinned. "Demolition practice," he explained. "You get to blow up a lot of stuff here."

They were taken through to a bare office where a colonel with a bristling mustache and cold gray eyes was studying a stack of papers. He acknowledged their salute and introduced himself as Colonel Cator. He had a very haughty upper-class British accent and looked them up and down in such a disdainful way that Teddy wished he had thought to neaten himself up after the long train journey.

"I believe you've been stuck on Crete," he said.

"Yes, sir," Teddy said. "We were left behind when our battalion was evacuated. I was taken prisoner but escaped. Jack . . . I mean, Lieutenant Hawke . . . he was injured and missed the boat."

"I see." Those frowning gray eyes looked them over. "Why did you not try to escape the island earlier?"

"Oh, but we did, sir. We tried several times."

"You failed each time?"

"Yes, sir."

"Many of your countrymen managed to escape Crete. One lot used blankets for sails, tied together with their bootlaces. Another used flour sacks and the straps from chocolate tins, with a mast made with an old fishing spear. Another group rowed the whole way in an old leaking dinghy. They showed great daring and initiative. None of these solutions occurred to you?"

"No, sir." Teddy shifted uncomfortably.

"Hmmm," the colonel said. "What about you, Lieutenant Hawke? You are very quiet. Does your friend always speak for you?"

"No, sir," Jack replied. "But be assured we have c-come to use our hands and not our t-tongues."

The colonel smiled. "Ah, a man who knows his Shakespeare! And you are right, a still tongue is not a liability in these times. Very well. You've been sent to me for assessment, so Smith-Hughes must've seen something in you. Private Thompson will take you to your rooms. We shall see how you get on."

D-School began at dawn every day. Teddy and Jack were part of a group called the Crete Squadron, made up of young men from the island who were being trained to work with British officers in the underground resistance on the island. The mornings were spent in fitness exercises and racing each other over an ever-changing obstacle course. The afternoons were spent in the firing range, competing with each other to shoot out the shape of the swastika on a Nazi flag. The evenings were for Morse code and map reading and listening to long lectures on strategy and tactics.

Competition was fierce among the trainees, many of whom had suffered terribly under German occupation. Teddy pushed himself to the front whenever he could, determined to stand out from the crowd, but it was hard when everyone was so keen. Colonel Cator often came and watched them, along with his second-in-command, a stocky hard-eyed Greek. They took notes, issued terse orders, and frowned if Teddy tried to warm them up with a few jokes.

They were given leave over Christmas. Teddy and Jack caught a train to Jerusalem and explored the ancient city, guidebooks in hand. They walked the Via Dolorosa, visited the Church of the Holy Sepulchre, and watched as black-clad men with long beards and side curls prayed and sang and lamented at the Wailing Wall. Every crack and crevice had a little roll of paper inserted within. On Christmas Eve they went along to the Church of Nativity in Bethlehem, along with a great many other young men in uniform, many of them on crutches, or with arms in slings, or heads bandaged.

"Happy birthday, mate," Teddy said at midnight, as he had done every year since meeting Jack at the age of eight. "Let's go find a pub."

"D-d-do they have pubs in Jerusalem?" Jack said.

"There'll be a bar somewhere. We'll try the Christian quarter."

Jack was very quiet, and Teddy suspected he was thinking about their Christmas in Crete a year ago. "I wonder how Alenka is doing?" he said when they were finally settled.

Jack flashed a look at him, then returned his attention to his glass. "I h-h-hope she . . . she . . . she's o-k-k-kay."

When Jack stuttered badly, it was always a sign of strong emotion. It was his tell. Teddy finished his drink, called for another, then said casually, "So what did you say to her, that last night on Crete?"

"N-n-nothing."

"Why won't you tell me? Come on, Jack, what did you say?"

"Just g-g-goodbye."

"I know it was more than that."

Jack shrugged. "W-w-w-what does it matter? We might never see her again."

"But you want to."

Jack looked up at last. "Of c-c-course I want to!"

"Is that what you said to her, that night on the beach? My God, that's what you said to her, isn't it? That you'd go back for her one day." He laughed and drank down the rest of his whiskey. "Bastard! She's my girl . . ."

"She isn't anybody's but her own s-s-sweet self!"

Teddy stared at him, then laughed. "As if a girl like Alenka would ever look at a bloke like you! You're dreaming."

"A man's allowed to d-dream," Jack replied, with scarcely a stammer at all.

He and Teddy hardly spoke on the train journey back to Haifa.

Teddy brooded over his words. She's my girl, he kept saying to himself. I saw her first. I bet she hasn't let you kiss her. I bet you've been too scared to even try. Hell, I practically got her into bed at one stage.

I'll show him, he thought.

Back at D-School, training continued, intensifying every day. Teddy did his best to beat Jack at everything, but for once Jack did not give him the chance. It was infuriating.

The first week of the new year was spent undertaking a series of tests, from shooting skills to the ability to solve mathematical problems to a series of questions that Teddy guessed was designed to see if they had the inner grit to succeed. He lied to some of the questions:

Can you sit still without fidgeting? YES.

Do you ever feel you are suffocating? NO.

Did you have a happy childhood? YES.

Afterward, Teddy was called in to Cator's office. His palms were sweating, but he stood to attention and listened as the colonel went through his results. No punches were pulled. Teddy was impulsive, hot-tempered, a daredevil. Teddy could not help grinning at this, but he did his best to compose his face when Cator looked up, frowning. "You clearly have trouble with authority," he said, "a trait not usually favored in the British army."

Teddy's grin faded away, and his gut churned. He was going to be sent home in disgrace, he thought.

At last Cator came to the end of his list of Teddy's faults. "Luckily for you, we are not the regular British army. We like daredevils here. I am glad to be able to say that we have accepted you for further training."

Teddy looked up, smiling. "Yes, sir! Thank you, sir!"

"I can't tell you what you are being trained for, except to say it's very secret and very dangerous. If you have second thoughts, no one will think the worse of you. You can go back to your regiment as if nothing had happened."

Teddy shook his head. "No, thank you, sir, I'll stay."

"Very good. You must now sign the Official Secrets Act," Cator said. "Any talk of what you have seen or done here, or in the tasks that follow, will be considered treason and you'll be imprisoned if you are lucky and shot if you are not. Understood?"

"Yes, sir." Teddy signed where he was directed.

"Excellent," Cator said, taking back the signed paper and folding it neatly. "Now that's done, I have one final question for you."

"Yes, sir?"

"Do you have any objection to murder?"

VI

"This is more like it," Teddy said, looking around at the Crete Squadron's new mess hall. It was liberally stocked with books, records, and alcohol.

Only a handful of men had made it through the assessment trials. Jack was, of course, one of them. In his secret heart, Teddy was relieved. He hated the strain between them. *Over a girl*, he thought a little contemptuously. *A girl we've both left behind.*

"So did Cator ask you if you had any objection to murder?" Teddy asked the other squad members, lowering his voice.

They all nodded.

"What did you say?"

"Well, I said, 'No, sir.' Didn't everyone?" asked a young Cretan named Sifis.

"I told them I was eager to do God's work, whatever he willed me to do," said an older man named Father John Skoulas, crossing himself. He was a Cretan priest who had been given permission by the church to be trained as a guerrilla fighter, and so had cut off his long hair and beard for the first time in his life. He was the eldest of them all, being almost forty, and had left his wife and family behind in Crete.

"I said not as long as it was a Nazi!" cried a young man with dark curls and fierce eyes whom everyone called Viko. He came from Chania and had seen his family die of starvation in the black winter of 1941. "Why, what did you say? I hope you said the same, Lloyd."

"I said, 'yes, sir, no, sir, three bags full, sir,'" Teddy said with a grin.

"What about you, Jack?" Father John asked. He seemed to have taken a liking to Jack, the two of them spending many an evening playing chess or talking about books.

Jack looked up from his journal. "I-I-I asked him to define murder. We had quite an interesting discussion about it."

Teddy laughed sardonically. "Typical Jack! What did you conclude?"

"That whoever fights monsters needs to take care they do not become a monster themselves." Jack met his gaze steadily.

"Well, good to get that settled," Teddy said. "Another round?"

Long before dawn the next day, they were roused from their beds and sent out on a long desert run. Teddy's head pounded as if being bashed with a sledgehammer, and his mouth was so dry his tongue felt like sandpaper. His legs trembled under the weight of the heavy pack and weapons.

To his dismay, he was among the last to return to base. Jack had been the first.

"How could you finish so fast?" he demanded. "After all that bloody whiskey, I had a humdinger of a hangover."

"I thought we'd probably have an early start, so I didn't drink that much. They like to test us on everything here, hadn't you noticed? I thought the bar in the mess hall was probably another test."

"You could have said something!"

"Would you have listened?"

There was no chance for rest and recovery. The men were driven hard all day, then—hot, sweaty and exhausted—shown into a long room with rows of desks and a blackboard.

A British officer was waiting for them, leaning against the desk. He was a mild-looking man with an impressive mustache and piercing blue eyes, aged in his midthirties.

"Congratulations on making it so far," he said. "My name is Nicholas Hammond, and I need to warn you that this is your last chance to change your mind and return to your own battalion. If you decide to stay, then change your mind tomorrow, you will be sent to the Cooler. Don't look so scared. It's not prison exactly. It simply means you will spend the rest of the war kicking your heels somewhere out of the way where you can't blab about what you've seen and heard here. Understood? Anyone want to quit now?"

"No, sir!" they chorused.

"Excellent. Then let us begin. You have all been trained and tested, but most of you do not know why. The answer is that we work for a clandestine organization called Secret Operations Executive. Sabotage and subversion are our business. The prime minister himself called for the Firm to be established. He calls us the Ministry of Ungentlemanly Warfare. Our only mission is to set Europe ablaze."

Teddy felt a thrill all through his body. At last! After all these months trapped on Crete, the chance for adventure and glory.

"The first thing you need to know about working with the Firm is that you must forget all the rules of fair play and sport you've ever been taught. There's no room for the Marquess of Queensberry rules in this war. Your aim will be to kill your opponent as quickly and as silently as possible. You must be like a phantom, appearing out of the darkness and disappearing back into it, leaving no trace. Do you understand?"

"Yes, sir!" they chorused.

"The type of fighting you'll be taught is dirty, no-prisoners-taken, gutter fighting. Prisoners are a handicap and a danger to you. They will slow you down and make a noise. You must learn to surprise, kill, vanish. I can see from your faces that some of you find this idea distasteful. This is not sport. We do not do this for fun. We are fighting a war, the cruelest and most crucial war ever fought in the history of the world. We must win because the cost of losing is unthinkable."

Hammond looked about the room, studying their postures, their body language, the expressions on their faces. "Over the next few weeks, you will be taught how to kill with your bare hands, how to lie your way out of a tense situation, how to escape handcuffs with a length of wire hidden in your sleeve, how to withstand torture as long as is humanly possible, and how to kill yourself if you are unable to escape. I think that gives you some idea of what you are likely to face once you leave us. Once more, I must ask if any of you wish to be released from the SOE?"

Hammond looked around the room.

"No, sir," the men all answered, but with much less certainty than before.

"Very well. Our first lesson will be on how to blow stuff up. It's a subject that anyone with even an ounce of the schoolboy left in him is bound to enjoy. I'm sure you all know how to throw a grenade, but tell me: do any of you know how to make one?"

As the weeks passed, Hammond showed them many different ways to sabotage and destroy a target, including using explosives cunningly concealed inside everyday items like tins of bully beef or pencils. Hammond called these hidden explosive devices sweets and toys. Teddy loved it.

Close combat fighting and small arms were taught by an older officer by the name of

Hector Grant-Taylor. He always had a different story to explain how he had learned one skill or another. "My father took me to see Buffalo Bill and his Wild West show when I was a boy," he told Teddy one day. "I was thrilled to see real live cowboys riding broncos and doing tricks with ropes. I saw Annie Oakley shooting dimes out of the air and a cigar from between her husband's lips and knew I had to learn how to do the same."

Another time he let slip he had learned a certain dirty trick working undercover with the Chicago police, bringing down a famous mob family. He had also, apparently, studied martial arts working in Peking with the Emperor's bodyguards. Teddy did not know whether to believe him or not.

Grant-Taylor had a theatrical way of teaching. "Hold your gun closer than that. As close as a lover you do not trust. Keep your wrist tight and squeeze the whole gun, not just the trigger. Imagine you're wanking! That's it! Keep your legs bent. Squat down, make yourself as small as possible! Now let the target have it. Double tap him! Bang, Bang! Okay, that was a piss-poor effort. Let's do it again."

He taught them to strip and reassemble all kinds of guns blindfolded. To Teddy's surprise and secret dismay, Jack was the quickest and most proficient at this task.

"Must be from practicing the lyra in the dark," he said with a grin.

"You play the lyra?" the defrocked priest Skouras said.

"All the bloody time," Teddy said with a rather forced laugh. "When he's not knitting."

"Knitting?" Viko said in surprise.

"Embroidering," Jack said shamefacedly. "It helps pass the time."

"Ah, yes, fancy work," Grant-Taylor said with approval. "My dad was taught to do that when he came home from the last war. They taught all the men who were badly wounded. My father helped embroider an altar cloth for St. Paul's Cathedral, and they hung it up for the service of thanksgiving at the end of the war. The king and queen were there and shook his hand and told him how beautiful it was. He embroidered a big red rose on it. No wonder you can strip a gun so fast, Hawke, you must have nimble fingers if you can embroider."

Teddy couldn't believe it. The man who had taught them how to break a man's neck was praising Jack for sewing like a girl. Teddy glowered at Jack and decided he had better put in some extra practice stripping his gun.

The next day, the men were taken down to the harbor where they spent the afternoon and evening swimming out to attach limpet mines to ships at anchor. To Teddy's dissatisfaction, Jack was able to swim faster and dive deeper than any of them.

"My nana taught me," he explained to the others. "She swims every dawn in the river near where we live, even in winter. She was a singing teacher, you know. She says endurance swimming is the best exercise for singers. It builds up your lungs, strengthens your rib muscles, stretches your throat."

"So you sing as well as play the lyra?" Skouras asked.

"Oh, yes," Teddy said. "Jack used to be a regular nightingale when he was a kid. Always tra-la-la-ing about the place. He soon had that knocked out of him at school."

"That is a shame," Skouras said. "In our church, we honor greatly those who can sing. Nothing in our liturgy is ever simply said. Our prayers are sung or chanted, for worship is at its heart like a song, and singing is always a way of worshipping God."

Viko said. "I like to sing too. Perhaps you will play your lyra after dinner, Jack? I miss the music of home."

"Okay," Jack said, looking pleased. "I'd like that."

Teddy couldn't understand it. He had always been the leader, Jack his reliable wingman. When had things changed so much?

That night Jack played some Greek folk songs on his lyra, and all the men gathered around and sang. Some had tears in their eyes. Teddy found the Greeks hard to understand. So fierce and tough in so many ways, but so soft in others.

He decided he had to thrash Jack in all the other classes.

A retired burglar taught them how to pick a lock and crack a safe. Once again, Jack's slender fingers flew faster than anyone else's.

A reformed conman taught them the art of lying, cheating, and stealing. "It is an art in life to be a good liar," he told them in his smooth smiling voice. "So invent a false history for me, persuade me it is true." Teddy thought he was bound to win this time. The Lord knew he had plenty of practice at lying. But Jack—whom he had always thought so naive and guileless—trumped him once again. He thought so fast on his feet and did not forget what lies he had already told, unlike Teddy, who talked too much and then got himself in a muddle.

A professional magician taught them sleight of hand and misdirection. Nimble fingers won again. A pensioned-off policeman taught them how to shadow someone and how to shake off someone who was shadowing you. Teddy was too tall, too noticeable with his bright hair and forget-me-not blue eyes. And Jack seemed to have the knack of making himself invisible.

It made Teddy grind his teeth.

There were no visits to the local nightclubs, no weekend leave. All their time was spent in class or building up their fitness and fighting skills. In the evenings, the men read, or played chess or backgammon, or did the crossword, or listened to music. Teddy was so bored he couldn't stand it. He began to drink heavily again and played poker with a few of the other men for stakes that grew ever higher.

The worst part of D-School was the parachute training, done at the RAF airbase at Ramat David. Despite all his best intentions, Teddy could only do it with a fierce shot of whiskey. As the jumps grew higher, the shots grew bigger. One day, hesitating at the edge of a long drop, he said to the instructor, "What happens if my parachute doesn't open?"

"Don't worry, just go to the quartermaster store and get another one," the instructor said reassuringly, clapping him on the back.

Teddy didn't get the joke until he saw everyone laughing.

That evening, their class was taken by a supercilious young woman in a neat tweed suit and high-heeled Oxfords. She smoked incessantly, her index and middle fingers stained yellow with nicotine.

She was the first female any of them had seen in months, so most of the men tried in various different ways to flirt with her. She was icily impervious to them all.

"You may call me Miss Yorke. Our subject this evening is secret communications. We shall begin with testing your proficiency with Morse code. Please take your places."

She only warmed up when she heard Jack.

"Well done, Lieutenant Hawke," she said. "You have the fingers for it. You should have been a pianist. Or a surgeon!"

"That's w-what my father would have liked," Jack said with a rueful grin. "But I went in for C-classics instead."

"*Such* a rebel." Teddy meant it as a joke, but somehow his tone was scathing.

They discussed different ways of sending messages secretly. Miss Yorke taught them a simple device called, for some strange reason, a 'barn code.'

"It's a straightforward-looking letter that conceals a message within it, usually by having the first letters of innocent-looking words spelling a keyword when put together."

"An acronym, you m-mean?" Jack said eagerly. "Agatha Christie uses that d-device in one of her stories."

"Does she? I don't think I've read that one. I thought I'd read them all!"

"It's a sh-sh-short story, one of her early ones. A former spy is murdered, and there are only four people who c-could have done it. He'd g-g-got a letter that day which mentioned several people he'd never heard of. When Miss M-M-Marple sees the letter, she wonders why the word honesty is spelled with a c-c-capital. She w-works out four of the names in the letter are the same as dahlias, a flower that means treachery. When you put the first letters of the names together, with the "H" for honesty, it's an acronym for "DEATH." It was really c-clever."

"Yes, that's a perfect example of a barn code," Miss Yorke said. "I shall see if I can find a copy of that story. You're fond of word games, Lieutenant Hawke?"

"Well, I like the crossword. My nana used to g-g-get *The Observer* every week just for the cryptic crossword by Tor . . . Torquemada." Jack grinned. "So clever the way he chose the name of a Spanish inquisitor as his codename! He is really quite f-fiendish."

Teddy stared at Jack. He had not known his best mate liked the crossword, or read detective novels, or was so good at Morse code. It was as if he didn't know him at all.

In the dead of the night, Teddy and the other men of the Cretan squad were woken from a deep drunken sleep and hustled out the door without time to do more than pull on their trousers and boots. They were taken deep into the desert and, one by one, left there alone with nothing but a dead radio, a flat battery, a broken charging engine, a soldering iron, and a code sheet.

Shivering with cold in the half-light before dawn, Teddy had to figure out how to fix the charging engine, charge the battery, repair the radio, then send a coded message of his whereabouts to HQ. It was a baffling and frustrating task, and his day was not improved when he finally walked into the mess hall and found he was the last one in.

Jack had, of course, been first.

VII

"Wh . . . where are we?" Jack looked about him curiously.

Brown flat fields, mountains like purple bruises, a round hill crowned with ancient ruins. His driver turned the car down a dusty rutted track that led to a cluster of low buildings. "This is . . . or rather, it *was* . . . the American School of Archaeology."

"W-what am I doing here?"

He shrugged. "I will allow them to explain that to you. It is . . . how do you say? Above my pay grade."

Jack looked about him curiously. He had been given no clue as to where he was going, or why. He had simply been roused from sleep by a silent servant in a white robe and taken out to a waiting jeep, his kitbag handed to him. He was rather thick-headed, having spent the previous night celebrating the end of their training after two weeks at the old Crusader castle near Haifa where the SOE's so-called finishing school was located. The men of the Crete Squadron had spoken only Greek, eaten nothing but Cretan food, learned when to spit three times, how to cross themselves the Orthodox way, and how to dance the *pentozali*. It had made Jack grin, remembering how Smith-Hughes had said he must add Greek dancing to the curriculum. Jack had thought he had been joking.

The driver drew the jeep to a halt and Jack clambered out, his kitbag slung over his shoulder. The sun was only just rising. An elderly man with white fluffy hair and a mustache came out to meet him. He was dressed in a shabby tweed coat over a primrose-yellow waistcoat and peered short-sightedly through a pair of thick spectacles.

"Welcome, my dear boy, welcome. I am Professor Jones. Come in, come in."

Jack followed him rather hesitantly, looking about him. A small lobby, crowded with statues. Glass cases filled with pot shards and broken figurines, all neatly labeled.

"Tea? Something to eat? I have marmalade."

"T-t-tea, please."

The old man led him into a small study, furnished with deep leather armchairs and bookshelves overflowing with hundreds of books and scrolls. A yellow skull was being used as a paperweight on a huge wooden desk stacked with haphazard piles of paper, all threatening to topple over and slide to the floor. A small table was pulled up before the fire, set with a teapot in a badly knitted tea-cozy, some fine bone china teacups, plates patterned with roses, a silver rack of toast, and jam and marmalade.

"Shall I play mother? How do you like your tea?"

"Please, sir, I'm afraid I m-m-might be in the wrong place."

"Oh, no, I don't think so," the old man replied, pouring out the tea. "Lieutenant Benedict John Hawke, nicknamed Jack, codename Pilgrim?"

It was Jack's turn to be surprised. "Yes, sir. But . . . w-where am I? Why am I here?"

"This is Armageddon. The place where the world is meant to end."

Jack stared at the professor in bafflement. "I'm sorry, sir, I d-d-don't understand."

"Nowadays it is called Megiddo. More battles have been fought here than any other place on the face of the earth, and people have worshipped here since God was invented."

"That is v-very interesting, sir, but it still does not explain what I am d-d-doing here?"

The old man smiled beatifically. "I've been told you love music?"

"Yes, sir."

"And know a great deal of Shakespeare off by heart?"

"Yes, sir."

"And you're good at crossword puzzles?"

"Well, I like to t-try my hand at them."

"And you have a flair for mathematics."

"That's k-k-kind of you, sir. I mean, I like math . . ."

"Believe me, that counts as a flair."

"Then thank you again, sir. But I'm n-n-not sure . . ."

"One final question. Do you write poetry?"

Jack flushed. "Yes, sir," he admitted.

The old man rubbed his hands together. "Excellent. Then you are just what we are looking for."

Jack wondered if he had fallen down a rabbit hole. "I . . . I'm sorry, sir, but I'm afraid I don't q-q-quite understand . . ."

"We need poets if we are to beat that madman Hitler. Poets will win this war for us!"

Jack was beginning to think Hitler was not the only madman in his life. The professor saw his expression and laughed in delight. "Let me explain to you. One of the most difficult problems of this war is the transmission of knowledge. We live in an age like no other. The great generals of the past—Alexander the Great, Caesar, Napoleon—they could look out across their battles and see for themselves how they surged and broke. They could send a runner with a message, or a man galloping on a horse, and pass on their orders at once. Now we fight a war that stretches over oceans and continents, over high mountains and vast ever-changing deserts. Our enemy guards the railways and docks and airports of the lands they have conquered. They tap our telephones, they listen to our wireless and telegraphs, they infiltrate spies into our very halls of power."

The old man paused, patting the pockets of his coat and trousers till he found his pipe and tobacco pouch. "Our problem is how to send a message that can only be deciphered by its recipient. That is where you come in."

"S-s-secret codes?" Jack asked with keen interest.

The old man nodded, stuffing his pipe. "Indeed. The ancient art of cryptography. Every day, thousands of messages are sent and received by us, from our agents in the field, by our generals and brigadiers, by our politicians and officials, and every day our messages are intercepted and decoded by our enemy." He lit his pipe and puffed away, a dreamy expression on his face.

"You were s-s-saying?" Jack prompted.

"Yes, yes. Of course. What was I saying?"

"Messages decoded by the e-e-enemy."

"Ah yes. That's right. We intercept and decode theirs, of course, but we don't want them decoding ours. We have all sorts of clever ways of hiding messages and smuggling them out. We hide radios in suitcases with false bottoms, we conceal reports in collar studs, matchboxes, and toothpaste tubes. We set up dead-letter drops. I believe you did so in Crete?"

"D-d-did I?" Jack said, startled.

"Yes. In a roadside shrine."

"Oh. You m-m-mean, the little shrine where we hid notes and things? Is that called a dead-letter drop? What a weird name. Why is it c-c-called that?"

"Who knows? It's delightfully sinister, though, isn't it? We have used every conceivable kind of hiding place. Inside hollowed-out logs, or fence posts, in false bottoms of cans of olive oil, inside the heels of shoes, baked inside bread, concealed within bodily cavities . . ."

Jack gave an involuntary wince of revulsion, and the old man laughed. "Makes quite a mess getting those out! The problem is the Gestapo have wised up to that one, and our poor captured agents now have to suffer the indignity of an enema on top of the usual interrogation and torture."

Still puffing away on his pipe, he lathered a piece of stone-cold toast with butter and marmalade, then took his pipe out of his mouth to take a huge bite. He munched with evident pleasure.

"Of course, the main way of transmitting messages is by wireless. Every secret circuit includes a wireless operator, as well as the lead agent who writes and codes the message for them to send. Our problem is . . . or, at least, *one* of our problems is . . . wireless operators today only have a life expectancy of six months if they are lucky. Most of the poor sods are only your age, or younger. They are killing them faster than we can train them."

His voice broke. He dabbed at his eyes with a handkerchief. "Sorry. The smoke, you know. Damn filthy habit. I'm meant to be giving up."

The professor brooded for a while in silence, then went on in a low, husky voice. "They have these machines now, you know. The Huns. Direction-finding transmitters. They can track down anyone sending secret wireless messages. Often they seize two agents at once, the one sending the message and the one who gave it to him to send. We've done our best to help. At the beginning of the war, the wireless sets were so bulky and heavy you could hardly carry them around. They are smaller and lighter now. But we are still losing so many brave young men. So we are hoping to train our agents to be both the coder of the message, and its transmitter."

"So you . . . you only lose one agent, not t-t-two?" Jack did not mean to be accusatory, but he could not help it.

The old man nodded sadly. "Yes. It would be better to lose none, of course. But all we can hope for now is to reduce the number who are seized. It only takes twenty minutes for the Gestapo to locate an operator, so anyone transmitting a message needs to be quick. The quicker, the better. I hear you are."

"I am . . . w-w-what?"

"Very quick transmitting Morse code."

"Oh. Well, I've been a b-b-bit of a ham since I was a kid."

"Nowadays we ask our wireless operators to send messages of less than five minutes. Then they have to get out fast, concealing their radio first. If the Gestapo find any kind of secret code on their person, they're dead . . . after they've been tortured into betraying the rest of their circuit or sending fake messages to us that could lead to the death of many thousands of our brave soldiers."

"I can see that w-w-would be a . . . a problem. Is there a s-s-solution?"

"I hope so, my dear boy. I hope so. We need to change the way our agents code their messages. Up until fairly recently, the Playfair code was popular. An agent would memorize a short line of verse, then write it out in five lines of five letters each, omitting any letter that had been used already. *I* and *J* counted as the same letter, so our alphabet of twenty-six letters fits into a grid of twenty-five squares."

The old man grabbed a scrap of paper and drew a square divided in five rows and five columns. Then he scrawled the letters of the alphabet in rows of five next to it, with I and J together in the same square.

"What is your favorite line of Shakespeare?"

"The one about the b-b-band of brothers, I suppose."

"Can you quote it to me?"

"W-w-we few, we happy few, we band of brothers; for he to-day that sheds his blood with me shall be my b-brother."

"Well done." The old man wrote the quote down, then carefully inscribed the letters into the squares, in the order in which they appeared. "Lots of repeating letters, that's one of the problems with Shakespeare. All codebreakers know to look for repetitions and patterns, and the Bard is full of them. Plus, he's one of the few writers our agents know well enough to quote, so the Huns have learned him by heart too."

He tapped out his pipe in the grate, then sucked on the stem as he finished writing in the letters. "As you can see, with so many repetitions of letters we are only using seventeen squares. So we fill in the gaps at the end by whatever letters of the alphabet did not appear in the line of verse, in alphabetical order. The problem with that, of course, is that we end up with the least used letters as a cluster at the end, as we do here. That makes it easier to break the code too."

"Didn't Dorothy Sayers use this code in one of her b-b-books?" Jack said.

He could not have delighted the old man more. "She did! In one of her best books. *Have His Carcase.*"

"With the acrostic poem that reveals the s-s-secret of the murder."

"I heard you loved detective novels."

"From whom?" Jack demanded. "Who t-t-told you?"

The professor tapped his nose. "That would be telling. And one thing we like about you, Lieutenant Hawke, is that you do not talk too much. Anyway, the main problem with the Playfair code is that it's easily cracked, particularly since our agents all tend to like the same lines of poetry, ones that are easy to memorize. So we began to use the double transposition code. It's similar to the Playfair code, in that the agent uses a poem they have memorized, but the code is transposed twice, once into letters and then again into numbers."

Once again he drew the scrap of paper toward him and swiftly illustrated his points as he spoke. "The agent picks five words from the poem to act as a key, then lets their handler know which word it is by assigning it the number of its position in the poem. The first word would be one, the seventh word seven, and so on. Then he simply transposes the numbers back into the alphabet. The first word is A. The seventh word is G. And so on. The receiver then simply follows the procedure backward to decrypt the message."

"Yes, v-v-very simple," Jack said sarcastically. His head was whirling.

"Sadly, that has not been foolproof either. One problem we've had is that sometimes agents cannot spell. Let me tell you a story to illustrate my point. One of our agents chose an extract from Edgar Allen Poe's poem *The Raven*."

He thought for a moment, sucking on the stem of his pipe. "How does it go? Oh, yes. "While I nodded, nearly napping, suddenly there came a tapping, as of someone gently rapping, rapping on my chamber door." Our agent sent, as his indicator code, the five words "came," "chamber," "my," "rapping" and "door." However, when our cryptanalyst tried decoding the message, all he got was rubbish. Many long frustrating hours later, he realized that the problem was not in the coding at all. The agent had misspelled one of the key indicator words. He had dropped a *p* from *rapping*, which turned it into *raping*, and so he screwed the lot of us."

The old man smiled, but Jack was too overwhelmed to appreciate the joke. It made him think of Alenka and the terrible story of her mother.

"We've had a few other problems," the old man went on, after an expectant pause. "Book codes have been a favorite method, since each one has thousands of words to choose from, instead of only a dozen. However, it means the agent and their home station need to have the exact same edition of the book. And, believe me, that can cause trouble. We broke a spy ring in Cairo this year where the German agents were using that book by Miss du Maurier about the house and the fire. What was it called?"

"*R-Rebecca?*"

"Yes. *Rebecca.* And even seemingly secure networks can be infiltrated. Washington was greatly embarrassed last year by the discovery that their ambassador to Cairo was sending back full reports to the US that were read by the Germans before they even reached the president. We've blocked that leak, thank God."

"Really?"

"Oh, yes. People think Rommel had some kind of psychic power, always knowing exactly how and when to strike, but the truth is he was simply reading the American ambassador's secret dispatches with his morning coffee every day. So we've moved to using the one-time pad system, but that too has its problems."

"Of c-course," Jack said wearily.

"Oh yes. In theory, it's fine. A pad of random figures and letters, with the agent and home station holding the only copies. After each one was used, it was burned. The problem is, if you are snaffled by the Gestapo, it's very hard to explain why you have a haversack full of secret codes. No, no, it's very inconvenient."

"So what's the s-s-solution?"

"You. And agents like you. Quick, smart, good at Morse, and able to write poetry. Do you think you could compose a poem, memorize it, and use it to quickly send secret messages?"

Jack smiled.

That night, Jack sat on his bed and drew his journal out of his pocket. It was full of scribbled lines. He began, slowly and laboriously, to fit some of them together into stanzas.

"You don't want to write anything that rhymes," the professor had
warned him. "But that will make it much harder to remember. So you
want some kind of organizing principle, something to help you memorize the poem and never forget it."

Flicking through his journal, it fell open on the page where he had
sketched out the Fibonacci number sequence for Alenka. An idea came
to him. Jack began to try to find syllables that fitted into that sequence.
1-1-2-3-5-8-13 . . .

He thought about code names. Pilgrim. Hunter.

He thought about Alenka, whose name meant *bright*. Standing on
the tiny beach, bidding her goodbye as he prepared to sail to Egypt, he
had said to her, "You have the brightest spirit I have ever known. Don't
let it be dimmed." She had thrown her arms about him and pressed her
body to him. The memory of it sent such a quiver of desire and longing
through him that he had to lay down his pen and go to the window,
opening it wide so the frosty wind swept in and cooled his heated skin.
Outside, the sky was luminous with zillions of stars. He looked for the
Corona Borealis, the curve of seven bright stars said to be Ariadne's
crown, set in the skies to guide those who were lost home. "Ariadne was
the earthly face of the bright goddess," Alenka had said.

Thinking about Ariadne made him think of the minotaur in the
labyrinth. He found the poem he had been writing the day he had
seen Alenka practicing the foxtrot in the ruins of the old palace. *Minotaur . . . mad and blind . . . longing for the light but so afraid of what
is to come . . .*

Jack had always thought the minotaur symbolized humanity's deepest fears or darkest desires. To walk the labyrinth was to face those fears,
those desires. And then Paddy had told him that story about his German
friend, who had thought the minotaur meant war. And wasn't war, in
all its blood and filth and terror, the most awful expression of human
fear and desire? And weren't the Nazis like the minotaur, driven mad
by their lust for power, their fear of impotence?

He began to write, adapting some of the many love poems he had
written to Alenka: *O bright girl, dancing . . .*

But *girl* had only one syllable. He needed two for his rhythmic pattern. So Jack changed the line to *O bright goddess, dancing* . . .

The professor had told him to use as many letters of the alphabet as possible. Jack changed "afraid of what is to come" to "afraid of the great beyond," and described Alenka's crown of stars as "blazing." Many hours later—dazed, exhausted, exhilarated—he had the rough shape of a poem, set in seven stanzas to reflect the seven circuits of the Cretan labyrinth.

It began:

O
blessed
pilgrim
the first step
on the spiral path
snaking down to the secret place
the point of pivot the darkness where your shadow hides

PART VI:
CASTING THE CIRCLE
SPRING–AUTUMN 1943

O
bold
seekers
hand in hand
casting the circle
the marvelous sacred spiral
a double-twisted crimson thread leading us safe
home

I

Two Germans came for Alenka one bitter morning while she was chopping wood for the fire. She thought of fighting them, hurling the ax at them and fleeing, but her blade was old and blunt, and they had rifles.

Pretending composure, she walked through the barbed-wire-strung gate and into the Nazi compound. She was taken to the villa's comfortable drawing room. The new divisional commander, General Müller, sat in a big chair by the fire, drinking coffee and looking through some papers. The delicious smell of the coffee was unbearable. It had been a long time since Alenka had drunk anything except a gritty beverage made with ground acorns.

Müller was a thick-necked man in his midforties. He had a pugnacious jaw and heavy jowls and wore an impeccable field-gray uniform hung with a great many decorations, including the Iron Cross which he had won fighting in Russia. His head was curiously square, his eyes small and deep set. He and Bruno Bräuer, the new commandant-in-chief of Fortress Crete, had been appointed the previous winter after the former generals had been dismissed because of their failure to stop the sabotage raids on the airfields.

Müller had already gained a reputation for brutality, with constant raids and reprisals since his appointment. Alenka knew that one of the

British wireless operators had been caught, tortured, and shot, and that many Greeks had been locked up in the infamous Agia Prison, where they were beaten and starved. Just being near him made her feel faint with terror.

Müller looked up as Alenka came in and lit a cigarette as if knowing what torture it was to smell the smoke. "Fräulein Klothakis, I am in need of a confidential secretary."

She stared at him, bewildered.

"Your brother has recommended you to me."

A sharp twist of nerves in the pit of her stomach.

"Your father is German, I believe."

Not mine, she wanted to say. My father is Greek.

But she could not claim to be proud of her father. So she kept silent.

Müller did not seem to expect her to speak. "I believe you can type and take dictation and speak German reasonably well. It is convenient that you live so close, and that you speak English too. We have British terrorists to root out and will need a reliable translator to help with the interrogations."

Alenka's senses swam. The room was too hot, the smoke too heady.

Beside the fireplace was a copy of the famous bull's head found in the ruins at Knossos. It was carved from a single block of black stone, incised with spiraling curls between the two immense golden horns. The eye was made from white rock crystal, painted with a black iris and a red pupil, and rimmed with fiery red jasper. Those wild bloodshot eyes seemed to stare at Alenka as pitilessly as the man with the iron cross about his throat.

"I will expect you to be punctual and conscientious, as well as utterly discreet. Any loose talk will, of course, be severely punished."

He stopped, obviously expecting a response.

"Yes, Herr General." Her lips were stiff and cold.

He waited till she had almost escaped the room, before calling her back. "One more thing, fräulein."

"Yes, Herr General?" She turned back to face him.

"As my confidential secretary, you will need to dress more appropriately. You have not always been so . . . shall we say, outmoded?" As he spoke, he picked up an old photograph from the desk and studied it. Alenka recognized it at once. It was a photo of her and Phyllia, taken the summer before the invasion. Dressed in flimsy summer dresses and sandals, hair in loose waves, they were laughing. She felt sick. Where had he got the photo from? It must have been from Axel.

Müller smiled at her. "I understand that some of the luxuries of life are hard to come by for young women here. So I have taken the liberty of ordering you some little treats."

He held out a small brown paper parcel. Alenka had to come close to him to take it. His hand was very large and thick in comparison to her own. She tried not to brush her skin against his. As her fingers closed on the parcel, he suddenly gripped it tight so that she could not take it. "I am sure you will be a most agreeable confidential secretary, fräulein." He let go of the parcel so suddenly Alenka stumbled back.

She managed to thank him and leave, but her legs were trembling so much it was difficult to walk normally. She was escorted from the grounds and somehow made it back to her own house without fainting or being sick. She sat down on her bed and opened the parcel.

Inside were scarlet lipstick and silk stockings.

———————————

"Is it a trap?" she asked Micky and Phyllia that night, crouched by the fire in their kitchen.

It was very late, and the rest of the family was asleep. The low flames flickered over the big loom, the spindle hanging on the wall, the gleaming icons in the eastern corner. The shutters and door were barred, and they spoke in whispers, but Alenka could not stop herself from flinching at every rustle.

"Maybe," Micky said slowly. "Perhaps he hopes you will lead him to the resistance. Perhaps he hopes you will be caught leaking secrets and you will be shot."

"But why would the general want to shoot Alenka?" Phyllia asked.

"I was talking about Axel," he answered shortly.

"But he's just a kid," Phyllia protested.

"He's fourteen years old," Micky said. "And he's fixated on Hitler, we all know that. He's a collaborator and a traitor, and we can't give him any opportunity to betray us again."

"But you can't work for that horrible man!" Phyllia cried. "Can't you just politely refuse the job?"

"I wish." Alenka shivered. "But I don't think he's a man who likes to be refused. Besides, I need the money! I'm hoping that's why Axel put my name forward. Because he's hungry."

"You can't turn the job down." Micky spoke with absolute conviction. "We need someone on the inside. This is a golden opportunity."

Phyllia was aghast. "But, Micky, it's so dangerous! What if they want to catch Alenka leaking secret information? What if the general wants more from her than just typing?"

Alenka's stomach lurched. Her greatest fear. But she had to make some kind of amends for her brother.

She set her jaw. "It's a risk we need to take."

II

Jack missed Teddy more than he could express. He was working on the Cretan desk in Cairo with Major Smith-Hughes. He did not know where Teddy was. Working somewhere dangerous in Northern Africa. They had not spoken in quite some time. Jack's loneliness was difficult to bear. It reminded him too much of his childhood, so cold and gray and forlorn. Meeting Teddy had changed everything for him. It was Teddy who had nicknamed him Jack since he was so nimble and quick. Teddy had taught him to play cricket, shared marbles with him, and warned the bullies to leave him alone or he'd spread the rumor they had penises the size of bees' dicks.

They had been best friends since they were eight years old. Yet now it seemed as if their long friendship had broken. Over a girl he could never have.

The tension between his longing for Alenka and his loyalty to Teddy was ratcheted to breaking point. Jack wanted both. And it looked as if he could have neither.

"W . . . when will it be my turn to go to Crete?" he asked the major, whom everyone called Smithy. "I want some action t-too!"

"I know it's hard being stuck on a desk when everyone else is having adventures," Smithy said sympathetically. "I need you here, though,

Jack, I need your brains. I promise you that your work here is vitally important too."

He hesitated, then said, "Actually, Jack, we have a sting going that—if we can pull it off—could really bamboozle the Huns. It's absolutely top secret so you can't breathe a word of it to anyone. They're calling it Operation Trojan Horse at the moment. They'll have to get a better name for it than that because it's a dead giveaway."

"W . . . what is it?" Jack felt a quickening of excitement.

Smithy glanced around, then scooted his chair closer. "The plan is to drop the body of a tramp off the coast of Spain, dressed in the uniform of a British officer, with secret documents on his body that hint broadly at us landing in Crete and Greece, when the true objective is landing in Sicily. The idea is that German agents in Spain will get hold of the documents, read them, believe them, then pretend they never saw them."

Jack could hardly believe it. "Isn't that a bit risky? What if they realize it's a bluff?"

"It's our job to make sure they don't. We will be supporting the sting with all sorts of activities to make the Germans believe that the second front will be opened in Greece, and not in Italy."

"B-b-but the dead body of a tramp?"

"Well, it has to be someone no one will miss. They've got the body already. It's in a cooler somewhere. The idea is to bring it to the Mediterranean in a submarine and throw it overboard."

"They'll have to make it look convincing," Jack said. "Otherwise, the G-G-Germans will smell a rat."

"They'll be smelling a lot more than that," Smithy said. "Our tramp will be reeking by then."

A lot of ideas were thrown around for new names for Operation Trojan Horse. Many of them were jokes, designed to alleviate the strain of trying to pull off such an audacious bluff. In the end, Operation Mincemeat was chosen. Its grim gallows humor appealed to the agents involved, while still satisfying the need for an easily remembered name that gave no hint of its purpose. "Apparently, the chap who first came up with the idea is a keen fly-fisher," Smithy said, "and the body of our dead tramp is our bait."

"And the Jerries are the big fish we hope to land," Jack replied.

Every detail was meticulously worked out. The dead man not only carried top-secret documents in a briefcase handcuffed to his wrist but also forged ID, fake letters supposedly written by his father and girlfriend, sham receipts, and phony photographs. A single eyelash had been hidden in the fold of one of the secret documents. If the dead man's belongings were returned to the British and the eyelash was missing, they would know the papers had been read.

Jack and Smithy and others in SOE Cairo were, in the meantime, working hard to set up various other schemes designed to trick the Germans into believing the Allies were planning an assault on their southern flank through Crete and Greece. The hope was that they would reinforce their garrisons in Greece, rather than in Italy and, perhaps, even divert resources such as weapons, ammunition, food supplies, and transport away from the bitter fighting in Russia.

All sorts of trickeries were employed. Greek resistance fighters were recruited and trained and dropped back in their homeland to cause whatever damage they could. Aerial reconnaissance was ordered, and detailed maps drawn up by cartographers known to be funneling information to the Nazis. Jack kept the wireless radio sets in Crete busy with instructions and reports, so the German garrison would report increased traffic. He bought millions of Greek drachmas on the foreign exchange and asked bootmakers in Cairo to make dozens of the distinctive knee-high Cretan boots, crafted from toughened goatskin with sturdy soles and only one seam. Commandos were dropped into Greece to blow up railways, bridges, and viaducts. Leaflets on hygiene in the Balkans were printed and given to soldiers to casually leave on tabletops in *kafenions* and restaurants. Battalions of sham tanks and planes were constructed out of painted canvas and plywood.

In mid-April, news came that the body of the dead tramp had been hidden aboard a submarine in Scotland and was on its way to the Mediterranean. On April 30, the captain of the submarine read a brief prayer over the corpse, and then he was dumped overboard. A Spanish fisherman found it a few hours later.

The next few weeks were a time of acute anxiety. The whole operation would only work if the Spanish leaked the documents to the Germans. Spain was ostensibly neutral, but there were many German spies there who kept the wheels of information well greased.

News came that the letters had been returned to London. The eyelash was missing. But no one knew if the Germans had seen the secret papers, or if they believed the ruse. Not knowing was excruciating.

On May 14, British codebreakers decrypted a "most secret" message sent from the German High Command to forces in the Mediterranean. It warned them that a major Allied Offensive was planned for Crete and Greece and ordered defenses to be reinforced. A telegram was instantly dispatched to Churchill in Washington:

Mincemeat swallowed rod, line, and sinker.

In Cairo, Jack and Smithy celebrated by going to Shepherd's Hotel and ordering gin gimlets.

"Confusion to the enemy!" Jack cried.

"May they rot in hell!" Smithy returned.

Even as Jack tossed back his drink, he thought of Alenka and wondered what it would mean to her, this trick they had played on the Germans with such gusto.

Every day was an ordeal. Müller would come and stand behind her while she worked, so close Alenka could smell his sweat. Sometimes he laid his heavy hand on her shoulder or bent over her shoulder to correct her. Alenka could not help flinching. She wondered if he suspected her of being part of the resistance and tried to reassure herself that he liked to keep everyone around him tense and afraid, on edge, in his power.

One day Alenka was taking notes in a meeting when Müller announced he had received a message from General Alfred Jodl, Chief of the German Operations Staff. "He says a large enemy landing is projected in the near future here in Crete, as well as on the mainland."

Alenka's heart leaped in her chest like a dolphin. Mechanically she kept on taking notes, her face impassive, but she could scarcely breathe for excitement and joy.

"The führer says that Greece must be held at all costs. He is diverting forty-five thousand troops here from Russia as reinforcements."

A murmur arose from the officers. Everyone knew how important the Soviet Union was to Hitler. It seemed inconceivable that he would risk weakening his forces there when he had already wasted so many millions of German lives on Russian soil.

"In the event of an invasion, we must defend Crete to the last man and the last round. So we must begin to prepare."

Müller began to outline the proposed arrangements for the defense of the island. Tanks were to be flown in. Bridges mined. Underground command bunkers built. Ammunition stocks increased. Food requisitioned. Forced labor gangs pressed into service. German units on garrison duty must commence combat training and practice street fighting.

"And any resistance must be ground out now," Müller concluded. "We shall instigate a new policy of aggressive patrolling. Platoons must systemically cordon off each village, lock every inhabitant in the church, and search every building thoroughly. Dig through the gardens and fields and examine every outhouse. I want all illegal arms and all alien soldiers found, and those that have hidden them severely punished. Do I make myself clear?"

"Yes, Herr General," the officers chorused.

Alenka's pulse was pounding so fast, it vibrated all through her body. She had to warn the resistance, she had to make sure Paddy and Tom and the other British officers were safe, and all the weapons hidden in rafters secreted away.

They're coming! she whispered to herself. *We'll be saved!*

III

27 May 1943

Axel crouched in a tree, his binoculars clamped to his eyes. The field glasses had been a gift from General Müller and gave Axel hope there would be many more rewards. Axel greatly admired Müller, whom everyone called the "Butcher of Crete." He was very strong. Axel had decided he must learn to be strong too. He spent an hour every morning and an hour every night lifting weights he had made himself from sacks filled with sand. Already, the muscles in his arms and legs were thick and powerful. He was growing tall too. Taller than his mother, but not so tall as the general.

He was fourteen years old now. A man. His birthday had been a great disappointment. Axel wanted jackboots and a motorbike like the German soldiers. Instead, his mother and sister had baked him a honey cake and made him a new pair of shorts. It made him angry every time he thought about it. They wanted to keep him a little boy.

Axel had hoped Alenka would lead him to where the British officers were hiding out, and then he could tell the general and win a much bigger reward. But she knew he was watching her. She did nothing but work and study and sew. So Axel had taken matters into his own hands.

He was pretty sure that Alenka's old school friend George Doundoulakis and his brother Helias had something to do with the resistance.

They were always sneaking around at night. Sometimes they went out with full haversacks and came back with empty ones. And they always seemed to have cigarettes.

So Axel wrote them an anonymous note.

I know you work for the British. If you don't pay me a million drachmas, I'll tell the secret police. Put the money in a bag and hide it in a jar at the shrine of the double axes, or you'll pay with your lives.

He was pleased with the result. He had slipped it under their door last night, and now he was hiding in a tree, watching the Doundoulakis house.

The door opened. Helias came out. He was only a few years older than Axel, and not nearly so strong and tall. Despite the heat, he wore his coat and carried a bulging haversack. His parents followed him out, bidding him farewell. His mother was weeping. She hugged him hard.

Axel wondered if the bag was stuffed with his money. A thrill of excitement ran through him. He watched closely as Helias wheeled out his bicycle and strapped the haversack to it. Then an old Greek soldier came hurrying up the pathway. Looking about furtively, he whispered something to Helias and passed him a note. Helias quickly pulled off one of the rubber grips on his bicycle's handlebar, rolled up the piece of paper, and slipped it inside the hollow metal tube. Then he reattached the rubber grip.

Clever, Axel thought. *I'd never think to look in there.*

The old soldier shook his hand fervently. His mother hugged him again. An uneasy feeling stole over Axel. Anyone would think Helias was going away.

At last Helias mounted his bike, and rode down the road toward Knossos. Axel wriggled down the pine tree and jumped on his own bike. It was a rusty old thing with no tires. He had to pump the pedals hard to make the steel wheels turn. He imagined the motorbike he would buy when he had his million drachmas.

A German soldier saw Helias racing past, and stepped into the road, shouting "Halt!"

Axel quickly swerved to a stop and drew his bicycle out of sight, grinding his teeth in rage and frustration. What if the soldier searched the haversack and found the money? He would take it. And if he found the note hidden in the handlebars, he would arrest Helias and get all the glory and rewards, not Axel.

Helias had not stopped. He pedaled even faster, his bike flying along the dusty road. The German soldier ran after him and grabbed the handlebar to slow him down. The rubber grip came off in his hand, and the bike jolted so roughly Helias was almost thrown off.

Axel groaned. Now the game was up!

"Where are you off to in such a rush?" the soldier said. "Take care on the road, young man, else you'll come a cropper." He bent and picked up the rubber grip.

Helias thanked him, calmly took the rubber grip, and pushed it back on the handlebar. Then he pedaled off again.

"Keep to the left side of the road, and don't forget to signal when you turn," the German called after him.

Axel followed, keeping well back.

One of the buckles of the haversack had torn, and a shirt sleeve flapped free. Axel fixed his eyes on it. It made him uneasy. If the haversack was stuffed with a million drachmas, there'd be no room in there for clothes. Then a toothbrush bounced out. Doubt began to harden into certainty.

Helias rode past the ruins of the palace and swooped down the road toward Heraklion. Axel pedaled after him, anger fueling his legs. He followed Helias all the way through the old town until they came to a small house near Chania Gate. Helias dropped his bike on the cobblestones and unstrapped his haversack. He saw the buckle hanging loose and quickly checked inside. Axel was crouched in a doorway nearby, but he could see Helias clearly in the window of a shop opposite. The haversack had nothing in it except clothes.

Helias surreptitiously removed the note from the handlebar, then knocked on the door. It was opened by George's best friend, John

Androulakis. John let Helias in, looked up and down the street, then shut the door.

Rage surged through Axel. George and Helias were not paying the ransom money. They were running away!

He clambered back on his bike and raced to the headquarters of the German secret police. Axel had been there a few times, delivering information to Sergeant Friedrich Schubert. The Germans called him *Fritz*, but the Cretans had dubbed him *the Turk* because he spoke Greek with such a strong Turkish accent. His father had been a Greek from Smyrna, it was whispered, but he had been brought up in Germany and had taken his mother's name. *He's a mongrel like me*, Axel had thought, when he first heard this rumor.

Like Axel, Schubert worked hard to be a good Nazi, perhaps because he did not look Aryan, having swarthy skin, dark receding hair, and very thick glasses. He had been imprisoned after torturing and murdering a Cretan. However, the new commandant Bruno Bräuer had released him and ordered him to set up a paramilitary force to destroy the resistance on Crete. Schubert had enlisted the most sadistic German soldiers he could find and recruited local Cretan hooligans from the prisons.

Schubert was pleased with Axel's information. "Good boy! If we catch them, there'll be a reward for you."

He called up his company of thugs. Full of excitement, Axel showed them the way to the Androulakis house. Schubert hammered on the front door with the hilt of his pistol.

John's mother opened it, her scarf wrapped about her face, her eyes filled with fear. Schubert pushed past her, jerking his head at his men who thundered inside the house. Axel could hear the sound of smashing china and breaking furniture.

"Where is your son?" Schubert shouted.

Kyria Androulakis cowered away, clutching her crucifix. "I don't know! He's not here!"

"Where have he and his friends gone? We have information they are carrying messages for the resistance." Schubert threatened her with a clenched fist, and she flinched, weeping.

"I don't know! They are just boys. They know nothing, we all know nothing. God Almighty, save me!" She fell into a chair, weeping.

Schubert joined his men in searching the house, but they found nothing. There was no sign of the three young men.

Reluctantly they left, slamming the door behind them. Axel ran to meet them, protesting. "They were there! I saw them!"

Schubert struck him to the ground and kicked him. "If you ever bring me false information again, I will kill you!"

Bruised and aching, Axel picked himself up off the cobblestones. Silently but with intense fervor, he swore revenge.

Next time, he'd make sure there was no escape.

Alenka slid up her window and climbed out, jumping down to the cobblestones below. It was long after midnight, but she could feel the heat of the ground through her thin soles. She crept along the narrow street till she came to the ivy-hung wall that hid the secret garden. Micky was holding the door open for her. She slipped through and felt Phyllia's hand grasp hers. The two young women huddled together, waiting.

A few moments later, there was the sound of a blow, a muffled cry, a thud.

"Quick, help me tie him up," Micky whispered.

Working as quickly as they could in the darkness, Alenka and Phyllia helped immobilize Axel, then together they carried the unconscious boy down the laneway and along the road, leaving him near the entrance to the Villa Ariadne.

"Do we really have to do this?" Phyllia whispered.

Alenka nodded, though she felt sick.

"I didn't hit him hard," Micky said impatiently. "And we can't risk him following us and finding our HQ. Come on, let's go."

"I wish we didn't have to hurt him," Alenka said unhappily, as they ran back up the road toward the old mill.

"So do I," Micky replied. "But we have no choice. We need to meet and talk about all that has happened, and we can't have that little sneak spying on us."

Crouching near the mill, Micky whistled the opening notes of Beethoven's Fifth. An answering whistle came, and the door opened just a crack. They ran inside and the door was shut and bolted behind them.

Inside the mill's cellar, a crowd of men and women crouched around an oil lantern that cast an unstable light on the maps and reports spread on an upturned barrel. Paddy Leigh-Fermor stood on the stairs, addressing the circle of listeners with a cigarette in one hand and a cup of *tsikoudia* in the other. With his commanding height and fair skin, he looked very English to Alenka's eyes.

He seemed to have no fear of being caught by the Germans, though. She remembered Helias telling her that the first time he had accompanied Paddy through the checkpoint into Heraklion, two guards had mocked their baggy breeches and the black beaded headscarf bound about their brows. Paddy had whipped off his headscarf and said to one of the guards in his broken Cretan, "Here, try it on. It will look good on you!" Helias had almost fainted with terror, but the guards had just laughed and said "*Nein, nein!*" and waved them through the barricade.

Alenka wondered how George and Helias were getting on in Cairo, and if they had seen Jack and Teddy. She sighed. It was strange having them gone. For so many months, her every thought had been how to protect and guard and feed them. Then they had simply disappeared out of her life as if those months of friendship had been a mirage.

Manoli Bandouvas sat in state on the only chair. The *kapetan* of the local *andartes*, he wore a belt of ammunition around his ample waist, a curved dagger in his purple cummerbund, and rested a rifle upon his knee. He was flanked by his five brothers, all of them sporting thick mustaches waxed into perfect crescents.

"The Huns are scared of an Allied landing, that's for sure," Paddy said, "and afraid the people of Crete will rise up and fight against them as savagely as they did when they first invaded."

"And so we will!" Micky cried, and the others shouted their agreement.

"We can work with that. Listen to the propaganda report I've crafted."

Paddy pulled up a scrap of paper out of his pocket, assumed a theatrical pose, and read, in a sinister voice: "Germans! You have now been two years on our island. Your rule has been the blackest stain on the pages of your already besmirched history. You have proved yourself savages and as such you will be treated. But not yet. Wherever you go Cretan eyes follow you. Unseen watchers dog your footsteps. When you eat and when you drink, when you wake and when you sleep, we are there watching you. Remember! The long Cretan knife makes no sound when it strikes between the shoulder blades. Your time is running out. The hour of vengeance is drawing near. Very near. Signed, Black Dimitri!"

Alenka laughed in delight, and Micky said, "We'll impale it to the door of the Villa Ariadne with a knife."

"We could print off copies of it," Alenka said, "and stick them all over Heraklion."

"Oh yes!" Phyllia clapped her hands. "Let's do it."

"How?" Micky asked.

"We'll think of a way." Alenka's mind was already racing.

"Who is this Black Dimitri?" Manoli demanded. "I do not know this man!"

"Well, no, I made him up," Paddy said. "I've got a whole list of them with menacing names. Siphi of the Red Beard, Panagioti the Germano-phage, and so on."

"*Po-po-po-po!*" Manoli said in disgust. "Too many words, not enough action. When will the British come? We have suffered under those devils long enough. Can you not tell them we are ready and willing to fight?"

"Well, yes, I've told them you will dig your rusty old rifles out of your gardens, stick a dagger in your belts, and charge off to kill as many Germans as you can, the minute you hear the British have landed. They won't do much good against Mauser MKs and Panzerwerfers, I'm afraid."

"We need arms!" Manoli cried, shaking his old rifle.

"Agreed. I've asked them to drop us as many guns as they can, as well as ammo and hand grenades. In the meantime, let's practice our cricket so we know how to throw the damn things when we get them."

"What can we girls do when the British come?" Phyllia asked.

Paddy smiled at her. "There will be work for everyone. We will need teams of boys and girls to cut telephone wires, spread broken glass on the roads, lock gates, and generally cause trouble and havoc."

"I can do that," Phyllia said, dimpling.

"I'm sure you can," Paddy replied with a grin.

"The British will never come," one of the Bandouvas brothers said pessimistically. "They will land in France, or in Italy. They have forgotten us. We will never be freed."

Paddy reassured him, saying with great solemnity that he was speaking nonsense, and he had no doubt that Crete would soon be attacked and set free.

"When?" Manoli demanded.

"*Avrio, methavrio*," Paddy answered, tilting his hand from side to side.

Everyone laughed.

"It had better be soon," Manoli said darkly, "or we shall rise up and throw off the yoke of the oppressors ourselves."

The meeting broke up, and Alenka hurried home as fast as she could. She had only just dove under the bedclothes when her door creaked open. She lay still, eyes shut, trying to breathe slow and deep. She heard Axel's heavy step, then felt him standing over her. She could not help the frightened quickening of her breath.

He bent and picked up a strand of her hair. "You will pay for this," he whispered in her ear.

IV

27 June–17 September 1943

Alenka was caught on the horns of a dilemma. She was afraid of her brother, afraid of what he might do, and yet she still feared for him and prayed that he might be saved. The guerrillas were shooting anyone known to be a traitor or a collaborator, and Axel made no secret of his Nazi sympathies.

Alenka and her friends met whenever they could to listen to Jack's homemade radio. She had carefully cut out the inner pages of an immense old Bible and hidden the radio inside, knowing Axel would never think to look in there. Whenever Axel was out, she would take the Bible down from its shelf in her bedroom and signal to Micky and Phyllia to come over. They would slip in and crouch around the radio, one keeping a lookout and the other two listening to the news and taking shorthand notes.

Alenka would then smuggle it in to work the next day, type up a report on her typewriter, and print off dozens of copies on the office ditto machine. No one paid any attention to her as she hurried to and fro, her arms full of papers. Still, it made her sick with anxiety, standing there, waiting for the copies to spew out into the tray, proof of her defiance vividly printed in purple ink for all to see. Once, she'd forgotten to remove her master copy and had to run back and seize it seconds before one of the general's staff began to use the machine. It took hours for her pulse to steady.

They called their little newspaper *Eleftheria i Thanatos*. Freedom or death. Every time Alenka stenciled those words at the top of her bulletin, she felt her determination harden. She had to smuggle the still-damp pages out under her clothes. It left purple stains on her skin like bruises.

As soon as she got home, Alenka would hide the sheaf of papers in the shed. Someone would slip by and pick them up, and that night runners would shove them in letterboxes or slip them under doors or glue them to telegraph poles. It was acutely dangerous, with so many new German reinforcements on the island, but Alenka was determined to do everything she could to fight.

The news was thrilling. In the first weeks of July, there had been a series of sabotage attacks on the Greek mainland. Five railroad bridges were blown up, airports destroyed and the commander of the secret police in Thessaloniki assassinated. Everyone was sure that this meant the British would be landing any moment. Alenka could hardly sit still or sleep. Soon, soon, the Germans would be driven away. Her homeland would be free, her family would be safe.

The invasion of Sicily on the tenth of July hit her with all the force of a blow. There was no hope of salvation now. The resources and energies of the Allies were totally focused on Italy. There was to be no liberation of the Greeks, no driving the Nazis from their shores.

The Germans were angry and humiliated. They had been taken completely by surprise. As Alenka walked to and from the villa, she saw how they looked at her, the pent-up rage in their bodies. She carried her dressmaking scissors with her everywhere she went.

By the end of the month, Mussolini had been deposed and arrested. In early September, the new Italian government surrendered to the Allies and sought peace agreements. Müller at once ordered the Italian garrisons in Crete to hand over their weapons and surrender to the Germans. Soon after, Micky heard from the commandant of the Italian garrison, General Angelico Carta, who had no wish to become a German prisoner of war. He offered to hand over his weapons to the Cretan resistance in return for help from the British. Micky was kept busy organizing secret meetings between Paddy and the Italians.

A few days later, Manoli Bandouvas decided it was time to act. Paddy had arranged weapons and ammunition to be dropped by parachute, and the *andartes* were itching to use them. First, his men killed two soldiers at a garrison outpost in Viannos. Their bodies were thrown into a ravine. When news came that the soldiers were missing, Müller sent an infantry company to investigate. Bandouvas set an ambush for them on the road and launched a blitz attack. More than four hundred German soldiers were killed, and many more wounded.

As soon as Müller heard the news, he ordered two thousand troops to march in retaliation. White with rage, he dictated his orders to Alenka whose fingers were trembling so much she could hardly type.

Destroy Viannos and promptly execute all males beyond the age of sixteen as well as everyone who was arrested in the countryside irrespective of age and gender.

The German soldiers formed up quickly and marched through Knossos on their way. They were followed by Fritz Schubert and his terror squad, called the *Jagdkommando* or 'man hunters.' Alenka watched them from the flat roof of the taverna, her stomach twisting with dread. She had heard Müller on the telephone, ordering Schubert to "get the boy to guide you and tell you what villages to target." She was so afraid that the general meant Axel.

Everyone in the village cowered inside their houses, their doors locked and shutters bolted. Led by men on motorcycles, tanks and trucks and jeeps were followed by long lines of marching soldiers, weapons at the ready. The sound of the soldiers' revving engines and marching feet was terrible. At last she saw Schubert in the passenger seat of a truck, his round glasses shining in the light, his burly thugs crowded in the back. Among them was a tall boy in shorts, his blond curls bright in the sunshine.

Alenka's stomach flipped. She ran out to the road, calling "Axel, Axel!"

He turned. Looked at her. Laughed.

Schubert gave Axel a dagger with a twisted handle, its grip forged in the shape of an eagle carrying a swastika.

"Time you were bloodied, boy," he said.

The German troops reached Kato Viannos first. Everyone was rounded up into the village square. The houses and church were looted, then sowed with handfuls of white powder and set alight with flame throwers. Smoke spewed into the summer sky. The villagers wept and prayed. Some of Schubert's men beat them to make them shut up. A few of the girls were taken away into the fields. Axel could hear them screaming. Their brothers and fathers struggled to reach them and were mocked and taunted and punched to the ground.

"Do you want to watch, boy?" Schubert asked.

Axel knew the correct answer was yes. Schubert took him to watch. Afterward, the girls were let go. Some ran sobbing back to their families. Some crept away and hid. The men were all lined up against a wall and executed. Some were only a few years older than Axel. He felt very strange. Aroused and excited, but also sick.

Ano Viannos was next. It was a larger town, so it was harder to subdue. Many people had already fled into the hills at the sight of the pillar of fire and smoke. Axel and some of Schubert's men were given the job of rounding them up and driving them back. It was fun.

Methodically they moved down the road, destroying each village till nothing was left but smoldering rubble. Goats and sheep and pigs and chickens were loaded onto trucks. Dogs were shot. Each house was searched, and all the valuables taken, before being burned to the ground. Axel had to requisition a haversack to contain all his loot.

In Vahos, he found a girl cowering under a bed. He dragged her out and gave her to the men. That time, he took his turn with the others. Afterward, Schubert told him to stick her with his dagger. One was almost as pleasurable as the other.

Eventually, they needed to stop and rest. The air was brown-hazed with smoke. Axel's body ached, his limbs trembled, his eyes burned.

He sat with the other men, comparing their trophies, laughing over the day, then he lay down and slept. The killing continued all night in his dreams, so that he woke stiff and hard and longing to do it all again.

For three days, the killing rage drove them on. At last there were no villages left to burn. Axel went reluctantly home.

His sister was crouched by the fire, waiting for him. It was only when her eyes widened in horror that Axel realized his arms were bloodied to the elbow.

"Get me some hot water," he ordered her. "And food. I'm hungry."

She said something imploringly, hands stretched out to him.

He drew his dagger. "Now!"

V

23 September 1943

The sharp peaks of the mountains of Crete rose against the twilight sky. The last of the gloaming faded, and stars began to tingle. Around the boat's prow, water churned white. The intoxicating scent of wild thyme on the wind. Jack looked up, searching for the seven stars of the Corona Borealis, pointing the way home.

"To think we're going back voluntarily. We must be crazy." Teddy turned and grinned at Jack.

Both were once again dressed in shabby breeches and long black boots, a black fringed scarf bound about their heads. This time, though, they carried Colt semi-automatic pistols tucked into the back of their silk sashes and cyanide pills sewn into the points of their shirt collars.

These were not the only tools the two men had been given. One of the buttons on their coats unscrewed to reveal a tiny compass. A box of matches concealed a miniature camera. A double-edged blade was hidden in the stem of a pipe, and a long, narrow spike—useful for puncturing tires and throats—concealed under the flap of their coat lapels. They had special utility knives with many different types of blades, saws, and wire cutters, plus a garrotte wire sewn into their hems. The tiniest gun Jack had ever seen was hidden in a secret pocket in the waistband of their breeches. It looked like a child's plaything, which is why, perhaps, their equipment was nicknamed "sweets and toys" by the Firm.

Jack had been thrilled when he had heard he was being sent back to Crete. He had been afraid he would see out the rest of the war desk bound. Word had come that Churchill wanted Crete and Rhodes and the other Dodecanese islands liberated, to give Allied forces another route into Eastern Europe. Crete was too well defended, though, so the SOE had been given the job of undermining the German garrison on the island. Jack had not known that Teddy was to join him until he had heard the sound of his laugh as he walked into the Firm's "toy shop" in Cairo.

Jack had stopped short, not sure what to say, but Teddy had looked up, smiling and saying, "Good to see you, mate. Wait till I tell you what I've been up to—you won't believe it. Blowing up tanks with mule dung! We have to take some with us to Crete."

"As long as you c-carry it," Jack had replied.

Teddy clapped him on the back, saying, "It's not really dung, idiot, it's dynamite in disguise. Take a look! Doesn't it look real? The explosive camel turds are even better. Shame there's no camels on Crete."

Just like that, all the tension and silence of the past few months fell away as if it had never been. They had spent the next half an hour laughing over elegant cigarette holders that were actually mini-telescopes and fountain pens that fired tear gas. Unfortunately, none were any use to spies disguised as Cretan peasants. The moment of laughter and comradeship had helped break the ice between them, though, much to Jack's relief. He vowed he would not even mention Alenka.

The island loomed above them, black against the swarming stars. A torch blinked out a brief message in Morse.

"A-OK," Jack deciphered. Excitement surged in him.

The motor launch was pitching wildly, and the crew were struggling to launch the rubber dinghies. The boat's captain frowned and checked his watch. Jack knew that the timing was tight. If they didn't manage to land soon, the captain would turn the launch around and head back to Egypt, racing the rising sun and the Luftwaffe's lift-off. It might be weeks before they could try to land again.

"I could swim to shore with a long rope," Jack offered. "Then we could haul in the dinghies."

The captain looked at him in amazement. "It's as rough as guts out there."

Jack grinned. "I've swum in rougher."

"But the rocks . . ."

"I'll be careful. Once I get between the headlands, it'll be smoother. The Mediterranean is very b-b-buoyant, it's easy swimming."

"If you say so," the captain replied dubiously, looking at the black churning waves.

Jack stripped down to his shorts, looped a rope about his waist, and dove into the water. A shock of cold, the sting of salt. He swam slowly, following the blink of the torch on the shore. He could hear the slap of the waves against the rocks and see the faint white frill of the break. Then his foot touched pebbles. He rode the wave into shore and was dragged up by helping hands.

"Jack!" Paddy cried. "Welcome back, old chap. Christ, you must be cold. Here, have my cloak."

He flung his heavy goatskin cloak over Jack's shoulders. Jack staggered up the beach. His teeth were chattering. Someone gave him *tsikoudia* as the men began hauling on the rope, dragging the rubber dinghy in to shore. "*Trava, trava!*" they shouted. Pull, pull.

Overhead was a pitted roof of stone, for the tiny beach was hidden within a sea cave. It was crowded with men with flourishing mustaches and fringed headscarves, all talking and gesticulating wildly. There was also a cluster of men in Italian dress uniforms, surrounding a plump, dandified man with round glasses.

"That's General Carta," Paddy said, sounding very pleased with himself. "He's surrendered to us, to avoid getting into bed with the Huns. We've had a fine old time trying to get him off the island. Thirty million drachmas offered in reward for his capture, dead or alive. Luckily, the only use for drachmas these days is wiping your arse, so I wasn't tempted to hand him over."

He lowered his voice, bending a little closer. "Besides, I've been given a satchel full of German defense plans for the islands. I think of it as my own particular bit of Cretan plunder. It could be worth its weight in gold."

"So you've been having a b-b-bit of fun then!"

"Oh, yes. The past six months have been just one long game of hide and seek with the Huns, false alarms, treachery, arrests, and friends getting shot. Fun, fun, fun."

Jack looked at Paddy quickly. There was real strain in his voice. "I . . . I'm sorry."

Paddy tried to grin. "Don't mind me. I'm feeling bad about leading them up the garden path over the invasion plans. It was a bit of a shock when they landed in Sicily instead of here. We were all raring to go. I've hated having to tell them that help is not on its way. They feel we've let them down, and with reason."

He made a restless movement. "The truth is, I wish it was Müller we were getting off the island. He's a brute. No one really cares much about Carta, but seizing Müller would be a real punch to Hitler's nose. And it'd really boost everyone's spirits here. Everyone is feeling very low after what Müller and his terror squads did in Viannos."

At that moment, the rubber dinghy was beached. Teddy crouched among crates of Tommy guns, ammunition, wireless sets, batteries, tins of food, and cartons of cigarettes. The guerrillas began to unload, passing the boxes along a chain of hands to a rift in the cave's roof, where they were hauled out by rope. Up on the clifftop, more men lashed the boxes to the backs of mules.

Paddy said his farewells and ushered the Italian general onboard the rubber dinghy. Teddy brought Jack his clothes, and he dressed quickly, then they went to greet Tom Dunbabin, the Tasmanian archaeologist turned secret agent who ran the SOE operations on the island. He was talking to a great bear of a man with a ferocious mustache and a rifle hung with a great many silver plaques. Jack recognized him as Manoli Bandouvas, one of the *kapetans* of the resistance.

Tom smiled at them wearily. "Good to have you back, diggers! How was Cairo?"

"Bloody hot," Teddy said.

"We are suffering a different kind of heat here," Tom said. "You've heard about the massacres at Viannos?"

Jack and Teddy nodded.

"The Germans have got the full hue and cry out for our friend here," Tom said.

"*Po-po-po-po*," Manoli said disdainfully. "They won't catch me."

"Let's hope not, my friend," Tom said, clapping him on the shoulder. "Come on, you two. Let me show you the heart of our operations here."

The guerrilla fighters were hiding out in a narrow valley high in the mountains behind the coast. Teddy was surprised at the scale of the enterprise. It was like a small village, with goats, sheep, and chickens in pens, and wooden huts guarded by lithe young men with rifles, hand-rolled cigarettes hanging from the corners of their mouths. A tall monk with his hair coiled in a bun and a cartridge belt slung over his robe led a church service in a cave, its rocky walls hung with cheap religious prints and gilt icons. Women in black dresses and headscarves cooked over fires or sat cleaning their machine guns. One carried a baby on her other hip. There were old bearded shepherds polishing the silver plaques on the butts of their ancient rifles, young men in town clothes with carefully groomed mustaches packing hand grenades into boxes, and ragged children playing ball while they waited to run messages for the *kapetan*.

Most of the men slept on the ground, wrapped in their goatskin cloaks. Room was made for Tom and Jack and Teddy by the fire, and a sheep killed for their supper. One young man brought them pillows made from parachute silk stuffed with wool, but Tom Dunbabin shook his head. "Not necessary, thank you."

When Teddy looked at him questioningly, Tom explained in a low voice, "They think us soft. We need to be as tough as they are."

After eating roasted mutton that was half raw and half burned, the *andartes* brought out their musical instruments and began to sing old songs full of longing and sorrow. Jack was coaxed to play his lyra.

"You must have Cretan blood!" they told him when he had finished, and he laughed and thanked them.

"A compliment of the highest order," Tom said, lying on his back and gazing up at the stars.

"I-I-I know," Jack said with a smile.

Teddy was called upon to sing too, but he declined politely but firmly. "I don't know any songs," he said.

"Oh, you must know this one." Tom sat up and called, "Change-bug, sing for us!"

A slender young man broke into a huge grin. He had huge dark eyes, one of which wandered slightly, a tiny boyish mustache, and a thick thatch of black curls under his beaded headscarf. He began to sing, in a very thick Greek accent:

> Hitler has only got one ball
> Göring has two but very small
> Himmler is rather sim'lar
> But poor old Goebbels has no balls at all!

As he sang, he made appropriate comic gestures. Everyone roared with laughter.

"It's the only English he knows," Tom explained. "Oh, not quite true. Paddy also taught him to say, "I steal grapes every day." It cracks us up every time he says it."

"What did you call him?" Jack asked.

"Changebug. His real name is George Psychoundakis, but we nicknamed him "Changeling" because he's such a Puck-like figure. Over time it shifted, in the way nicknames do."

Changebug stood up and bowed with an exaggerated flourish to his audience, one hand tucked behind his back as if he wore tails.

"S-s-so what plans have you got for us, Tom?" Jack asked eagerly. "What can we do to help?"

"I want you to go undercover in Heraklion, Jack," Tom answered. "Our circle there was betrayed, and the leader and his brother had to be evacuated. It'll be very dangerous. The secret police have eyes and ears everywhere, it seems, and they are led by a madman they call Schubert. It was him and his men who committed the atrocities at Viannos."

Jack nodded. "What's my cover?"

"You'll be a lyra player at a nightclub in the old quarter. It's built above a network of old crypts, with a passage that leads into the tunnels of the Venetian aqueduct so that you have a way of escape."

"What about me? What's my cover?" Teddy asked.

"I'm sending you to support Xan Fielding in the White Mountains." Tom saw Teddy's expression and said quietly, "I'm sorry, Teddy. Your Greek is just not good enough."

Teddy grunted something, his disappointment so thick in his throat he could scarcely speak. The White Mountains! Those soaring peaks and plunging ravines haunted his nightmares. And no girls, no cafés, no tavernas, no fun. He rolled over, his back to Tom and Jack, and brooded over it till he fell asleep.

He was woken much later by the sound of a desperate, pleading voice. "Please don't kill me! Please, *kapetan*. Don't kill me. I've done nothing."

Teddy sat up, looking around him.

It was almost dawn. The guerrillas were drawn around a man who knelt on the stony ground, his hands tied behind his back. Firelight flickered over his face, catching the sheen of sweat, and the metallic glint of the guns and daggers of the men interrogating him.

"I am told it was you who betrayed us to the Germans," Manoli said, lifting the prisoner's chin with the tip of his long dagger.

"No, *kapetan*, it was not me. I said nothing."

"Then why did you try to run away?"

"I was afraid I would be accused. I have enemies in the village."

"Not anymore. They're all dead."

The prisoner gave a terrified jerk. "I didn't kill them, it wasn't me."

"No, but the information that you laid with the Germans caused their deaths. The whole village was burned, and all your enemies with it. And now I am on the run, and all my men with me."

"Please, *kapetan*, I could not help it. I had no choice. If I had not helped the Germans, they would have killed me. You understand, don't you?"

"You have betrayed your country," Bandouvas said, his broad face set in such an expression of hatred and contempt that the prisoner hung his head in shame. "You should have been proud to die for Crete!"

"What's going on?" Teddy whispered to Tom who sat nearby, wrapped in his goatskin cloak, a somber look on his face.

"They caught a man spying on the camp. Someone says he is an informer for the Germans."

"What will they do to him?"

"They'll kill him."

"You should not have attacked the Germans," the prisoner said. "It is your fault all those villages were burned, not mine. What was I to do? They threatened my family, my livelihood. The Germans are here to stay, we cannot defeat them. We have to find some way to live with them."

"*Malakas!*" one hissed.

"Are you a Cretan?" another cried. "We do not give in! We fight and we fight till the cuckolds are gone, like everyone else who has ever tried to conquer us."

Bandouvas gestured so wildly with his dagger the prisoner shrank back in alarm. "Yes! We fight! The struggle needs blood, my lads, and if the British will not fight on our behalf, we must fight on our own."

"I feel bad," Tom said quietly. "We led them to think they were to be saved and then sent our men elsewhere. No wonder they don't trust us anymore."

Suddenly a shot rang out. "To arms! To arms! Germans!" the sentry cried.

"Kill the traitor," Bandouvas ordered. "We cannot risk him giving us away."

One of his men nodded, drew his weapon, and shot the prisoner through the head. His body was kicked over the edge of the ravine. Bandouvas made a sweeping gesture with his arm, and the partisans at once began to bound down the path, shooting as they ran. Teddy and Jack and the other agents were already on their feet, pistols in their hands.

"Follow me!" Tom ordered. "Whatever you do, don't be taken alive!"

VI

24 September 1943

Hesper bent over her loom, wiping away slow tears. She was so thin, her cheekbones were blades pressing under the skin. Alenka did not know how to comfort her. How could one comfort the mother of a monster?

Alenka sat sewing, one rhythmic repetitive stitch after another. She was embroidering a young woman wrapped in coils of barbed wire made up of black swastikas. She did not know why. It had become a weird compulsion, the only thing that kept her from breaking.

Everyone knew what Axel had done. An old woman had spat at her at the marketplace that morning. Someone else had spray-painted the shape of the swastika on their front door. Alenka had scrubbed it till her hands were raw, but she could not eradicate it.

She did not know where her brother was. He made no pretense of going to school anymore or observing the common civilities of life. He strutted about, in his new *Jagdkommando* uniform, his new knife stuck through his belt, the swastika brazenly displayed. He had shorn off all his curls, in imitation of the other thugs of the terror squad, and came home only to demand food. His mother would bring it to him, her whole body shrinking away from him, and Axel would taste it, then spit it out, throwing his plate on the floor. "Pig food!" he'd shout. "I'm a man now. I need real food."

You're not yet fifteen, Alenka wanted to retort. But she did not dare.

She was so ashamed. What had she done wrong? How could her own brother, her own flesh and blood, be so cruel, so misguided? What should she have done differently? The questions tormented her.

There were few refuges for her. Days spent typing up directives for what Müller called "atonement measures," which meant murders. Nights spent drifting in and out of terrifying dreams, her scissors under her pillow in case her brother came for her. Alenka's only source of comfort was her embroidery. She carried her sewing bag about with her and took out her needle and thread every chance she could. One whole edge of her *sindoni* was now embroidered with images of the battle and occupation of Crete. Burning houses, weeping women, rows and rows of black crosses.

It was time for her to go to work. Alenka unfastened her hoop. As she folded the linen sheet, she saw the seven knots of protection sewn above the dancing figures of her family. In sudden rage, she caught up her seam ripper and slashed at the red cross-shaped stitches so savagely she tore the fabric. Then she flung her *sindoni* across the room. Hesper rose and rushed to her, enfolding her in a close embrace, stroking her hair, soothing her with soft broken words. "My little Alenka . . . my heart, my star . . . do not weep."

Hesper spoke so rarely, Alenka always treasured every word. She took what comfort she could, before giving her mother a strained smile, drying her eyes and tidying up her tumbled sewing. She powdered her face, reddened her mouth with the lipstick the general had given her, and walked with her mother toward the Villa Ariadne, each step an effort of will. As they reached the gate, the sentry greeted them both with a smile and lifted the bar without having to be asked.

No wonder the villagers drew aside from her or whispered cruel accusations to each other. *Her brother is a traitor . . . she is a whore . . .*

For what else could she be, with her scarlet lipstick and silk-clad legs, her job as the Butcher of Crete's confidential secretary?

No one knew that Alenka carried in her bra shorthand reports of the war which she and Phyllia had scribbled down over the past few days, crouched around the radio Jack had made. Mussolini had been rescued by German paratroopers, and the Germans had invaded Rome. The British were fighting in the archipelago of Greek islands known as the Dodacanese, hoping to strike at Germany through the Balkans. Surely, surely, Crete could be next?

Slowly, over the course of the day, Alenka began to mock up the next edition of *Eleftheria i Thanatos*. She did a little at a time, hiding the master sheet among her other papers whenever the general's aide-de-camp came near. He was a fervent young man named Hans-Ulrich Hoffman, who liked to linger near her desk, scrutinizing her closely, making subtly suggestive remarks.

Most days, General Müller and his aide-de-camp traveled to the Wehrmacht's divisional headquarters in Ano Archanes, and Alenka often accompanied them there in the general's large and comfortable car. Today, however, the general was working from home, so Alenka was able to eat her lunch in the villa's kitchen with her mother, then go out into the garden to sit in the sunshine and sew. Hoffman came down from the terrace, smoking a cigarette and watching her.

"Very housewifely," he said sarcastically.

"Thank you," she answered, sewing another row of black crooked swastikas.

"But you sew images of war, fräulein. Surely not a proper subject for the feminine arts?"

"I sew what I see."

"And is what you see so very black? What is it with you Greeks and that color?"

"Black is the color of sorrow."

He made a derisive sound and reached out to stroke her silken leg. "You seem to be doing well enough for yourself, fräulein."

She moved her leg away. "My family needs to eat, Herr Hoffman."

"Yet you seem to be watching your figure, fräulein. You are very thin. The general prefers a more womanly shape."

"Then I wish him luck in finding one."

"We will have to go back to Germany for that."

"Soon, I hope," she said sweetly and sewed another swastika.

He lit another cigarette, took a deep drag, then offered it to her. Alenka shook her head. "You do not seem to welcome the general's attentions," he said with studied nonchalance. "I warn you, he is a bad man to cross."

"Warning noted."

"Perhaps, if you had another protector, the general would look to find someone more to his taste."

"I do not need a protector."

"Don't you? I do hope you are right. Feel free to call on me if you find yourself mistaken." He flicked his cigarette butt into the bushes, and went away, leaving Alenka feeling sick and frightened. *Does he suspect me?* she wondered. *Or is he yet another man who thinks he can have any woman he wants?*

Hoffman came back early that afternoon, almost catching her half-way through stenciling *Thanatos* in the header of the newsletter, one of the last things she did before printing it off. She stood up, hurriedly tidying the desk so that the mock-up was hidden by other papers. "Yes, Herr Hoffman?"

"The general wishes you to call a meeting at once. He has news."

Alenka obeyed, then sat quietly in a corner of the drawing room, ready to take notes, as the general's staff filed in. All she could think of was the master file for the underground newspaper, still on her desk, easy for anyone to find.

"We have been ordered to the Dodacanese islands!" Müller said in a voice of deep satisfaction. "Some action at last! We are to go to Kos, drive off the British, and secure the airfield for our führer."

Alenka did her best to keep her face still, but it was hard. Müller was leaving Crete! This was news indeed.

Hoffman stood up, clicked his heels, and congratulated the general. "A chance to show what we're made of at last, Herr General," he said crisply. "We will need to commence training at once. Our men have grown undisciplined. Too much wine and soft living." He cast Alenka a look of dislike as if she was to blame.

"First, a toast!" Müller said. "Fräulein Klothakis, fetch us some schnapps. We must toast our new campaign."

Obediently Alenka fetched the bottle of schnapps and some glasses and poured it out for the men.

"Join us, fräulein," Müller said, passing her a glass.

"Thank you, Herr General, but I still have a great deal of work to do."

"I insist."

Alenka reluctantly took the glass.

"Drink! To driving the British out of the Greek islands."

She pretended to sip.

"Not like that. Toss the whole glass back. That is how schnapps must be drunk." He clinked his glass with hers. Though he was smiling, the general's cold eyes were watching her closely. She drank as ordered, the fiery liquid burning its way down her gullet, then put her glass down.

"If you'll excuse me . . ."

"Not so fast, fräulein. Surely, you can stay for another drink?"

"Perhaps when I have finished my work, Herr General."

"You are diligent indeed. Very well. Come back here when your work is done. We shall have ourselves a little party."

Alenka hurried from the room. Her legs were trembling. She went to her desk, slipped the mock-up out from under her papers, and quickly slid the shiny wax-coated piece of paper into her typewriter. BUTCHER OF CRETE TO LEAVE! GERMAN GARRISON CALLED TO FIGHT IN KOS! she typed at full speed along the bottom of the paper.

As soon as the last word was typed, Alenka snatched the paper out and made her way to the ditto machine, laying the master file on the drum and cranking the handle as fast as she could. Pages printed with blurred purple ink began to slide out, the sweet intoxicating smell of the spirits making her dizzy. When at last the pigment was exhausted, she hurried back to her desk, slid the thick sheaf of papers inside her bag, and went quietly out into the hallway. The general's staff were all going back to their desks. She had only a few seconds to get away.

Alenka had her hand on the front-door handle when the aide-de-camp came out of the drawing room. "Herr General wishes to see you," he said coldly.

Hoffman showed Alenka into the room, then went out, shutting the door behind him. Müller was standing by the fire, pouring himself another glass of schnapps. The bottle was almost empty.

Very aware of the weight of her bag on her shoulder, Alenka stood by the closed door, hands clasped before her. "You wanted me, Herr General?"

"Yes, Fräulein Klothakis. We are having a little party at the villa tonight, to celebrate our deployment to Kos. I would like you to come." Müller came toward her, carrying a flame-orange cocktail dress. "As it is a special occasion, I have a little gift for you. I would like you to wear it."

Her mouth was dry. She swallowed, managing to whisper, "Yes, Herr General."

Taking the dress, Alenka turned and groped for the door handle. He laid a heavy hand on her shoulder. "Why don't you try it on? Though I am sure it shall fit. I have taken note of your measurements."

Why did that simple statement sound so very threatening? Alenka could scarcely manage a breath. "I . . . I'll just go to the lavatory."

"No need. The door is closed. No one will see."

She backed away. "No. I can't do that."

Müller put one hand on the door behind her, trapping her. He reeked of sweat, cigar smoke, schnapps. Slowly he ran one thick finger down the skin of her throat and chest, sliding it into the cleft between her breasts. "You are quite lovely, fräulein, and I am a long way from home. I have been patient, but soon I will be gone from here and I do not wish to wait any longer. If you please me, I can help you and your family. If you displease me, however . . ."

He slid his finger inside her bra and stroked the soft curve of her breast. She jumped, and her bag fell to the ground with a thud. He pushed her against the door, his weight pressing upon her, one hand inside her blouse. Over his shoulder, Alenka could see her bag gaping open and her papers beginning to spill out. If he saw them, she would be shot.

Alenka struggled to be free. "Please . . . Herr General . . . I cannot! Stop!"

"You cannot?" he said thickly, in utter incredulity.

"Not here. Not now. They will hear. Everyone will know."

"We can be quiet."

"No. No. They will know, the *andartes* will find out, and they'll shave my head. Please, I don't want them to shave my head."

He hesitated, then stepped back, straightening his jacket. "Well, yes, that would be a shame. Come back to the villa tonight. After the men have gone. Wear the dress I have given you."

"Yes, yes, Herr General." Alenka hardly knew what she said. She grabbed her bag and stuffed the papers back inside. The smell of the spirits on the damp paper seemed very strong. She scrabbled to open the door, her palms so slippery she could not turn the knob. At last she got the door open. Alenka ran out into the hallway. Hoffman was standing right outside, and she barrelled into him. "Sorry, sorry!" she gabbled and ran down the corridor. She knew her hair was disordered, her blouse gaping open, her lipstick smeared. She kept her head down, hurrying through the twilight garden and down the driveway. The aide-de-camp called after her imperiously. She did not answer. The sentries opened the bar for her, and she raced out into the road. She heard Hoffman hurrying after her, calling her name again angrily.

She had to find a way to get rid of the papers.

It was the feast day of Panagia Mirtidiotissa, Mary of the Myrtle. The street was filled with people carrying candles and myrtle branches. Many were walking the long pilgrimage to the monastery of Paliana where an immense ancient myrtle tree was said to hide an icon of the Virgin. Others would simply honor her here at the little church of Knossos, then return to their own houses for a feast of bread and wine and lamb cooked with myrtle and rosemary.

Footsteps pounded behind her. Alenka ducked down a little alleyway and came out in the village square where the almond tree was heavy with green, velvety nuts. Women were basting the lamb, turning on its spit above a pit of smoldering coals. They looked at her in surprise.

"Help me . . . please . . . if he catches me . . ."

She pulled out the sheaf of papers, and they scattered from her hand. One glance at the distinctive purple ink, and the village women knew at once what she carried. Alenka ran, catching up the newsletters and shoving them into the fire. Dozens of eager hands helped her, some using long-handled forks to push them into the flames. One of the oldest and fiercest women in the village poured oil onto the coals. Flames leaped high, and Alenka sank down exhausted onto a gnarled root of the tree.

The aide-de-camp raced into the square. "Fräulein Klothakis! How dare you ignore me. What's in your bag?"

"Nothing," she panted. "My embroidery."

He seized her bag and emptied it out on the cobblestones. A shower of silk skeins, packets of needles, her thimble and scissors and her bedspread, unfurling to show a creeping purplish stain at its center. Time seemed to slow. Alenka could not take her eyes off the stain. She waited for exposure.

But Hoffman did not notice. He rifled through the bag, then threw it down in disappointment. "Why did you run?"

"I . . . I was late to the Virgin Mary of the Myrtle's feast day," Alenka replied. "I did not want to fail to honor Our Lady."

A long pause. The women all stood around Alenka. The flames roared, blackening the underside of the lamb.

Hoffman drew himself up, straightened his uniform, and said, "The general expects you to attend his celebration tonight."

"It would be wrong," Alenka said, "on the night of the Virgin of the Myrtle's feast."

VII

A quick rat-tat-tat on the door. Alenka flinched. She dropped her embroidery and jumped up, nails digging into her palms. She was afraid to answer it. The general would be so angry. Hesper stood up and went slowly across the room. She opened the door a crack. Then she glanced at Alenka and made a slight shrugging motion. Alenka came and looked out. The street was empty. On the step lay a feather and a small white stone.

Alenka bent, picked them up, and retreated to her room. Her heart was thudding in the hollow of her chest. A secret meeting at the old windmill? But who had organized it? She had heard nothing from Micky or Phyllia. Could it be a trap?

She did not decide to go until it was almost too late. But in the end, she crept out her window and hurried through the darkness, looking behind her every few seconds.

The old windmill was dark and silent, its sails creaking in the wind. She eased open the door and stepped within. In her hand she held her scissors, ready to stab.

"A-Alenka?" The faintest hint of a stutter.

"Jack?"

A match flared up, as Jack lit a small lantern. He smiled at her.

Alenka flew across the room, casting herself into his arms, sobs shuddering through her. He held her gently, stammering worried questions. She only shook her head, clinging to him more tightly. At last the storm of tears subsided, leaving her exhausted, but somehow eased.

"You've come back," she said wonderingly. "I thought you were gone forever."

"Both T-T-Teddy and I are back. We wanted to help." Jack looked down at her with frowning eyes. "What's wrong? Are you . . . have you been hurt?"

She shook her head. "It's just been a hell of a day."

"What happened?" He drew her to sit down on the narrow steps that led to the upper floor where the big grinding stones hung and took out a hipflask of *tsikoudia* to share with her.

So Alenka told him how she had been using the Wehrmacht's ditto machine to create their underground newspaper.

He frowned. "It's far too dangerous! You'd be shot if you were c-c-caught."

"I had to do something!"

"Th-there has to be a better way."

"What? I'm the only one who can do it. I have the little radio you made, and I'm the one who works for the general. It's hard for me to tell anyone what I hear because Axel spies on me all the time. I have to get the news out somehow. Until now no one has paid any attention to what I carry in and out of the villa. But they suspect me now. Or at least, the general's aide-de-camp does."

"What if we f-f-found another way to print the newspaper?" Jack said.

"How?"

"I could get us another d-ditto machine."

"Could you? Where?"

"I'll ask Smithy to send us one. We'll f-find somewhere safe to hide it, and organize a roster of people to work it, and runners to bring the news. The . . . the p-problem will be finding enough ditto paper and spirits to run it. The Huns keep meticulous records of the sale of paper and ink and so on, d-d-damn their eyes. But we can improvise. At least you will not be in such d-danger then."

She heaved a great sigh. It was an unutterable comfort to know she did not have to keep trying to produce the underground newspaper under Hoffman's suspicious gaze. "But I'll need to go back to work, won't I?"

"Only if you w-w-want to. Micky has told me the intelligence you are g-g-gaining is very useful to us, but it's not worth risking your life."

Alenka knew she had to go back. She told him so, and he nodded. "I-I knew you would. You're very brave. What will you do about the general?"

"He is leaving any day now. I will pretend I am ill until then. It's true enough, the very thought of going back there makes me sick to my stomach."

Jack looked troubled. "Are . . . are you sure you w-want to go back? We've seen just how merciless the Germans can be."

"Oh, Jack, it's so awful. My brother helped them!"

"In what way? As an informant? Or did he actually take part in the m-massacre?"

"He had blood splattered all over him."

"But he's only a b-b-boy."

"Almost fifteen. And he's big as a man. And as brutal, it seems."

"N-not all men are brutal."

"Aren't they?" she said bitterly.

Jack did not speak for a long moment. "I like to think we're not," he said at last. "B-b-but we live in brutal times. I . . . I'm afraid the only way to stop this war is by k-k-killing more of them than they kill of us. If we don't f-fight, they will win. And the whole world will live in terror. I don't want that to happen, and so I must fight. I w-w-wish it wasn't so."

She made a helpless gesture. "I know. I'm sorry. I just can't bear it any longer."

"I'm s-s-sorry," Jack said. "War does terrible things to men's souls."

Alenka nodded. It was such a comfort to have him there. She had been feeling very alone. With Axel spying on her so closely, she had not even dared to go next door to see Phyllia and Micky, in case she led the *Jagdkommando* there too.

"I am to be b-based here in Heraklion," Jack said, "and so I will be near to hand if you need me. We can set up a system of signals so you can let me know if anything is wrong. And we p-plan to cause so much trouble the Jerries won't have time to do anything but ch-chase their own tails."

"But what kind of signal? How will I let you know I have information?"

"We will n-n-need to devise some kind of secret code."

Jack sat, thinking, and she studied him covertly. He looked different somehow. Still dark and slender, but hardened into lithe strength, with an air of tough competence and self-assurance that was entirely new. He glanced up, catching her gaze, and she looked away, flushing hotly.

"You say you t-take your embroidery to and from work? And the g-g-general's ADC hardly glanced at it when he was searching your bag?"

Alenka nodded.

"I w-wonder if you could use it to send messages?"

"Sew it? Instead of writing it?" She was puzzled. "But they would see the message if they looked at my embroidery."

"Not if it was sewn in secret c-c-code."

Her pulse quickened. "What? Like Morse?"

"It'd be easy enough to sew a message in dots and dashes, w-wouldn't it? It'd just be a series of running stitches and French knots. I've seen how fast you can sew those."

"I'd have to learn it. I only know a few letters." She remembered how he had tapped out a dot and a dash on her knee for the first letter of her name and blushed again.

"I c-c-could teach you."

"Okay."

He grinned and reached out to tap swiftly on her wrist. Dash-dash-dash. Dot-Dash-Dash. "That's "OK" in Morse code. We may as well begin right now."

She practiced tapping out OK till she felt she knew it by heart, then Jack taught her "A" and "B."

Dot-Dash.

Dash-dot-dot-dot.

"Th-that's enough for one night," he said. "If you can learn three or four a day, you'll have mastered the whole alphabet in two weeks."

"Won't it be suspicious if my *sindoni* is suddenly covered in dots and dashes?"

"You'll have to conceal it somehow. P-p-perhaps as a kind of border beneath your dancers and musicians?"

She looked away. "It's a long time since I've sewn anyone dancing."

"M-maybe begin again, to deflect attention." He stopped as a thought struck him. "Alenka, do you remember how you lent me a Sherlock Holmes book to read one day, in the secret garden? D-d-do you still have it?"

"It's from the villa."

"Could you smuggle it out to me again? Do you dare?"

"I could try," she said stoutly, though her stomach sank at the thought. "Why?"

"There was a s-s-story in it, called "The Adventure of the Dancing Men." Holmes has to crack a c-case in which secret messages are being sent in the form of little stick figures, all in different positions. Left arm raised, right leg bent, or both arms raised, one leg bent, that k-k-kind of thing. It's a simple monoalphabetic substitution cipher, but I'd say the Jerries would be unlikely to recognize it as a c-code if it's sewn among other images."

"It'll take much longer to sew dancing figures than dots and dashes," Alenka said.

"Yes. B-b-but one will help disguise the other. And we can devise shorthand codes for long words."

"Perhaps we could draw the design with tailor's chalk if we are in a hurry, to be sewn later?" she suggested.

"Good idea. Though we don't w-want to risk it being brushed off. One of your bedroom windows looks toward the m-mill. Perhaps you could hang the quilt out that window as a sign there's a new message? I could creep down and read it when there's no one about."

"Are you hiding out in the mill now? But it's so close to the garrison!"

"I'm using the windmill's sails to charge my radio battery, so the Germans can't track where I'm sending my reports from by turning off the electricity grid."

"You're using the windmill to charge your radio?" She was astonished.

He nodded. "I've r-r-rigged up the shaft of the millstone to a little generator. I've got a c-c-copper wire running along a beam and out to the sails as an antenna, and the radio hidden up in the b-beams. It means I have an off-the-grid power source. The Germans track an agent's location by turning off the electricity grid in sections and seeing when the signal dies. That won't work with my radio. And the Gestapo can only track to within one kilometer using their direction-finding vehicles. After that they need to search on foot. I can see for miles from here, and the *Funkabwehr* are easy to spot. All I need to do is stop transmitting, and then they can't track me. So it's a perfect hideout for me. Plus, I'll get to see you." He grinned at her.

She smiled back, marveling at his cleverness. "What about if you need to send me a message?"

"If you give me some fabric and a needle and thread, I'll sew the message to you in the dancing-men code. It will just look like a sampler. I could leave it hidden here in the mill, or in the roadside shrine outside the ruins. I'll leave a stone or a feather so you know where to look."

"How will I remember the code, though? It sounds a bit complicated."

"W-w-we could make up our own code, rather than copying Sherlock Holmes. Then you don't need to try and get the book from the villa." Jack drew his notebook and pencil out of his pocket. "*A* could be for you." He swiftly drew a stick-figure girl with a triangle for a skirt, arms upraised, a crown of seven stars on her long hair.

"*B* could be for you, Benedictus." She took the pencil from his hand and drew a stick figure in breeches holding a lyra in one hand. "Do you still have your lyra?"

"I will t-t-treasure it till I die. What shall we do for *C*? I know. How about my mother Celia playing the Chaconne?" He took back the pencil and sketched a woman with curls like his, playing a cello. "*D* can be you bringing me dittany and *E* can be the eagle dance." Jack scribbled a girl carrying a bunch of heart-shaped leaves, and another girl with arms outspread like wings.

"But *zeibeikiko* is a man's dance."

"Not for me. The first time I ever saw it was when you were d-d-dancing all by yourself in the throne room, in your wine-red dress. I've never seen anything so fierce and b-b-beautiful."

Alenka felt a tingle all though her. If it had been Teddy speaking, she would have thought he was flirting with her. But Jack had never bantered with her like Teddy did. She sneaked a look at him. Jack was gazing at her with his usual dark, steady, grave expression.

"You had a fever," she retorted, trying to speak lightly. "That's what we'll do for *F*. You in bed feverish." She drew a stick figure in bed, with a thermometer in his mouth.

"It's meant to be d-d-dancing men, not sick-in-bed men. How about *F* for *fate*? The fate that brought me here to Crete."

Alenka flushed. She remembered how she had told him once that he had been saved from death so many times because there is something he was meant to do. *Fate?* he had asked. *You think fate brought me here to you?*

She glanced at him again.

Again his eyes met hers, dark and intent.

"How does one draw fate?" he asked.

Alenka thought of her Yia-Yia's stories, which always began: *Red thread bound, in the spinning wheel round, kick the wheel and let it spin, so the tale can begin.*

"An old woman spinning." Alenka drew the image as she spoke.

A thread of tension humming between them.

"What shall we do for *G*?"

"My granny." Jack took the pencil from her hand and drew an old cross-looking lady with a hunched back and a walking stick. "And if we d-drew a man with a Charlie Chaplin mustache, goosestepping, one hand raised in the Nazi salute, is that too obvious for *H*?"

"I don't want to have to embroider Hitler," she protested with a shiver.

"Any other ideas?"

"My mother's name is Hesper. It means *evening star*." Alenka sketched a woman on her knees praying, a star hanging over her shoulder.

"How about *I*?"

"Icarus!"

"G-g-good one." Jack drew a man upside down, arms and legs spread wide as if falling.

"*J* for *Jack*?" She took the pencil from him, but then found herself suddenly shy, not knowing how to draw him.

"*I* and *J* can be the same, to make it easier to remember. What shall we do for *K*? How about kissing?" He drew a boy in breeches and a girl with long hair facing each other, hands entwined, mouths just millimeters apart.

Alenka could not look at him. Jack was almost as close to her, their heads bent together over the paper, the light shed by the lantern a tiny halo of radiance about them. If she leaned a little closer, she could have kissed him. But she did not dare. She still remembered how she had held out her hand to him, asking him to dance, and he had shaken his head and turned away from her.

"*L*?" she asked, her voice not quite steady.

This stumped them for a moment. "How about the bull leaper?" Jack suggested at last. "From the f-fresco at the palace?" He drew a stick figure standing on its hands, back arched almost into a hoop.

"*M* for *minotaur*?" Alenka suggested.

"Too obvious? We don't want anyone guessing that each figure represents a letter. It wouldn't take long to break the code after that. L-let's make it *M* for *Micky* and save the minotaur for *N* for *Nazis*."

"But what's the link?" she asked, puzzled.

"In the poem code I wrote, to help me encrypt radio messages to Cairo, *minotaur* is my codename for the Germans."

"What's a poem code?"

"It's just a way of communicating in cipher. Agents used to use well-known verses from Keats and Shakespeare and Tennyson, but they are too easy to crack. So I wrote my own."

"I always knew you were a poet. Can I read it?"

"It's n-not written down. I had to memorize it. Too . . . too dangerous otherwise."

"Maybe you could recite it for me one day?"

"One day I will." His voice had deepened. Alenka glanced up and met his gaze. Jack smiled at her, and her heart gave a weird kick. She was very aware of him, his smooth olive skin and warm brown eyes, his slender long-fingered hand so close to hers. She had missed him so much since he had left Crete. There had been so little to hope for. But now Jack had returned, and it felt like the break of light through looming thunderclouds.

She looked away, fidgeting with the pencil. *I'm just tired*, she told herself. *These past months have been so hard. Don't read too much into a smile.*

"What shall we do for *O*?" Jack asked. "Odysseus? Orpheus? Oceanus?"

"Too obvious," Alenka said. "We need something only we know."

"Something personal. I know. How about my nana? Her name was Odette." Jack sketched an old woman with one hand raised high, her mouth opened in a round *O* shape. And then he made Alenka smile by telling her how his nana used to play opera at high volume when she was in the bath, and the dog who lived next door used to howl along. "Patch liked *La Boheme* the best. Particularly the bit where the soprano dies," Jack said solemnly.

He set himself to amuse her, coming up with more and more ridiculous ideas for their code alphabet. He drew a jitterbugging *Teddy* for *T*, an upside-down girl for *U*, an upside-down boy for *V*, and a double-tailed mermaid for *W*. Finally, he sketched a swing-dancing Zephyra for *Z*, making her arms and legs so wild Alenka had to laugh.

"Can you remember all those?" Jack said when at last they had finished. "For we should eat this bit of paper."

"I will never forget them."

Or this night, she thought.

She could not remember the last time she had laughed.

PART VII:
SEVEN BLAZING STARS
APRIL 1944–APRIL 1945

O

wise

old way

step by step

she finds her way free

cradling her own shadow within

she rises, radiant, crowned with seven blazing

stars

I

10 April–15 May 1944

Alenka sat, sewing. Her fingertips throbbed and her eyes ached, but she dared not stop. She had to finish embroidering the last stretch of dancing figures, so she could hang the *sindoni* out her window before it got dark.

She had news. The Soviet army had liberated the Romanian port town of Odessa after nine hundred and seven days of German occupation. It was the biggest German defeat since Stalingrad. The German Seventeenth Army had been crushed.

Alenka was bubbling over with joy, but she had to try to keep her face calm. Axel sat opposite, his boots stretched out to the fire, his face sulky. It was hard to be near him. What had happened to the little curly headed boy she had known? He seemed a stranger to her now. His jaw was long and hard, his chin bristled, his Adam's apple protuberant, and his voice had cracked. In ten days, he would be fifteen years old.

"Get me something to eat," he ordered.

Silently, Alenka laid down her *sindoni* and got him a bowl of bean soup and some acorn bread. He ate morosely, then pushed the empty bowl away and got up. He put on his coat, strapped his dagger to his belt, and went to the door, kicking over her sewing basket on the way. A few moments later, the roar of his motorcycle broke the evening peace. Alenka quickly sewed the last few stitches, then rushed to her bedroom, flung open her window and hung the *sindoni* over the sill.

At once she heard a soft whistle. Her heart jumped. She whistled back the all-clear. Jack slipped up to her window, almost invisible in the gathering twilight. "Alenka, I have news. Paddy and Teddy are here, at Micky's house. Can you come?"

She nodded and jumped down from the window into his waiting arms. "What's up?" she asked, her heart beating hard in excitement.

"They have a plan. Such a plan! Wait till you hear."

Micky's house was just next door, with a loft window that looked straight onto the villa. Micky and Phyllia were sitting on his bed, while Teddy and Paddy knelt on the floor, taking turns to peer through binoculars. Teddy jumped up at the sight of her.

"Alenka!" He hugged her. "What a sight for sore eyes. You're more beautiful than ever! Did you miss me?"

She felt the usual rush of conflicting emotions he aroused in her. Annoyance at his presumption, embarrassment that he was so forward with her in front of others, and—despite herself—a warm glow of pleasure.

He's too charming for his own good, she thought. Then, very quietly, in the back of her mind, *I wish he wouldn't kiss me when Jack is around to see.*

"I hear you've been doing great work for us," Paddy said. "Well done."

She ducked her head in acknowledgment. "It is better now Müller is gone. He was a pig!"

"It's rather a shame for us," Paddy said. "Because we wanted to kidnap him."

Alenka stared at him in astonishment, then broke into laughter. "Kidnap Müller? You mean, take him off the island? Oh, I wish you could!"

General Müller had recently returned from the Dodecanese islands, where—it was rumored—he had ordered the murder of hundreds of Greek civilians, the razing of their villages, and the destruction of their harvests and livestock, just as he had done in Crete. He had been rewarded by a promotion to commandant of the whole island, and so was now stationed in the capital city, Chania. Another general, Heinrich Kreipe, had replaced him as divisional commander in Heraklion.

Alenka had continued with her duties, smuggling out information to Jack whenever she could.

"I wish we could too," Paddy responded. "Müller is the true minotaur of Crete, and I'd love to chop off his head, metaphorically speaking—the way Theseus did in the myth. But we won't be able to get him out of Chania, it's too well guarded. So we're thinking we'll take Kreipe instead. I know nothing of the man, but he's German and he's a general."

Alenka shook her head in amazement. "You really think you can get away with it?"

"We have to do something to show the Cretans we've not abandoned them. They've all risked so much to shelter and hide us. I hate them thinking we've forgotten them just because the war has moved elsewhere."

"We will just have to make sure the Germans know that the locals had nothing to do with the kidnap," Micky said. "We don't want any more reprisals!"

"But . . . how?" Alenka could still hardly believe it.

"Th-th-that's what we need to decide," Jack said. "You know his movements best. Could we burgle the villa? Go in at night and take him from his bed?"

"The villa is very well guarded," Alenka said doubtfully. "All the walls are strung with triple rows of barbed wire, some of them electrified. The guardhouse is right next to the gate, they patrol regularly, and they have dogs."

"And it'd b-b-be impossible to take him from HQ at Archanes—the town is thick with Jerries," Jack said. "W-we'd need an army."

"What about an army of *andartes*?" Teddy suggested.

"No." Paddy spoke with absolute authority. "The reprisals would be too savage. We want them to think this is a purely British operation, and no Cretans were involved."

"So we n-need to be swift and silent and t-take him by surprise," Jack said.

"Could you stop his car?" Alenka asked. "He drives back to the villa every night. Often it's just him and his driver."

Paddy nodded. "I was hoping that was the case. We could come up with some kind of ruse. Dress up as German soldiers and flag him down."

"The best ambush spot would be where the road from Archanes meets the road to Heraklion," Micky said. "It's steep there, and cars need to slow down almost to a walking pace to navigate the turn."

"What if he suspects a trap and accelerates?" Phyllia asked.

"We'd have to improvise. It'll have to be when it's good and dark."

"We could create a diversion," Teddy said. "Gunfire and flares going off."

"A mule cart blocking the road?" Alenka suggested.

"Or a log?" Phyllia put in.

"We'd have to move the log before we could escape. We'll need to get away fast, and we'll be lumbered with the general himself."

"Why don't we just shoot him?" Teddy said.

"No bloodshed!" Paddy said sharply. "Our job is to extract him and take him to face justice. Do I make myself clear?"

"Yes, sir," Teddy said sulkily.

"I'm thinking we'll use his car as our getaway vehicle, then dump it somewhere so the Jerries think we've got him away by submarine. Then we can sneak over the mountains to the south coast and get taken off by boat from one of those lonely beaches once they've stopped looking for us. We'll have to start a whispering campaign, spread rumors, talk about it in earshot of informers, that sort of thing."

"That'll be Alenka's job," Micky said. "Her brother's an informer."

Paddy looked at her quickly, frowning.

"I'm sorry," she whispered. "Please believe me, I don't condone what he does. I'd do anything to stop him."

Paddy looked at her with pity. "You may have to."

On a chilly evening in late April, Alenka and Phyllia crouched together in her bedroom, taking turns to watch the Villa Ariadne through a tiny pair of binoculars.

All was quiet.

"If they don't manage to grab the general tonight, they'll have to call the whole plan off," Phyllia said. "Too many people know now, we just can't risk it."

Alenka nodded, biting at her thumbnail. This mad scheme to kidnap General Kreipe was the most dangerous act of resistance yet attempted by the SOE agents and their supporters, and it was very close to home.

They had already faced many setbacks. Paddy's co-conspirators—a young Englishman named Billy Moss and two local Greeks, Manoli Paterakis and Georgi Tyrakis—had been unable to land on Crete for weeks thanks to the wild weather. Paddy's hideout was raided by German soldiers, and he barely managed to avoid detection. Rumors had begun to spread, some even wilder than the truth. Then the conspirators had spent the past three nights lying in a damp ditch by the side of the road, Paddy and Billy dressed in uniforms of the German military police which Micky had found for them. The general's car had, however, failed to make an appearance.

"I can see headlights," Alenka said suddenly.

She leaned forward, her nails digging into her palms, as a long-nosed black limousine drove through Knossos. It slowed as it came near the villa. She could just see the sentries saluting and the bar being lifted. But the car sped past the villa, racing down the hill toward Heraklion.

"It kept going!" Phyllia cried. "Do you think . . ."

"They must have the general!"

Alenka and Phyllia jumped up and down with joy. Then they sobered, gripping each other's hands. "What will happen now?" Phyllia whispered.

They both knew the plan. Seize the general, steal his car, drive it through Heraklion and then along the coast road where it would be dumped, with Player's cigarette butts, a British army beret and a paperback copy of an Agatha Christie murder mystery on the floor, and a note from Paddy stressing that the general had been kidnapped by British forces.

Then the general would be taken through the mountains, picked up from a little beach on the south coast by motor launch, and whisked back to Egypt. If they pulled it off, it would be one of the most audacious operations of the war, second only to the German rescue of Mussolini after the fall of Rome.

"There's twenty-two checkpoints between here and the other side of Heraklion," Phyllia said, white with fear. "Oh, I wish Micky hadn't insisted on being a part of it."

"He wanted to spit in the general's face," Alenka said.

"I know . . . and part of me wishes I could have been there to do the same."

"Me too," Alenka said. "But we have our own job to do."

The villa was quiet. No one was raising the alarm.

"They must think the general has decided to go out in Heraklion," Alenka said. "It's movie night for the garrison, perhaps they think he's decided to go to the flicks."

Phyllia laughed.

Half an hour passed. "They must be safe through Heraklion by now," Phyllia said. "Oh, God, I hope they haven't been caught." She crossed herself three times.

It was close on midnight before lights sprang to life in the villa's windows. Distant shouting, men in boots running. "They've realized the general is missing!" Phyllia cried.

"You'd better go home," Alenka whispered. "Go to bed, pretend you're asleep. Just in case they do a house-to-house search."

She did the same but could not sleep. Her jaw ached from clenching it so hard, and her heart was fluttering away in her chest like a trapped bird.

In the morning, she rose and dressed and went to work as usual. It was very hard. She feared being questioned by Hoffman, who still regarded her with suspicion. She would have to try to pretend she knew nothing.

But Hoffman was not at the villa.

"He's been arrested," one of the general's officers told her. "Along with the sentries from last night. They think it must be an inside job, for who else would know when the general would be driving back from Archanes?"

Alenka's legs weakened with relief. She put one hand on her desk for support.

"The general's chauffeur was murdered," the officer said grimly "' will make sure his death is avenged."

The news dismayed Alenka. What could have gone wrong? Paddy had been insistent that no one must be killed. The Germans would retaliate for sure.

"I need you to print up a leaflet," the officer ordered. "We shall drop it over all the towns and villages. Someone must know where the general has gone! He cannot have simply disappeared."

So Alenka typed up the leaflet as he had dictated, and printed off hundreds on the office ditto machine. It read:

To all Cretans:

Last night the German General Kreipe was abducted by bandits. He is now being concealed in the Cretan mountains and his whereabouts cannot be unknown to the inhabitants. If the General is not returned within three days, all rebel villages in the Heraklion district will be razed to the ground and the severest reprisals exacted on the civilian population.

It made her feel sick and shaky. She could only hope it was nothing but bluster.

Afterward Alenka was sent home, for no other work was being done in the office that day. As she walked through the village square, she could hear voices calling out in excitement and incredulous joy. "Just think, their general's been stolen! The cuckolds won't dare to look us in the eyes! How could it have happened? Who did it?"

We did, Alenka thought proudly.

For days, rumors and conjecture flew. The kidnappers had taken the general over Mount Ida, the tallest peak in Crete, by foot. They had hidden in a cave, in a cheese hut, in a ravine, they had had a dozen close escapes. Planes flew constantly overhead, and thousands of German soldiers searched every village and guarded every beach. Four villages on the southern flank of Mount Ida were dynamited, the men arrested and taken to work on the forced labor gangs. But no one betrayed the resistance. The SOE agents were hidden and helped by the Cretans every step of the way. The general was not found.

One night in mid-May, more than three weeks after the kidnapping, Alenka found a feather and a white stone on her windowsill. Her heart did a handspring. At midnight she crept out and met Phyllia under the almond tree, then they hurried through the darkness to the old windmill, taking great care they were not followed.

Micky and Jack were waiting in the cellar, hungry, dirty, unshaven, and bursting with news. Alenka embraced them both, kissing their bristly cheeks. "You're safe! Thank God!"

"What happened?" Phyllia demanded. "We've been going crazy with worry."

"Tell us everything!" Alenka cried.

"W-well, it was a grand old game of hide and seek," Jack said. "But we d-did it. The general's on his way to Egypt now."

"How did you do it?" Phyllia asked, clasping her hands together. "Tell us everything!"

So Jack did. It seemed like something out of a spy novel. Chases, close escapes, near misses. They had indeed crossed Mount Ida, bent double against the driving snow, and hidden in a secret cave, hearing the Germans blundering past. Somehow, they had made it down the far side of the mountain, hidden by a thick mist that seemed to spring up from nowhere. Time and time again, they managed to slip through the German cordon, but their radio was broken, and they had no way to send HQ news of their whereabouts.

"L-luckily George Psychoundakis, the runner they call the Changebug, ran all the w-way from the White Mountains and back, so we were able to get a dispatch through to Cairo," Jack said. "What a run! M-m-much further than the original marathon, and much, much harder, uphill and downhill the whole way."

"He is a hero," Micky said simply.

"The g-general was quite glad to be safely handed over by that time," Jack said. "He told us he'd been sent to Crete as a nice rest cure after f-fighting on the Russian front! I have to say I'm g-glad we kidnapped the wrong general. Can you imagine being on the run for weeks with Müller?"

II

Alenka knocked on a low door in the side of a half-ruined building in the old quarter of Heraklion. The door opened, music and smoke swirling out. She stepped inside, and the door was quickly shut behind her.

The *bouzoukia* was filled with young people, smoking, drinking, talking, dancing. At the far end of the room, five men sat on stools playing long-necked string instruments, trilby hats tilted down over their eyes, accompanying a singer in a low-cut black dress. Alenka made her way through the crowd to the end of the room to watch the musicians. Her eyes met the gaze of the lyra player. She looked away, then leaned over the bar. "Got any *rakomelo*?"

"Got some out the back," he answered. "Come and take a look."

Alenka followed the barman into the wine cellar. A wine rack swung aside noiselessly on a well-oiled pivot. She slipped through the narrow aperture, and he shut the secret door behind her. She lit a small lantern hanging from the roof and held it high as cautiously, she went down the tight spiral of stairs into a vaulted crypt, deep below the city streets. A stone tomb stood in the center of the room. Within lay the crumbling bones of some long-ago saint. The stone lid of the grave was piled with coins and tiny gilt icons and hand-knotted crosses. Alenka crossed herself three times, took a flower from her hair, kissed it, and laid it on the tomb.

"W-what are you wishing for?" Jack said from the staircase.

She turned and smiled radiantly at him. "You know I can't tell you that!"

"You have n-n-news? Good news?"

She nodded. "They've landed troops in Normandy! More than one hundred-and-fifty thousand of them. The Second Front has begun!"

Jack rushed forward, seized her in his arms, and swung her around. "At last!"

Alenka clung to him, laughing. "We have to get the news out. Will you help me?"

The printing press was set up in a cellar on the far side of the crypt. The *bouzoukia* helped conceal the *kachunk-kachunk-kachunk*. The newspaper was smuggled out in barrels of wine with false bottoms and distributed by runners all over Crete. Alenka wrote most of the stories, illustrated by photographs taken with Jack's miniature camera. She concealed the film inside reels of embroidery thread and carried them through checkpoints to the *bouzoukia* where Jack developed them in the tiny darkroom he had set up in the warren of tunnels and cellars behind the crypt.

By the time the last bus to Knossos was leaving, she had typed up the master sheet and left it with Jack to print. He would run it through the ditto machine overnight, and by dawn hundreds of copies of *Eleftheria i Thanatos* would be disseminated through the countryside, hastily read, then passed on from hand to hand.

A few days after D-day, Alenka heard through the grapevine that the island's Jews were to be shipped off, no one knew where. They had been arrested in late May, the ancient Jewish Quarter of Chania cleared out in a single night. Apparently, they had been taken to Agia Prison and kept there in the most barbaric of conditions. Now they were being driven in open lorries to Heraklion. Alenka rode her bike down to the port and found a hiding spot among chimney pots and lines of washing on a roof and took as many photographs as she could as the lorries rumbled past. So many people crammed together. Many were still in their nightclothes, their feet bare, as if dragged from their beds. Children wept and clung to their parents, who struggled to comfort them. They were taken to the port and pushed onto a waiting ship. The soldiers guarding them were smiling.

The next day, news came that the ship had been blown up and nearly everyone on board drowned. No one knew if the Germans had done it on purpose, or if it had been hit by a torpedo from a British submarine. Alenka had a great lump in her throat as she laid out her photographs for printing. That young woman in the fur coat, weeping and trying to comfort her elderly father? Dead. That little boy, staring out so defiantly? Dead. That old woman, frightened and humiliated, huddling a shawl over her nightgown? Dead.

All dead.

As the summer passed, Alenka had to write the story of many atrocities. It was as if Müller was determined to punish the Cretans for the losses the Axis forces were suffering on every front. Many nights, Alenka did not get home till very late. Her mother would be waiting up for her, a pot of soup keeping warm by the hearth, a hot-water bottle tucked into her bed. Alenka would eat, creep under her blankets, and listen to the radio Jack had made. As Alenka listened, she scribbled notes, then sewed a message to Jack, burning her notes in her candle. At dawn the next day, she would leave her *sindoni* hanging out her bedroom window as if to air.

One evening in mid-September, Alenka received a message from Jack sewn in Morse code. It said simply, "throne room midnight." Excitement thrilled through her. At the appointed hour, she climbed out her bedroom window and hurried down the road to the ruins of the old palace. The throne room was full of people. Small lanterns illuminated the blood-red walls with their frescoes of griffins and lilies. Cries of greeting and welcome, exuberant embraces, kisses on cheeks. A buzz of excitement. "What news?" everyone kept asking. Alenka felt proud to see their little newspaper being passed from hand to hand.

She rushed to greet her friends, kissing and embracing Phyllia and Micky, and giving Jack a quick glad hug. Then she saw that Teddy was there too and greeted him just as warmly. He did not get down to Heraklion very often. Teddy slid his hand around her waist, kissing her cheek and whispering in her ear. She stepped away, shaking her head at him. "Teddy," she warned. "I don't want to have to slap you again."

"But I haven't seen you for so long! I was hoping absence had made the heart grow fonder."

"Have you been absent? I'm sorry! I've been too busy to notice."

Teddy pretended her words had pierced his heart like an arrow.

Jack was watching them, his face unreadable.

Micky clapped his hands. "I have news! Allied troops have entered Germany!"

Everyone cheered and embraced each other.

"It looks more and more likely that the war will soon be over," Micky said. "Romania has surrendered, which means the Huns have lost control of their oilfields. One of Hitler's main reasons for invading Greece was to safeguard those oilfields. Surely, now, there is no reason to keep troops here, when they could be fighting to defend the fatherland?"

"Let's drive the cuckolds out now!" someone shouted.

"They are still too strong," Micky said. "There is one German for every five of us, and their fire power is far superior. In the past few months, we've seen brutal reprisals for even small acts of defiance. I was at a meeting with the British liaison officers a few days ago, and they've had orders from Cairo to desist from all acts of sabotage and sedition. It's our job now to try and keep order."

"Why do we have to do what they say?"

"It's our homeland, we can defend it if we wish."

"Bloody British, think they rule the world."

Micky waited till the catcalls had died away, then said, "I think they're right. If we lie low for a while, the Huns might leave of their own accord. We don't want them doing any more harm. What we need to do now is start thinking about what needs to be done once they are gone and we have peace once more."

"Peace," Phyllia whispered, her dark eyes shining. "Just think of it! What shall we do, Alenka?"

She shook her head, unable to imagine a world at peace again.

III

Alenka went home in a happy glow. As she came up the hill from the ruins, she saw a blaze of light from her front door and heard shouting. Her stomach lurched. She began to run.

Her home was full of Germans. They were emptying drawers and cupboards, smashing bottles of wine and oil, slashing open sacks of flour, disemboweling mattresses. Hesper crouched on the floor, clutching her cross and praying. Axel watched with a scowl. With him was the head of the Secret Field Police in Crete, Ferdinand Friedensbacher. He looked bored.

"I tell you, she's part of the resistance," Axel said.

"What proof have you got?"

Axel made a restless movement. "She goes out late, after curfew."

Friedensbacher raked Alenka with a cold glance. "Perhaps she has a lover?"

"She does, I tell you! A British officer!"

"Indeed? Where does she meet this lover of hers?"

"I don't know! I have tried following her, but she always gives me the slip."

"That does not bode well for your work with us," Friedensbacher replied.

"She goes to a nightclub in Heraklion!"

"There is no law against dancing."

"She's not dancing! She's carrying messages for the resistance."

"We raided the nightclub and found nothing. And now we raid her house and still find nothing. Much as I would like to break the resistance ring in Heraklion, I sadly need some evidence before I can arrest her and question her."

Alenka felt faint and giddy. She clung to the doorframe.

"Look in her sewing bag," Axel said.

Friedensbacher jerked his head. One of the soldiers came toward Alenka, jerked her bag off her shoulder, and emptied it on to the floor. Her *sindoni* tumbled out, along with her embroidery hoop, scissors, pincushion, thimble, needles in little paper packets, and a shower of brightly colored bobbins.

She could hardly breathe. Only a few minutes ago, her reel of crimson thread had hidden a spool of photographic film. She had given it into Jack's care just before she came home.

Axel charged forward, grabbing her bedspread and shaking it out impatiently. Alenka saw her dancing figures ripple. She knew the secret code so well now, she could read it at a glance. *US troops reach Siegfried line. Le Havre liberated. 12,000 Germans captured.*

Beneath the line of chain dancers was a border of black swastikas and double-headed eagles, designed to deflect attention from the row of dots and dashes below. She wondered if the secret field police knew their Morse code. She braced herself for discovery.

.Friedensbacher glanced at the bedspread. "There is no law against sewing either. Indeed, she looks like a good dutiful hausfrau."

Axel rummaged through the rest of her bag, slashed open her pincushion with her scissors. Nothing. He threw them down in a rage.

Alenka began to breathe again. Friedensbacher bowed to her, and then to Hesper. "My apologies, Frau Klothakis, fräulein."

He was turning to go when one of the soldiers called out sharply from Alenka's bedroom. "Herr Feldpolizei-Sekretär!"

"*Ja?*"

The soldier came out carrying the old Bible. He opened its worn leather cover and showed Friedensbacher the homemade radio hidden within. He exclaimed in surprise and cast Alenka a sharp look. "Very clever! Look, it's made with old wire and razor blades, and a lead pencil. I'm surprised she knew how. Very well. Arrest her."

Axel laughed and shot Alenka a look of gleeful triumph. She felt as if she had been kicked in the stomach. The soldier grasped her arm and jerked her forward.

"It's mine."

For a moment Alenka did not realize who had spoken.

Hesper stepped forward. She clutched Yia-Yia's black hand-knotted cross. "It's mine," she said again, her voice husky with disuse. "I made it. She knows nothing."

For a moment no one knew what to do.

"She's lying," Axel shouted. "It's not hers. It's Alenka's."

"I was a girl guide. We were taught how to make a radio. How would my daughter know how to make one?"

Alenka had not heard her mother say so much for many years. She met her mother's eyes in despair. Hesper smiled, reaching out and pressing the cross into her hands. She turned to Friedensbacher and offered him both her wrists. In moments, she was handcuffed and taken away.

As soon as the soldiers were gone, Alenka darted forward, seized her dressmaking scissors, and plunged them down toward her brother's heart. Axel managed to jerk back in time, but the sharp point of the scissors tore his shirt and drew blood. She stabbed at him again. He tried to seize the scissors from her, but she was gouging at him in a frenzy. He hurled her away, but she was on her feet in seconds and hurtling toward him, scissors raised. He scrambled backward.

"I will kill you!" she panted. "Traitor! Murderer!"

He punched out, but she ducked, and he missed. She plunged her scissors into his arm. He screamed and scrambled away, and she tried to stab him again. He kicked her, and she fell to the floor. Both scrambled up, but Alenka still had her scissors in her hand, raised high and ready to strike. Axel stared at her. "I hate you!" he shouted.

Then he turned and ran. Moments later, she heard his motorcycle roaring away.

Alenka stood, panting, sobbing. Her fingers were clenched on the scissors' handles. The blade was red and sticky with blood. She let them fall.

Her mother would be taken to the Agia Prison. Alenka had heard rumors of what happened there. Torture, humiliation, starvation. She did not know what to do. Her first impulse was to chase after them. But it was very late, and the prison was a long way away. Too far to walk. There would be hundreds of checkpoints. She needed to make a plan.

Alenka bent and picked up her bedspread. She threaded a needle. Her hands were shaking so much, it was hard to get the thread through the tiny eye. She sewed a message in red thread. She hung the quilt from her bedroom shutter, then closed and locked the window. Systematically, she went around the house, barricading every door and window. She was so afraid Axel would come back.

She tidied the house, washed the floor, smoothed her mother's pillows and blanket so all would be neat and comfortable for her mama when she came back. Still, she could not rest. She climbed the steps to her brother's room. She searched through it methodically. She found a tin hidden under a floorboard. It held a pistol, bullets, a pair of binoculars, Nazi badges and buttons, a pile of much-handled Nazi cigarette cards, and an ancient ivory figurine of a man with a bull's head. Alenka sat on her heels for a long while, examining the golden horns and sword, the delicate carving of the clew of thread reddened with ocher. She realized the bull's head was a mask and carefully lifted it. Underneath was a man's face.

The figurine was very valuable, she knew. Her brother must have found it in the ruins of the Palace of Knossos and stolen it. He was no better than those Nazis who had come and plundered the ruins, seizing whatever they liked and carrying it away from its rightful home.

She had to take the figurine back. She would hide it in the ruins, and one day someone would find it again, and it would be acknowledged as one of the great treasures of the Palace of Knossos. It would be saved, studied, and displayed in a museum for everyone to see with eyes of wonder.

Alenka wrapped it carefully and put it in her bag. Then she loaded the pistol and put it in her pocket. She incinerated the cards and badges and buttons till nothing was left but ashes and unrecognizable twists of metal. Then she crept out the front door, locked it behind her, and went as quietly as she could to the ruined palace, clambering over the broken walls till she reached the maze of small crypts behind the shrine, where many treasures had been found. Alenka carefully hid the minotaur statue within a small gap at the foot of the wall, concealing it with a broken wedge of rock.

It took her all day to get to the prison. A high wall topped with barbed wire, a glimpse of some kind of watchtower. She went to the gate. She pleaded with the guards, she bribed them, she offered them her body. None of it did any good. They had heard it all before.

Alenka did not know what to do. She stood outside, gazing up at the immense walls, hoping for a glimpse of her mother. Nothing.

There were many other women there, waiting outside the prison walls just like her. One told her that Müller had been recalled to Berlin. He was determined to make Crete suffer as much as possible in the days he had left.

"Once he has gone, perhaps then we can free our loved ones," the woman told her.

It made a strange kind of sense. She had not been able to understand why Axel had betrayed her now, after so long. She had done nothing, she had thought. Nothing new. But perhaps he had heard Müller was leaving. She remembered how distressed her brother had been when General Ringel had been recalled. He had bitten her. Perhaps he felt betrayed and abandoned. Perhaps he simply wanted revenge.

She had a lot of time to ponder the mystery of her brother, waiting outside the prison. Like the other women, she camped there, hoping against hope that she could free her mother. Everyone shared what little food they had, along with terrible stories of cruelty and injustice. Fires were lit in old petrol drums, and Alenka slept on the ground wrapped in her winter coat.

Three days later, Alenka was startled awake by the sound of screaming punctuated by a dull rhythmic *thwack* of an ax. Terrified, she ran to the gate, begging to be told what was happening.

"They're executing prisoners," the guard said. He seemed a little sorry.

"But who? How?" There had been no gunshots.

"They're chopping off their heads." He shrugged a little at the horror on her face. "Saving on ammunition?"

It was too horrible to be real. Alenka could only hope it was a trick, a lie, a cruel joke. But they started bringing out bodies to bury in a field. Then she could only pray it was someone else's mama or papa, someone else's sister or brother or lover or child. A list of the names of the executed prisoners was posted outside the gate. Sixty people, chosen at random, to have their heads hacked off as General Müller's last memorial.

Hesper Klothakis was one of those beheaded.

Alenka went that night to the mass grave in the field. She knelt and dug her hands into the freshly turned clay. She filled Axel's old tin with the grave dirt and took it home.

She had a vendetta of her own to enact.

Alenka found her brother's comb. It had a few strands of pale hair caught in its teeth. She pierced her finger with a pin, then rubbed her brother's hair between her fingertips till it was darkened with her blood. She unknotted the cord of her grandmother's cross, cut a length of black yarn, and knotted it together with her brother's hair. With each knot she tied, she chanted a curse her *yia-yia* had taught her long ago:

I will bind my enemy

In blood and in ashes

Down with the shades of the dead.

I bind your hands, your tongue,

your mind, your soul,

I bind you to hell.

Seven knots, the final one tying the cord into a circlet. She buried it with her mother's grave dirt in the shadow of her grandmother's tombstone.

IV

1 October–8 December 1944

The Germans began withdrawing in early October. The Kriegsmarine and the Luftwaffe took off soldiers in their thousands every day. After the first week, the Heraklion airport was bombed by American B-24s, making Teddy cheer in jubilation. It had been hard to watch the retreat and do nothing. He ached to strike another blow, to take some kind of revenge, but the orders from Cairo were clear. The people of Crete had suffered enough. It was time to start rebuilding.

Müller had flown out in the last week of September. The resistance discovered the time of his flight and radioed the details to Cairo, requesting the deployment of long-range fighters to shoot him down. The dispatch was marked *XXXX*, which meant a message of the highest priority.

"Keep Calm. Use Less *X*'s," was the only response. Müller landed safely in Athens and was flown to the eastern front to fight against the advancing Red Army. "May his bones be blackened by the tars of hell," the old men of Crete said.

Cairo did send Spitfires, though, to strafe the long lines of German troops retreating along the coast road, and so many Junkers were shot down from the sky that the garrison soldiers begged for another way to get off the island.

"Like Icarus," Jack said. "They flew too close to the sun and now they are paying the price."

The Villa Ariadne was abandoned, and Tom Dunbabin at once took it over as the new headquarters of the British Military Mission. "Much more comfortable than a cave!" Teddy said. The place was a mess, but many of the villagers gladly came to help clean and repair it.

Alenka did not come.

"She's still grieving for her mother," Jack said.

Teddy frowned. He hated it when Jack acted like he was the one who had the right to know what was going on in Alenka's life. It was infuriating. Just because he'd seen more of her during the last few months. Teddy was sure there was nothing more between them. He had never seen Jack kiss her or touch her, had never seen them exchange the warm intimate glances of lovers. Alenka seemed to act toward Jack in the same way she acted toward everyone. Friendly enough, but not allowing any kind of flirtation or familiarity.

Alenka had told Teddy once that wartime was not the time for kissing. Well, the war was almost over, wasn't it?

She would have to let him kiss her then.

On October 11, the German garrison withdrew from Heraklion. The infantry marched out the Chania Gate first, followed by lorries and tanks. The SOE agents dressed themselves in their British uniforms and went openly into the town for the first time, saluting the departing garrison ironically. Smithy was there, having flown in from Cairo, along with Jack, Teddy, and as many of the other agents as they could gather together.

As the last German tank rumbled out of the gate and down the road, the town erupted into wild celebrations. People sang, danced, drank, and shot their pistols in the air. Greek flags were waved from every window and rooftop, and the cathedral bells rang. Known collaborators were dragged out and beaten, their homes looted. Quite a few women had their heads shaved.

Teddy got thoroughly drunk. "Where's Alenka?" he kept asking. "She should be here. We fought for her. Germans gone now. Should be here celebrating with us." He drank down another half bottle of *tsikoudia* and announced, "Gonna go get her."

Jack tried to stop him, but Teddy swung a wild punch and then lurched out into the night. He liberated a motorcycle from its owner, and zoomed up the hill to Knossos, crashing it into the wall of the villa. He left it there, and staggered up the laneway, calling, "Alenka, Alenka. Where are you?" He banged on her door.

After a while, he heard her voice. "Go away, Teddy. Leave me alone."

"Won't go 'way. Come celebrate with me. C'mon, Alenka, open up."

"Please, Teddy, just leave me alone."

"Won't. You owe me a kiss. Open the door, Alenka!" He hammered his fist on it. "Open up! Give me my kiss. You owe me!"

Suddenly a window above his head opened, and he was drenched in a deluge of icy water. "I owe you nothing!" she cried. "Go away! Leave me alone!"

At that moment, a jeep roared up the laneway, filled with tipsy SOE agents. Teddy, dripping wet, was illuminated by the jeep's headlights. They all roared with laughter, gathered him up, and drove him off to bed at the villa.

For days after, he was teased relentlessly. "Need another bath, Teddy? Better go find some poor girl to kiss."

It was humiliating.

––––––––––

Only five thousand Germans were left on the island. They had retreated to Chania and its strategic installations at Suda Bay and Maleme Airport. These facilities had been the first to fall to German forces three-and-a-half years ago and were now the last to be defended.

Kapitulation! became the new slogan for the resistance. Boys and girls were recruited to paint the letter *K* on sentry boxes and barrack walls, and the letter was cut into the windscreens of German vehicles with acid.

Posters were printed with the word in capital letters above drawings of defiant fists and pasted to telegraph poles. Crowds gathered outside the Chania compound at night, chanting "Capitulate! Capitulate!"

Life was still very hard on Crete. The retreating Germans had stolen and destroyed so much the country was in ruins. Tom Dunbabin paid a bribe of eighty gold sovereigns to one German officer so he would not blow up the long stone breakwater that protected Heraklion harbor. The officer had then mockingly ordered every bridge on their way to Chania to be blown to smithereens.

The UN Relief and Rehabilitation Administration took up residence at the villa, and Teddy, Jack, and the other agents were kept busy helping deliver food, clothing, and medicine, and rebuilding homes and shops.

In late October Paddy arrived by boat from Cairo, laden with British gold sovereigns, the only currency trusted in a country in which everyone ironically used the German-issued paper drachmas to light their cigarettes. He came at once to Heraklion, and a grand reunion took place at the basement bar at the Knossos Hotel, near the lions' fountain. He was thin and pale, having spent several months in hospital with rheumatic fever after the mad abduction of General Kreipe. "Too many cold nights in damp caves," he said in explanation. "They had to come and pin my medal onto my pajamas."

"What happened to the general?" Teddy asked.

"Oh, he was interrogated in Cairo. He said the German garrison in Crete would fight to the last cartridge to hold the island. I do hope he's wrong. The Germans have fled Athens, and the swastika no longer flies above the Acropolis. Why is Crete still occupied?"

"The German garrison are afraid," Tom Dunbabin said. "They think the Cretans would gladly slit their throats in return for all the blood they have split here. And they have a point. Crete may not have invented the vendetta, but they certainly have brought it to a fine art."

"So what are the Germans hoping for?" Paddy asked.

Tom shrugged. "Maybe that the tide of the war will turn again? Or that they can surrender to a British invasion force? I don't know. The buggers are certainly not trying to make it up with the Cretans. They've sowed the whole place with landmines. The hospitals are full of injured locals who were simply trying to till their fields or repair their walls. It's criminal!"

"What can I do to help?" Paddy asked.

"Keep an eye on the German garrison in Chania for me? I've my hands full here in Heraklion. And I'm afraid they're not beat yet. It wouldn't surprise me if they try for one last hurrah."

So Paddy went back to his hideout at the little village of Vaphé in the foothills of the White Mountains, taking a haversack of sovereigns to help his friends in the local resistance. Teddy went with him. He was restless and bored, hoping for some action. He had still not seen Alenka, and the villa was filled with do-gooders and top brass. Again, he felt as if the war had passed him by, and all the glory was being won elsewhere. Soon, he would be demobbed and sent home, back to his father's farm, to spend the rest of his days shearing sheep. The thought made him sick.

One chilly evening, when the men were weary after their day's labor and bleary-eyed after their first bottle of *tsikoudia*, a sudden cry of alarm rang out. "Germans! Quick, they are coming!"

The rat-a-tat-tat of machine gunfire. Teddy leaped up, seized his rifle, and raced outside. Tanks roared up the narrow, winding road toward the village, followed by about four hundred soldiers in lorries, rifles at the ready. Motorcycle troopers zoomed alongside, goggles over their eyes, many with sidecars.

Men ran from every home, carrying antiquated guns and long daggers. Women hurried away toward the soaring crags behind, children in their arms or clutching at their skirts. Someone began to ring the church bell in alarm.

Paddy had been issuing quick, clear orders. The SOE kept its weapons and funds in the old schoolhouse, which was the most probable target of the attack. A long chain of young women and children passed the vital stores up the hill to caves in the cliffs, including their precious radio, while the men kept up a hail of bullets at the advancing Germans.

A house was blown to smithereens. This only angered the men of Vaphé. One leaped on to the back of the tank, raised the hatch, and dropped a grenade inside. He barely jumped free in time. The German soldiers blazed away at him, but he ran, swift and low as a hare, zigzagging across the field, and into the forest.

"Retreat!" Paddy cried. "Teddy, grab the guineas!"

He caught up his precious satchel of papers and raced toward the cliffs, firing back at the Germans as he ran. Teddy hefted the haversack of British sovereigns onto his shoulder. It weighed a ton. He wondered how much gold was in it. Enough to set him up for life, he thought. He could go back to Cairo, buy a palace, live the high life.

He glanced about. By the blaze of the burning house, he could see German tanks rolling into the village square, giving cover to the soldiers who ran behind, machine guns at the ready. The Greeks were retreating fast, shooting as they went. If Teddy was quick, perhaps no one would see him creeping the other way, toward the road that wound up into the mountains, toward the south coast.

Keeping his head low and his shoulders hunched, he crept along the wall of the schoolhouse. The weight of the haversack was making his shoulder ache. He didn't much like the idea of having to carry it all the way over the mountains.

The villagers had reached the shelter of the cliffs and were taking pot shots with their pistols and rifles. Bullets ricocheted from the metal sides of the tanks, finding many an unintended mark. In the darkness and confusion, the Germans did not see him.

A young man raced up on a motorcycle with an empty sidecar. He did not wear goggles or a helmet like the other motorcyclists. He was big and blond, with muscular shoulders and a thick neck. Something about him nudged Teddy's memory. The color of his hair, so pale as to be almost white.

The young blond man parked his bike, then—gun in hand—ran into one of the biggest houses in the village. Teddy looked at the motorcycle consideringly. It would make his escape much easier. He began to creep toward it. Then the blond man ran out, his arms full of loot. He slung it into the empty sidecar, then went into the house next door.

Teddy ran forward, jumped onto the motorcycle, and kick-started it. He was just accelerating when the blond man raced out, shouting in rage. He caught Teddy by the back of his jacket and hurled him off the bike. Teddy hit the ground hard. Winded, he gasped for breath. He was hauled up and punched hard in the stomach. He fell again. The young man grabbed the haversack.

"*Po-po-po*, what do we have here?" he exclaimed in Greek.

Teddy staggered up, one hand to his stomach. Sudden recognition blinded him. His attacker was Alenka's brother.

Axel had opened the haversack and found the stacks of sovereigns, all rolled in Bank of England paper. He grinned. "Thanks, mate," he said in a broad parody of Teddy's Australian accent. "This will get me to Berlin!" He casually punched Teddy to the ground again, flung the haversack into his sidecar, and mounted the motorcycle, revving the engine. Seconds later he was off, speeding across the fields to the road.

For a moment Teddy could only watch him go, his hands clasped over his aching stomach. Then he scrambled up and ran after him. Another motorcyclist had paused and turned to see what was happening. Teddy shot him and seized his bike. In moments, he was racing after Axel.

The road wound down the rolling foothills, through stony fields and olive groves toward the sea. Teddy expected Axel to turn left, toward the German garrison at Chania, but instead, he swerved to the east, heading along the winding coast road toward Heraklion. Teddy followed him. On the wider road, their speed increased. His world narrowed down to the roar of the engine, the cold blast of the wind, the skid of his wheels on the corners, the crouched figure racing ahead.

"Just you wait, I'll get you!" Teddy said through his gritted teeth. "And my gold!"

V

Alenka sat by the fire, her head resting wearily on her hand. Grief was a wave of black water, swamping her. She could not forget that her mother had died trying to save her. It was all Alenka's fault. If she had not kept the radio hidden in her room, if she had not made her own brother hate her and want revenge on her, if she had spoken up in time, confessed her crime, Hesper would still be alive.

A knock on her door. Alenka raised her eyes but did not stir.

"A-A-Alenka?"

It was Jack again. He came by most evenings, with some kind of little gift for her. A book, a posy of flowers, a warm slice of honey cake wrapped in a cloth. She never opened the door to him. She wished she had never met him, never joined the resistance, never put her mother's life at risk.

"Is there anything I c-c-can do for you? Do you n-n-need anything?"

She did not answer.

"I've got something for you. I-I-I-I . . ." Jack was stammering badly. He had not done that for a while. He managed to force the words out. "I will leave it here for you. If you n-n-need me, hang your quilt out your back window. I will see it from the villa. I-I-I . . . I'd do anything to help, Alenka, I'm so very . . . so very sorry."

She heard his footsteps leaving. She went back to staring at the fire.

Some time later, Alenka had to rouse herself to get some more wood. She got up, went to the door, brought in an armful of split logs, and the little gift Jack had left for her on the step. She fed the fire and sat, turning it in her hands.

It was her copy of Sappho's poems that she had lent to him so long ago. A feather marked a page. She opened it, and read the words that had been faintly underlined in pencil:

> *Yea, my tongue is broken, and through and through me*
> *'neath the flesh impalpable fire runs tingling;*
> *nothing see mine eyes, and a noise of roaring*
> *waves in my ears . . . I falter, lost in the love trance.*

As she read the words, her own body responded in kind. Fire rushed through her veins, blood boomed in her ears, electricity sparked across her skin. *He loves me*, she thought. *He loves me!*

Alenka started to her feet, the book pressed to her heart. She looked about. Her quilt! She must hang it out her window, she must wave it like a flag.

The sound of a step on the cobblestones, a knock on her door. Gladly, Alenka flew to unlock it.

It was not Jack who stood in her doorway.

It was Axel.

She tried to slam the door in his face, but he shoved it open, sending her staggering. Alenka threw the book at him. As he ducked, she fled to her room, dragging her chest across her door. To her surprise, Axel did not try to break through but ran instead to the ladder and climbed up to his room. He was looking for his tin of treasures. Alenka threw up her window and tossed her quilt over the windowsill as a signal to Jack. Then, with shaking hands, she found the loaded pistol, shoved back the chest from her door, and went through it like a rocket. He hurtled down the ladder. "Where's my minotaur?" he roared.

She fired at him. Her aim was wild. He flinched, then leaped forward once again. In seconds, he had her by the throat, the point of his knife pressed up under her chin.

"Drop it!"

She struggled to bring the pistol up, to shoot him, but he was too strong. He easily wrenched the pistol from her hand. "Where's my minotaur?"

"I took it back to the ruins."

"Why?"

"It's not yours. It's Crete's."

He laughed. "Do you know how much it's worth?"

"It's priceless."

"It's my ticket out of here. I will take it to the führer, and he will know I am a good and loyal Nazi."

"You idiot," she said furiously. "How can you be such a fool? The Germans have lost, your precious führer has lost. He will not care about some old statuette!"

He squeezed her throat mercilessly. "That's where you're wrong. The führer will strike back any day now, and he'll crush all those who tried to stand against him. And I want to be there to see it! Where's my minotaur?"

Alenka could not speak. She yanked at his arm with all her strength, but her senses were swimming, she could not breathe. She let herself go limp, sagging against him. He released the pressure, and she managed to gasp a breath. He repeated his question menacingly, moving the blade of the knife so it pressed against the artery throbbing in her neck.

"I hid it," she managed to say.

"Where?"

"I'd have to show you." He meant to kill her, she thought. One thrust of that knife, and she'd be dead. She had to delay him. When Jack saw her quilt hanging out her window, he would come at once, he would save her.

She heard the roar of a motorcycle. Axel's head jerked around. "Take me there. Don't try any tricks or I'll kill you." He began to push her out the door.

"Go ahead! If you kill me, you'll never find your minotaur." She struggled, kicking a chair over with one foot, knocking a photo off the wall so it fell with a crash of broken glass.

He bent one arm up behind her back, so she cried out in pain. "I'll break it if you don't come quietly."

She subsided, knowing the signs of struggle would alert Jack that she was in trouble. But how would he know where to go?

She put up her free hand and pushed the knife away from her throat with all her strength. The keen edge sliced deep into the soft skin of her palm. The pain made her gasp, tears springing to her eyes. Axel looked at her questioningly.

"Get your knife away from my throat, it frightens me! What if you stumbled?"

"Then you'd be dead," he jeered.

"And you'd never find the figurine."

He grunted and lowered the knife. "Don't make a sound as we go through the village." He bent and picked up a haversack that he had dropped by the door, throwing it over his shoulder.

Alenka kept quiet as instructed. It was a dark, cold, wintry night, and every house was dark and shuttered. She squeezed her hand shut, then opened it, then squeezed it again. Blood dripped down her cold fingers. She imagined it falling behind her, leaving a trail of crimson drops. When they came to the last house in the village, she pressed her hand against the wall, leaving a bloody handprint. As Axel pushed her through the gap in the fence, she brushed her sore palm against the wood.

Stumbling through the ruins, Alenka squeezed her hand harder and harder. The blood flow was easing, her palm was sticky. She dug her nails into the wound. The sounds of the motorcycle had died away. All was quiet and still. She felt very cold and very alone.

"Which way?" Axel asked.

Alenka pointed toward the West Porch. That way led past three deep circular pits. Perhaps she could shove Axel into one as they passed.

But her brother knew the palace as well as she did. As they passed the yawning pits, he kept well away from the lip. She would have to try to push him off one of the many broken walls within the main part of the palace.

Up the Corridor of the Procession. The waning moon glinted between the clouds, showing the ghostly shapes of musicians and priest-esses painted upon the walls. Alenka looked behind her desperately, but there was no sign of movement, no one racing to help her. She would have to save herself.

She waited till they had crossed the vast expanse of the Central Court, then jerked free of her brother's grasp and sped across to one of the dark apertures that led to the maze of low dark rooms behind the shrine, pressing her hand to her breast to try to stop the blood from dripping and leaving a trail.

In seconds, she was hidden in shadows.

VI

Teddy found Alenka's door ajar, the room in chaos, a trail of blood leading down the laneway.

He followed it, keeping his flashlight low so it would not flash a
warning. Every now and again the trail disappeared, and he would need
to cast around before he found it again. He followed it along the narrow
stone road, and into the palace.

The drops of blood were now wild and widely spaced as if she had been
running. He followed them through dark narrow crypts. Ahead he heard
footsteps and drew his gun. The *click* as he cocked it seemed very loud.
He came to a flight of steps and went down it cautiously. Suddenly, Axel
charged him from below, driving his shoulder into his gut, winding him.
They struggled on the steps, then Teddy heaved him over the edge. Axel
fell. Teddy flashed his flashlight down and saw the boy had tumbled several
stories and now lay spreadeagled on his face at the bottom of a kind of pit.

He raced down the steps. "Alenka!"

"Teddy?"

He flashed his torch about and saw he was in the blood-red throne
room. His light wavered over the white throne with its strange sinuous
lines, the paintings of eagle-headed beasts and delicate flowers. At the
far end was a doorway. He ran through and found Alenka crouched in

the corner of a small, dark room. She said his name in a sob and then cast herself into his arms. He held her close. The feel of her body against him aroused him painfully. He kissed her.

A rush of sound, a heavy weight hurling against him. Teddy dropped his torch. The light spun. He saw Axel's face, mouth stretched in a snarl, a flash of steel in his hand. He ducked and punched hard. His fists connected with ribs, which cracked satisfyingly. He punched again. The boy fell hard. His knife flew from his hand and skittered across the floor. Alenka rolled over and kicked it toward him. "Teddy!"

Teddy bent and caught the hilt, driving the blade deep into Axel's body. Again and again, he stabbed, till the boy lay still. Teddy kicked him, then lifted Axel's head to check he was dead. Blood dribbled from the corner of his mouth, staining his shirt. Teddy dropped the knife. His hand was black with blood.

Alenka sat up. Her dress was crumpled about her thighs, her black hair tumbled down her back. Teddy stood and gazed at her, then knelt before her. "It's done," he said. He kissed her. A kind of shudder went through her. She turned her face away. He pushed her down, kissing her, pressing her beneath him. "Teddy, no," she protested, trying to hold him off. He did not listen. Her shudder, her whimper, all were oil to his flame. He undid his belt, dragged up her dress, and drove inside her, again and again and again. The relief was exquisite. For a few moments, the world was lost to him. His ears roared. Then he was spent. He lifted himself up, smoothing one hand over her long bare thigh, curling a tendril of hair about his fingers.

Alenka lay still, one arm flung over her face.

"Well, that was a long time coming," Teddy said, doing himself up again.

Alenka did not speak.

Teddy got up and went across to where the corpse of her brother lay in a slick of blood. He searched him quickly, pocketing a few items, then picked up the haversack Axel had been carrying, hoisting it onto his shoulder. "I'd better get rid of him. I mean, he was a traitor and all, but we don't want any awkward questions." He bent and tried to lift him. "He's bloody heavy. Can you give me a hand?"

Still, she did not move. He frowned and looked at her. Her breast was rising and falling raggedly, he could hear the shallow gasp of her breath.

"I had to kill him," he said reasonably. "Otherwise, he would have killed me. You saw him come at me with the knife. He would have done for me, then finished you off too. I saved your life."

Teddy came to lift her up, but she scrabbled away from him. "Don't touch me!"

For a moment, he stood without moving, regarding her narrowly. Then he bent, picked up the knife, and carefully wiped it clean on her dress, blade first, then hilt. He forced her fingers open and laid the hilt upon her bloodied palm, closing her fist upon it. She struggled against him, but he would not let her cast the knife away.

"I'll get rid of him. Don't tell anyone what has happened here, or I'll tell them it was you. I'll tell the world you tricked and seduced me, so I'd kill your brother for you, and then, when I wouldn't do it, you killed him yourself."

She stared up at him with great, dark eyes.

He bent and whispered in her ear. "I warn you, if you tell a soul, I'll kill you."

Then he picked up his torch, thrust it through his belt, and began to drag the dead boy away. He left Alenka alone in the darkness, the knife still gripped in her hand.

———————

Jack found her in the pale light of the dawn, crouched against the wall of the inner sanctuary.

The bloody knife, the long rust-red smears on the floor where a body had been dragged, her torn dress and haunted black eyes told him a terrible story.

The knife, the stain of blood, her torn dress, and haunted black eyes told him a terrible story.

Jack took off his coat and knelt beside her, wrapping her in its warmth. "I'm here," he whispered. "I'm here."

VII

Alenka felt as if she had been turned to stone. She lay in her bed, unmoving, hunched around herself. Her thoughts grinding around and around in a deep ceaseless groove. *It is all my fault. If only I hadn't . . .* So many things she had done wrong. So many stupid, stupid mistakes. She had brought it all on herself.

Jack had tried to care for her as much as he could. Alenka did not want him. Angrily, she had told him to go away. To leave her alone.

He did as she asked. Then she wept and wept because he had left her.

The day dragged past. She had managed to wash herself and bind up her hand, but after that she was utterly spent.

The sun was sinking into bloody smears of clouds above the dark hills when Jack came back. She heard him knock on the floor, but she did not respond. After a while, she heard him sit down on the step.

"A-A-Alenka . . ." he said in a low voice. "P-p-please . . ."

She had not heard him stutter so badly for a very long time.

Alenka crept a little closer. She sat on the floor, leaning her face against the wood of the door.

He must have heard her, for he went on. "A-A-Alenka . . . I n-need to tell you . . . Teddy is dead."

She jerked. Could not speak.

"He . . . he w-went off the edge of the road . . . m-must've been going too fast . . . tried to correct himself . . . you . . . you . . . you can see the skid marks.' Jack took a deep shaky breath. "I . . . I'm sorry. There was no sign of Axel. Teddy must've . . . he must've d-d-d . . . got rid of him . . . somewhere else."

There were so many cracks and crevices and caves in the mountains. Axel could have been dumped in any of them. Alenka wondered dully if she would ever find her brother's body. Ever be able to bury him. He was still her brother. She remembered the little boy he had been. Naughty and cheeky and full of curiosity. When did he begin to go wrong? What could she have done to save him?

"It was the w-w-war," Jack said. "War does terrible things to people's souls."

Yes, she thought.

"He was . . . he was n-not a bad kid, I swear," Jack added. "A bit wild. He h-hated being told what to do, hated anyone trying to curb him. Maybe I should've . . . I don't know. I should've done something. I never thought . . . I'm so, so sorry.'

Alenka realized Jack was talking about Teddy.

"They . . . they're bringing up his body. He had a haversack full of loot . . . icons and candlesticks and stuff . . . it m-might've unbalanced him . . ."

The holy relics of Crete would not wish to leave their home, she thought. The great mountains of Crete would guard their own.

"Teddy . . . Teddy hated the m-m-mountains," Jack said in a rush. "It was . . . it was . . . it was like he knew what was g-g-going to happen."

His voice broke. He stammered another apology. Jack was grieving the death of his oldest friend, she suddenly understood. Not the man he was, but the man he should have been. Just like she was weeping for her brother.

Alenka swallowed, moistened her dry lips, tried to speak. The words came with great difficulty, as if her tongue was broken. "I'm sorry too . . . sorry you've lost your friend . . . you are right . . . war makes so many into monsters . . ."

But not you, she thought.

She could hear Jack's ragged breathing, as he tried to gain control of his tears. "I'm terribly sorry," he whispered at last.

She could hear Jack's ragged breathing, as he tried to gain control of his tears. "I'm terribly sorry," he whispered at last. "I wish . . . I wish I could have stopped him. Can . . . can I do anything? To help?"

Alenka shook her head. No-one could help her.

After a while, Jack got up slowly. "If you need me . . ." His voice trailed away. He waited a long moment, then Alenka heard his footsteps fade away. She put her face in her hands.

An hour or so later Jack came back, knocked on the door, and put something on her step. He did not try to speak to her again. When Alenka eased the door open a crack she found a bundle of firewood and an earthernware pot of chicken and lemon soup wrapped in a warm shawl.

She had thought she had cried herself dry. She was wrong.

Every day, Jack put a little gift for her on her step. A little bunch of rosemary tied with a ribbon. A jar of honeycomb. A loaf of freshly baked bread. Something different every day.

On Christmas Eve, he left her childhood copy of *The Secret Garden*. A feather marked the passage when Colin cried, "I shall get well! I shall get well! Mary! Dickon! I shall get well! And I shall live forever and ever and ever!"

Alenka began to weep, deep guttural sobs that shook her thin frame. Afterward, she sat by the fire and read her favorite book from beginning to end for the first time in years. She cried many times in the reading of it.

That night, as dusk was falling, Jack brought a chair and sat in the street outside her window. He played the Chaconne on his lyra. As the haunting music lilted through the air, many people came to listen, candles and lanterns in their hands.

Alenka stood by her window, listening. Tears crept down her face, and she found it hard to breathe. When the last heartbreaking note had died away, she opened her shutter just a crack, so that she could look out at him. Their eyes met. He stood and took a few steps toward her.

"Happy birthday, Benedictus," she said. Her voice was low and husky from disuse.

"Alenka . . ."

She shook her head and closed the shutter.

He came closer, one hand on the windowsill, speaking softly so no one else could hear him. "Alenka, I'm so s-s-sorry. Please forgive m-me."

She was surprised. "Forgive you? Why?"

"I . . . I should've known . . . I should've stopped him."

"How could you know? How could anyone know" He had kept his true face hidden, she thought.

Jack said, stammering badly: "I-I-I w-w-would d-d-do anything to m-make it up to you, Alenka. A-a-a-anything."

"There is nothing you can do."

Jack sighed. When he spoke, the words came broken and difficult. "A-a-a long time ago, when I was a b-b-boy, I read this poem. It had this line that stuck in my memory. *Life's little lantern, between dark and dark.* Alenka, you are my l-l-lantern, my light in the dark. I told you, when I left Crete, that you had the b-b-brightest spirit I had ever known. I c-c-can not bear to see your . . . your light blown out. D-d-d . . . don't let him."

Alenka could not reply. After a while, she heard him walking away. She sank down onto the floor and bent her face down into her hands. Then she heard it. A few pure notes singing out into the frosty air. A phrase of notes repeating itself again and again. She recognized the melody. It was the music Jack had played on the grand lyra in Heraklion, the time he had saved her life. She did not remember its name. Except that he played in the key of benediction.

She stood, opened the shutter again, listened. This time, when his bow had stilled on the strings, she nodded at him. "Thank you," she mouthed and managed a little smile.

The crowd applauded him. Jack bowed in thanks, then kissed his fingers to her. It was a declaration, an avowal of love made before the whole village. She smiled again, more easily, then closed her shutters and went to bed.

Her lantern glowed in the darkness. Such a small light, yet such a comfort to her. She had been afraid of the dark since the night her brother had died. She lay in her bed, watching its golden dancing flame, waiting for her grief to grip her by the throat once more, her first Christmas without her mother. Instead, she slipped easily into sleep. She did not wake once.

The next day Jack brought her a little Christmas pudding, dense with fruit and brandy, wrapped in cheesecloth with a sprig of holly on top. It was hot and surprisingly delicious. It must have come straight from the kitchen of the villa, where Jack was living with the rest of the British Military Mission. She wondered how much longer he would be able to stay. Panic clutched her at the thought he would have to go.

Winter passed; the frost melted. Jack plaited her a red-and-white *martis* bracelet. Though Alenka still did not open the door to him, she sat on one side and he sat on the other, and they talked through the wood. Alenka told him stories of her *yia-yia* and he told her stories of his nana, and she smiled a little. The almond tree began to bud, then burst forth in fairy blossoms. The swallows returned from Africa. She passed him the *martis* bracelet through the window, and he hung it on the almond tree for her.

The spring equinox was her twenty-third birthday and a hard day for her. She did not get out of bed. Jack brought her a little cake, but she would not open her window to take it. He tried to cajole her, but she turned her face into her hot, damp pillow and would not answer. He had to go. He had work to do. But he came back in the evening and sat in the square under the blossoming almond tree and he played his lyra for her. Once again, all the villagers came to listen, carrying lanterns in their hands. It was Bach's birthday too, he told her, so he would play all his favorite Bach music for her. Alenka lay in the darkness, the haunting music weaving a web of enchantment about her, and wept till she had no more tears left within.

The fairy blossoms fell, and the living wood budded with fresh green buds. Leaves sprang out, carrying within them velvety-soft kernels of almonds. Every day Jack came for a while, sometimes only to hear her voice for a few moments, to know she was well. Alenka still would not come outside. She could not bear the thought of anyone seeing her. Such shame, such soul-corroding guilt.

One day he brought her a posy of wild dittany, just beginning to bud. She wondered if he knew, in Crete, young men plucked the heart-shaped leaves as tokens of love. He must have climbed high to gather it for her, he must have braved the dizzying heights. Alenka remembered how she had brought him a bunch of leaves when he had been dying. He had kissed her. She pressed one finger on her lips. It had shaken her to the core, that kiss. She should have known what it meant.

She made herself dittany tea and sat on her doorstep and raised her face to the sun.

That evening Jack brought his lyra, and serenaded her with Greek love songs:

> *What a burst of flame I have in my heart,*
> *As if you had cast a spell on me,*
> *My sweet Alenka,*
> *As if you had cast a spell on me . . .*

Alenka opened her shutters so she could hear more clearly. The listening villagers gave a welcoming cry at the sight of her. The fierce old woman who had helped Alenka on the feast day of Mary of the Myrtle called out to her, "Come out, my child, come out and join us." But Alenka shook her head and shrank back into the shadows.

Jack finished the last chords and rose to go. Alenka could not let him go without saying something. She leaned forward and held out her hand, softly calling his name. He came at once, taking her hand, looking up into her face. She had meant just to say a few words of thanks, but the expression on his face smote her to the heart.

Alenka bent and kissed him.

When at last they broke apart, both were breathing quickly, unsteadily.

"I'm sorry. I can't," Alenka said.

He nodded. One hand reached up and stroked her dark, loose hair away from her face.

"I-I . . . I will wait for you if you want me to," he said.

She drew back. Shook her head.

"Do you want me to go?"

Again, Alenka shook her head. "I'm sorry," she said again.

"I will wait till you tell me to go." He smiled at her very sweetly, and she could not help it, she had to bend and kiss him again.

The Great Fast began. Greeks were forbidden to eat anything with blood in its veins.

It was easier than it had ever been. Alenka seemed to have passed beyond hunger. Phyllia brought her pots of vegetable soup, Micky cut her wood and fed her chickens, and Jack brought her a different flower every day. Alenka cleaned her house again. Sometimes she opened her shutters so she could feel the faint warmth of the sun upon her face.

On April 30, Hitler committed suicide in his underground bunker in Berlin. It was announced to the world two days later. Alenka heard the running of feet in the street, the shouts of incredulity and gladness, the joyous peal of the church bell. She rose to her feet, went to the window, listened. *He's dead*, she thought in amazement. *The monster is dead.*

And I want to live . . . oh, how I want to live!

The following day was Holy Thursday. The anniversary of the Last Supper, the day of betrayal. All over Greece, people would be grieving, as they had done for thousands of years. Alenka watched through her shutters as the effigy on the cross was brought out from the church and paraded around the streets of Knossos. The priest walked behind it, chanting. Black-clad women fell to their knees and wept.

The church bells tolled mournfully all day on Easter Friday. At nine o'clock, a funeral procession walked slowly through the village, following the glowing *epitaphios*. All was quiet and somber, the candles casting strange shadows on the faces of the faithful. Alenka watched the little parade. *My mother should have been walking with them, a candle in her hand, my mother should have been praying with all her heart too.*

Hesper had not had a funeral procession. Alenka grieved as if it had been hers.

At midnight on Easter Saturday, the whole village walked to the church, carrying unlit candles. Jack came to her house. "Alenka," he said through the closed door, "will you n-not come out now? It is spring! The war is over. It's t-time."

She could not bring herself to open the door.

"Please, Alenka. I've stayed as long as I c-can. They . . . they will make me go home soon. I do not want to go without you. You know that."

Alenka did not answer.

"Then . . . then I will need to say g-g-goodbye." There was agony in his voice. "I love you, Alenka. I think I always will. I'm sorry I . . . I'm sorry I failed you."

She heard his slow footsteps, moving away.

Alenka flung open her door and ran outside for the first time in months. She followed the procession, lagging at its rear, a thin haggard figure all in black. A few people turned to her and smiled. She saw Jack and ran to him, slipping her hand in his. His warm fingers closed over hers. He looked down at her and smiled but did not speak. The candles were being doused. The church was all shadows. The bells began to ring out. One frail light flickered into life. The priest stepped forward, holding up his candle. "Christ has risen!"

"Indeed, he has risen!" the whole congregation shouted, surging forward to have their candles lit. One by one, the candles took flame. People embraced, weeping, laughing. Outside, fireworks began to bang and flower.

She and Jack ran outside, gazing up at the sky. Phyllia came to hug her, Micky close behind. "Alenka-mou," they crooned. "Are you well, my heart, my star? Are you better?"

"Yes," she answered. "I am better."

"Christ has risen! Indeed, he has risen." Phyllia kissed her, then turned to embrace Jack. "You are a good man! A golden man! And we liked your serenades!"

"You've made it hard for the rest of us poor fellows," Micky said. "All the girls want to be serenaded now."

Jack grinned, putting his arm about Alenka's waist. She looked up at him, and he kissed her, very gently. She felt the same shifting of the earth under her feet that she had felt the last time. She clung to him. "Let's go home," she whispered.

Hand in hand, they ran back through the blazing night. Many times they had to stop to kiss. They fell in through the front door, somehow made it to their bed.

In the morning, Alenka woke. She lay curled against Jack, skin against skin. She turned a little in his arms so she could gaze at him. His dark eyelashes fluttered. He opened his eyes and looked straight into hers. He smiled.

They danced all day, in each other's arms, sometimes breaking free to embrace and kiss their friends, always finding each other again. It was the beginning of the Bright Week, the most joyful time of the year in Greece.

Three days later, the German commander-in-chief signed his country's unconditional surrender in the dining room of the Villa Ariadne. It was the last act of the war on European soil.

"It's over, it's really over," Alenka said.

Jack nodded, drawing her naked body closer to his. "What d-do you want to do?"

She shook her head. It seemed impossible to plan. He drew circles on her skin.

"I'd like to go away from here," she said at last. "Start somewhere new. A little house in the country where I could have a garden."

"I'd like that." He kissed her throat.

"Somewhere safe."

"Mmm-hmm." He kissed her collarbone.

"Maybe we could have a family of our own?"

"I can think of nothing I want more." He kissed the hollow of her shoulder.

"Maybe we could open a taverna. I'd cook, and you could play the lyra."

"It sounds like heaven." He brought his mouth to hers. For a long time, neither spoke.

"We could go home," Jack said, much later, lying on his back with Alenka nestled by his side. "To my home, I mean. I'd like you to meet my nana. She would love you so much."

"Would she truly?"

Jack smiled at her. "How could she help it?"

"We'd need to be married first."

"I'm willing and eager."

"I'd need a dress."

"You could wear the white dress you were wearing the first time I saw you. I don't mind, I'd marry you naked if I could."

"I need a dagger too."

"A dagger?"

"Yes. All brides are given a dagger by their bridegroom in Crete."

"Then I will give you a dagger."

"I have no dowry." She sighed, thinking of her *sindoni*, sewn all over with secret codes of war and tyranny and death.

"Neither do I," Jack said comfortably. "I can't offer you anything except what you see right here." He spread out his arms and she smiled, and nestled closer to his bare chest.

"That's all I want," she answered and kissed him.

It was the twenty-first of May. Four years earlier, a young Australian soldier had saved her life playing a lyra amid the smoking ruins of Heraklion. Now she was to marry him and leave her homeland forever.

Their wedding had not been easy to arrange, but Alenka had found they had many friends eager to help. While Jack dealt with the logistics, she had embroidered her white dress with spring flowers and found her mother's wedding crown of porcelain lemon blossoms and her grandmother's white handwoven veil. She touched them gently as she went out the door, walking through birdsong to the churchyard. She knelt beside her grandmother's tombstone and filled a tin with soil from her grave. She knew it carried her mother's ashes as well as her grandmother's dust.

When Alenka got back to the little cottage among the ruins, a package had been left on her doorstep. A small, black-hilted dagger tied to a folded length of white linen with red ribbon. Alenka unfolded the cloth. It was a *sindoni* embroidered with two dancing figures. A man in breeches held a lyra in one hand. His other hand was linked with the hand of a young woman with a crown of stars on her head. Entwined around them was an intricate design of blossoms and leaves and birds and snakes and beasts, all wound about with the blood-red thread of fate, spun by an old woman hunched over a spinning wheel. Around the edges was sewn a daisy chain of dancers, some of them standing on their heads.

Alenka could read the secret code easily. It was the love poem Jack had written for her. She read the last lines with tears burning her eyes:

O

wise

old way

step by step

she finds her way free

cradling her dark shadow within

she rises, radiant, crowned with seven blazing

stars

AUTHOR'S NOTE

Once, when I was a girl, I found some old children's books hidden away on the top shelf of a cupboard at my grandmother's house. It was the summer after my parents' divorce, I was spending my school holidays with my grandparents, and I had already read every book in the house. I stood on a chair to reach the shelf, ran my finger along the battered volumes, and selected a few to read, at random. One was *Tales of the Greek Heroes* by Roger Lancelyn Green, chosen because his name seemed so magical. The other was *The Chalet Girls in Exile* by Elinor Brent-Dyer.

It was a sizzling hot summer. I spent most of the day lying on my bed, reading, drinking iced water with sliced lemon in it from my grandfather's tree. I read *The Chalet Girls in Exile* first. It is set in Austria after the Anschluss and tells the story of a group of schoolgirls who flee from the Nazis through the Alps. It made a deep impression on me, not least because the heroine Joey was a dark-haired girl who wrote stories.

I told my grandparents about it at dinner that night. My grandfather said my great-uncle Gerry had retreated from the Nazis through the towering, snow-clad White Mountains of Crete when he was just twenty-four years old. He barely managed to escape, having fought desperately for days after the Germans invaded the Greek island from the sky. I was enthralled with this story, made even more poignant by the fact that my father's nickname was also Gerry. Pleased by my interest, my grandparents told me many more stories about the war during my stay with them.

My grandfather Arthur Humphrey was one of three brothers. The eldest, Stanley, fought along the Kokoda Trail in Papua New Guinea. Arthur was the next born. A self-taught musician, he could play any music he heard, on any instrument. His favorite was his beloved double bass which he often played for me. Granps had to leave school young—his family was very poor. He was a ham radio enthusiast who taught himself Morse code. When war was declared, he joined the Air Force as a warrant officer and worked in signals deciphering Morse code messages sent by the Japanese. Radio operators were called pianists, he told me, because they needed long, supple fingers and an ear for rhythm.

The youngest brother, Jack Humphrey, joined up when he was only twenty. Like many in his family, he was dark-haired and dark-eyed with an olive complexion and described in his war records as "somewhat quiet . . . sincere and serious." He, too, fought in Papua New Guinea.

Two of the Humphrey sisters married brothers, Reg and Gerry Quirk. Reg was a prisoner of war at Changi Prison, while Gerry fought in Greece, Crete, and the Middle East, and was one of the famous Rats of Tobruk. After the war, both the Quirk brothers suffered shellshock. One day, the elder brother Reg went out to buy a loaf of bread from the corner shop. He never returned.

The story of my great-uncle who disappeared one day and was never heard of again hooked deep into my imagination. I always wondered what had happened to him during the war that caused such profound, lasting harm.

A few days after hearing about my great-uncle's dramatic escape over the White Mountains, I read *The Adventures of Theseus*, Roger Lancelyn Green's retelling of the minotaur in the Labyrinth myth, which fixed Crete in my imagination as a place of danger, mystery, and wonder. I was particularly enthralled by Ariadne, with "her dark, wild beauty" and her cleverness in coming up with a scheme to safely navigate the labyrinth. I was also intrigued by the story of Icarus, the boy who flew with wings made of feathers and wax. Later that year, I read Mary Renault's *The*

King Must Die and Mary Stewart's *The Moon-Spinners,* both of which strengthened my fascination with the island where Zeus was born.

I began to think about drawing on Greek myths and history in my own work quite a few years ago. My interest was quickened one day when I found a photo of a mother and her daughter in Crete, both carrying machine guns. The mother was dressed in a black dress and headscarf and looked so sorrowful. Her daughter was so young and dressed in a pretty, flowered dress. The photo illustrated an online article about the untold story of the brave women of the underground Cretan resistance. I knew at once I wanted to tell it.

The Battle of Crete was one of the most remarkable struggles of the Second World War. It was the first airborne invasion in history and the first time that the Enigma code was broken by cryptoanalysts at Bletchley Park. It was also the first time that the men, women, and children of a country took up arms and fought against their Nazi invaders, fighting against machine guns and tanks with kitchen knives tied to broomsticks, scythes, spades, rocks, ancient rusty rifles, and the small Cretan dagger traditionally worn tucked into a man's sash. One German paratrooper was even clubbed to death by an old man wielding his walking stick.

Almost four thousand Germans died in the first few days, more than had died in the whole of the war to that date. The struggle lasted for ten days and was followed by the Allied forces hurried retreat over the White Mountains, strafed with machine-gun fire by the Luftwaffe. Fifty-seven thousand men were rescued from Crete's stony beaches in a mass evacuation as desperate and dramatic as that of Dunkirk a year earlier. Almost seven thousand soldiers were left behind. Most were taken prisoner, but a few evaded capture or escaped the prisoner of war camps. The people of Crete risked their lives to help and hide them and set up an underground railway to smuggle them off the island. General Alexander Andre, the German commander of Fortress Crete, wrote: "Nowhere else have I witnessed such love of freedom and defiance of death as I did on Crete."

Alenka, Jack, Teddy, and their families are entirely fictional, but nearly everyone else in the book once lived and loved and suffered and sorrowed. The names of the SOE operatives who worked with the Cretan resistance are well known, in particular Patrick Leigh-Fermor, William Stanley Moss and Xan Fielding, partly because they all wrote books about their time on the island. However, the names of the Greeks are less known. I hope that my story will in some small degree alleviate that injustice.

In particular, I want to highlight the true story of Micky and Phyllia Akoumianakis, who grew up next door to the Villa Ariadne. Micky was head of counterintelligence for Force 133, the codename for the Greek arm of the SOE. His sister Phyllia worked closely with him, bravely working in the office of the German divisional commander and smuggling out a great deal of information. She ended up marrying an SOE agent, Johnny Houseman, and moving to London, and so her real life is uncannily like that of my imaginary Greek heroine, Alenka, though I did not know that when I planned my story. I am indebted to her son Peter Ormrod for much information about his family and their incredible courage. If you would like to see what Phyllia looked like, she plays herself in *Ill Met by Moonlight*, the film inspired by Billy Moss's wartime diary, appearing about twenty minutes in (along with a brief snippet of a lyra being played and a mantinada being sung).

Faith Naughton-Green, the Australian nurse who befriends Alenka when the Villa Ariadne is turned into a field hospital, is one of the few other fictional characters. She was named after one of my readers who won an auction to raise money for the fire brigade after the cataclysmic 2020 bushfires in Australia. This is the only occasion in the book when I have bent the facts a little, since all Anzac nurses were evacuated from Crete a few days before the battle. Thank you so much to Faith for her generous contribution, and for the use of her name.

The story of Ariadne and the minotaur in the labyrinth is ancient. Multiple versions of her story exist. Many scholars believe she was originally an aspect of the Great Goddess worshipped in Minoan culture, either the goddess herself or the high priestess of her cult. As guardian of the gateway to the labyrinth, she was also the gatekeeper to the underworld, and so a powerful goddess of death and resurrection. The journey through the labyrinth reveals the classic initiation quest of Descent-Search-Ascent seen so often in Greek mythology.

In most versions of the tale, Ariadne falls in love with Theseus and gives him a "clew of red thread" so that he may find his way out of the labyrinth after he has slain the minotaur, her half brother. Theseus betrays and abandons her, but Dionysus, the god of wine and epiphany, is "drunk with love" for her and marries her and makes her immortal, casting her wedding crown into the sky as the constellation Corona Borealis. In some versions of the tale, she is turned to stone in her sorrow and he must travel to the underworld to save her. In other versions, she hangs herself.

Almost two thousand years ago, the Roman poet Catallus described Ariadne's tale of love, abandonment, and consolation embroidered upon a wedding quilt, her story embedded within another tale. This first gave me the idea of telling Ariadne's "shadow story" through embroidery. Researching Cretan textile crafts, I discovered the story of Major Alexis Casdagli who was forced to surrender at the Battle of Crete and spent the rest of the war in a German POW camp. After his death, his daughter found her father's war box in the attic. It contained a secret diary written on scraps of paper and a hand-embroidered sampler that contained the message "Fuck Hitler" sewn in Morse code. This story inspired me with the idea of sewing messages in secret code.

I first wrote the "labyrinth" poem when I was playing with the idea of visual poems. I decided to try my hand at a poem laid out in a spiral and filled a page of my notebook with disconnected lines and images inspired by the idea of spirals, from spinning galaxies to defensive coils to the double helix of DNA. This led me to the *spira mirabilis,* the miraculous spiral, which led me to read about the Fibonacci number sequence. I thought it would be interesting to write poetry in the same pattern, and began to play with fitting some of the lines I had written into the proper syllabic sequence. The idea of it being a poem about the minotaur in the labyrinth came to me quite unexpectedly. I did not have time to play with the idea anymore; I was going into hospital that day for a procedure that required a general anesthetic. I have spent too much time in hospitals. They make me anxious. Usually, I silently recite poetry to keep myself calm. That day, I thought about my labyrinth poem as I sank down into the darkness. I woke up some hours later with the poem bright and clear in my head. I scribbled down six stanzas, almost exactly as they appear in the book. It was quite eerie and magical.

As always, in a novel of this size and complexity, I have many people to thank. Firstly, of course, my darling husband and children who never fail to support me. They traveled with me to Crete, explored the labyrinthine ruins of the Palace of Knossos, drove through the staggering vertigo-inducing heights of the Cretan mountains, and imbibed large quantities of roast lamb and *tsikoudia,* all in the name of research. Special thanks to my daughter Ella who took a break from her final school exams to help me devise the secret code of the dancing figures.

As always, my love and thanks to Tara Wynne, my agent at Curtis Brown Australia, who champions me in all my wild dreams and escapades, and is always there for me, no matter what happens; and to my wonderful publishing team at Penguin Random House who gave me all the time I needed to research and write this book—much longer than I could ever have imagined! Thank you in particular to Meredith Curnow, my publisher, and Patrick Mangan, my editor, for your patience, your kindness, and your keen insights. I am so blessed to have you! Thanks also to Stephanie Koven and the whole team of

Blackstone Publishing for your faith in me and my story. I'm so glad to be working with you.

My heartfelt thanks to my beautiful sister Belinda Murrell, for many long walks by the sea talking about books, writing, and Greek adventures, and a very special thank you to my father, Gerry Humphrey, Uncle John, and my aunts Trish, Helen, and Kathy for answering all my questions about our family history.

The character of Jack Hawke in my novel is very much inspired by my grandfather (though I gave him his younger brother's name). Granps was a very kind and loving man who helped give me my deep love of music and my fascination with secret codes. After the war, he played double bass in one of the first jazz clubs in Melbourne and once performed with Louis Armstrong. He'd come home long after midnight, pile all his tips on Nana's bedside table, and go to sleep. She would get up early, gather up the coins and use them to feed the family. My grandfather's tips paid for my father Gerry to go to university in Sydney, where he met my mother.

Granps was also a great craftsman and used to make us toys out of bits of old wood, once making us a model of a Spitfire aeroplane. He loved his garden and grew a lot of the family's food. My most enduring memory of Granps, though, was of him playing his double bass. He would close his eyes and move his bow over the strings, and the most thrilling, deep, moody music would rise like magic into the evening air. I wish I had inherited his gift.

Jack's stutter and his struggle to overcome it is inspired by my own life. I wrestled with my words all through my childhood, until my mother took to me to a speech therapist who taught me to sing my words and gave me rhythmic poetry to recite out loud. Realizing I did not stutter so badly when I sang or recited something incantatory was a wonderful revelation. Every night, after a long day working full-time and caring for our family on her own, my mother would listen to me read poetry out loud until I, at last, achieved some semblance of fluency. I am so grateful to her for that; I believe my passionate love of poems began there.